SWORD AND SORCERESS XII

AN ANTHOLOGY
OF HEROIC FANTASY

Edited by
Marion Zimmer Bradley

D0172700

DAW BOOKS, INC.
DONALD A. WOLLHEIM, FOUNDER
375 Hudson Street, New York, NY 10014

ELIZABETH R. WOLLHEIM
SHEILA E. GILBERT
PUBLISHERS

Copyright © 1995 by Marion Zimmer Bradley

All Rights Reserved

Cover art by Monica

DAW Book Collectors No. 993.

Introduction © 1995 by Marion Zimmer Bradley
Demon in Glass © 1995 by John P. Buentello
Does the Shoe Fit You Now? © 1995 by Carolyn J. Bahr
A Lynx and a Bastard © 1995 by Karen Luk
Dragonskin Boots © 1995 by L.S. Silverthorne
Truth © 1995 by Lynne Armstrong-Jones
Skins © 1995 by Heather Rose Jones
Though the World is Darkness © 1995 by Lisa Deason
Hemparius the Trader © 1995
by Valerie Atkinson Gawthrop
Chance © 1995 by Tom Gallier
Touched by the Gods © 1995 by Deborah Millitello
Promise to Angel © 1995 by Stephanie Shaver
Shadow Harper © 1995 by Cynthia McQuillin
The Stone Face, the Giant, and the Paradox
© 1995 by Vera Nazarian
Wormwood © 1995 by Laura J. Underwood
Silverblade © 1995 by Deborah Wheeler
A Dragon in Distress © 1995
by Mercedes Lackey & Elisabeth Waters
Stone Spirit © 1995 by Diana L. Paxson
Garden of Glories © 1995 by Jennifer Roberson
Stealing the Power © 1995 by Linda J. Dunn
The Lost Path © 1995 by Patricia Duffy Novak
Winter Roses © 1995 by Patricia Sayre McCoy
Amber © 1995 by Syne Mitchell

First Printing, July 1995

1 2 3 4 5 6 7 8 9

DAW TRADEMARK REGISTERED
U.S. PAT. OFF. AND FOREIGN COUNTRIES
—MARCA REGISTRADA
HECHO EN U.S.A.

PRINTED IN THE U.S.A.

Suddenly the track opened up into a clearing. She urged her battlemare into it, disliking the whimpering trees and eager to put some distance between herself and them—and then reined the mare in abruptly when she saw what stood in the center of the clearing.

It was a doorway without a building, a beautifully formed arch of white stone taller than three tall men, and wide enough for a cart to pass through with space on either side. There was only one problem.

It shouldn't be here.

Kethry brought her mare up beside her partner's, surveyed the clearing, and wrinkled her brow in consternation. "The path ends here, doesn't it," she stated.

Before Tarma could respond, the space inside the doorway suddenly changed. Instead of the other side of the clearing, there was nothing there but darkness, a black void that Tarma shrank from without knowing why she did so. Whatever *that* thing was, she wanted no further part of it!

But suddenly Kethry gave an all-too-familiar cry of pain, and spurred her mare straight at the archway. In a heartbeat, she was swallowed up in the blackness between the white stone pillars.

With a heartfelt curse, Tarma spurred her horse after, and followed.

CONTENTS

INTRODUCTION
by Marion Zimmer Bradley

Every year, I get more and more good stories, and the problem of final selection becomes a little harder. (This is part of the reason I started my own fantasy magazine in addition to editing these anthologies.) These days I have much tougher standards for *Sword and Sorceress*; *Marion Zimmer Bradley's Fantasy Magazine* is an easier market for beginners. Some of the writers who had stories in the early volumes of *Sword and Sorceress*, although most of them have gone on to sell novels by now, still submit to me; this volume has stories by Mercedes Lackey, Diana L. Paxson, Jennifer Roberson, Elisabeth Waters, and Deborah Wheeler. Most of the other stories also come from writers who have sold to me before, although in some cases the sales were to my magazine and they are making their first appearance in *Sword and Sorceress*. Only a handful of stories in this volume are by new writers. Over the past twelve years, the market has changed.

When I first began editing these anthologies, there was no market for this sort of story except mine. People were not yet accustomed to female heroes; I practically had to create the genre and establish the market. I remember some of those early stories were fearful and wonderful things.

I still remember one manuscript with a nostalgic kind of wonder; it wasn't even badly written, simply preposterous: a college of priestesses— sadistic lesbians, if you can believe it—and this is one reason I suggest that you skip lesbians unless you know what you're doing; the author of this story might possibly have recognized a lesbian if one had come up and bit her. But I wouldn't have bet on it. And, to add, I suppose, to the fantasy quality of this story, each woman in the college was mentally linked (as with Anne McCaffrey's dragons) with a gigantic purple rhinoceros! This woman actually had a good imagination for writing sword and sorcery. What a pity she didn't stick to it long enough to learn her craft!

Everybody writes a few clunkers—my early stories, like those of—say—Harlan Ellison or Robert Silverberg, revealed no indication of any talent whatever. All three of us have since achieved at least respectable status as novelists. So I always say that if you have sufficient discipline, anyone can learn plotting; but when it comes to ideas, you have to bring your own. And anyone who could imagine telepathic purple rhinos has the kind of imagination we really need. So if the young writer who perpetrated that story had kept writing, I'd have been happy to keep reading and rejecting her wild ideas till she learned to plot and wrote something salable.

That's probably the secret. "Good writing" is a drug on the market. Good writers, or at least those who can turn out luscious prose, are turned out by the dozens in high schools and college magazines; "good writing" doesn't mean a blessed thing, except to English teachers—who have probably spoiled more good writers than "the devil drink." I nearly had my own career aborted before it began by a so-called teacher of "creative writing." He marked down several of my early stories (some of which later sold), because his only model for fantasy was James Branch Cabell! My own first story was about astronauts, and my teacher expressed wonder about whether anyone would be interested in such a story.

I said demurely that no doubt he was right, produced reams of poetry (which is why I am less interested in fantasy poetry than I probably should be), gathered my A plus for the course, and have spent forty years since then telling young writers to stay out of college creative writing classes. I had sense enough to go back to reading the best fantasy I could, writing it very much in the manner of C.L. Moore and Leigh Brackett, sending it in to Sam Merwin and Tony Boucher, and finally selling my first long stories to Tony Boucher at *F&SF* and Don Wollheim at Ace—and the rest is history in our field. And I still say that reading the best for long enough, you will teach yourself.

This is still the best writing class you can have.

1) Read the best.
2) Write your own work.
3) Submit what you write to your favorite publication.
4) Repeat as needed until you sell.

Number Four—repeat as needed—is the real secret of writing. You'll get tired and discouraged, but keep it up long enough and you won't fail. Ask any selling writer how long he worked before he started selling.

But that's where many people fail; about half the people who submit to me stick around for two or maybe three rejections and then disappear, never to be heard of again.

Develop a professional and undiscourageable attitude. Become indifferent to rejection and keep coming back for more. But don't get rejected for reasons which could have easily been avoided. *Read* the markets you are trying to sell to, and always send for guidelines before submitting a story. For guidelines for these anthologies, send a #10 SASE (Self-Addressed Stamped Envelope) to me at PO Box 72, Berkeley CA 94701. For guidelines for my magazine, send a #10 SASE to *Marion Zimmer Bradley's Fantasy Magazine*, PO Box 249, Berkeley CA 94701. I have always said that anyone who could write a literate English sentence could sell category fiction—but I never said it was easy!

DEMON IN GLASS
by John P. Buentello

John Buentello is one of the rare males to find room in this volume. Somehow, an idea has taken root in the public mind that I am reluctant to use stories written by men. It is true that I refuse bad stories by men, but it is also true that I refuse bad stories by women. I am not very receptive to the feminist argument that I should use bad stories written by women because bad stories written by men are used every day by supposedly "anti-woman" magazines and anthologies. In my book, if a story stinks, it stinks, whether it was written by a man, a woman, or a telepathic purple rhinoceros. I feel that no one of either gender should be allowed to write bad fiction. There is too little true excellence around; we can't afford to print bad stories by anyone.

Like almost every writer, he's working on a novel, and when he finishes it, he probably won't have time to write short stories even for these anthologies. I guess that's the penalty for discovering writers; they grow up and leave their first markets. It never fails. But I'll have my revenge—demonic cackle—I'll just go out and discover more, heh heh heh.

About his writing, Buentello says, "It's been nice to find out that there are people out there who are willing to read what I write. For me, that's the biggest thrill of all."

John Buentello lives in San Antonio, Texas, with his wife and children.

L eska listened to the sound of the fountain spray hitting the water in the pool below. She skirted the square where the fountain stood, staying well away from the face of the pool, and made her way to a long, narrow alley sided by dull brown buildings. She let her eyes adjust to the dark of the windowless corridor, then slowly advanced into its depths. Counting the doors on her left side by the feel of the wood, she continued until she came to the sixth one. Pausing in front of the closed door, she listened to the sound of glass being broken from within.

Clearing her mind, Leska concentrated on the rod of iron she felt barring the opposite side of the door. She whispered a spell of opening, hoping the release of magic was not enough to draw her adversary's attention. The mirror that lay carefully wrapped and stored in her pack rattled in its frame, then was still again, Leska pushed open the door and went inside.

The room she stepped into was darker even than the alley itself. The gloom was cut by a hot, orange fire that blazed in an iron crucible standing in the center of the room. A thin shape sat hunched over the bowl of light, turning a long glass rod in hands wrapped with burlap. The figure stood abruptly, revealing herself to be a young woman, whose dark hair blended with the shadows surrounding the fire. She pulled the rod from the fire and held it close to her face. A frown appeared on her forehead, marring the smoothness that had been there before. The woman cursed and threw the glass wand from her, shattering it on the wall at the opposite end of the room. The shards fell to join a pile of others littering the floor.

"The piece looked perfect to me," Leska remarked as she drew close to the crucible.

The other woman turned. Leska saw that her eyes were the color of the flames that danced above the coals in the urn. The Adept's own eyes were darker than the shadows surrounding them. The rich folds of her ceremonial robes caught the other woman's attention. Leska touched the Adept's medallion at her neck and gave a greeting of peace. The woman relaxed and looked back at the pieces of glass laying on the floor.

"There was a bubble the size of a sand grain at the lip of the wand," she said. "Such imperfection isn't something I'll put my name to."

Leska nodded. "What are you called?"

"Jelin," the young woman answered. She bent to a lamp on a low table standing beside the crucible, lighting a twig and touching the flame to its wick. The lamp flared into brightness, revealing a room with a series of shelves and boxes filled with odd bits and pieces of glass. Leska caught the smell of sulfur and other noxious odors. One wall held a shelf of some of the most beautiful glasswork she had ever seen. No Adept, no matter what his or her power, could have commanded glass to flow into the strange and delicate shapes that stood before her. She wanted to go closer to see them, but she drew back from the pale reflections cast by the lamp.

"I see what you mean." She took off her robe and carefully set the pack she carried on the table beside it. "I am Leska, an Adept of the Chosen, and I need your help."

Jelin frowned and sat down on the stool sitting next to the crucible. The heat from the fire had already made Leska uncomfortable. The glassmaker didn't even break a sweat. She crossed her arms and regarded her visitor once more. "What kind of help are you asking?"

"The kind you can give."

"And if I don't?" Jelin asked.

Leska turned away from her. "Then I will be dead very shortly, and you will have done nothing to help me keep a demon from being loosed on the land."

The glassmaker's shop became cooler once Jelin allowed the fire beneath the crucible to die down. She poured herself a cup of water and offered the same to her visitor. Leska took the cup and shut her eyes tightly, draining the water in a single swallow. Jelin noted that she kept well away from the glass lying about the shop. In fact, she stayed in the shadows as much as possible. Jelin decided it must be in the tradition of an Adept and thanked her god again for a profession where light and warmth played so vital a role.

"So what is this about a demon? Do you have one after you?"

Leska smiled and drew farther into the darkness. "You could say that. Have you heard of the Chosen?"

Jelin nodded. "Some of the most powerful sorcerers in the realm. They always carry a familiar with them, do they not?"

"They do." Leska drew a bundle from her pack and laid it on the table between them. "The Chosen gain their power through years of study. We learn under the tutelage of other Adepts, and from magical beings as well."

"You mean demons?"

Leska shook her head. "Not anymore. Those Chosen who called on darker gods have all been—" She smiled again. "Exorcised. We train with beings who only wish to serve. A familiar is such a spirit. Even the most ignorant among us knows to stay away from demons."

"Then why is one after you?"

"He tricked me," Leska said. She pointed a slim hand at the bundle on the table. "I was building my power, learning to expand on it. It was time for a familiar. They are our channels, the guides for our power, and they can come in any form. Some of us have staffs, some pets, some are followed by strange clouds. We call them and wait for an answer."

Jelin shivered at the unfamiliar cold that filled the room. "And you called upon a demon?"

"I called for a friend. I laid the proper invitation, and the next day a silver mirror lay on the table in my study. I picked it up, and almost lost my soul." She closed her eyes, her face losing some of its hardness at the memory. "A demon was waiting inside. He wasn't strong enough to force his way into our world, but he did establish a link, binding his magic to mine. Now I cannot cast a spell without one of his own emerging to warp it and bend it to his will."

"Can't you simply cast him out?"

"There's more," Leska said. "The demon is a reflection in this world. *My* reflection, twisted and made corrupt. He can appear on any surface I look into. Each time he appears he steals a little of my power. He wants to kill me, so he can claim my body."

Jelin looked down at the bundle. "Is he in the mirror now?"

Leska nodded. "He is always there. Waiting."

"So why not just break the mirror?"

"It is his portal and his prison. It's his way into this world, but it keeps him out, too. Break the mirror, and he is free. Other Adepts have tried to help me. They cannot loose the bond between us. I can feel my life ebbing. In a few days I will be dead, and he will be strong enough to break the mirror himself."

Jelin let out a cold breath. "So you figured a glassmaker could help you with your demon in glass."

"If you cannot, then I must go." Leska's eyes flashed in the lamplight. "I must be alone when he comes for me."

Jelin went to the crucible and began to stoke the coals under it. "I'll need time to get the fire hot enough. You'll need to make yourself ready by then."

Leska joined her by the urn. "Ready for what?"

"Ready to use your power. If the demon is to come into this world, the time must be of our choosing."

"And what do we do once he gets here?" the Adept asked.

Jelin shrugged. "Give him what he wants. Your power."

Leska rested while Jelin worked at the crucible. She listened to the sound of the woman moving pieces of glass about the room, and tried to calm her mind. It had been a long time since she'd had a good night's rest, and her fatigue was going to be a factor in this battle. The demon would try to kill her quickly once he was free. She would have to have all her strength to fend off his first at-

tacks, in the hope she could survive long enough
to put Jelin's plan in motion.

She turned her head and watched the glassmaker work. The woman seemed incredibly
young. The only glassmakers Leska had known
were dried and burnt from years of standing next
to flames hot enough to turn glass to liquid. The
woman looked as if she had just left her family's
care. The only sign of age was the look of discipline on her face. She had no doubts about her
role in their upcoming trial. They both knew the
risks they took and what would be forfeited if
they failed. Leska felt she should leave the girl in
peace. She was asking more than perhaps even
she herself would willingly give. But if she left
now, how long would it be before the demon
came for her?

She must have slept, for when she woke it was
to a feeling of deep, intense heat. The entire room
seemed awash in waves of hot air, and as she rose
from the bed Leska saw that the glassmaker had
been hard at work. Tall, rippling sheets of glass
rose from the floor of the shop. They formed a lu-
minescent screen around the crucible where Jelin
stood. The Adept saw a pale reflection in one
sheet of blue glass, and a warped, rictus-faced image of herself appeared, laughing at her. Leska
felt the familiar sensation as the demon reached
out to claim another part of her soul. She turned
away and stood, calling out to the other woman.

"Jelin, he is here. He must know what we're
doing."

"Pray he does not," the glassmaker said. "Can
you make your way to the center of the room?"

Leska nodded and stepped forward. She kept
her eyes to the ground, carefully stepping around
the screens of glass. She knew all around her the
demonic images of her other self were laughing

and reaching out to her. She willed the fear from her mind and joined the woman by the crucible.

"Can you bring him to us?" Jelin asked. Leska looked up to see her holding a bowl of steaming liquid. "I don't have enough of this to try a second time."

"Nor I the strength," the Adept replied. "Let us begin."

She waited until Jelin had stepped behind one of the screens and pushed it close to her. Raising her head, Leska opened her eyes and stared full into the glass screen in front of her. The back of the glass had been covered with silver by the glassmaker, and the image she stared at was fully her own size. That was where the resemblance ended.

As she stood and stared, Leska looked into the mad eyes of her own face. The demon had pulled and molded her features into a dark leer. The once sharply lined face had melded into a bloated caricature that hissed at her with raw anger. The desire to cast against such a creature was almost overwhelming. The Adept did not raise her power. She stood and waited for what was to come.

The demon laughed and stretched toward the surface of the glass. His body flowed through the opening, becoming solid in front of her. He wrapped a burly hand around the Adept's wrist and leaned close to her.

"You made it too easy, girl." His voice was a low echo of her own. "I would have waited to come through the mirror. Have you accepted what is to be? Are you ready to die?"

Leska wasted no time on words. She held up her hand and cast. The demon made a motion to block her power, but the Adept's magic swept past him, heading for its true target. The screen behind the demon moved forward, locking beside the screen next to him. As Leska watched, her demon image stopped and looked around. Both he and Leska were now completely surrounded by a cylinder of silvered glass.

"You expect that to stop me? I'm already in your world, sorcerer. You can never send me back again. Now give me your power!"

Leska closed her eyes. "Take it," she said. She raised her hands and opened herself to the demon, dropping all defense against his power. She heard the creature laugh and then his hands were on her. She felt a pulling sensation course through her body. At first it only affected her strength, as though she were having all the muscle drained from her. Then the thing reached her soul, the source of her power, and she felt a rending pain like nothing she had felt before. She screamed, a high, piercing cry that echoed through the small room.

"Jelin! Help me!"

She opened her eyes in time to see the glass-maker push one glass screen aside and close it behind her. The demon turned at the sound, and she saw how bloated and gorged his body had become from draining her power. The demon stared at the other woman and growled.

"You brought company, Adept? More for my appetites."

As the demon moved toward her, Jelin brought her hands up, revealing the glass bowl she held. At first Leska did not recognize the mirror she had carried for so long. Under the glassmaker's hands, it had been warped and bent into a deep-shaped bowl. It caught the reflection of the demon, throwing his blood-red gaze back to her.

"Take all of the power!" she cried out. The last of her strength left her then, and she freed her power to the air around her. It flowed from her like a vapor, drifting toward the demon. Before he had time to turn and absorb it, the ethereal cloud had swept past, drawing the demon along with it.

"What is this?" he screamed. The demon slammed into the surface of one of the mirrored screens and rebounded from its surface. The creature struck a screen on the opposite side of the circle and went spinning past the Adept. "Stop this!" he bellowed as he smashed into another mirror and was pulled away by the swirling cloud of magic. "Stop, I say! There are too many mirrors!"

Leska stood on shaking legs and faced the demon. She caught the edge of the whipping stream of power and pushed it deeper into the creature, causing him to bounce and crash again and again against the mirrored walls. She turned to the other woman, who stood in the center of the circle, and nodded. Jelin raised the bowl and waited.

"Now, demon, back to where you came from!"

The demon flew into her, almost knocking her over. Leska felt the power seep back into her soul. Taking hold, she built it back up to a solid wall of magic and sent it back into the demon who struggled against her. The creature screamed and broke free. While he struggled to keep his feet, she stepped forward and laid her hands on his face.

"Take my power," she whispered, her image reflected over and over by the wall of mirrors. "It's yours now."

She pushed the last of the magic from inside her, propelling the demon backward. He fell toward Jelin, carried by the force of the Adept's casting, and was swept into the mirrored bowl. His face contorted into a mask of rage and pain, and then it was folding, shrinking into itself. The cloud of magic collapsed with him, absorbed into the bowl. He raised a clawed hand toward her and then he was gone, vanished into the surface of the bowl.

"Leska! Help me finish it!" The glassmaker pushed one screen aside and stepped toward her crucible. The Adept struggled to keep her feet and took the bowl from the other's hands. The object felt hot, trembling with the rage of the thing caught inside it.

"That bowl won't keep him trapped for long." Jelin said. As the Adept watched, she took another bowl from the crucible. It held a steaming silver liquid in its depths. Jelin poured it into the glass bowl, being careful not to singe the Adept's hands. Leska felt the heat touch her fingers, and she used that bridge to shape the shadow of power that surrounded the bowl. She caused the liquid to cool and flatten, sealing the inner surface. There was a sound from within the glass itself, like an angry wail of betrayal. Then the trembling in her hands ceased.

"Here, let me take that."

The bowl was taken from her hands and she watched as Jelin set it on one of the shelves along the far wall. Leska let herself sink to the floor and let out a long, trembling breath. When she looked up again, the glassmaker was kneeling beside her, a worried look on her face.

"Are you all right?"

The Adept nodded. "The power I lost will take a long time to replace. For a time, I will be like anyone else."

Jelin smiled and helped Leska to her feet. "Is that so terrible a thing?" she asked.

"No, it's not," Leska replied. Then she smiled too. "As long as I'm not consigned to being stuck in a place like this. How do you stand the heat, woman?"

Jelin laughed. She helped the Adept to the alley and out into the cool night air. "Is that better?" she asked.

Leska nodded. "Much better." She took the other woman's hand. "Come. We have the rest of the night to celebrate. I want to walk in the light this night. Let the darkness tend to itself for a while."

DOES THE SHOE FIT YOU NOW?
by Carolyn J. Bahr

Almost everyone who sells to my anthologies or to *Marion Zimmer Bradley's Fantasy Magazine* finds out rather soon that I have a list of clichés which I usually reject as soon as I spot them. One of these is the rewritten fairy tale; but this story is proof that I will occasionally buy something that violates one of my taboos, *if* the story is fresh enough. This one is, giving a totally unexpected view of Cinderella's life after she married Prince Charming.

Carolyn shares a house with a friend and four cats in Burbank. She says her day job—another crazy job for writers—has been as Assistant Music Editor for feature films such as "Teenage Mutant Ninja Turtles," and adds that her "true glory and passion" is horses. I confess the charm of those four-legged beasts still eludes me. After all these years, I'm beginning to suspect that it's because I saw most of them from the wrong end—not as pets, but as just more work for a farm girl.

It does make a difference whether you're riding the horse or cleaning up after it.

Carolyn states that she would like to acknowledge the help of her writing partner Rochelle Marie, who appeared in *Sword and Sorceress XI*. "Without her criticism, patience, support, prodding, and creativity, I would never have finished or submitted my story." They are, of course, collaborating on a novel. Who isn't?

Once upon a time, not so very long ago, there lived a young girl who dreamed of a better life and got it. *Or did she?* thought Cinderella. She walked to the edge of the castle turret and gazed out on the late evening activity of the kingdom below. Certainly her stepmother and stepsisters thought she had gained more than she deserved. Every young girl in the kingdom dreamed of the day when they, too, like Cinderella, would be swept off their feet by a charming prince on a white horse. *I wonder what they would think if they knew what my life was really like? Would they even believe the truth?* Cinderella sighed, and headed back into the castle. *Probably not.* The day had been long, but then all of her days were long.

Cinderella's day started when she took the royal hounds for a walk. It was a pleasant spring morning, but nothing could shake her gloomy mood. She thoroughly disliked this duty. The Prince, remembering her skill with animals, thought she would enjoy exercising the dogs. What he failed to understand, no matter how many times Cinderella told him, was she was extremely sensitive to the beasts. Her skin would itch all over, and she couldn't stop sneezing. They made her ill. To make matters worse, the large hairy hounds appeared to take a perverse pleasure in jumping all over her. By the time she got back from her walks with the hounds, she could barely breathe.

Cinderella rarely had a chance to breakfast after these morning excursions. By the time she recovered enough to think about food, the morning was nearly past, and she still had more than a full day's worth of chores ahead of her. It didn't help much that her next stop was at the food cellars when all she had had to eat was a bit of bread.

The cellars were dark and smelled of mildew. Their cool temperatures ensured food storage year round. The Master of the Cellars had insisted on her help in checking on the supplies and inventory.

Next came the visit to the Mistress of Laundry. The Prince complained of his shirts being stiff and scratchy, bothering his royal person. The laundress did nothing different than Cinderella would do herself, but the Prince insisted that only Cinderella could make his shirts feel soft and silky. It wasn't long before she was up to her elbows in suds. There was more work than the washing women could handle in the little time they had. So being the person she was, she jumped in to help, thereby washing her way through lunch.

After a snack, Cinderella stopped to help the cleaning maids. The Prince constantly complained about a stain on the hallway carpet runner. Knowing her background in housecleaning he asked her to intervene. It wasn't the first time, and it wouldn't be the last. She had been down on her hands and knees for hours before the stain finally gave way and disappeared.

Even after a grueling day of labor, Cinderella entered the kitchen smiling and greeting her fellow workers. She tied on her apron and began to work. The Prince was very particular about his food. He trusted no one else to prepare it. That had started not long after their wedding day.

There had been a string of assassinations throughout the country which had set his royal nerves on edge. The Prince, simply put, was paranoid and a bit of a hypochondriac. (The slightest fatigue or sniffle would send him to bed, complaining he was too weak to move—until some buxom servant would wander by.)

That particular evening the Prince had sat down to a meal prepared, as always, by his faithful cook. The meal, however, wasn't up to the cook's usual standards. The cook was preoccupied with plans of bedding the new kitchen maid and had accidentally overspiced the meat. The Prince took one bite of the offensive meal and immediately began to choke and gag. With tears streaming down his face, he collapsed to his knees shouting, "I'm poisoned!" The guards hearing the commotion rushed to his side. As they helped him to his bed, the Prince blamed the cook, who was then summarily executed. The Prince never felt remorse even after it was proven the meal was untainted. He shrugged it off as a little accident. It was then that Cinderella realized that everything was not roses and romance.

The sweat was beading on her forehead. Cinderella wiped it off with the back of her hand. It was hot working in the kitchen, but one did such chores for the Prince of the realm. One did *a lot* of chores.

The Prince barely acknowledged Cinderella as

he left the dinning table. He was off to the library for cigars, cards, and drinks. Plenty of drinks. Slowly, she began to clear the table.

She helped with the dishes and wished everyone a good night. She grabbed another bit of bread, which she munched on as she made her way up the stairs. Tired, she was going to her favorite place of quiet, the castle turret. It had been one of those days. Each day was longer and worse than the next.

Cinderella climbed down the winding turret steps and made her way to the Prince's chambers. She truly was not in the mood tonight, but she had begged off too recently to refuse again. The Prince, hopefully, would be his usual inept self, so the evening would be short and bearable.

She opened the door greeted by a drunk and slovenly Prince. What a complete change in her husband since they first met. Where he had been trim, fit, and handsome, he was now obese, weak, and repulsive. She had kissed her Prince and gotten a pig.

"Ah, my Cinder-rel-ly! You have come to me at last." He let out a burp and patted the bed next to him. "My vision, my dream, let us populate the nursery."

Cinderella walked over to the Prince, and began helping him to bed.

"Rella, Rella, I've got an inspired idea," the Prince singsonged. "Fetch your glass slipper. It will be the sluck, uh, luck charm that we need," slurred the Prince.

She walked over to the wardrobe that stored the slipper. Opening the door, she stared at the symbol of her life. She picked it up carefully and gave it to the Prince.

"Do you remember, Rella? Do you remember how you felt when the slipper fit you?"

"Yes," was all Cinderella could reply.

"Come, sit and let me slip it on your foot. It will be like old times again."

Cinderella sighed and sat down, extending her still slim and dainty foot. The Prince, attempting to leave the bed and kneel at her feet, lost his balance. In his drunken stupor, he tried to catch himself with his hands, causing the glass slipper to hit and shatter on the floor. Cinderella stared in dismay. The Prince paused for a moment, unhurt, and looked up at Cinderella.

"Well, Rella, I guess that's it. We really didn't need it anyway." The Prince lurched to his feet and fell on top of the bed. Before passing out he managed to say, "Oh, and sweetheart, don't forget to walk the dogs."

Cinderella exited the castle gates with the four hounds frolicking as usual. She continued to walk far from the surrounding town and deeper into the woods. When she had gone some distance, she stopped, and took a deep breath. She thought of the shattered glass slipper. The Prince was right. She didn't need it, or him. She laughed as she let the dogs loose. Without looking back, she continued down the path, following it to wherever it would lead.

A LYNX AND A BASTARD
by Karen Luk

Karen is seventeen and, like most students, is stressing out over college before she even finishes her junior year in high school. In her senior year she will be Assistant News Editor of her school's newspaper.

She adds that she's also finished one novel and is working on her second—surprise! Well, good luck; my first novel didn't get published till I'd sold about forty others. Good writing and technique means a lot less than being aware of market requirements. When I was nineteen, I knew I could write better stories than most of what I read; it took me years to realize that what commercial markets want is not better stories, but stories that really fit their formula. Once I learned to do that—look Ma, no more rejections.

Shadow's lean figure lounged in his chair surrounded by rows of bookshelves. His long face showed the lines of his age—the crow's feet at the eyes, folds about the thin lips, and the furrowing of his brow. He arched an eyebrow at the sound of his requested guest entering the library, deftly marked his place in the book he was reading, and smiled in welcome.

His guest was one of the most promising Guild members. She approached him with a nod of deference. But indigo eyes glinted with wariness. Cropped ebony hair did not ruffle as she walked. She settled uneasily into the chair across from Shadow.

"Good morning, Lynx," greeted Shadow. "I trust you found the initiation ceremony to your liking."

"Thank you for giving me a Name in the Guild so soon," said Lynx. "I didn't think I was *that* good. I thought that I had more studies to come, before I became initiated as a full thief . . . that's what my former instructor believed."

"I was the one to make that judgment, not him," replied Shadow calmly. "And I have my reasons. I required a skillful thief worthy of my trust."

That silenced Lynx. She hadn't expected personal interest from the Guild master at this early stage in her career. She was merely a thief fresh from the Naming and still untried in the Guild's eyes.

"I'm the one you're looking for?" Lynx finally asked in disbelief.

"Yes, there is nobody who can match your growing skill," said Shadow. "Guild thieves have been vanishing from Cant Borough. Our fair city is losing its criminal population to an unknown phenomenon or person."

Shadow rose and crossed to the balcony. His eyes scanned the city below.

"I had intended to choose someone with more

experience for the task," he continued, "but I waited too long and now my choices are few. Besides, you were raised on the streets, that and your inate talent will help to compensate for your lack of experience."

"I take it that I have been chosen to find the missing thieves?" Lynx asked.

"Yes, Lynx, but not without help," Shadow replied. "I have assigned you an experienced partner for this expedition. I know his talents will complement yours well." There was a knock at the library's door. "Ah, here he is now."

The wooden door swung open to reveal a tall man with hazel eyes and brown hair. An open satchel was slung from his left shoulder to his waist. It was stuffed with scrolls and parchments. He also smelled of dried herbs. Lynx rolled her eyes.

"Great. A conjurer, right?" she sighed.

"A *mage* at the service of Shadow." He bowed, taking Lynx's right hand and pressing his lips to it. "I would have gladly responded to Shadow's summons earlier, if I had known she was such a vision of beauty."

Lynx snatched her hand free from his grasp and wiped off the kiss on the corner of her tunic. She scowled indignantly at the mage, but Shadow seemed amused. He smiled and gestured for the mage to sit at the table. Shadow resumed his seat and pushed the book aside.

"*I* am Shadow and *this* is Lynx," Shadow corrected. "Lynx this is Damien."

The mage grinned sheepishly as he shook hands with the real Shadow. Lynx looked disgusted.

"Oh, I've heard of him, he's the one whose mother was too stupid to know who his father was," Lynx said. "What makes you think he's going to be able to help us? Stupidity usually runs in the family, you know."

Damien smiled at her and said, "Gods, you're *so* cute when you're angry."

Lynx turned to Shadow with a glare. "Do you want me to work with him or kill him?" she asked. Shadow gave her a stern look.

"As you know," he began, "there have been more disappearances of Guild members in the past few months than in the last three years alone. My sources have reported that these are not random 'business' encounters, but calculated removal of the Guild members. It has gotten to the point that we have few informants left in the various fields. It has now become of paramount importance to reveal our unseen adversary."

"And you have considered that there might be magic involved?" asked Damien.

"Yes. Witnesses outside of the Guild have spread word of sorcery being used by the abductors," replied Shadow. "That is why I have employed your talents—" He nodded toward the mage, eliciting a small snort from Lynx. Damien glared.

Shadow waited, then went on, "—and Lynx's connection with the Guild will also be useful."

"Shadow, I don't need to work with a *mage* to discover who's behind this," scoffed Lynx. "His magic won't help me in the least."

"I wouldn't be so quick to judge, Lynx," Damien defended. "I'm a mage of no small talent, and I do have some training as a thief."

He got up and looked down at Lynx. She remained undaunted by Damien. The mage-thief's face was calm.

"I'll have you know that I am considered a very accomplished mage," he added. "Very prestigious among my peers, entering my prime."

"Prime of what?" Lynx laughed. "Puberty? You could have fooled me with that idiotic flattery when you waltzed in here."

"Both of you will have to cooperate to defeat whoever is behind the kidnappings," said Shadow flatly. "It will require all the skills and talents you both possess to uncover this mystery, and it will require your cooperation." He paused. "With each other," he added. "I will forward the rest of the information to your rooms. I *strongly* recommend that you both reconcile, or you will fail. Together."

However, Lynx wasn't through yet. "What binds me to this . . . this ego on two legs!"

"What binds you to this man? Your word as a named member of the Guild to carry out this errand," said Shadow. "One of your notable faults, Lynx, is your inability to work with a partner. I am ordering you to work with Damien, and that is all. Now, if you will excuse me," Shadow smiled, and left the library.

Lynx shoved her chair away from the table. She paced the library. After a moment, the mage walked over to Lynx, who ignored him. He grabbed one of her hands. She glared at him.

"As a sign of good faith, my *real* Name," he said. "It's Ralstone, and yours?"

"Lynx, just Lynx," she snapped, breaking free of him. "You're lucky I'm not a mage, or I would use your Name's power against you."

"Does that mean you're not going to tell me your real Name?" he asked, irritated.

"What do *you* think?" she shot back. "Look, if Shadow wants me to work with you, fine. But if he thinks I'm actually going to spend an indefinite time sharing the same air as you, he's dead wrong."

He started after her as she tried to leave the library. Lynx turned to tell him to stop following her, and somehow found herself in his arms. Damien, grinning, pinned her against the door. His eyes locked with hers.

"I can see why they named you a wildcat," Ralstone smirked, leaning forward suggestively. "Maybe I'll tame a Lynx yet. . . ."

Lynx let his lips drift ever closer to hers. Smiling sweetly, Lynx snapped a knee into his groin. Ralstone released Lynx, wincing in pain. "Tame *that!*" taunted Lynx, and then she was gone.

Ralstone sagged against the wall, gasping for air. A knock at the door startled him, but it was merely a servant to lead him to his room. It took him a while to get up. The servant seemed oblivious to Ralstone's agony. As they left the library for the stairway ending in the courtyard, Ralstone looked up to the balcony. Shadow was there. His eyes tried to focus on him, but Shadow vanished from view. The mage-thief thought he heard Shadow's laughter drifting from the balcony.

The following day, food rations, water canteens, and two saddled horses were at Shadow's home entrance, waiting for their owners. Lynx arrived first, followed by Ralstone.

"Good morning, Lynx," he said, after exchanging greetings with Shadow.

She didn't respond.

"Well, for some of us it is," he said and shrugged.

Lynx mounted her horse. She did not intend to pay attention to Ralstone. Shadow stood in front of them, holding the reins of both horses. Ralstone gave Shadow his full attention, while Lynx could barely look at the Guild master.

"Your task should not take you far," Shadow began. "Although if it should, there is a pouch of gold coins located in each of your saddlebags for any other expenses you deem necessary during your search. I expect you *both* to collaborate in this effort—"

Lynx stayed unresponsive, but she listened.

"—or there will be no more Thieves' Guild in the Realm," he finished. "I wish you the success that will light your path, and the rewards that come from achievement."

Shadow released the reins. Without a farewell, Lynx abruptly turned her mount away and headed off. The mage-thief hurried to catch up.

Shadow watched as the two disappeared among the other inhabitants of Cant Borough. He sighed, as if another burden had been added to his shoulders.

"And may you come back alive, Marial," he whispered. "The survival of the Guild rests upon your shoulders."

Lynx rode ahead of Ralstone, certain of her destination, while the mage-thief stopped to look around. She spurred her horse forward as she entered an empty alley. The mage-thief snapped out of his trance and rushed to keep up with her. His horse shied away from the many rats in the alley. Ralstone noticed that Lynx seemed oblivious to the creatures.

"I didn't think there would be so many rats in such a fair city," he remarked, as he finally reached Lynx's side.

"Doesn't surprise me, they come in by the cartfuls these days," she curtly replied. "A *rat* slinks in every damned day."

Ignoring the insult, Ralstone added, "Perhaps Shadow should acquire more cats. I'm sure that one *cat* could easily rid the city of more rats."

"Believe me, if I were a cat, I'd know what rat

to devour first," Lynx returned. Ralstone found himself liking the sound of her laughter, even if he disliked her words.

Eventually, Lynx stopped in front of an inn. She didn't bother to see if Ralstone was following her, but slid off her saddle and let a stable boy take charge of her horse. The mage-thief quickly did the same and went into the inn, a few steps behind her. The common room was not crowded. Tables and chairs were scattered. Lynx strolled to where the innkeeper stood behind the bar and showed him the Guild's seal on the palm of her right glove. He nodded and handed her a room key.

Ralstone caught up with her and trod on her heels as she unlocked the door to the room. He grasped her arm, forcing her to look at him.

"I'm going to share the same room with you— it's safer that way," he said. "We have no idea what we're up against yet, so we should stay together."

Lynx brushed his fingers off her arm.

"Don't you think I can defend myself?" She glared at him. "I chose this inn because most of the reports have said that the disappearances happen in inns like this one, sympathetic to the Guild. Besides, I was going to ask you to stay in the same room with me anyway, but not for your reason. I want to see what you have thought of the information Shadow provided."

With that, Lynx turned the key and the door swung open. Inside were two beds and a table with two chairs. She claimed the closest bed and began to unpack her things. The mage-thief dumped his gear on the floor and gazed out of the window. Lynx pulled up a chair and started to lay out Shadow's information on the table. She examined several maps and articles, then grouped them together in different categories.

Without looking up from the table, Lynx asked, "Are you going to help me, or are you going to vanish into thin air like the others? Not that I would mind."

"I'll help you," Ralstone came away from the window. He slumped in his chair. "The view's better here," he added, leering at her.

"Haven't you ever been in a city before?" Lynx asked.

"None as intriguing as Cant Borough—the thieves' capital in the Realm," he replied.

Lynx chose to ignore that comment and continued to sort through the papers. Ralstone picked up a couple of them, while Lynx watched him.

"Well, did you go over the information last night?" she inquired, not expecting an affirmative response.

"Yes, I did," replied Ralstone. "I figured out that most of the kidnappings must have occurred in Cant Borough."

"Why?" Lynx said.

"Because a teleportation spell to move all those people would take a tremendous amount of strength and endurance from even a powerful sorcerer. Also, the maps show that the vanishings all happened in Cant Borough."

"But it doesn't mean the thieves are still here; this sorcerer could have hidden their presence—or gotten rid of them."

"I think he could have cloaked their presence, but not gotten rid of them altogether; your informants would've found traces of their bodies."

"True, but the losses are all over the city. How am I—are we—going to track down this sorcerer?"

"I don't know, Lynx. I can't imagine how he

could be in so many places, unless he had some loyal apprentices or demons to serve him. If he does, there is no way we are even going to catch a glimpse of him."

After the briefest of knocks, an inn servant walked in with a tray of food, set it on the least cluttered area of the table, and left, closing the door behind him. Lynx gestured for Ralstone to keep quiet as she expertly inspected the tray and utensils on it. She found a small, magical contrived listening device on the bottom of the ale pitcher. She set it carefully on the table. Ralstone nodded. The mage-thief destroyed it with a word.

"Well, we have someone's attention," Lynx said.

After eating the food and drinking the ale, the pair went back to pondering the clues that Shadow had acquired. Ralstone was glad that Lynx was cooperating, despite her earlier protests and insults. He kept on his guard, though, not quite trusting her change in attitude. They had another pitcher of ale sent up along with some fruit later in the afternoon and made sure they examined the dishes for more listening devices.

The pair spent a few days locked in the room, examining the information. They were not disturbed by someone trying to listen to them again. Lynx was developing a genuine dislike for Ralstone and his near-constant flirtation. She had kicked him several times and then ignored his attempts to annoy her, having noticed that he enjoyed seeing her infuriated. The mage had checked with Shadow for any new information, but there was none.

It was late one evening when Ralstone recommended that they resume work the next day. "What good will it do us if we're exhausted before we actually go anywhere?" he asked.

"Fine," replied Lynx.

The mage-thief stretched, loosened his brown hair from the ponytail, kicked off his boots, and climbed into his bed. He took one last pull from his mug of ale, blew out the lights on his side of the room, and then settled into slumber. He turned a couple of times, then began to snore.

Lynx sat with all the papers and maps laid out in front of her. She didn't feel like sleeping yet. Her eyes studied each bit of information again—there had to be something they had overlooked. Propping her head on a hand, Lynx stared at the marked map of Cant Borough. Her free hand began to absently trace the streets on the map to each place of a disappearance.

She found she was tracing the outline of a hood, the same design as Shadow's seal, which he used to mark every document in the Guild.

"The thieves' kidnappings match Shadow's mark!" Lynx breathed, comparing it to an original mark on one of the papers. "Wait, the one on the map isn't finished."

Taking an inked quill, Lynx started to connect the various places together until there were no more left on the map. She held the map at arm's distance to compare it better with the actual mark. Finding the missing part on the map, she circled the area. Lynx gasped when she studied the area inside the circle. She had no idea how current the information was, but if it was more than a fortnight old. . . .

"I'll be too late," she murmured.

A rope and hook, lock picks, and a dagger were all she needed for the night's prowling. Lynx scooped up the map and tucked it into her inner tunic. Right before she stepped out of the window, she remembered the sleeping mage-thief. Her dark eyes drifted over to Ralstone's bed.

"I don't need him for this," she muttered, blowing out the candles on her side of the room.

Lynx kept to the dark alleys and shadows cast by the street lamps. She ran swiftly under the night's cover, only stopping once to refer to the map to make sure that she was in the right area. Lynx judged the time to be past midnight already. A few hours of traipsing past Cant Borough's night guards brought her to her destination. Before her, Lynx noted the heights of and lack of light from the buildings. She would have to be careful.

Lynx silently covered the distance between her position and the first building in the marked area from the map. Crouching beneath a window, her ears strained for sounds of people inside. She heard no indication of occupants. Wary of danger, she opened the window a crack. Again, she heard nothing, so she slipped inside the window.

She remained still, waiting for her eyes to adjust to the building's darkness. Her ears caught the squeaking of rats. She cautiously worked her way through the rooms, trying not to step on rats or make any other sound.

Arriving at the roof, Lynx noticed lights flickering in another building four down on the same street. She pulled out the map—the building was in the circled sector. Stuffing the map back into her tunic, Lynx backed up, ran, and then leaped to the next rooftop. Skidding to a stop, she decided to jump the remaining roofs as well. At the last building beside the one with light, she hooked her rope to a secure chimney, then lowered herself down to the alley.

Lynx left the rope where it was, planning to use it as a means of escape. She crept around the lighted building until she discovered a door with no light seeping around the frame. After picking the lock, Lynx entered the building. But she was unprepared for what greeted her.

She was engulfed in searing light which scorched her closed eyelids. Lynx attempted to shield her eyes with her arms, but a red haze still blinded them. She felt a hand shove her forward. She sprawled on the floor and lay there, until she felt herself being bound with ropes. Suddenly the radiant light lowered in intensity.

Lynx blinked rapidly to try to regain her eyesight. She saw the fuzzy form of a man standing nearby and staring at her. With a simple gesture of his right hand, he levitated Lynx to a standing position. She struggled against her magical bonds, but to no avail. When she was finally able to focus on her captor, she saw he was wearing long, flowing robes with intricate designs sewn on the hems. Neatly cut blond hair hugged his neck. His beady, brown eyes narrowed in malicious amusement.

"Another thief from Shadow," said the man, "and the most enchanting one yet."

Lynx kept her face blank despite the rising anger she felt as the man's eyes roamed her body. His satisfied laughter grated on Lynx's ears. His right hand cupped her chin as she tried to avert her face from his devouring eyes. The man sniggered all the more at her futile attempts at defiance. She tried to show as little disgust as she could, but she hated the way he looked at her.

"You know, you won't be needing your clothes anymore," he mused aloud. "When I'm through with you, wearing clothes will seem to be only a former way of keeping yourself warm."

"If you even *think* I'll be easy, you're wrong," Lynx shot back.

"Feisty, aren't you?" he chuckled. "I do enjoy

that particular trait in my women. But then again, you're allied with my adversary. What a loss."

While his eyes lingered on Lynx, the man retreated to his throne in the center of the room. She noted that, despite the building's shabby exterior, the interior was elegant. The stone floor was meticulously polished. It had a mirror reflection of everything standing on it. The design on the man's hem was duplicated everywhere. The door to the room had vanished, but Lynx knew there had to be one. How else did she get inside in the first place?

"Oh, how forgetful of me—my Name is Ignatius." He smirked. "Not that it matters, once I deal with you as I did the others. Since I have given you my Name, would you care to give me yours?"

"You said it wouldn't matter, so why do you care?" snapped Lynx.

"Exactly, but I do make exceptions." Ignatius grimaced arrogantly. "And to prove my point. . . ."

Ignatius held out his right hand, and slowly clenched it.

The rings of magic wrapped around Lynx tightened their hold. She gasped for air as the bonds constricted about her chest. Ignatius approached Lynx with his fingers closing toward his open palm. Lynx's steady gaze met his brown eyes till she nearly lost consciousness. He relaxed his hand suddenly and glared at her. She coughed, then breathed heavily. Ignatius pulled back the robe sleeve covering his left hand, but there was only the end of a wrist. The sorcerer thrust the stump in Lynx's face.

"This was taken from me by Shadow," his voice colored by indignation. "I was training under him as a thief in my internship. Back then,

I was his top student, Lynx. Yes, I know your name as I know the Names of all the Guild's members. To earn my Name, Shadow sent me to capture a priceless jewel.

"Easy, I had thought. Of course, I was certain of my ability not to get caught, as all thieves are." Lynx said nothing. "No, I did not get caught," he continued, "but there was a simple trap I had overlooked. I was distracted by excitement when I finally held the jewel in my right hand. I was slow in removing my other hand, and so I lost it.

"Upon my return to Shadow, I triumphantly showed him the jewel, but he refused to consider me successful because I had lost my hand. He cast me out of the Guild, saying that with only one hand I was useless as a thief.

"So I turned to magic, where my lack did not hinder my apprenticeship. Though as I advanced to higher levels, I discovered that certain of my sorcerous potential had been lost with my lost hand. I was forever denied that power.

"So I'm taking Shadow's power away from him," he whispered. "Yes, his power. The loyal thieves that flock to his Guild and his influence over the Realm. I have drained him—his thieves are *my* loyal creatures now."

Ignatius snapped his fingers once. Lynx could hear the scampering of tiny clawed feet on the stone floor. Then she saw them come out of every nook, every crack of the room. Rats of every size and color piled on top of each other at their master's command. Their squeaking filled the quiet of the night. Ignatius appeared to be pleased at Lynx's calm composure toward the rats.

"You see these rats? These are the same rats that have been overrunning Cant Borough—" Ignatius smiled. "—the former thieves that will destroy Shadow's home. Sweet isn't it, to be crushed by one's own power?"

His deranged cackle hurt Lynx's ears. Suddenly her bonds vanished and she landed on a carpet of writhing rat bodies. Ignatius walked quickly toward her, the rodents parting to make way for their master. The sorcerer loomed over Lynx. He knelt to look into her eyes once more.

"A pity. It would not do justice to you, if I were to change Shadow's favorite student into a rat, so I will change you into something more fitting—something to devour some of the other thieves."

Lynx attempted to break free of the sorcerer's gaze, but it was too late. Ignatius' brown eyes bored into hers, and he spoke the words of Change, even as he touched her forehead. At his touch, Lynx shuddered, feeling rising nausea in her stomach. She wanted to cry out with agony, but her voice was snatched away by the incantation.

Grinning in satisfaction, Ignatius plucked the clothes from Lynx's changed body. The rats scurried away, afraid. The sorcerer leered all the more as he grabbed the scruff of Lynx's neck. She was too disoriented to fight. He cruelly tossed her out the nearest window, his laughter echoing in the morning's first light.

Ralstone awoke from a fitful slumber. From the amount of light in the room, he guessed it was noon. The mage-thief stretched and tumbled out of bed. Tying his hair back in a ponytail, he glanced at Lynx's bed. It was neatly made.

"She probably went out for some fresh air," he said to himself. "Well, I'll just order some food."

A few moments later Ralstone was enjoying a piping hot stew and a pitcher of ale. He didn't give much thought to Lynx's absence until he finished his meal and glanced at the papers spread on the table. When the mage-thief saw that the marked map of Cant Borough was missing, he nearly choked on his bread.

"Of all the hot-headed idiots!" he exclaimed. "Don't tell me that she went off on her own! Damn it, Shadow told her that we had to work together."

Ralstone knew that without the map he would have no chance of finding Lynx in Cant Borough. He slumped back into his chair, racking his brain for a way to follow Lynx's trail. If she had left more than an hour ago, her track would be cold to his magic.

When a black cat stumbled through the open window into the room. Ralstone did not notice it—he was too absorbed in his thoughts. The cat leaped onto the table and devoured the remains of the stew ravenously, then started on the ale pitcher. Ralstone finally pulled the cat away before it could tip over the pitcher.

"How'd you get in here?" he asked, holding the cat level with his hazel eyes. Then Ralstone noticed the odd color of the cat's eyes—they were a very dark blue, very much like. . . .

"Lynx!" he shouted in disbelief and dropped the cat on the floor. She landed on all fours and meowed irritably. "What happened?"

She merely meowed.

"Wait a moment, I have a spell that will enable us to communicate," Ralstone said. "But you'll have to give me your *real* name for it to work."

She nodded her whiskered head reluctantly.

"I'll recite the alphabet, and you meow when it's the right letter," he suggested, grabbing paper and a quill. Shortly, Ralstone had her true Name.

"Marial. A pretty name, for a pretty cat," he

crooned and patted her head. She hissed and swiped at his hand with her claws. "All right, all right, I'll perform the spell."

Ralstone flexed his fingers and drew in a deep breath. He closed his eyes as he recited the spell. With his mind, he tried to grasp Marial's thoughts. Beads of sweat formed on his forehead as he concentrated. When he felt a cold flush, the mage-thief knew that the spell was completed. Suddenly, Ralstone opened his eyes. Marial was digging her claws into his chest.

"Ow!" he yelped.

I couldn't think of a better way to snap you out of it, came her voice. *You fool.*

"At least, *I* didn't get turned into an animal," Ralstone pointed out. Marial's claws dug deeper as she hissed again. The mage-thief jumped up in pain, dumping Marial to the floor.

Can't you change me back? she growled.

"I can't," he replied. "Only the person who cast the Change can return you to your former self. I take it this is the handiwork of our sorcerer?"

Marial nodded. *He's changed all the missing thieves into rats. I tell you, it was very tempting to chase and eat some rats. If one of them were you, I wouldn't have hesitated at all.*

"Thank you for the honor," Ralstone remarked.

He's going to use the rats to overrun Shadow in his home. Marial went on. *Tonight, I think.*

"Then let's get going," the mage replied, shouldering his backpack. Marial leaped onto the top of it.

"You know, I could really get used to your being this way," commented Ralstone, reaching back to scratch her head. He withdrew his hand quickly, not wanting Marial to slash it.

Shut up and get moving, you bastard, came her angered voice.

"How did I know that was coming?" He shook his head in amusement as he left the inn and headed out into the bustling streets of Cant Borough.

Marial directed the mage to the sorcerer's building. It took them a while to reach the area—during the day, Cant Borough was one huge marketplace filled with pushy traders and desperate merchants, even if the contracts that made the most money were negotiated at night. So by the time Ralstone and Marial reached the building, it was early evening.

Marial jumped off Ralstone's backpack and led the way through the area with her tail twitching back and forth. The mage watched the suppleness Marial possessed as a feline. He wondered if she carried the same subtle grace as a woman, but he hadn't noticed before. Despite all his flirting he hadn't really paid much attention to her.

Would you stop gawking, and watch where you're going? she scolded. *You nearly fell through a sewer hole—not that I care if you smell.*

Ralstone shrugged, then moved away from the hole. He followed her to the building. It was surprisingly near Shadow's own home. Ralstone carefully checked all entrances to the building. Deciding that it would be best to break in through the top window, he collected Marial in his arms to use a levitation spell.

She jumped onto the windowsill, while the mage pried it open. Marial went in first, then indicated that Ralstone could follow. The floor was coated with heavy dust and there were cobwebs in the corners. Ralstone found a flight of stairs that led down. Marial reached the next floor before the mage did. A door with runes decorating the doorway and knob stood between them and the sorcerer's throne room.

Ralstone read the warding runes silently, then unraveled them. He knelt at the door knob and picked the lock. Marial had braced herself for another trap, but nothing happened. As soon as they passed through the doorway, the door slammed behind them. It was the same room that Marial had been in earlier. She meowed in discomfort.

"Welcome back, Lynx," boomed Ignatius, "and welcome to your associate."

The sorcerer appeared in the center of the room, sitting comfortably in his throne. His triumphant smile seemed too perfect. He rose to stand and then threw his arms wide. The rats appeared at his command, surrounding Ralstone and Marial. She hissed violently and tried to fight her instinct to attack the rats—her fellow thieves.

His Name is Ignatius, Marial spoke through clenched teeth.

"Well, *Ignatius,* you are so dependent on your rats that you can't recognize another mage?" Ralstone asked. The sorcerer looked startled at Ralstone's use of his Name, then, remembering Lynx, he scowled. His eyes narrowed.

"So . . . you are indeed a mage, despite your dress and your tastes in allies," sighed Ignatius, obviously not impressed.

"I, Ralstone, challenge you, Ignatius, to a duel."

"Pah. Challenging me would only gain you your death," responded Ignatius, undaunted.

"Are you afraid that what I can accomplish with *two* hands can defeat you?" baited Ralstone.

Ignatius was angered. Ralstone could see him clenching his hand. When it opened, the rats retreated to their hidden holes and cracks and Ignatius stepped forward.

"I accept your challenge, *Ralstone,*" he said.

"And as a sign of my sincerity in this would-be duel, I will return Lynx to her former self."

The air sighed as Marial returned to her human body. She clutched her mid-section as a wave of nausea hit her. Her head was splitting. She would not be able to do anything, except perhaps witness the duel. She felt too wretched even to reach for her clothing, which was piled near her in a heap on the floor where Ignatius had dropped it the night before.

Ralstone looked at her in concern. "Are you all right?" he asked. Hunched over and lying on the floor, Marial nodded.

Ralstone turned back to Ignatius. "What are the terms?" he asked.

"The terms are by any magical means, within these walls, and the duel lasts until only one remains standing," answered Ignatius.

It began. The two men circled each other, each testing the other's ability. Ralstone knew he was not as strong as the other, but he already knew Ignatius' weakness from Marial and also knew that the sorcerer had expended significant energy beforehand.

Still, Ignatius' attacks wore down Ralstone's defenses. The mage-thief fell to the stone floor and scrambled to ready himself for another spell. But before he could utter the words, Ignatius' next offensive caught him squarely in the side. Ralstone staggered backward against a wall.

"Child's play," taunted Ignatius, raising his right hand to finish him.

"Not quite," said Ralstone.

Five long needles came from the forearm cuffs on his shirt. They flew true and embedded deep in Ignatius' chest. The sorcerer fell back. Pulling his ritual knife from his belt, the mage tackled Ignatius. The sorcerer muttered another spell just as

Ralstone hacked off his right hand, and with it the last of his power. Ignatius shrieked in horror then slumped to the floor, dead. Ralstone stood, nursing his side.

"Magical forearm bracers," Ralstone smirked. Then he disappeared as his clothing dropped to the floor.

"Ralstone!" yelled Marial, pulling on her tunic and dragging herself to her feet.

She walked unsteadily over to the pile of his clothes, knelt and pulled out a brown rat. Then Marial felt a tap on her shoulder. The room's appearance had changed, the symbols had vanished, and it became an ordinary common room. She looked up. A couple of men, naked and looking very embarrassed, stood shakily beside her.

"Were you the first changed into rats?" she asked.

"Yes; I believe it was several months ago," one man replied.

"Well, Shadow's home is near, and I'm certain he'll be glad to get you some clothes," she said.

They nodded, and left, some of the other rats following them. Marial held Ralstone in her hands and smiled.

"I guess you'll be the last to change back," Marial grinned. "I'm going to take *such* good care of you."

The rat squealed in horror.

Marial was giving Ralstone a bath in a bowl when he finally reverted back to human form. The mage ended up standing on the broken shards of the bowl. He howled, and jumped off the table. Marial merely watched as he plucked the bits of bowl out of his feet. When she finally could no longer contain her laughter, the mage-thief blushed darkly.

He swore as she laughed harder. "I'm going to get back at you for all you did to me!"

"All I did to you was keep you safe," shot back Marial. "Think about it, Ralstone. I could have fed you to the cats, owls, let you get captured by a rat trap. . . ."

"Fine, I see your point," he grumbled. "But a *bath!*"

"If you insisted on sleeping on my pillow, you should have expected I would wash you," smirked Marial.

The mage-thief chuckled.

"Oh, Ralstone, are you hungry?" she asked sweetly. "Because I have some cheese for you."

She shoved it in front of his face and bolted with her laughter trailing behind her. Ralstone knocked the cheese off the table, and started after her, oblivious to his nakedness.

Shadow watched in silent amusement as the mage-thief chased Marial, cursing all the way. He smiled from his balcony above the courtyard. Sometimes solutions came in the most unlikely guises.

"A Lynx and a bastard," he laughed.

DRAGONSKIN BOOTS
by L.S. Silverthorne

Ms. Silverthorne has now had four sales to
us; in addition to these, she has made 17 or
so sales to semi-pro markets and a sale to
Galaxy. She wrote her first novel in the sixth
grade, and adds that many of her "early stories have been buried as a public service to
the community."

As the church bell tolled the noon hour, the
Queen swung a delicate dragonskin boot
out of the coach door and stepped out of
the coach. The boots had been a gift from the
cobbler, so she had decided to wear them on her
official visit to the village. As she paused in front
of the Red Hand Pub, a screech pierced the afternoon calm. A bald-headed woman rushed at the
Queen, shrieking something about the toll of a
bell, and flung handfuls of ash at her feet. A puff
of gray smoke billowed up toward the Queen's
face, settling on her burgundy skirt and even in
her dark hair. She coughed, the smell of stale

charcoal clinging to her nostrils. When she glanced around, the woman was gone.

"Fire!"

One of the Queen's attendants, a stout, bearded man, hurried her away from the pub door as a thick stream of black smoke rolled out from under it.

"Reginald," she shouted. "What's going on?"

Reginald shook his head. "They've set another fire, m'lady."

"They? Who is responsible for—this?" She held out her arms, the ivory sleeves smudged with soot.

"Perhaps it was the Virgins Guild? They have been out of work since the sacrifice of virgins was decreed unlawful."

Suddenly, a crowd of white-robed maidens clamored out of the pub, their dresses and faces smeared with ash. Each maiden wore a dainty silver pair of dragonskin boots. As they paused in front of the door, coughing and gagging from the smoke, three bald-headed women rushed at them with buckets. Furious, the maidens lunged at the women.

"Repent your evil ways," one of the bald-headed women shouted and dumped a bucketful of ashes on them.

"As you can see, m'lady," said Reginald. "They were not pleased by your ruling. I've heard rumors that they are disbanding."

Across the street near the inn, clanging and banging echoed above the shrieks of the maidens. Two hoarse men's voices rose above the clamor. "Sacrifice or Death! Sacrifice or Death!"

The Queen craned her neck to see two ragged-looking men in torn leather jerkins and brown dragonskin boots. "Sacrifice or Death? What are they talking about? Who are those men?"

Reginald sighed. "They are what's left of the Heroes Guild. They, too, are upset about your ruling. They've launched a bitter campaign against it."

A frown overshadowed the streaks of soot across her face. "Some campaign. They're down to two members. And what sort of silly battle cry is that?"

Two villagers dashed between the coach and the Virgins Guild members, carrying pails of water. Thick coils of black smoke billowed into the sky from the burning pub.

"Who is responsible for these fires?"

"We believe it was the Dragon Foundation."

"What Dragon Foundation?" demanded the Queen.

"The women who have shaved their heads say that with every toll of the church bell, a dragon dies," answered Reginald. "They vow to set a fire with every toll of the bell to remind us when a dragon dies."

The Queen's eyes widened. "Is that true? I don't recall the knights having much luck on their dragon quests."

"Hard to say, m'lady. I'd ask the knights, but as you already know, most of them have died or quit."

The Queen scowled at the Virgins wrestling with the bald-headed women, the sound of the Heroes' chant driving her wild with irritation. "I want all of them arrested!"

"Arrested?" Reginald glanced sheepishly at his ash-covered boots. "It—it isn't possible."

"Why not?"

"Because some of the Foundationers have chained themselves to the blacksmith's forge. They have shaved their heads to symbolize the horror of dragon-skinning and they heckle any knight who tries to purchase a sword. Some of them were even camped in front of the Virgins Guild to convince them to stop their evil ways."

The Queen's eyes widened. "The Virgins?"

"The Foundationers say they have lured so many dragons to their deaths that they are bordering on extinction."

"The virgins?"

"No, m'lady, the dragons."

"What sparked the Foundationers' crusade?"

He pointed at his feet. "Dragonskin boots."

"Reginald, I want a meeting with all parties involved—immediately."

In a short while, the Queen arrived at the town hall. On one side of the room, a handful of knights clanked and creaked in their seats. In front of them sat the Virgins Guild, their robes soot-gray now.

On the other side of the room sat two rows of Foundationers, their shaved heads making the Queen nervous. Gently, she rapped on the lectern with a gavel.

"My loyal subjects," she began, "I have called this meeting in order to put a stop to the violence plaguing our town."

"The violence will stop when the killing stops," shouted a Foundationer, her hard brown eyes boring holes through the Queen.

"M'lady," cried one of the Virgins, "you must repeal the sacrifice law. Without our meager shares of treasure received for our sacrifices, we will starve."

A knight clanked to his feet. He raised a hand and opened his mouth to speak, but the visor of his helmet snapped over his eyes. With a squeak, he awkwardly shoved the visor open. "Our Order is being ravished by the dragons, m'lady. Something must be done. I say kill the dragons before they kill us!"

"Who will speak for the dragons?" said a voice from the other side of the room. "Who will stop the killing—and the wearing of dragonskin boots?"

The voices mingled into a dull roar, accented by the Heroes pounding and chanting, "Sacrifice or Death." Angry, the Queen smacked the gavel against the lectern.

"Silence! Enough of this bickering!"

Abruptly, the room fell silent except for the raucous chanting of the Heroes Guild outside.

"I will think carefully about this matter and rule on it one week from tonight. Until then, I want no more fires and no more trouble. Agreed?"

The Foundationers nodded their burnished scalps toward the Queen and filed out of the hall. Creaking and clanging, the knights also agreed as they made their way to the door. After the Virgins had whispered among themselves, they, too nodded their agreement and flitted out into the street.

"How will you solve this, m'lady?"

She shook her head. "I don't know, Reginald. I don't know."

The next day, the Queen sat at her desk by the window, gazing out at the castle lawn. How could she appease all the Guilds and the Activists? Toward afternoon, there was a knock at the drawing room door.

"Enter."

One of her servants rushed in, carrying her light blue pair of dragonskin boots. "I polished them for you, Your Majesty. Cleaning the ash off them was hard, but I managed." She pointed at a scratch across one of the scales. "Must have gotten scratched during the cleaning, Your Majesty. I beg your forgiveness."

The Queen stared at the scratch for a moment. "Odd," she said. How did one scratch dragon scales? Something seemed peculiar about that scratch. It seemed too deep for dragonskin. She reached over to her quill pen and dragged it across the other boot, leaving a deep gash on it.

"Your Majesty!"

The Queen smiled. "Call my driver immediately. I need to go into the village."

The attendant frowned. "What for, m'lady? The cobbler won't be able to fix this."

"I think he can," she answered and rose from her chair.

She put on the boots and followed her attendant down the stone stairs. In a few moments, her carriage jostled up to the front door. She rushed out of the castle and into the carriage.

The ride to the village was dusty and bumpy, but the Queen endured it in silence. When the carriage squeaked to a stop at the cobbler's doorstep, she hurried out of the carriage and into the store.

The slight man behind the counter pressed his wire-rimmed glasses against the bridge of his nose and bowed his head. His hair was thick and his build was slight, matching his quiet demeanor.

"Good afternoon, Your Majesty. What may I do for you?"

The Queen reached down and pulled off one of the boots. She plopped it onto the counter. "Do you see this?" she asked, pointing at the scratch.

His face flushed pink. "Yes, m'lady. Would you like it repaired?"

"No," she said and crossed her arms. "I would like it explained."

"Explained?"

She nodded. "Explain to me why you are passing off leather boots as dragonskin?"

The cobbler sighed. "Sales have been bad, Your Majesty."

"But these were a gift . . . like the ones you gave the Virgins Guild."

He dropped his head into his hands. "I confess. The boots are merely carved and dyed leather."

The Queen shook her head. "Why would you do this?"

"With all the hype about hunting dragons, I wanted to boost sales. They've sold well since the Foundationers shaved their heads."

"So you created all these dragonskin boots."

"Yes, m'lady," said the cobbler, looking her in the eye. "When the Foundationers saw the boots, they thought many dragons had been killed. Of course, when Virgin sacrifices were outlawed, most of the dragons left the area. The Foundationers are the only ones taking these boots seriously, m'lady."

She smiled. "You've just given me the solution to the problem, cobbler." The Queen slipped her foot back into her dragonskin boot and started toward the door. She paused, finally turning back to him. "And you will make no more fake boots, understood?"

He nodded. "You have my word, Your Majesty."

At the end of the week, the Queen returned to the Meeting Hall. The Heroes Guild, all two members, sat in the front row, their hands poised over their shields. The Virgins Guild sat across from them, the Knights squeaking and clanging behind them. In the back of the room sat the Foundationers.

The Queen, carrying her pair of dragonskin boots, walked up the aisle to the lectern. She set the pair of boots on the lectern and cleared her throat.

"After careful assessment of the situation, I have decided to do two things. First, I have rescinded the law prohibiting the sacrifice of Virgins Guild members to dragons." The Virgins Guild chattered among themselves while the Knights and the Heroes Guild cheered. She noticed how the Foundationers glared at her and crossed their arms in protest. "Second, from this day forward, all dragonskin boots are considered illegal." Snatching the boots from the lectern, the Queen turned toward the hearth. She dropped the boots into the fire as the Foundationers clapped and whistled.

One by one, the Virgins and the Heroes filed toward the hearth and tossed their boots into the fire.

"Your Majesty," said one of the Virgins, "we accept your compromise. There won't be any more fires."

"Good," said the Queen. "Then we are finished here." She stepped away from the lectern and left the town hall. Her coach awaited her, Reginald standing beside the door.

"Did it go well, m'lady?" Reginald asked.

She nodded. "Yes. There will be no more fires and no more dragonskin boots."

"That's wonderful," said Reginald. He reached into his vest pocket and pulled out a pair of glistening green gloves.

The Queen gasped and pointed at the gloves. "What are those?"

Reginald's brow furrowed. "They're dragonskin gloves, m'lady. I bought them from the cobbler while you were in the Town Hall."

Just as the Queen opened her mouth to protest, the church bell rang.

TRUTH
by Lynne Armstrong-Jones

Lynne and I go back a long way. I've bought several stories from her for various anthologies, and for *Marion Zimmer Bradley's Fantasy Magazine*. She has also sold to other markets. So many of the young writers I see submit to me once, or maybe twice, and then go away and are never heard of again. While, in theory, I agree that if they don't like the heat they should get out of the kitchen, I hate the idea that if they don't sell right off, they will ride off on their high horse and never be heard from again. The right thing to do is stick around and try again—and try other markets. There may be nothing wrong with your story—I may just be a little over my wordage for the book.

Lynne has two children, a boy just over eight and a girl of two, and is teaching adult English—which I found out I couldn't do. After a day spent teaching I couldn't even read, let alone write. I got my fill of words teaching and never managed to do both at once.

Lynne is a brown belt in karate. Well, better

her than me; my interest in the martial arts is watching wrestling on TV—and some people claim wrestling's not a sport. Maybe that's why I like it.

He was ugly, by the heavens he was ugly! Or so he seemed to Lucia. But then, Lucia's judgment was clouded, her vision blurred. In fact, she was fortunate to have any will left at all. . . .

She closed her eyes once more, tried to soothe away the throbbing, the aches and stings of her injuries—her torture—which she'd received at this brutal man's commands. But her earlier attempts to heal herself had only drained further her energy and strength.

"Tell me, Mistress Lucia." The man's voice was soft, gentle. He was very close; she could smell the sweet, fruity wine on his breath.

Tell him, she thought, *tell him, tell him—oh, indeed!*

And what would he *do* if she enacted the spell to release the Secret of Great Power? Would he use it for the betterment of humankind? Not likely! She almost laughed aloud at the notion.

"Lucia," he said again, his voice just a *wee* bit sharper this time.

But the little sorceress heard the difference; he had spoken just that way the last time he'd ordered further "persuasion" for her. Her brown eyes flew open, stared into his green ones—

I am a sorceress of the Three Towers, she reminded herself sternly. *I shall fight to the death to protect the world from Evil.*

A shiver raced through her nonetheless, leaving a cold trail along her spine. She tried to hold his stare with her own, but she couldn't control the trembling. Her teeth burrowed into the inside of her lower lip; somehow it seemed that, if she could just control *it,* perhaps she'd gain control of the rest.

He was smiling. Too broadly. Torchlight accented the flaxen streaks which brightened his brown hair, his perfectly-trimmed beard, and set the golden earring glittering. He reached a manicured hand down, gently stroked the sweaty brow of the woman with his soft fingers. Clicking his tongue, he shook his perfume-scented head from side to side.

"Ah, Lucia. Dear, dear, dear. Look. Your brow is soaked, you ache, you wish nothing more right now than just to fall asleep. Don't you. Yes, yes. . . ."

She fought. Oh, *how* she fought. It took every bit of will she could muster just to keep her eyes from closing. Yet the voice was so soothing, so comforting, so. . . .

"NO!" His voice was like the boom of a cannon.

She jerked, eyes wide. Another of his ploys.

He stared once more into her eyes, then shouted again. "NO! No, no, NO! Don't you think I'd *like* to let you rest? Do you think I *enjoy* this? Surely you must know that I only do what I must!"

Lucia swallowed, licked her lips with a tongue so thick it seemed to fill her mouth completely. *The game begins again.*

And Lord Armand the Powerful (or so he liked to call himself) once more filled the dungeon area with his sarcasm, his words echoing throughout the tunnels: It was almost as though his lies truly went on and on, forever without end—

A shiver seized Lucia again, this time holding

her, keeping possession as though it would never release her. Teeth chattering, she considered the one element of truth in the dictator's words. He wanted power. Power, power and more power. It was like a demon possessing the man's soul, only to discover that this was not enough. Hunger. Eating away at him from the inside out.

What if she *did* give it to him? But there was no point in even considering it. His history showed him to be a ruthless man, selfish; human life meant nothing to him—

Then the only alternative, the only way out of her predicament lay in either rescue . . . or death. The first was quite unlikely. Yes, there were those who knew she was missing, who'd search for her. But there was not much chance that they'd venture into Armand's territory: He had a strict rule about trespassers. And, as she was the only magician from the neighboring county . . . well, her chances simply did not look good.

Only one way out. As she sighed, her bruised and cracked ribs complained bitterly. And she felt that she was not all that far from her one way out. If only her death could be easier, quicker. . . .

"Ayeee!"

He'd yanked her into a sitting position, every part of her body crying out with pain. His eyes bored into hers, seemed to burn tiny holes right through her.

"Kill me," she whispered, her lips thick and dry.

"What?!"

"Kill me," she repeated, a little more clearly this time. "I can't give you the spell you want—"

He held the edge of her sweat-stained robe in his hands, pulled her so that her face was almost touching his. "I will kill you, you know. But not until you've suffered more. Do you *want* to suffer? *Do* you?"

She tried to reply, to say *something*, but a huge lump blocked her throat. *No*, she wanted to say. But would not.

"If you—if you," she began, her voice hoarse. "If you kill me, you'll never get what you want. And—and if you keep torturing me, I'll be too weak, too ill to use *any* spell to help you."

Abruptly he released her. A moan burst from her as she fell back onto the platform. He turned away, fists clenching, unclenching, clenching once more.

"All right, then, Mistress Lucia." He turned to face her again, stepping closer. "I guess we could say that you win. You have, indeed, presented me with a problem."

She turned her head to see him more clearly. Had she really heard him say that?

He continued, his voice velvety soft. "No. I won't take further action against your person. You're quite right. If I hurt you more, you'll be too weak to do my bidding. And I certainly don't want *that!*"

Closer still he moved, until he knelt by her side. Gently, gingerly, he took her small hand in his smooth one. "No, my dear. I'll not harm you further." He grinned. But the smile's brightness proclaimed that the worst was yet to come. "Instead, dear one, I'll send my army into your county with orders to kill every female they can find."

He stood then, letting her hand fall. Arms crossed, he fixed his gaze on her, and smiled again. "And so you see, my dear. Two can play at this game."

Her head swam, the room seemed to turn, turn in one direction and then another. She tried to control her breathing, slow it down, yet her breath came almost in pants. And all she could hear was the *thud, thud, thudding* of her heart.

There must be a way; there HAS to be!

She could see their images—the women of the villages and countrysides. Her friends, neighbors. She could not let this happen, and yet—

And yet she could not, *must* not give him the spell he requested. In fact, her desire had nothing to do with it; she was simply too weakened now to give the energy the Great Spell demanded.

She had to rely on something *else*. And a memory lit her mind; the memory of a lesson *not* learned inside a tower. Yes. She was a sorceress. Yet sometimes spells alone were not enough. She must think.... From somewhere deep, deep inside, she could feel a spark of strength. At first it was just a flash, but it grew, grew slowly until a soothing warmth drifted gently through her. Yes. She had a reply for him now.

She cleared her throat, tried again to lick her lips with an equally dry tongue. "We have—we have a problem, powerful lord, but there might be a solution of sorts. A drink, please, if you would?"

He studied her, this woebegone slip of womanhood. Her robe was tattered, stained, her short brown hair drenched with sweat. Her light brown eyes seemed to have sunk deeply into her thin face. She did not look very impressive.

But she was of the Three Towers, a powerful sorceress. And those of the Three Towers were incapable of lying. Everyone knew that as fact....

And by the Great Gods, he wanted that power!

Lord Armand stroked his beard and nodded to an aide. In a second, the sorceress was sipping cool water from a ladle. Grimacing, she held herself up, supported by her elbows.

"There is—there is a spell I can do for you. Something that will give you much of what you seek—"

"What is this spell?"

But she shook her head, motioned to him for patience. "We must venture to the outside. For the spell I have in mind, I must be able to call upon what nature can provide."

"*Oh*, no. No, my dear, I'll not fall for that one," he guffawed, shaking his head.

"Hear me out." She stared at him, and he blinked, for there seemed suddenly to be a bit more strength in that gaze. She continued. "You have robbed me of much strength. Allow me, please, to use the strength of the natural elements in its place. And anyway, you may bring as many armed guards with you as you wish. So what do you fear?"

"*Fear?* From you? *Nothing,* I can quite assure you."

"Then take me outside. And I will create a spell which will bring you something no other human has—"

"What?"

"Something of which other men can only dream—"

"Tell me, sorceress. *Now.*"

There was silence a moment as Lucia moved her head in a circular motion, stretching out her cramped neck muscles. She could hear the rattle of his jewelry as he moved closer, and she turned her gaze to him once more. "You shall have a longer life than any other living mortal. You shall outlive all your enemies, have many, many decades in which to use your power. Imagine what you could do with such a gift! I can even offer you a unique protection against spears and arrows. What say you, Lord Armand?"

His eyes were not focused on the sorceress; he seemed to be studying something far, far away.

Immortality? Not quite, perhaps. But he had much, much power already ... and more time to use it, add to it ... the opportunity to watch his enemies die—

But he turned to her, glaring. "You must give me your word that I'll not be helpless. Or crippled. Or—"

She raised a hand to stop him. "I promise perfect health."

He studied her. "You'll not frighten my guards away with illusions. And you promise that all of this is truth. By your word of the Three Towers."

"Truth," she nodded. "All. By the Three Towers."

It was his turn to nod.

Truth or not, she certainly had not gained all of Armand's trust. She gazed at the many soldiers surrounding them. And the spears, axes, and swords. But the breezes were wonderful coolness on her cheeks, refreshing her beautifully as they dried the perspiration on her brow.

And she gazed not at the lord or his soldiers, but at the heavily treed area just ahead. She urged the pony onward, and was not surprised to find soldiers quickly in front of her to prevent her from moving on.

"That's far enough," came Armand's baritone voice from just behind.

"As you wish," she said softly, knowing that his words were quite true.

"Now," he ordered. When she turned to him, he was smiling. "And, by the way, the wood is filled with quicksand, and deep bogs which will suck you up should you try to escape. Oh, did I not mention that before? Just a little secret, my dear."

She nibbled on the inside of her lower lip. When she replied, her voice was very soft. "Indeed."

"The spell. *Now.*"

Lucia breathed very deeply, enjoying the pine scents, the sweet smells of the grasses. She filled herself with what the forest offered, let nature give her strength. . . .

She was inside her mind, watching the Book of Spells open, open, to spill forth the enchantments she needed. A moan escaped her as she felt her insides quiver, for soon she would change—

But first, a bit of show for the soldiers. It would be more impressive that way. Not to mention safer.

An enormous fog suddenly deposited itself firmly over the area. One could barely see an arm's length ahead of oneself. . . .

Indeed, Lucia almost had difficulty finding a suitable branch on which to perch and watch the fun. She folded her wings and settled just behind a row of pine needles.

The fog cleared almost as quickly as it had come. The men were still shouting, brandishing their blades, certain that a new and terrible enemy lurked near. But, when all was clear once more, they saw themselves and nothing more.

No great beast or other threat. And no Great *Lord,* for that matter. Not at first, anyway. . . .

But then the soldiers' captain spied a strange creature which was unusual in these parts. They watched curiously as it ambled slowly through the grasses.

A tortoise.

Lucia fluttered upward, turned east toward her beloved home. She would have to rest before she arrived there, before taking her own form again, for she was still weak. But that was all right.

Indeed, everything was.

SKINS
by Heather Rose Jones

One of the clichés of which I get far too many every year is the story of the shapechanger; I've decided that everyone has a story of this kind, and it usually lands on my desk. Heather works in the office for *Marion Zimmer Bradley's Fantasy Magazine* and is a very fine songwriter and singer, appearing on at least one tape in my collection. She is also a full-time graduate student at the University of California at Berkeley.

Psychologically speaking, the story of a shapechanger is an indication of an obsessive desire to change one's life. Or perhaps in a writer, it is a substitute for changing one's life. To me the best thing about writing is the way in which one can live more lives than one. I am constantly reminding myself that, "He who lives more lives than one/More deaths than one must die." Does this mean that I have nine lives like a cat? Or does it mean that the nice young lady who works in my circulation department goes out at the full moon and becomes something else? Time will tell, I guess. Meanwhile, who—or what—is up in my office logging in those subscription orders?

The ground raced by under our feet, damp and rotten with last year's litter. The trees crowded closely overhead, blocking the moonlight. It was so dark that even with wolfeyes I could barely follow the path. And with the other senses parceled out to the boys ... I didn't miss the scents, but the dead silence made everything unreal to me.

"Dyoan, what do you hear?" I could feel him struggling to put things into words. Words were necessary even when we shared a body like this.

"Only two riders ... far behind ... fallen back."

I swiveled our ears. "And ahead?"

"Nothing ... wait! To the right." I turned our head momentarily to focus. "They've circled around ! Laaki, run!"

"Wait. Ale'en, that's upwind. What do you smell?"

His thoughts wailed at me. "I want out! Laaki, let me out!"

I prayed for patience. He was only seven—too young to have the discipline to be carried senseless inside, but it wasn't much easier to be limited to smells. "Soon. Shall we be caught because you're such a baby? Now tell me, what do you smell?"

"Horses. Horses and men. They're sweating a lot."

"No dogs?"

"No. Laaki, let me out!"

"Be still!"

Dyoan leaped to his brother's defense, as usual. "You let him be! It's easy for you!"

Easy for me—those were the words that had gotten us into this....

We were in the kitchen-yard of the White Swan; I fetching water from the well and Dyoan sneaking a break from cleaning tables. Now, I've never minded hard, honest work, and we were lucky that Ercin would take on strangers as he did. But Dyoan thought it all beneath us, somehow, and the customers could tell and sometimes couldn't resist poking at his touchy pride.

"I want my skin-song—now!" he said, as if I could produce it at will.

"You'll have it when I've made it, and not before. And if you don't let me do my chores, I won't have time to work on it at all tonight."

"You haven't worked on it for months."

And he was right. But then it was months since I'd had a day to myself, to go off in the woods with the wolf-skin he had inherited from his mother and think wolfish thoughts and craft wolf-ish rhymes. Our kind are few enough as it is, and fewer still of us have the talent for making the songs that bind skin to man. It was not an easy task.

Nearly a year ago, their father had left these two in my care, then wrapped himself in his eagle-skin and fled some nameless stalker. We are often hunted. He never returned, and I was left with an angry youth who had not yet learned to wear his mother's wolf-skin, and a child who had not even that much. Their father might have hired me to craft them songs. A year's time with no worries for food and a roof—maybe even a bit of coin at the end—and I'd have had them both wearing skins. But here I was: father and mother

and singer, all three. And five years might not be
enough. There was one thing I could give him
now, though.

"Would you like to go hunting? I can give
Ercin some excuse."

He looked at me as if I had offered a starving
man a sugared violet. "I want my *skin!* It's easy
for you! All you do is throw it over me and say,
'Wear thy skin.' and you think that's the same.
It's not the same when I have to come whining
back and wait for you to take it off me. You have
your feathers—you can't understand."

But I did. And the thought of how lost I would
be without my owl-skin was a cold place in my
soul. How could he have patience? He was fifteen
years old.

He took my silence for something else and had
opened his mouth to continue when a sound in the
main yard made us freeze. Dyoan turned pale,
knowing he had broken the rule, talking of skins
where someone could hear.

There was silence, then a horse stamped and
snorted and a low voice called, "Halloo." A customer, then. Dyoan was also part-time stable boy.
He sighed and slipped through the gate to the
main courtyard.

I would have dropped the incident entirely
from my mind if not for the way the new customer stared when I brought his food, not that I
wasn't used to rude stares from some of the men.
I schooled myself to a bland look and was relieved when he examined Ercin just as closely
later on. Maybe it was just his way.

But then Ercin had pulled me aside at the end
of the evening, when the kitchen fires had been
banked and the customers had all gone to their
beds.

"That fellow—he was asking questions about

you and your brothers." (They weren't my brothers, of course, but it was the simplest explanation.) "Like, where you were from, and did I know your folks, and how long had you been here. You haven't run away from something have you?"

It was a reasonable guess, although runaway bondsmen usually headed for a town. "No, I told you true. We're freeborn, just lost our land."

"He asked something funny, too: did you have a cloak of fur or feathers." My mind raced to the skins, hidden carefully under our sleeping pallets. "Now fur I can understand—wouldn't mind one myself when winter sets in—but what would anyone want with a cloak of feathers?"

I shrugged, trying not to shiver. "For pretty, maybe? I heard a story once about a queen with a dress of peacock feathers."

Ercin scratched his head and shrugged in return. "Well, if he bothers you, you let me know. I don't want to lose you."

But I knew then that he would lose us, and soon.

I roused the boys from their sleep; Dyoan alert and wary, Ale'en yawning and sleepy-eyed. "We have to leave. That man was asking questions—he knows too much." Guilt rose in Dyoan's face with a flush. I stopped a useless apology with a squeeze of his shoulder. "Get your skin, we can't afford to carry anything else."

That wasn't entirely true, for I did fetch our thin coinpurse out from under my bed along with my owl-skin. I bundled them up and tied them, leaving a loop of cord long enough to go around a wolf's neck. Paws were faster than wings and we couldn't afford to get separated.

We slipped out the back, through the kitchen court and over the garden wall. I thought we

would be free and safe, but someone must have
been watching for us. There was a muffled
whinny from the roadway and an answering one.
Who were the others? He'd come in alone. Had
he hired other travelers for his hunt?

There was no time to wonder. I shook out the
wolf-skin and flung it around us as the boys
pressed close to my sides. This was different from
using a skin-song. This was the rough, crude
magic a singer could use in emergencies, forcing
a shape on a body, willing or unwilling. "Wear
thy skin!" I hissed, and then human speech was
ours no more. We would run in one body as a
wolf until I chose to release us.

The inn lay in a narrow valley, just down from
the pass into Ganasset—the better to catch the
trade. I might have run for the pass if I thought
we could beat the riders. Beyond, the land was
thick forest all the way to Karskar. The other way
lay fields and orchards, and a strip of wooded
land along the river. We took to the woods and
raced along the deer-paths, with the hoofbeats of
our pursuers falling farther behind. But then we
heard the other riders flanking us to the right. . . .

If I had known the land that lay in this direction
better, we might have avoided what came, but
when we hunted, it had been beyond the pass
where we would not disturb the local farmers. So
I veered to the left, closer to the river, and didn't
notice how the land rose in a steep bank between
us and the road. We could have swum the river,
but I feared it would slow us down too much. So
instead we were racing along the narrow track at
the base of the rise, up a bit from the water's
edge, when the ground crumbled under us and we

fell through woven branches into a steep, mud-bottomed pit.

One of them must have known the pit was there and simply herded us toward it, for how could they have known what that night would bring any more than we did? And there we were, bruised and muddy, with Ale'en shrieking in my mind to be let out, and the walls too steep for climbing or jumping, and in the distance the sound of the hunt. I drew the wolf-skin off us, bundling it quickly as I shook out the owl cloak.

"Quickly now," I called to the boys, spreading the cloak wide.

Ale'en wailed and scrabbled to the opposite end of the pit. "No! I won't!"

"We have no time for this!" I hissed, reaching for his arm.

But in that moment of confusion Dyoan's instinct was to protect his brother, and he pushed between us saying, "Let him be."

And all that I can offer in my defense is that the hunters were nearly on top of us, and there was only one way out, and I had been caged once before. . . .

I wrapped the cloak around me with my skin-song whispering in my mind, clutched the wolf-cloak in my talons, and fled.

Being that I had worn my skin for so long, and that I am a singer, I never needed the song itself to change. But still the echoes of my first creation came back every time I flew.

"Time to wear the feathers,
Time to fly the night,
No ground can hold me down now,
No one can stay my flight."

The dark pit shrank beneath me as I tried to stop my ears to the shouts of the hunters and the boys' frightened cries.

"Fetch the finely fashioned feather cloak
And clutch it close across me,
Feel the flesh reforming,
Fingers stretching,
Strong and starward striving. . . ."

I flew until the weight of the wolf-skin and my own grief bore me down. Then I found a dark place to hide and curled up under the skins, weeping for the trust I had betrayed.

Two days passed before I found the courage to return to the pit. The wolf-skin was hidden away safe and I flew unencumbered through the early dusk. The ground around the pit was still churned to mud, but when I followed the hoofmarks, they only led me back up around to the road and then disappeared in the mass of tracks. Where might they have been taken? Ercin might know, if they had gone that way, but would he tell me? Would he help me at all, knowing now what I am? Better, perhaps, to ask a stranger, who would be only normally curious.

I perched on a milepost, feathers fluffed in indecision, and didn't notice the shadow above me until it slipped steeply through the air. Even then I was frozen a moment in confused recognition, but the intent of the eagle's stoop was unmistakable. I cast forward, hoping to make the shelter of the trees in time. The wind of his turn buffeted me nearly as much as his fisted talons as he knocked me tumbling to the ground. I cast off my feathers, hoping to gain the advantage of size and to no surprise at all, my assailant did likewise.

"Dyoan! What does this mean?" He was not the person I expected to see beneath that eagle-skin.

He folded his arms and smiled smugly. "It means I've found a better singer than you ever were to help us. It only took him half a day to make the skin-song for me and you can't even make one in a year! Now give me back my wolf-skin and go your way."

"He gave you that skin?"

He snarled at me, but I could see the hurt behind it. "What do you care? You left us behind! To die, for all you knew—or worse. Just give me my skin and let us be."

"Dyoan." My voice dropped to a whisper. "The man who chased us wasn't Kaltaoven—wasn't one of us. Who gave you that skin?"

Something in my tone broke through, and he looked confused. "He only wanted to help us, you know, but you made us run."

"Dyoan, the last time I saw that skin was on your father."

I watched as he took that in, and the implications crossed his face like scudding clouds. "That doesn't mean. . . . He wouldn't have. . . ."

"How do you know?" I asked harshly. "What do you know of him, except that he collects skins and their wearers? And now he wants you to bring him yours—and mine, too, no doubt." I saw that last one hit home. Dyoan might have been content to let me go my way, but I guessed that those hadn't been his instructions.

"He has Ale'en," he said quietly.

I nodded, unsurprised. "Would you lend a skin and not keep something as a pledge?" I thought a moment. "How can I find Ale'en? Will you give me the eagle cloak to go fetch him? I might have a chance to slip in and out if he thinks I'm you."

Dyoan shook his head miserably. "He'll be kept close inside. The singer said he was afraid you would try to steal him ..."

". . . and then he'd have no hold on you."

"It didn't sound like that at the time."

But I knew even when I suggested it that running wasn't the answer. There was a man out there who hunted our kind and could sing to our skins better than we could. I could think of only one way to stop him, and it made me sick with dread. Before I could lose my nerve, I told Dyoan what to do.

He was staying at another inn, some miles down the valley. Perhaps he was unsure of our former employer. But he had arranged to meet Dyoan in a field nearby at moonrise. We glided down to meet him—I hanging limply in Dyoan's talons. The boy shed his skin and stepped away while I made a show of flopping clumsily as I changed, rising unsteadily to one knee.

The stranger came forward, saying, "She wouldn't give it to you, then? Just as I said! But we'll get it back."

At that moment I slipped the owl-cloak from my shoulders and flung it before me like a throw-net, crying, "Wear my skin!"

He blinked in surprise—large, golden, owl eyes. I think I held my breath for a full minute waiting for him to realize what had happened. Then with a cry he fled on soundless wings—wearing my feathers to the end of his days, for *I* would never release him.

Dyoan fetched his brother from the inn and, as he brought him back, draped the eagle-skin around the child's shoulders. Well, then, it should have come to him in the normal course of things.

I was content. The older boy looked up at me with troubled eyes.

"Laaki . . ."

I felt his sympathy but couldn't face it just yet. "So," I said briskly, "I'll have to get to work, with two new songs to make. Will you lend us all your feathers for a bit, Ale'en? I'd have you carry us, but you don't know where I've left Dyoan's skin and it's a bit dark for your first flying lesson, anyway. We had best be far from here by dawn, I think."

He ran his fingers possessively over the feathers, then grinned and handed me the skin.

THOUGH THE WORLD
IS DARKNESS
by Lisa Deason

Lisa Deason is another writer who has become one of our regulars. She has appeared in at least two previous anthologies: *Sword and Sorceress IX* and *X,* and had several stories in *Marion Zimmer Bradley's Fantasy Magazine,* as well as a few sales in the semi-pro market, both fiction and poetry.

Lisa says, "My credits are happily growing and, with a lot of hard work and persistence, it won't be long before I can include novel credits."

"Et tu, Brute?" Is there anyone who *isn't* working on a novel?

In Fianah MikRalisyn's world, there was no sun. She who had first been the rebel daughter of a minor lord, then later a young, brash member of the elite group called the Hounds, was now simply a woman who had gone blind.

She would have withdrawn completely into herself if not for her older brother's wife, Dree.

81

The pretty blonde girl was several years her junior, full of life and always urging Fianah to take part in the daily routine. It was by her doing alone that Fianah retained any small grip on the life that would have otherwise passed her by.

On one day, as the two were taking an afternoon walk, Dree's cheerful chatter cut off in mid-sentence and her guiding grip on Fianah's arm tightened.

"There's a man on a black horse coming over the hill."

The words weren't particularly ominous, but nonetheless a chill went from the base of Fianah's spine to the nape of her neck. "Is he wearing all black with a red insignia over his heart?"

Dree's tone somehow conveyed that she was squinting. "Yes, he is."

Then Fianah could hear the hoofbeats until they were drowned out by the sudden, rapid staccato of her heart. She shoved her friend in the direction they had come from. "Run, Dree! RUN!"

To her credit, the girl didn't pause to ask why, just grabbed her hand and the two ran for all they were worth. Fianah stumbled over terrain she couldn't see but managed to keep to her feet. The hoofbeats gained on them, booming like the pounding of a giant's hammer on the earth.

Knowing that no one could outrun a horse, Fianah tore her fingers away from her friend's and shouted, "Keep going! It's me he wants!"

She altered her course and the hoofbeats followed. She ran with only her arms thrust before her to tell if her path was clear. Instinct warned her to swerve and something brushed the back of her short dark hair. Damn! She cut to the side again, clinging to the thin hope she could outmaneuver her pursuer even if she couldn't outrun him.

Then something solid hit her head and sent her crashing to the ground. Pain and nausea swept over her in disorientating waves as consciousness fled.

She came to, gasping at the water that had been thrown in her face. Her hands flailed through the air, automatically seeking to grasp something, anything, that could tell her where she was. The ground beneath her was packed dirt. Her knuckles scraped the stone of a wall behind her.

"Who's there?" she demanded and heard the ugly sound of panic in her tone.

"Pathetic," a male voice drawled.

She wasn't familiar with the man himself but all the same knew who he was. "Have the Falcons become so cowardly that they have to chase down blind women now?"

A slap she couldn't anticipate sent her sprawling backward. "We'll see who's the coward here," he snarled, then with calculated scorn added, "Oh, that's not correct, is it? *You* won't be seeing anything ever again, will you?"

There was a rush of cool air and the click of a door closing. He was gone. Fianah's bravado fled as well and she couldn't stop the sobs that shook her body.

When she had been a Hound, she had been a holy terror when on the hunt. She had loved her work, loved stalking the opposing Falcons and turning them in. Only one more capture and return had been needed for her to reach the next rank and receive a royal blue vest in place of the tan one she still wore. She would have been the youngest Hound to have achieved the blue so quickly.

But all that was gone. An inexplicable illness caused her sight to dwindle rapidly, unstoppably away, leaving her little more than an invalid who needed help to dress and to feed herself. Shut out from life as she had always known it, her new world was only darkness and she was consumed by it. Self-reliance, self-esteem, self-worth, all were things of the past. She hated her blindness but hated herself even worse for being defeated by it.

A slight sound drew her attention and she choked back her useless tears. Without sight, she had to make the most of her other senses, so she listened intently.

Again, the sound. The rasp of breath, even and shallow. There was someone else in the cell with her.

"Who's there?"

No answer. From the slow, steady pace of the breathing, she suspected the person was unconscious.

Oh, please don't let it be. . . . She crawled toward the sound, one hand testing the ground like the flicking of a snake's tongue.

There, the solid warmth of a body, long, soft hair woven in a loose rope, tied with a thong that had a bit of hard smoothness dangling from it. In her mind, she saw the sun catch the clear, round glass as it swung at the end of a blonde braid.

Her fear was confirmed. "Dree," she murmured regretfully.

The girl stirred at the touch and came awake. "Fianah! I was so frightened when I saw him hit you. I thought you were dead! Then he knocked me out when I tried to help you. Who *is* he? What does he want?"

"He's a Falcon." It was explanation enough for anyone who knew her former trade as Dree did.

"But you're not a Hound any longer. I thought Falcons only turned in Hounds and vice-versa."

Fianah struggled to get past her helplessness, fought to think. Her mind hadn't been lost with her vision. To save both Dree and herself, she was going to have to make use of it.

Aloud, she began to reason it out. "I think he's trying to bend the rules. I still am technically a Hound, just retired, but because I'm blind, I'm easier to catch than one of the others. I think he's not sure they'll allow it, though, that's why he brought us here instead of taking me back for turn in. I don't know why he took you as well, but I can guess it wasn't for anything pleasant."

She stood. "We can't stay here. The Hounds and Falcons are run much the same way and I can't see my captain allowing something like this. I doubt his will either. Both groups frown on anything that stinks of laziness."

The nearly forgotten lump on the back of her head roared to painful life when she got her feet under her. She did her best to ignore it and continued wielding her best weapon, her mind.

"Tell me what you can see of this place we're in," she urged. "What does the door look like?"

Dree's tone was a bit sheepish. "I don't know. It's pitch-black in here."

"Then we'll just do this my way." She shuffled carefully forward until she found one of the walls, then began a methodical search from there.

"Good!" she exclaimed when she came to the door. "It's a key lock."

"How does that help?"

"It means that I can pick it." As she spoke, she ripped loose the hem of her vest's collar and pulled forth the slim metal instrument concealed within.

The delicate art of lockpicking didn't require sight and it took only a moment for the door to swing silently open.

Dree had followed her and linked their arms. "It's still totally dark," she said as they moved cautiously out of their cell. "Which way do we go from here?"

Fianah inhaled deeply, breathing in the dank earthy smell. Which way? Turning her head from one side to the other, she searched for some slight clue.

Then she found it.

"Do you feel that?" she said. "From the left there's a slight breeze. That might be our way out."

She found her usual position with Dree reversed as the blind had to lead the sighted. Keeping the wisp of air on her face at all times, Fianah navigated the series of twisting tunnels that began to gradually rise upward.

"It's getting lighter," Dree announced excitedly after the last turn. "You've done it!"

A few minutes later, the dirt of the tunnel floor gave way to grass and the damp air became fresh smelling.

"We're out," Dree whispered.

Then a blow from behind caught them both by surprise, sending them sprawling apart. Fianah managed to twist and get hold of the assailant, knowing that if she let go, there would be no way she could fight.

"And where do you two think you're going?" the Falcon snapped. "My master might not value you, but I'm sure you'll both fetch a few coins at the Slave Market!"

"You've got his left arm. He's facing you!" called Dree.

Feigning a punch with her right fist that positioned him where she wanted, Fianah slammed her forehead against the bridge of his nose.

The Falcon grunted and she chopped out with her free hand, angling for his neck. He twisted and she caught his shoulder instead. His hands locked around her throat and tightened. Levering her arms from within his, she struck up and out but miscalculated and the hold didn't break. Her lungs screamed for air and weakness began to pool in her knees.

"I've got him!" Dree suddenly hollered and there was a resounding crack. Abruptly, she was free.

Gasping for air, her throat feeling as though burning embers had been ground into it, she heard the thud of a body hitting the grass. Without knowing if he was down for good or merely stunned, she had to act.

Dropping to her knees, she flipped the man onto his stomach and pinned his arms behind his back. "Is there . . . anything we can . . . use to tie him?" The words stuck in her aching throat.

"Would my underskirt be good enough?"

"Yes."

While Dree used a sharp rock to rend the material into wide strips, Fianah regained better control of her voice, saying, "Good job. What did you hit him with?"

"A branch. I fell on it when he knocked us down. But if you hadn't kept him occupied, I would have never been able to sneak up on him like that. Here's the cloth."

The makeshift ropes were put in her hands and she fastened the unconscious man's wrists securely behind his back. She tested the bonds, then tied his ankles before standing.

"Are we going to go for help now?" Dree asked.

It was the practical thing to do. What else could

be expected from a gently-raised girl and a blind woman?

Fianah grinned.

It was early evening when the Hound Headquarters received their unusual visitors. The dark-haired, clearly blind woman firmly stated she was Hound Fianah, tan rank, bringing in the capture that would advance her to blue.

The Captain of Hounds was summoned to personally handle the strange case. "Hell, Fianah," he said, shaking his head, "if anyone can do it blind, then it'd be you."

She shrugged out of her vest and held it out for the man to take. "I had help," she said demurely and Dree squeezed her arm. "That'll be ten gold pieces and my new vest, if you would be so kind, Captain."

Doubtlessly, he was shaking his head at the whole proceedings; she could hear the metal Hound insignia he wore jingle slightly with the motion. "Jens, get Hound Fianah her things," he told his lieutenant, and in a few moments the vest was placed in her hands.

"Half the money goes to my associate," she said and the coins distinctly rang out into both of their palms. She pocketed the gold, then put on her vest. "Well? How do I look?"

"Very blue and very dashing," Dree replied.

"So tell me, Fianah," the Captain said. "Do the Falcons have cause to lose sleep again? Are you back in the game?"

Fianah smiled. "You never can tell, Captain."

Head held high, she turned and left the office with Dree at her side. Though the world was still darkness, she wasn't helpless or afraid any longer. Nor alone.

"We make a fine team, Dree. Remind me to

thank my brother for marrying you." She ran her fingers fondly down her vest and pictured its crisp royal blue color.

Then she smiled. "Come on, little sister. Let's go home."

HEMPARIUS THE TRADER
by Valerie Atkinson Gawthrop

Valerie says, "This is my first fiction sale and I can't possibly be nonchalant about it." Enjoy; thrills like a first sale don't come along very often in a lifetime. She's published nonfiction, but "otherwise I couldn't trade all my writing credits for a good cheeseburger." She lives in Tulsa, which she says is full of generous established writers and members of the MWA—Mystery Writers of America.

She says she is working on *several* novels, "and if I'm lucky enough to see them in print, so be it." Luck might have something to do with it; catching the editor in a buying mood can often be a matter of timing, and yes, luck. But luck—or timing—is only part of the game; it takes knowledge, hard work, and learning the markets. It also takes knowing how to do the work so that when opportunity knocks, you won't be asleep at the switch. And the best way to sell is to write such a good story that the editor can't resist it.

By now we all know that there is room for just about everyone in all fields. If a woman doesn't get published in s-f, it's not that the editor is prejudiced (Although I imagine that there are a few dinosaurs around who haven't yet gotten the message—but give 'em time.), it's just that she hadn't written the best story around or sent it to the wrong editor. Such fiction markets as still exist are fiercely competitive, so that one has to be good or better than the competition.

I heard the mask maker's voice, even though I'd covered my ears with my wings. What now?

"You know what, you lazy dracona. Wake up, we have work to do."

I'd forgotten that she could read my mind. I raised my left wing high enough to uncover one eye and blinked at the enigmatic figure seated on the ornately-patterned rug.

Bright scraps of silk strewn about her feet cast silver, fuchsia, and indigo shadows against the white of her robe. The ever present translucent blue veil shrouded her features from the nose down.

"Princess Claws, if you are to be my assistant, you have to learn not to dally when I call. We are expecting a visitor. Soon."

She had the voice of a cheery wood flute, one that had been played too late, too long, in a tavern too dark. Such a strange new employer.

"I regret that you find me strange. I rather enjoy your company, and with a little training. . . ."

There I go again. I really have to learn to think quietly. Actually, I liked the mask maker. When she didn't need me, she let me sleep. Besides, watching her make the masks was intriguing.

Sometimes they were beautiful, other times. . . . Anyway, she always knew what the client needed.

I stretched upward on my hind legs and extended both of my shorter appendages to eye level, where I paused to admire my perfectly manicured scarlet claws. Wings folded against my back, I ambled toward the mask maker.

I am lucky to have this job, I suppose. I'm small, even for a dracona, and the good jobs, guarding gold and virgins, were taken by my larger dragon cousins. If it weren't for the Queen pulling some strings, I'd be unemployed. But what are mothers for anyway?

"Princess!"

"Coming." I scuttled across the white marble floor and slid to a stop, tangling my right foot in the folds of the rug. Oh no. Head bowed, I raised my eyes and gave the boss my most pitiful look.

She clucked and shook her head, but I thought I saw the trace of a smile behind her veil. "Fetch the silver sequins and the crystal baguettes, medium size will do, and I'll need number ten gold thread and, let's see, a box of point three amethysts. Oh yes, and a new needle. Can you remember all that?"

I nodded and mentally scratched off the list. "Don't forget the silver sequins," she called after me.

"Darn," I muttered as I picked up a basket and started up the staircase.

My wings brushed against the cool white walls. Everything was white in the tower. Everything except the supplies for the masks, that is. The staircase spiraled along the walls, giving me access to thousands of sparkling jewels, silks, threads, and feathers that spilled out of ornate boxes. Those big dragons would be so jealous if they could see the hoard of the little dracona, Princess Claws.

I chuckled when I thought how my curious talents, and the Queen, had brought me to the richest tower in the universe. I couldn't fly very far, but I could hover between the staircase and the boxes to retrieve whatever the mask maker needed. I also have an eccentric type of memory that allows me to remember what is in every box. Even if I can't remember exactly what I'm looking for, I always know where it is. Tsk, tsk, now where was I?

"Silver sequins," came a voice from below.

Right. I scratched my head. Two flights up, three stairs over, first box on the left. Silver sequins, bravo. Let's see, do I have everything?

"Gold thread."

"Gold thread, gold thread," I mumbled. I half flew, half walked up two more flights of stairs and hovered over the box of thread. Finished. I started back toward the tower floor. I paused on the last landing and panted for breath. One of the twenty-two doors glowed with an apple green light. Our visitor had arrived.

"Hmm. We rarely have anyone come through that door," the mask maker said. "Interesting."

I poked my head over the railing and watched the door open. The visitor appeared normal enough. Human, male, bronze skin, slanted eyes lost in a round face. A royal blue turban covered his head, but I guessed his hair was the same white as his goatee. A green satin robe fell to his knees. The paunch of his stomach strained under a copper colored blouse. I crept lower on the staircase.

"Where in all of purgatory am I?"

So mundane. Why don't they ever say anything

original? I expected more from someone who came through door thirteen.

The mask maker looked toward me, then turned to the visitor. "Purgatory? No, this is the white tower," the mask maker said.

He rubbed his eyes as if trying to force the confusion out of them. He blinked and slapped himself but not hard enough to hurt, I suspected. "Awake. I command it." He slapped his other cheek.

The mask maker's voice sang cool and low. "You are not asleep."

I hesitated at the foot of the stairs, enjoying the chance to watch our guest unobserved.

"By all the gods, I must be dreaming." The stranger tugged at the gold ring in his ear. "On the ashes of my ancestors, if this isn't a nightmare, I must be . . ." Silence filled the tower as his bronze face paled.

Something about him reminded me of the Zandara merchant who taught me how to play bones my last summer at the palace. I should say, taught me how to cheat when playing bones.

"Please sit." The mask maker pointed to the rug in front of her.

"Sit? The lady tells a dead man to sit." The stranger pounded his ample chest. "Halt the caravan. I cannot be dead. This is unlike anything in the holy scriptures of my ancient ancestors. Not that I live a particularly holy life, but haven't I made all the proper sacrifices to you gods?"

His eyes narrowed into slits. "You cannot be a god, you're a woman. I would never stand before a woman on the karmic wheel."

Leaning over the mask maker, he smiled and the light bounced off a gold tooth. "Perhaps you are a new customer? Hemparius the trader is delighted to do your bidding. What is it you are looking for? Silk for a new robe? A young slave girl? That is my specialty."

Slave girls. Slave girls. I couldn't believe my ears.

"No thank you. You are here for a mask, and I am the mask maker. Sit and we'll talk while I make it for you."

"Princess!"

At her command I flapped down the last few stairs, slipped across the floor, and made a bumpy landing at my mistress's feet.

Hemparius clutched his throat with one hand and pointed at me with the other. "A demon."

I dropped my basket, stood as tall as I could, and spread my wings. I stuck out a hand and unsheathed five sharp claws. Tail thumping against the floor, I put my hands on my hips and pushed out my chest.

I snarled. "You don't refer to Princess Claws in that tone of voice. Indeed, I'll show you a demon."

The trader's mouth flew open, but from the vacant look in his eyes I could tell that the fool didn't understand a word I said.

The mask maker patted me on the back. "Calm down, Claws, he's never seen such a fantastic creature as you. Did you get everything I asked for?"

I nodded and handed her the basket without taking my eyes off Hemparius. What had the mask maker said? Never seen a dracona? Ha, I found that hard to believe. I reclined on the rug next to my mistress and leaned forward on my wings, putting my chin in my palms and keeping my claws extended for maximum effect.

"Never mind my assistant," the mask maker whispered, even though she knew of my superior auditory abilities. "She's a bit sensitive. High strung royal blood."

The uneasy fellow swallowed twice, a knot bobbing up and down in his throat. "I need no mask."

The mask maker hummed to herself and gave the visitor a look that would mesmerize a gaggle of castle swarmies. As if in a trance, Hemparius plopped to the floor.

He tried to sit cross-legged like the mask maker, but his bulk wouldn't permit it. Giving up, he stuck both legs straight out like plump sausages lined up at the fair.

"Who are you?"

"In the white tower, I'm known only as the mask maker." She selected a scrap of poppy-colored silk from her lap and drew the fabric through her fingers. "Tell me about yourself."

The man squared his shoulders. "I'm the most successful merchant in the civilized world. Hemparius the trader, perhaps you've heard of me." We shook our heads.

"But how can that be? I supply all the potentates, emperors, and kings with the flesh to meet their every desire. Everyone knows Hemparius." Again, we shook our heads.

"My merchandise is coveted in all the kingdoms. Men dream of buying just one of my slaves." His voice cracked.

I sniffed. His fear smelled like dead mackerel. My stomach churned. I hated the scared ones. I caught their fears like others catch the flu. Mother always lectured me, "Claws, you are a sponge for the fears of other beings. You must learn to protect yourself."

The mask maker spread the silk out on her lap and arranged some sequins across it. "What is the last thing you remember?"

The trader scratched his goatee. "The last thing? Allow me to ponder." His eyes flickered over the walls of the tower. I didn't like the way he stared at the jewels that overflowed their chests.

"I was coming back across the desert with a load of merchandise. The gods had blessed me with a most successful trading campaign." His face clouded with distant memories. "The slaves pitched the tents and fed the new slaves that stretched from one dune to the next."

He shook his head. "Just the money I've invested in chains alone would choke a camel. But that's the price of doing business and the women are worth it. Beautiful, all of them. The fortune they will bring I cannot calculate."

His greedy eyes squeezed shut. "It isn't as easy as it sounds. The journey is difficult. Some slaves will get damaged, and I will have to discount those to another trader. I have a reputation to maintain."

I flinched. Buying and selling women and then talking as if they were sacks of salt. If Mother could hear him, she'd have his head hanging in the trophy room of the palace. I shuddered, then scanned the tower as if expecting her to come swooping through one of the doors. All was quiet; Hemparius's fate remained in the hands of my mistress.

"Continue, please," the mask maker said.

How could she remain so calm, so polite? I wished I was back in the palace garden, basking in the sun eating moon pics.

"My favorite concubine brought my usual evening meal into the tent. She'd even fixed me a special new wine. Sweet of her, though it wasn't very good. Bitter aftertaste."

The mask maker and I exchanged looks. Her

fingers flew across the mask as she worked the trader's story into the fabric.

"And then?"

"I remember sucking on my hookah, I felt pain, I couldn't move. . . ."

The noxious odor of fear filled the air.

"A door appeared out of nowhere, and I was pulled through it. And here I sit talking to a strange woman and her pet dragon." He buried his face in his hands.

I growled. A pet, he called me. I've never been so insulted. He doesn't even know the difference between a dragon and a dracona. Hemparius looked up. I curled my upper lip to show my fangs. He broke out in hysterical laughter. A stare from the mask maker silenced him.

She held the mask she'd been working on at arm's length like an artist studying the model and the canvas at the same time. Quickly she made some adjustments to it.

"You make a living buying and selling humans. Correct?"

"Only the finest of females. Also oils, incense, gold, silk. Any goods of luxury. That is what Hemparius is known for." He stood and wiped the sweat from his brow.

She had him now. I wouldn't miss this for all the marshmallows in the universe. His soft slippers made no sound as he paced the marble floor. The silent fear started to seep into me. He turned to the wall of doors.

"I'll go now, unless I can interest you in something to make your life more pleasant. It must get boring, isolated like this. A pretty young girl would be more enjoyable than that creature; consider it my gift." He flashed his gold tooth and I bared my fangs.

"Perhaps another time," he said as he reached for a door knob.

The door wouldn't open. He went berserk, running from door to door and pounding on each one, twisting the knobs and screaming.

"Release me, I say. Hemparius commands it."

"Cut the racket," I yelled, but he ignored me. I drummed on the floor with one set of claws. The mask maker reached over and covered my tapping claws with her hand, raising a finger to her lips. One last tap and then I stopped. Hemparius gave up his pounding on the doors and whirled to face us. Silence, as white as the trader's face, filled the tower like fog at dawn.

The trader's fear clutched at my throat. I leaned back on my tail and flapped my wings. The mask maker scratched me under the chin. That's better, I thought, tilting my head back.

She stopped scratching me and held up the mask. I gasped when I saw how beautiful it was. I'd assumed that Hemparius would get one of the grotesque masks, but the mask maker never makes mistakes.

The mask came to life and bathed the tower in a fiery glow. Sparks of silver bounced off the walls and the crystal baguettes reflected its creator's face in pools of infinity. For a fleeting moment I thought I could see what the mask maker looked like behind her veil. She offered the mask to Hemparius.

His eyes, brimming with madness, gleamed like the silver sequins. "Get away from me you evil sorceress, I won't accept your mask." He held his hands in front of his face. "Ancient ancestors, protect me. Release me."

"You cannot leave without the mask. You must accept it." The mask maker gestured toward the doors. "I only make the mask, *it* opens the door."

He snatched the mask from her hand. "I'll play your game, evil one, but this had better unlock one of these doors or you will rue the day . . ." He shook his fist at the mask maker.

I hissed. "Now you've gone too far," I said. I lunged for his ankle and missed. I slid across the floor and bumped into the wall between doors six and seven.

"Ouch, that hurts." I rubbed my head where a knot was pushing its way through my scales. All this time, I thought I was hard headed.

"Now you've made me mad. I broke a claw." I flew to my feet and dusted myself off with my wings. In spite of my wounds, I prepared for another attack. The cretin ignored me as he covered his face with the mask. Then the strangest thing happened. A section of the tower wall changed into a mirror.

Hemparius looked at his hands. The fingers were long and slender. A broken chain of gold links dangled from his wrist like a bracelet. He felt his face, patted his chest and hiked his full skirt to get a look at his shapely calves.

His, I mean, *her* voice vibrated as if it had been forced through a hollow reed. "Sorceress, you've turned me into a . . . a woman."

Fascinated, I watched her reflection as Hemparius clawed at the new face trying, I guessed, to remove the mask that had already vanished. Hers was one of the most beautiful faces I'd ever seen. Hemparius threw back her head and howled like the soul of doom. I covered my ears with my wings, but I thought the wailing would drive me insane. My eight-one pearly white teeth chattered against each other.

"Princess, come here," the mask maker called.

I kept an eye on Hemparius as I inched backward toward my mistress. Almost there, I thought.

"Just a few more steps," the mask maker said as I fought for control. I trudged through the waves of fear, legs trembling in the wake.

What was Hemparius so frightened of? It seemed to me that living as a beautiful woman was an advantage not to be underestimated. Why, in some circles, I'm considered gorgeous. Doesn't bother me one bit.

I heard the boss's low voice. "That's right, Claws, talk to yourself, fight the fear. Think of better things."

I absorbed her advice and thought about the palace and the dances in the grand ballroom. I remembered how the Queen told me that the more I confronted fear the better I would be at controlling it. I took a deep breath and imagined I was back home with the court jester and his bouquets of magic roses.

All of a sudden door eighteen glowed with a deep purple light. The wailing stopped as I felt my tail swish against the mask maker. She pulled me into her lap.

Hemparius faced the door as it dissolved into purple energy. Through the opening I could see a tunnel of liquid silver. The air shimmered and so did Hemparius as she slipped out of the tower and into the tunnel.

A reedy voice rang in my ears. "May my ancestors damn you for all eternity, mask maker."

The light disappeared and door eighteen reappeared, closed. A scrap of poppy-colored silk floated toward me and I snagged it with a claw.

The mask maker cradled me and stroked my head. "That was an interesting case, was it not?"

I whimpered.

She felt the knot on my head. "You've been hurt."

"It's just a bump." I tried to sound brave. "But

look." I held up my broken claw for her inspection.

"Oh, that's too bad, but it will grow back." She squeezed my hand. "You chipped the polish on this one."

I chortled at all the attention. Then the mask maker turned from me and cocked her head, listening.

"So soon?" I asked.

She nodded. "I'll need lapis lazuli beads, the dark ones, medium blue rhinestones, two white peacock feathers and one large moonstone. Oh, yes, and a new needle. Can you remember all of that?"

No time to grumble.

I climbed the spiral staircase, going over the list in my mind. Whistling the "Battle Hymn of the Draconas", I flapped my wings, taking the steps three at a time.

Her voice floated behind me. "The white peacock feathers, don't forget."

Slave driver.

"I heard that."

I grinned. I hope I keep this job forever, at least as long as I'm with the mask maker.

"Don't worry, Claws," she sang out. "I will always be here. There is no mask for the mask maker."

CHANCE
by Tom Gallier

Tom Gallier is another of the men who regularly writes stories that I usually wind up accepting because they're the best stories around.

Tom works for a fiber-optics company. Well, there's another one for our collection of eccentric occupations, which now includes a female postman (actually I believe the proper title is "letter carrier"), an employee of a large municipal gas company, an employee of a large city's rat control board, a teacher of music (mostly trombone and tuba), assorted salespeople, and teachers of subjects from English as a second language to military engineering.

Brooding brown eyes stared out from the shadows of the hood. No movement, whether inside the alley or not, escaped her notice. She knew every route in and out of that alley, and every bolt hole. The Imperial capital's seedy Aagrin Quarter, in the city's northeastern corner, had belonged to her for the last three years. The prey wouldn't escape.

The cloaked figure loitered casually just outside the dark alley, near a vendor of sweetmeats. She ignored the succulent aroma of the warm treats and the fetid stench of human and animal waste in the narrow, twisting cobblestone street. Even the piles of maggot-ridden garbage in the alleys couldn't produce odors strong enough to overpower that open sewer called a street. Her dusty brown cloak, worn leather pants, and muddy soft-soled boots gave her the appearance of some peasant. But she was far more, or less, depending on your perspective. Chance was a janizary. And a highly trained assassin.

Orphaned as a babe, she had been turned over to the Imperial Ministry of Interior. The Ministry had uses for people like her. She was raised in an orphanage far from civilization as the Empire had no use for *civilized* janizaries. Especially within their corps of assassins.

It was a grueling, torturous twenty years, where all humanity and compassion was brutally beaten out of her and unquestioned loyalty to the Empire beaten in. For twenty years before coming to the capital all she knew was the learning of the art of stealth and murder. The Imperial Assassin Corps was the most highly trained, and most feared, organization within the Empire. The Minister of Interior, Baron Sorpose, personally saw to that.

The prey stood up, laughing amid frustrated shouts and groans. He apparently was a winner. For the moment. His fortunes were about to take a decidedly nasty turn. Chance watched as he turned her way. She turned away, rubbing her arms as if chilled, blending in with the gray, cold winter crowd with practiced expertise. He walked past, not giving her a second look. She followed discreetly.

He was tall and well-formed, with a thick shock of unruly brown hair and clear sky blue eyes. His clothes looked expensive though worn. He had seen better days. But his clothes were clean, his boots shined to a high gloss. He walked the dark streets of the seedy Aagrin Quarter with an air of confidence. Chance wondered if she had been told everything about the prey. He didn't look like a down on his luck gambler. Not exactly.

He soon arrived at a rundown flophouse. Its ground floor was of dressed stone, with the upper three stories of timber and wattle covered with clay. The whole structure looked to be leaning decidedly northward. A pair of drunks were sprawled in the doorway, singing in badly slurred voices. He gingerly stepped over them and started up the stairs just inside the door.

Chance hesitated. She could hear the loud protests of the steps as he made his way up. Her passage would be considerably quieter, but not quiet enough. She quickly scanned the building, then hurried around back. After placing in memory all the lighted windows, she began circling until a new window in back lit up. Smiling grimly, she walked up close to the wall and pulled two daggers from within her cloak. Using the daggers to good measure in the crumbling clay and wattle and rotting timbers, she climbed up to the newly lit window on the top floor. Peering through the threadbare curtains, she saw the prey sitting on the bed counting his winnings.

The small window was unlocked, if it even had a lock. Chance reached out one hand, pushed the window open, and slipped inside before her target knew anything was amiss. As she straightened before him, he stared at her with a measuring gaze. There was only the faintest hint of fear.

He looked her over carefully, missing nothing. She had thrown back her cloak and hood, revealing a shortsword—with the steel skull pommel and cross bone guard of an Imperial Assassin—strapped to her left hip, a garrote coiled on her belt, and a number of daggers. She was of average build, with long, lank hair, dark menacing eyes, and an olive complexion. With the right clothes and some cosmetics, he thought she could be rather pretty.

"I'm surprised it took so long," he said at length.

"I've been busy," Chance said quietly, without inflection. She didn't expect trouble from him. She knew him to be a fatalist. "Your time has come, Jon Hazard."

He shook his head sadly, "I knew better than to play Baron Sourpuss. Knew no good would come of it."

Chance had to suppress a grin at the use of Baron Sorpose's nickname. If word got back to the dour old cuss, he'd send out an assassin to silence him. But then, Jon Hazard was already prey. His death was at hand.

"You shouldn't have won so much," she said, looking almost sad herself. "You embarrassed him."

"My curse." He shrugged. "I never could throw a game. Hate to walk away with less than when I started." He looked up at her suddenly. "The funny part is I didn't cheat at all. Didn't dare."

"Cheating's no fun," she said, pulling the garrote off her belt. "No excitement if you know the end results beforehand."

He gave her that measuring glance again. He noticed the set of bone dice dangling from her sword's steel skull pommel like a topknot. A gambler?

"How about a little wager?"

"Your life is already forfeit," she said. "I can't give it back to you. My job is to take it."

"One last game before I go, maybe?"

"I don't gamble."

Pointing at the sword, "What of the dice?"

"My name is Chance. I received it for all the chances, risks, I'm willing to take. I have no fear." She stepped closer, gripping the garrote tightly. "Life means nothing to me. Not your life, not even my own."

"Lord, you're a fun one," he half-joked.

Chance hesitated. "And you are a strange one, gambler. Do *you* not fear death?"

"Damn right I do! But I know enough of the Imperial Assassin Corps to know running, or fighting back, would be less than useless. You'd probably get pissed off and torture me to death."

"Good thinking," Chance said. Though torture didn't bother her, it didn't particularly fascinate her either. She never tortured her prey, unless specifically told to do so. "Now, hold still and I'll make this relatively painless."

Holding up his hand, "Do you just *have* to kill me right now?"

Chance almost growled, suspecting some treachery on his part. The room looked secure enough against anyone barging in—the door's bolt was thrown, at least.

"I'm not trying to escape, Chance," he offered hopefully. "Just one last throw of the dice. One last wager before I meet my gods."

Chance studied him closely. He looked innocent enough. Then again, he was a gambler. Looking deceivingly innocent was his trade. But she didn't have any more assignments for tonight.

Lady Esmerina was to be killed at the stroke of midnight tomorrow night. She already knew how she would do the Lady in, and escape afterward. And there was something strangely compelling about the gambler.

Eyes narrowing, "What kind of wager? Your life is out of the question."

"My loss," he said, smiling sadly a moment. Then cheering up, he ran his eyes over her appreciatively. "How about wagering a night in your arms?"

Her snort was loud and contemptuous. For an instant, he thought he had gone too far. A ghastly vision of her ripping out his heart and feasting on it flashed before his eyes. It was well known that Imperial Assassins ate the still beating hearts of their victims.

"Do you expect me to fall in love with you after a night of passionate lovemaking? Is that it?" she asked, almost mockingly. Then, sneeringly, "All passion, love, and tenderness were taken from me years ago, Jon Hazard. Try again."

"I don't think that's true," he said quickly. "You're very beautiful, with the most gorgeous brown eyes I've ever seen." Letting his eyes drop lower, "And your body is shapely and firm."

Chance was startled by the assessment. No one had ever made any comment concerning her looks before. Never. It had been years since she had even considered such things. Beauty and other such trivial things had no place in the life of an Imperial Assassin. No place in her grim life.

"You're not *scared*, are you?" he taunted, a hint of a leer tainting his face.

Chance visibly bristled. Her dark eyes burned into him as she fought to control herself. No one—*no one*—had dared to accuse her of cowardice or fear in more than ten years. Was she not the

one who snuck into the Emperor's bedchamber
and stole a ring off his hand on a dare? And then
returned it the next night!

"If you're afraid I might try to escape, or even
attack you while you sleep . . ." he said, needling
her further.

Chance snorted contemptuously again. His soft
hands and body weren't a threat to her. She could
have killed him as a child. Easily. But his comment did spark something deep down. Pride,
maybe? Contempt for danger? Chance was her
name; it was how she chose to live her life. Only
danger made life worth living.

Suddenly, she flashed him a crooked grin. The
smile didn't totally reassure him. He wouldn't
have understood the thrill she felt anyway. Here
was a chance she had never taken. Never even
considered. Lie with the prey, dropping her guard
and opening herself up totally to him. Would he
try to kill her? Could she really stop him while in
the throes of passion? Suddenly, she *needed* to
know.

"The wager is accepted. One more night if you
win," she said. "Then you die in the morning
without struggle."

"Agreed, love, but don't forget the part about
you spending the night in my arms."

"I haven't, gambler," she said, placing the gar-
rote back on her belt. She held out her hand.
"Give me the dice. I don't trust you that much.
And I will decide the rules of the game."

She looked over the bone dice meticulously,
measuring their weight carefully. They seemed to
be perfectly ordinary. If there had been even the
slightest sign that he had tampered with them, the
wager would've been off.

"The game is snake-eyes, gambler," she said,
rattling the dice in her hand. It was a simple

enough game, first one to roll snake-eyes won. "I'll go first."

Both took several turns at the dice. On his fifth cast, Jon Hazard rolled snake-eyes.

Chance stared at the dice for a moment, still as death. In truth, she hadn't expected him to win. Wisely, Jon Hazard was keeping his joy at winning in check. Despite the thrill she felt at the chance she was about to take, the fact that she had *lost* grated on her pride.

"Shall we retire?" Jon Hazard asked. "Or would you prefer to spend a few hours on the town first? Maybe dinner?"

"I am not some painted courtesan who needs the illusion of being seduced, gambler. You won; I will submit to your touch now."

Without further ado, Chance straightened and began stripping off her clothes. Jon Hazard watched in stunned disbelief that he had actually done it, before starting to undress under Chance's stern look. When the gambler was undressed, Chance settled herself on the bed.

She tensed as he climbed atop her, expecting him to make his move to subdue her. He didn't, and instead began some foreplay. Slightly disappointed, but relaxing nonetheless, Chance lay back to enjoy the experience. She hadn't the slightest idea of what was expected of her, and didn't really care. The gambler would have her before dying; she had promised nothing more.

A scraping noise at the window alerted Chance. Shoving the gambler aside, she rolled out of bed and pulled her sword as a dark figure slipped through the window and crouched. She watched with rising fear and dread as Davic, a fellow Assassin, pulled his shortsword and grinned in triumph.

"So, Chance, dallaying with the prey, I see," Davic said.

"That is my business, Davic," she said, sliding over a step to get the room's lamp above and behind her. Davic would be forced to look into the bright light during any attack. "You have no right to interfere with my hunt."

"I have every right. The Baron is most dissatisfied with your delay in disposing of the prey. Now I see why it has taken so long. Are you two plotting his escape as well?" Davic asked, every word dripping with contempt. "You have betrayed the Corps, and the Precepts. *You* are now prey."

"Lies!"

Davic's face flashed victorious again.

"Who do you think the Baron will believe? Me, a loyal lieutenant, or some slut assassin who beds the man responsible for publicly humiliating him?" Davic chuckled darkly as he stepped toward Chance. "I will be handsomely rewarded for killing both of you."

For a bare instant Chance knew pure terror. She was now prey. Never had she thought it would come to this. Davic was a veteran assassin of twenty years in the capital, and widely thought to be the Corps best swordsman.

"I have violated none of the Corps Precepts."

"But you will not live to defend yourself," he said, lunging for her throat.

Chance swept the keen-edged blade away with her own, twisting and scrambling away. He followed, keeping her on the defensive. They fought in silence, as was the way of assassins. Only the whisper of their feet and the rasp of their blades betrayed their struggle.

As the seconds grew into minutes, Chance regained her confidence. He had not proven himself the ferocious fighter spoken of in their circle.

Though he was stronger, she now knew herself to be faster and at least as cunning. There were as many minor wounds bleeding on his body as hers.

Stepping back, Chance straightened and signaled a halt.

"We are evenly matched, Davic. Let us kill the prey and be gone as comrades. Neither of us needs this."

Davic's eyes seemed to glaze over a moment, dropping to stare at her feet. For a moment Chance thought he would agree. Then he smiled fiercely and lunged at her. Jumping back, Chance's feet caught on her own discarded clothes and she stumbled.

Kicking her sword out of her hand, Davic savored the moment a bare second before his blade leaped at her breast. In the last instant Jon Hazard kicked the sword aside.

Chance didn't hesitate, kicking Davic low in the belly and rushing to her feet. Grabbing him by the nape hairs, she punched him twice in the face and then ran him into the wall. She sighed heartily as he fell unconscious at her feet.

"That was a close one, Chance," Jon Hazard said.

He was gingerly examining the deep gash in his shin. Chance looked at him in disbelief. He had to be insane. Instead of saving her, he should have run for it. He wouldn't have gone far, but he should at least have tried.

"Why?" she asked.

"Why did I save you? I don't know. Maybe it was just I didn't particularly like the other assassin's attitude. Maybe I'm not as bright as I always thought I was."

She looked at him a moment longer, then turned back to Davic. Davic was her superior. He wouldn't be here unless highers were upset with her. His disappearance would mark her as prey. If he lived, he would hunt her till his last breath. Chance slit his throat.

"Gods! Why did you do that?" Jon asked, ashen-faced.

"I didn't care for the idea of him hunting me," she said. She quickly slipped back into her clothes, then paused. "Come along, gambler, we seem to be on the same side now."

"You'll help me escape?"

Chance's smile was grim. "You saved my life, so I'll take you with me. I owe you, and I always repay my debts."

"Very noble of you," he said, starting to dress before she changed her mind. "I realize that I'm not particularly impressive to you, but I think you'll be pleasantly surprised at what I'll contribute to our endeavors together."

Chance scowled at him before turning to the window and staring into the darkness that waited.

"Ah ... my love, look at this!" Jon Hazard said, looking through the shop window.

Chance walked up and glanced at the indicated display. It was a thin silver necklace bearing a set of tiny silver dice. She couldn't help but smile. A roll of dice had changed her life.

Taking her hand firmly, he led her into the small shop. Within minutes the necklace was being fastened around her slender neck.

"A small token of my undying love," he whispered in her ear.

"Our love," she corrected.

Smiling, she gently caressed the gift, thinking back on six months of total bliss. Well, maybe not the first two months of terror and running. But she still couldn't believe how one night of indiscretion had altered her life. Still didn't understand how more than twenty-three years of intense training, brainwashing, and casual death had been so easily washed away in the months that followed.

Chance wasn't the same woman. Gone were the brooding face and threadbare drab clothes, replaced by soft linens and silks, and a bright smiling face. Gone was the simmering rage she had lived with so long, replaced by a contentment she had never known could exist.

There had been a brief time when she feared the Corps would finally find and kill them. Indeed, she knew they had no choice in the matter. All prey must be downed. It was their First Precept. If one assassin failed, another was waiting to take on the assignment. Only her cunning and knowledge of the ways of the Corps had saved them. It had been four months since she'd seen any sign of them, though discreet inquiries had revealed the Corps was still hunting them. Especially her, their first deserter in sixty years. But she hardly even thought about her former life anymore. Just being Jon Hazard's wife of two months was all the excitement she wanted to handle now.

"Do you like it?" Jon asked hopefully.

A chill of joy ran down her spine. He was the first person to ever really care what she felt. "I adore it."

While he paid for the necklace, Chance checked her face in a mirror and smoothed her yellow velvet dress with the delicate lace trim at neck and wrists. She had never worn a dress or makeup until meeting Jon. At first he had gotten her to wear the silly stuff as a disguise, but now she truly enjoyed wearing such frills. It seemed that every day he showed her something new and exciting to do or wear.

Offering his arm, "My love."

They continued their stroll down the wide boulevard, peeking in the windows at the expensive merchandise. At first Chance had balked at walking about in broad daylight on busy streets. But Jon had insisted that life wasn't worth living if you had to constantly skulk around in the dark. He had even steadfastly refused to leave the capital. So Chance had moved them secretly to the upscale Larcharin Quarter, using all her old knowledge to erase their trail and build a new "past" for them.

Stopping before an alley, where a large mud puddle blocked their path, Chance acted as if she were trying to decide on a route to circumvent the obstacle. She already knew that he would sweep her up in his arms and carry her across the mud, thus saving her long velvet skirt and expensive shoes. But before any of that could happen, she heard a zeep and thud beside her face. They both grunted and jumped back.

Chance stared at the tiny red dart embedded in the wall, her worst fears realized. It would only take seconds for the assassin to load another poison dart. She doubted he would miss her a second time.

Turning to her husband, "Jon, we have to . . ."

He was leaning heavily against the wall and beginning to slide to the ground. A tiny trickle of blood oozed from a pinprick on his neck, just a finger's width from the jugular vein. He still clutched the red dart in his hand.

Chance's knees went weak and her stomach twisted in on itself. She knew her husband would soon be dead, killed by an Imperial Assassin. Their poisons were fast and none had antidotes. Stifling sobs of despair, she rushed to his side and eased him to the ground. For the first time in her memory, tears flooded down her face. Jon Hazard could only gape at her in astonishment and die in her arms. She lowered her face into his neck and cried. Chance no longer cared who saw, or if another assassin waited to kill her. She no longer had a reason to live. For the first time in her life, Chance felt the icy grip of loss.

Several bystanders crowded around and made to help, but then saw the red dart. They quickly moved away once they realized an Imperial Assassin had killed him. No one wanted to be associated with him or her.

After several minutes, Chance lifted her head and looked around. Passersby were doing their best to ignore her and Jon. No assassins were evident.

Strangely, she felt a certain embarrassment at being alive. Not because Jon had died so suddenly and violently, but because the assignment was obviously bungled. She was still alive. All she could figure was the assassin had panicked after missing his mark. Her reputation must have unnerved him, causing him to run for his life.

"A serious mistake," she muttered, studying her beloved husband's slack face. "My darling, I vow bloody vengeance on all those responsible."

Chance eased out of the cool river water, perching upon the thin shelf of earth between the dark waters and the massive building. Looking up, she judged the time to be three hours before sunrise. Removing the oiled skin bag tied to her back, she pulled out her clothes and slipped them on in the dark. After donning the black cotton pants, shirt, and soft-soled boots, she removed her weapons from the bag and belted them on. She was glad now she hadn't discarded the tools of her old trade.

That done, she turned to scrutinize the massive

white marble Ministry of Interior building towering over her. She knew the layout of the structure well, having worked out of it for most of the last three and a half years. There were five stories above ground and three below. The Imperial Assassin Corps was run from the lowest level, but its leader, heart, and soul—Baron Sorpose—had his office on the top floor overlooking the river. She stared at his dark office window with barely controlled rage.

Without hesitation, Chance began the climb up the side of the building. Any who saw the dressed and *polished* marble would have said it was impossible to scale. But Chance was trained to accomplish the impossible. Such acts helped to build and sustain the fearsome reputation of the Corps. Some believed them all to be sorcerous. Even demons.

Reaching the top level, Chance ignored the Baron's window. She suspected it was boobytrapped. Instead, she quickly stepped from window sill to window sill as if walking the street. She had no fear of heights. She had no fears. No reason to live—except revenge.

Rounding the corner, she hurried to the centermost window. It opened into the floor's wide hallway. Jimmying the window open, she slipped in and made for the Baron's office. She had no reason to hide her method of entrance. She wanted everyone to know of her deed.

The sound of booted feet echoing through the night-shrouded hallway stopped her. Easing over into a shadowy doorway, she watched and waited. Soon a night guard came strolling toward her. His crimson tunic and leggings said he was a simple City Guard, not associated with the Ministry of Interior or the Imperial Assassins Corps. Reaching into her right breast pocket, she removed her late husband's bone dice. She quickly rolled them. Dice had given her a new life. Dice had given both Jon and herself a brief chance at happiness. Dice would decide the guard's life. Any pair, he lives. Otherwise—

"A pair for fives, lucky dog," Chance muttered, surprisingly pleased with the outcome.

Her argument was with Baron Sorpose and the Corps. She pulled her foot-long blowgun from its sheath along the shortsword's scabbard, a red-feathered dart, and a tiny vial. Opening the vial, she dipped the dart's needle tip in before placing it into the blowgun. When the humming guard came within range, she sent the dart streaking into his neck. He slapped once, then collapsed in a heap. Chance dragged him to a closet, not bothering to bind or gag him since the drug would keep him asleep for at least twelve hours. And by the time he was discovered, she'd either be long gone or dead.

She quickly found Baron Sorpose's office door. She stared at it thoughtfully a moment, wondering what cunning defenses it held. Pulling out a feather, she ran it slowly over every surface of the door and door jamb. Chance found what she was looking for hidden in the lintel.

Chance hurried back to the unconscious guard and stripped off his tunic. Wrapping the tunic around the doorknob, she stepped back and slowly twisted it until it was taut enough to turn the knob. As the knob turned, poison darts shot down out of hidden chutes in the lintel. That done, she stepped to one side and kicked the door low, then fell to the floor and pressed herself close to the wall. The door flew open and she heard a sharp crack and felt a burst of dispelled magic. A common spell often seen in her line of work, designed to paralyze any would-be intruders until someone came to fetch them.

Picking herself up, she eased through the door with all senses alert. Ignoring the reception room, with its dark paneled walls and expensive paintings and sculptures, she entered his personal office. She found it dimly lit by moonlight flooding in through the large picture window. The office was large and well-appointed. One whole wall was nothing but shelves of rare books and personal mementos. She admired his collection of ancient swords and daggers bracketed to one wall for a moment, even considered using one of them to kill him. Studying his well-padded chair, she flirted with the notion of hiding a poisoned dart in the seat. It was a common enough ploy, and very effective. Also, the ploy would give her plenty of time to escape beforehand. But she wanted to see his eyes when she killed him. This wasn't business, it was personal. Very personal.

Knowing her entrance couldn't be hidden, she decided on a diversionary tactic. Taking a piece of stationery, she wrote the Baron a note and pinned it to his chair, leaving a set of dice in the seat.

BARON SOURPUSS, GREETINGS.
HOW DOES IT FEEL TO BE PREY? HOW DOES IT FEEL TO KNOW YOU CAN'T PROTECT YOURSELF AGAINST ME? BREAKING INTO YOUR OFFICE WAS EASY, AND ONLY A SMALL DEMONSTRATION OF WHAT I'M CAPABLE OF ACCOMPLISHING. WHERE WILL I SHOW UP NEXT TIME, YOUR BEDCHAMBER, THE STABLE, THE TOILET? TILL WE MEET FOR THE LAST TIME—CHANCE.

After preparing a very special dart for the Minister of Interior, Chance slipped up into the fireplace. It was summer, so she had no fear it would be used. Wedging her legs into the tight chute, she waited patiently for her prey to arrive. It wouldn't be long; she knew him to be an early riser.

It was barely past sunrise when Baron Sorpose, Minister of Interior and second cousin to the Emperor, arrived with his entourage in tow. The missing guard and open office door had caused a good deal of intense and angry shouting. Her note caused a great deal more. Chance smiled grimly as the Baron cursed her vehemently, ordering all hunts postponed until further notice. All Imperial Assassins were to hunt Chance down and kill her.

Chance waited in the chimney with her blowgun armed and aimed down at the spot where any curious face would appear. After the initial outrage cooled, the Baron assigned an aide to personally supervise the hunt for Chance and began his day.

After settling down in his overstuffed chair with a cup of hot tea, he began shooting out a myriad of orders that sent everyone scampering about. Chance was mildly impressed by the sense of urgency everyone moved with. So much for so-called lazy bureaucrats.

She waited until the lack of other voices indicated the Baron was alone. The only sound was the rustle of papers and an occasional sip of tea. Chance had excellent hearing. As quietly as she could, she worked her numb legs loose and eased out of the fireplace. The Baron was a mere twenty feet away, unknowing of the danger to himself. He was absorbed by what he was reading. Chance moved stealthily out of the open inner office door and locked the outer door to the hallway. Then she returned and locked his door. Baron Sorpose looked up as the lock clicked.

"Who are you?" he demanded imperiously.

She smiled without warmth.

"An errant child," she said quietly.

He took in her attire, especially the distinctive assassin's skull and cross bone shortsword, and knew who and what she was. And why she was there. He graced her with a look of undisguised loathing.

"Chance. You can't possibly think you'd get away with killing me," he said. "You'd be hunted down like a mad dog. Even the Imperial Army and City Guard will be looking for you, *if* you even get out of the building alive."

Chance looked steadily at the dour old man. He was rail thin with wispy white hair that refused to lie down obediently and a craggy face. His ears were too big and his icy gray eyes too small. He wore only the latest fashions, today a maroon velvet waistcoat and breeches. She thought the clothes looked too young on such an old man. Hopefully, his survivors would bury him in something more appropriate for his generation.

"I'm already being hunted by the Corps," she said. "Why should adding a few City Guardsmen and soldiers bother me?"

"No, you misunderstand. We're not hunting you," he said, watching her every movement. The blowgun in her right hand disturbed him. He knew what it could do. "We only want you to return. We have need of such an accomplished assassin as yourself. You're the most daring, most fearless assassin we've had in years. Your presence here proves that."

She ignored his lies. His own training had taught her how to see through such tactics. And she had overheard his orders concerning her. Besides, she knew the Precepts as well as anyone. Violating even the most minor Precept was death. And Chance had done far more than just violate the half dozen Precepts she could think of, she had threatened Baron Sorpose's life. If taken alive, her death would be excruciatingly slow.

"No, you don't understand. My life is nothing. You took the only thing that had meaning to me, my husband." She opened her left hand to reveal a set of dice. Jon's favorite dice. The only thing of his she had kept. "These dice changed my life. One cast, that's all it took. Now they will decide how you will die. Any pair, you receive a quick death. Otherwise. . . ."

With that, she shook and rolled the dice on his desk. She rolled a three and five. She smiled; his death wouldn't be easy. Not for him anyway. His look of growing fear showed he understood that, too.

"Wait! We can come to some kind of agree—"

Chance whipped her blowgun up to her lips and silenced him with a dart in the throat. He slumped in his chair. The dart had been dipped in a potion that only paralyzed the prey. Only his involuntary muscles worked now. But he was still brutally conscious, and could hear and see as well as ever. That was important.

"Those absurd rumors of assassins eating the still beating hearts of their prey are about to come back to haunt you, Baron *Sourpuss*. After I finish demonstrating how good and effective the Corps torturing training is, you will die when I cut out your heart and eat it before your eyes."

Chance began making good her promise. As an assassin, she was also trained to be an expert in torture. Many of her past victims had been similarly tortured before death. But this was the first time she had felt anything at all while doing it.

Halfway through, though, she became disgusted with herself. She didn't think Jon Hazard would have approved. With that thought, she ended it with a swift cut through the breastbone. With practiced ease, she cut out the still beating heart and watched the life leave Baron Sorpose's eyes.

Walking over to the window, she smashed out the glass with a thrown chair and watched as ten short steel bolts flashed across the window and embedded themselves in the sill. Poisoned, no doubt. The magic guarding the window was obvious as she stepped closer. An aversion spell. Very tricky, but quite effective, even against assassins. But it had little effect on her now, since it was aimed outward.

She tossed the heart into the river below. Let them think she ate it in truth. Give them something to think about should they decide to make the same mistake Baron Sorpose did. Maybe they would just let her go. Maybe, but not likely. But it really didn't matter, for she had no intention of letting *them* alone. Baron Sorpose wasn't the only one responsible. The hunt had only begun.

Without a look back, Chance stepped up onto the window sill and dived down into the river.

TOUCHED BY THE GODS
by Deborah Millitello

Deborah Millitello is "one of ours," having been published both in *Marion Zimmer Bradley's Fantasy Magazine* and in these anthologies. She has been writing since she was in fourth grade, and she lives in southern Illinois, has three children and four grandchildren, and loves to read aloud to all of them.

I strongly recommend reading your fiction aloud, not only does it help you catch typos that the spell-checker missed, but it lets you find out if your dialogue sounds wrong, your character names are impossible to pronounce, or you have used too many fanciful adjectives and adverbs.

Deborah collects dragon and unicorn figures, bakes angel food cakes from her grandma's recipe, reads, raises herbs, plays computer games, and spends "too much time on the GEnie computer network."

I woke up suddenly, aching as if I'd been trampled by cattle. My throat was dry as Zindol's Desert, but my hair and skin were damp. I didn't recognize the room I was in. The closed shutters let in little light, and the hearth fire had burned down to a dull red glow. Finally, my eyes adjusted enough to see a middle-aged woman sprawled like a plump rag doll in a chair beside my bed. Her clothes were a brightly colored patchwork.

Of course, I thought, my mind starting to work. That's the fashion in Thallingar.

I sat up, groaning, muscles punishing me for moving.

My companion yawned. "Are you awake, Elan?"

I groaned again, pulled a wool blanket over my breasts, and shivered. Who was she? She seemed familiar. Yes, Althea, the innkeeper's wife. I was in the Full Barrel Inn.

Althea touched my forehead. "Fever's gone. Tomorrow or the day after, you can get up."

I started to ask what she was talking about when I remembered. My twin sister Filea and I had come to Thallingar a few days before the autumn Full Moon Fest to look for work, Fi as a dancer, me as a sword-for-hire. Instead, I'd caught a fever. It must have hit me quickly, too quickly for me to use my healing power, and that made me uneasy. Usually, I felt an illness in time to heal myself. Not this time. I didn't know how many days I'd been in bed, but I stank of sweat.

"How long have I been sick?" I asked, smoothing my hair behind my ears.

Althea beat my pillow into a soft mound, then eased me back to it. "Ten days. Didn't think you'd survive. Many don't live past the third day. You've a strong spirit."

I shivered again, but this time from fear. Ten days? Where was Filea? Who'd taken care of her while I was sick? What frightened me was that someone might discover Fi's ability to see visions while dancing, might learn we weren't human. I could take care of myself in the world. But Fi, she was so vulnerable, trusting, I was always afraid for her.

We were identical twins with sun-gold hair and eyes like summer skies. I'd been born first, normal. Fi was born breach after a long and difficult labor. Her body grew to womanhood. Her mind didn't. Sometimes, I wondered if the gods had given her the gift of dance in recompense, as if they ever felt pity or remorse.

"Where's Fi?" I asked in a raspy voice.

Althea paused half a moment, less perhaps. Only a fighter like me would've noticed. She smiled and tucked the blanket under the feather mattress. "She's being well cared for. Save your strength. Don't worry."

Something was wrong. I read it in Althea's gray eyes, in the slight tremor of her mouth. "I want to see her," I said, trying not to betray my anxiety.

She didn't look directly at me. "Not safe for a visit yet. Wouldn't want her to catch Quick Fever, would you?"

At least, Fi wasn't ill. Somehow, I knew Althea wasn't lying about that. She tensed. Her fingers curled into her palm. She was hiding something. A warning screamed in my head, but I was still too weak to do anything about it, at least with Althea present. I decided I wouldn't push her. Better to be cooperative. "No, I don't want her to get sick. Just let me see her when it's safe."

Althea relaxed and managed a genuine smile. "Of course. Rest now. I'll bring food later."

"What time is it?" I asked in a tired voice.

"Early evening." She added wood to the hearth and stirred the coals to life.

I yawned and let my eyelids droop. "I think I need rest more than food."

Althea studied me. "Then sleep. I'll bring food in the morning. Water's in the pitcher."

"My throat's so dry, it hurts."

She poured me water, which I drank slowly. When I handed the cup back to her, she said, "Call if you need anything. I'll hear. My room's next door."

Good to know, I thought as she left.

Pretending sleep, I listened. Floor boards creaked in the hall. Hinges squeaked as someone opened my door but didn't enter. A moment later the door shut, the lock clicked, and footsteps faded away. Someone wanted me to stay here, but why? And who? Outside were the answers, and I meant to find them.

I lay very still and summoned the quiet fire hidden in my Jin soul. Warm, healing blue flames flowed through me, around me, chasing pain and renewing strength. As my body healed, my mind cleared. I remembered things I should've noticed before, that should've alerted me: the intense look in Dask's eyes as he spoke; the sudden interest Royan, chief priest of the Temple of Gedderin the Merciless, took in Filea; the wide-eyes citizens watching my sister dance, whirling like a blue and gold butterfly.

Fi was in trouble, I knew it. I felt no cry mind-to-mind in the Jin way, but I sensed danger. I'd tear down every building in Thallingar to find her.

Moving with the silent stealth I'd learned from the wild animals I'd played with as a child, I got out of bed and pulled on blouse, pants, boots, and cloak, all the color of forest shadows, just right for being unseen at night. My clothes felt strangely loose; the fever had made my normally slender body even thinner. Streaking my hands and face with charred wood to hide my lightly tanned skin, I strapped my sword to my back beneath my cloak, slipped daggers into wrist and belt sheaths, then crept to the window and lifted the latch. I was lucky. The shutter hinges were leather and didn't squeak when I pulled one side open a crack.

I was on the second floor, looking out on Merchant Street which ran from the North Gate to Temple Square. Twilight was fading into a clear autumn night on the Plain of Anrathoth. A crescent moon hung like a sliver of orange peel above the Yorbid Mountains on the western horizon. A few people hurried past, eyes watching everywhere. Though Thallingar was known for swift, merciless justice, thieves and murderers still lurked there. Only the foolish or desperate traveled at night. I wasn't foolish.

At last, no feet echoed on stones. No eyes or steel gleamed. I pulled my hood low over my face, eased the shutters open, and climbed out the window. Clutching the sill, I relaxed my legs to absorb the shock, then let go. I landed in a crouch with no more noise than a leaf, dagger in hand in case I was wrong about the street being deserted. I wasn't. I melted into the alley behind the inn and headed for Choley's Tavern and the one person I hoped could tell me what I needed to know—Dask.

Every city had a section where life was miserable and death was easy to find. Thallingar's was called Darkway, and Choley's Tavern sat in the center of it. There was little color in Darkway, even in daylight: light gray and dark gray, black and brown. Smells were much more varied, from mildly offensive to stomach-turning putrid. Darkway's denizens never noticed.

Actually, Darkway wasn't too dangerous during daylight if you carried weapons openly and walked down the center of the streets. At night, ten armed mercenaries might not be enough to keep you alive. Only Darkway's inhabitants and priests were relatively safe after sunset—the former because they knew every escape route; the latter because no one dared anger the gods.

I crept from shadow to shadow through filth-covered alleys, past limp bodies I didn't bother checking for life. At last, I reached the street beside Choley's. Rough voices and heavy footsteps made me flatten against the stone wall. Two men, swaggering drunkenly, argued as they passed down the street before Choley's. Shortly after, I heard the soft thunk of steel entering flesh. One or both wouldn't see sunrise.

I slunk around the corner and into a recess below a wooden sign, a frothy mug painted on it. I listened to sounds seeping through the wooden door, laughter, pounding on wooden tables. Someone was singing a bawdy tune. I rubbed off just enough of the char-black to look dirty but not disguised. Pulling my hood lower over my face, I pushed open the door and went in.

A few eyes turned in my direction, then dismissed me. Minding one's own business was normal at Choley's. The owner stood behind the bar, drawing mugs of beer and singing along with his customers. His voice was as rich and vibrant as the giant Bell of Seaside. Dask had told me Choley was an ex-mercenary. He was built like a blacksmith and needed no bashers to handle unruly drunks. His leathery face was square, marred by many lines. At least two weren't natural.

The tavern was dark, smokey, and smelled of

sweat, filth, and spilled drink. I scanned the crowd till I located Dask, Second Priest of the Temple of Gedderin. He'd been one of the first people to greet Fi and me when we'd arrived in Thallingar. His grass green eyes had made me nervous, but in a pleasant way. I'd played my silver flute; Fi had danced. Dask had followed every ching of her finger cymbals, every flutter of her veil. I'd worried about his interest, but after the dance, he'd turned to me.

"Are you and your sister staying in Thallingar?" he'd asked and leaned close to me. I'd pulled back a bit. "At least until the fest is over, unless I've found work by then."

"What kind of work?"

"Mercenary."

He'd raised a sandy eyebrow. "Perhaps," he paused and gave me half a smile, "I could help. I know the captain of the guard and most merchants. I'll inquire about work."

I'd thought he'd been concerned about us as part of his professional duties, but if he could help, I wasn't too proud to accept. Dask had been charming and amiable. We'd spent our time in his company, except when Fi'd danced and I'd played. He'd introduced us to his fellow priests, including chief priest Royan. I'd had the feeling Dask was flaunting us, but he'd treated us both with the greatest respect.

The last evening of the fest Fi'd wanted to go to bed early. Dask had escorted us to the inn, said good night to Fi, and asked me to join him for supper. I'd smiled and agreed.

Dask had hesitated a moment, then said, "Would you accept this?" He'd pulled out a black and red scarf and held it out to me. The followers of Gedderin wore such scarfs during the festival.

I'd looked at it, touched it, then shook my head. "No, I'm not a believer."

Dask had frowned, then gave me a weak smile. "Then keep it as a remembrance of me."

I sighed and smiled back. "All right."

We'd shared a good meal at a tavern near Temple Square. Dask told me tales of Thallingar while I'd eaten. I'd felt edgy, a vague sense he wanted something from me.

As we'd left the tavern, I'd shivered though the night had been warm. Before we were halfway to the Full Barrel Inn, I was shaking, dizzy, and barely able to stand. The last things I remembered before I'd passed out were Dask's arms around me and his quiet voice chuckling.

I wove my way through the tables to the unoccupied end of the bar and waited until Choley wandered my way. Plunking two copper coins on the wooden counter, I said softly, "A mug of ale for me and one for you, if you'll let me buy it."

A crow-feather eyebrow raised slightly as he stared hard at me. He picked up one copper with surprising agility, considering how huge his fingers were, then slid the other coin back to me. "I don't drink while I'm working, stranger, but thanks for the offer. Maybe later when Ramy takes over."

My hand froze above the coin. How did he know I was a stranger? Of course. My accent betrayed me. I clutched his wrist and said in a hushed voice, "I need some information."

His dark eyes narrowed, pulling at the scar on his left cheek. "Information's expensive." He held up his other hand as I stuck my free hand in my pouch. "Sometimes information costs more than coins."

I released him, my hand trembling from the

strength I felt in him. "I'll pay the price, but I need answers."

"Answers can kill."

"No, just unanswered questions."

He scrunched his thick lips. "When Ramy comes on duty, we can take a room upstairs." He grinned as I jerked back. "Just business, nothing more."

"All right," I said slowly. "How long?"

"About half an hour. Go up now if you want."

Should I watch Dask or stay out of his sight? "I'll wait."

"Suit yourself." Choley grinned as he went to wait on someone at the other end of the bar.

Dask seemed unaware I was watching him. I'd learned that the best way not to be noticed was to act as if you belonged, make no effort to hide. I didn't want anyone wondering about me.

Sooner than I hoped, crippled old Ramy limped in. Sidling between tables, he went to the bar where Choley handed him a rag and told him to make correct change. From Choley's tone, I figured Ramy couldn't count higher than the fingers on one hand.

Choley motioned for me to follow him. I didn't want to let Dask out of my sight, but I went. The stairs creaked as I climbed after Choley. I glanced at the crowd. No one paid any attention. My imagination was making me skittish.

Choley led me down a dim corridor barely wide enough for him, pushed open a door, and waited for me to enter. I glanced in and was surprised to see only a large table and six chairs. Choley grinned at me, obviously pleased with himself. I slipped past him and sat down, my back to solid stone. He closed the door with deliberate delight, sauntered to the table, and sat down facing me.

"Now, to business," he said. "Price will depend on what information you want."

I hesitated. How much could I really trust him? I leaned close enough so he could hear me and whispered, "I want to know where Dask has my sister."

A lecherous smile pulled at his lips. "I don't keep track of his women."

Barely controlling my anger, I tossed back my hood. "She's not one of his women! She's a dancer, my sister. You may have seen her at the Full Moon Fest. She looks exactly like me."

Choley grinned again. "Cleaner, I hope."

I gritted my teeth and continued. "She's very . . ." I searched for the right word, "child-like."

His eyes flew open wide. He sucked air through a space between yellowed teeth and stood up. "Can't help you."

I grabbed his arm. "You know where she is, don't you? Tell me, please!"

"Beyond help. Leave here if you want to live."

"I won't leave without her! Where is she?"

There was pity in his eyes as he shook his head. "Where you can't reach her. Where no one can."

"She's not dead. I'd know if she were."

Shoulders sagging, Choley looked down at me. "Not yet," he said softly. "Why'd you bring her here? Don't you know what they do to people like your sister?"

I shook my head, ice spiders in my stomach.

He sat back down, ran his hand through a tangle of blue-black hair, and gazed straight at me. "There's a sect of Gedderin, not officially sanctioned, called the Innocents." He frowned and spat on the floor. "They believe the childminded are touched by the gods, given visions too beautiful or too terrible for their minds to bear. They're given back to the gods on the moonless night after the autumn full moon. Of course, the Temple priesthood won't admit the sect exists, even though some of them are part of the Innocents—like Dask. I didn't think they'd find a victim this year because tomorrow night's the ritual. They probably thought your sister was sent by their god just in time."

"They'd have to kill me before I'd let them hurt Fi."

"Very likely," said Choley. "I'm surprised you're still alive. I'd have killed you first."

I jumped, startled, clutching the table until my knuckles turned purple-white. "I think they tried." I told him about my sudden illness.

His jaw tightened, and his eyes became slits of ebony. "Sounds like that scarf Dask gave you was infected with Quick Fever. Over half those who catch it die. You must be stronger than you look." He shook his head. "The innkeeper and his wife, never suspected they were Innocents."

"Where would they be keeping her?"

"In the Temple. You'd have to fight the whole priesthood to get her back."

"If I have to, I will." I stood up and turned to go.

I'd almost reached the door when Choley called, "Wait."

I looked over my shoulder at him and saw him digging his chipped nails into the table.

"I . . ." He paused, brows pulled together. "I've made a good life here and want to stay, but if you need another sword, mine's still sharp."

I gasped. "If you're found helping me, you'll be a fugitive—or worse."

His face crinkled even more. "Oh, well, never

did like the Innocents. Beside, Darkway's getting dull."

I stared at him incredulously. Darkway was probably more exciting, in a deadly sort of way, than any other place I'd ever been. I walked back to the table. "My name is Elan. I can't offer you much, but what I have is yours." I held out a leather bag containing all the money I had.

He took the bag, weighed it in his broad hand, and tucked it inside his shirt.

I assumed he accepted. "It has to be tonight, but first, I have to talk with Dask. Do you have a place we wouldn't be overheard?"

Choley's face looked like crinkled parchment as he smiled. "A room below my living quarters behind the bar. I use it for ... private ... business."

"All right. I'll grab Dask after he leaves here. Just be at your back door when I knock."

"Might make it easier for you." Choley reached deep in his pocket, pulled out a small hinged box, and opened it.

My mouth fell open. Silver-gray dust half filled the container. Dream Dust. Possession was death in Thallingar. One pinch relaxed a person, gave him exquisite pleasure; two made him unconscious, brain damaged; three killed him. Choley had enough to make half the population of Thallingar happy for a year or dead in one night.

He closed the box and slipped it into a pocket. "I'll put some in his drink. You'll have no trouble with him."

I swallowed hard. "Let's hope he hasn't left yet."

Dask was sitting at his table, drinking with three companions, as we descended the stairs. I watched Choley amble through the crowd, greeting those who were leaving and welcoming new arrivals. He spoke to the table directly behind the priest, turned, and stumbled against Dask's back.

"You shhpilled my drink, Choley!" Dask sputtered while his companions leaped out of the path of flowing mead.

Choley looked apologetic. "Sorry, priest. I'll get you another. No charge."

Dask glowered as Choley called old Ramy to sop up the mess. Choley took the mug, refilled it, and returned it to the red-haired priest. As Dask drank, a contented smile bowed his wide mouth. Green eyes clouded. Freckled skin flushed. His head wobbled from side to side like a huge, burnt orange flower on a spindly stem.

Dask's friends wandered away since he ignored them. After a while, he looked around the vacated table and lurched to his feet. Walking as if the floor constantly shifted, he reached the door and sagged against the wall. His hand inched toward the latch, grasped it, and raised the bar. He staggered outside into Darkway. Choley looked at me, barely nodded, and vanished through the curtain behind the bar. I waited a few moments, then walked to the door and left.

My eyes took half a second to adjust to the darkness, but my ears picked up the unsteady shuffle of feet on cobblestones. I peeked around the corner and saw Dask zigzagging down the street, holding his head steady with one hand, smothering laughter with the other. I checked the shadows for lurkers but saw no one. Like a night hawk, I glided silently toward my prey until I was an arm's length behind him.

Suddenly, Dask looked back over his shoulder. His face turned so pale, it looked like a full moon in Darkway's streets. He tried to step away from me, tangled his feet in his robe, and fell hard on his hip.

I dropped to a crouch. That much noise would attract people I'd rather not meet. I tied his hands and feet, stuffed cloth in his mouth, and heaved him over my shoulder. I nearly gagged. He smelled as bad as the rest of Darkway. It wasn't easy to stand up. Dask was heavier than he looked. On the third try I made it, but my back ached from the strain.

I heard soft leather against stone, the barest rustle of cloth. Darkway's inhabitants were coming to investigate. I headed quickly for Choley's back door.

I tapped against the wood. The door made no sound as it opened from dark alley to darker room. I hurried inside. Moments after the latch clicked into place, yellow sparks glittered like star showers from a flint-struck steel. A candle sputtered to life and gave the room a translucent golden glow.

"Follow me," Choley said. Candle in hand, he led me through heavy curtains to another room.

Embers in a fireplace cast crimson light. Choley set the candle on a table, threw back a frayed rug, and tugged open a hidden trapdoor. Retrieving the candle, he climbed down a wooden ladder, set the candle in a lantern, and came back to the ladder. "I'll take him," he said.

Dask squirmed as I transferred him to Choley's broad shoulder. The wooden rungs creaked from the added weight but held. I grabbed the trap door, flipped the edge of the rug over it, and pulled rug and door together over the opening as I descended to the hidden cellar.

Choley tied Dask to a chair, made a slip knot in a rope, and looped it around Dask's neck. I stood before him until his eyes fixed on me with clear recognition.

"You thought I'd die, didn't you?" I asked, my voice soft as snowflakes.

Dask struggled against the ropes until Choley tightened the noose. "Still," Choley whispered in Dask's ear. "Stay very still."

I moved a chair in front of Dask and sat down. "I'm going to take the gag from your mouth. Tell me what I want to know, and I may let you live." I removed the cloth. I should've guessed Dask would scream.

Choley jerked the rope so tight, Dask turned nearly as red as his hair. Bending close, Choley said, "No one can hear you, so speak quick and soft."

Our prisoner panted as the rope loosened around his throat. I could read my death in his eyes.

"Where's my sister?"

He didn't answer, just glared hatred at me.

Choley pulled the rope just enough to worry Dask. "Where is she, priest?"

"In ... in the temple," he growled.

I took out my dagger and ran the flat side of the blade along his cheek. "Where?"

His eyes opened so wide, they looked like they might fall out of their sockets. "At the top of the central tower. Six Innocents guard her. If you try to save her, she'll be killed. You're helpless to stop it." His smile cut deeper than his words.

"If she dies, you will, too."

He laughed. "If I die, you won't leave alive either."

"Don't!" Choley grabbed my arm.

Blood leaked down Dask's face from a shallow cut, a cut I hadn't realized I'd made. I dropped the knife and fled to a dark corner. My heart thumped hard against my ribs. I wanted to kill Dask, to see his blood soak into the ground, and those thoughts made me sick. The world had taught me to fight, to kill to survive, but my ancestry taught peace. Sometimes, I thought the conflict would shatter my mind like crystal handled too roughly.

A firm hand on my arm made me jump. Choley stood beside me, creases in his forehead. I swallowed hard and blew out the air that fear had trapped in my lungs.

"Sorry," he said, one brow raised. "Didn't mean to startle you. What's troubling you?"

Only a handful of people knew Fi and I weren't human. Could I trust Choley that much yet? If I hoped to save Fi, I had to. "Watch and listen," I said, then strode to the chair before Dask.

Facing him, I reached toward his red-stained cheek. He flinched, fear in his eyes. With a corner of my cloak, I dabbed the blood away from the wound. I touched his face, then reached inside myself. Faint blue flames flowed from my hand and licked at the cut until it healed without a scar.

"H—how'd you do that?" Choley stammered as he clutched the ladder.

I looked straight at him, knowing I was putting my life and Fi's in his hands. "I'm Jin. So is Fi."

His face scrunched in a puzzled frown. "But Jin are just stories, tales for children."

"No, we're real. So are our powers. I'm a healer. Fi sees visions while dancing. My people had many gifts."

"Had?" He paused as if he were repeating my words to himself. "Where are your people? Why are you here?"

"Dead." I told him of my people, massacred by humans who'd feared our gifts. I still heard my mother's screams, saw my dear friend Jenise run through, felt my little brother die—always with me, even after eight years, as fresh and raw as the day it happened. I shuddered, drove the painful memories back to the dark cell in my heart, where I kept them locked away. I looked at Choley and waited for him to speak. He didn't, but Dask did.

"It's true your sister has visions?" His eyes took on the gleam of religious fervor. "Then she's truly sent to us. She'll be an excellent sacrifice, the perfect expression of our devotion to Gedderin. The believers would die rather than let her escape."

I'd always been afraid of Dask's type of fanaticism. I sent a pleading look to Choley.

He looked from me to Dask. "He's right."

"What?" I sputtered. "How can you say that!"

"Even if you rescue her from the temple, the Innocents won't give her up. They'll trail us till we recover Fi. Unless we offer them something they want," he smiled as he stared at Dask, "like their priest."

"A trade? Fi for him? Would they really do it?"

"Never!" Dask spat. "When they know your sister has visions, they won't exchange her, even for me!"

Choley strode to him and bent down until they were face to face. "The Innocents don't know she has visions. Only the three of us do. I won't tell them. Elan certainly won't." Choley's eyes took on a gleam that made me as jittery as it did Dask. "And *you're* not going to tell them anything."

Dask's eyes widened. He started to speak several times, his mouth opening and closing like a beached fish, but no sound came.

"All right," I said, breaking the icy tension. "I'll rescue Fi tonight, then we can leave the city."

"No," Choley said.

"No?" I gaped at him. "We can't stay here after I've invaded the temple!"

"Oh, we'll leave," Choley replied, then poked my chest, "but you're *not* going to rescue Fi."

Anger made my voice like cold steel. "Yes, I will."

Choley shook his head. "I won't let you."

"Why?"

"Because it's suicide."

Disgusted, I turned away, but he grabbed my arm and jerked me back to face him. "Look, Dask has already told you there's no way you can reach Fi without alerting her guards. She'd be dead in seconds—and so would you. Let's go for a straight exchange. Best chance with least risk."

I started to argue, but he was right. Slowly, I nodded. "How will we get a message to the Innocents?"

Choley rubbed his square jaw. "One of the Alley Cats."

"Alley cats?" Had he trained cats as messengers?

"Darkway's orphans. They call themselves the Alley Cats. Quiet, fast, deadly, know every back alley, rooftop, and unlocked door and window in the city. We give them a message for the innkeep, since he's an Innocent."

I nodded. "Good. Set the exchange point outside the city, somewhere we'll have the high ground and a quick escape route. Make it at least an hour's ride west of the city and late in the day. That way the sun will be in their eyes, and they'll have to make the trade fast and hurry back before the city gates close for the night. Only problem we have is getting out of the city ourselves."

Choley gave me an appreciative smile. "No problem. We'll just take one of the carts I use for my, uh, other business and drive out at first light. I'll handle the rest since I know this city better than you do."

Suddenly, I felt very tired. I'd healed twice without resting. "Can I sleep here for a few hours? I need a little rest, and I can't go back to the inn."

Choley nodded toward the ceiling. "Sleep in my bed."

I gasped, embarrassed.

He held his hands up to stop my reply. "Don't hear words not spoken. I said 'you,' not 'we.' I won't be sleeping tonight, too many things to do."

I gagged Dask again, then followed Choley up the ladder. His room was separated by a dark velvet curtain from the room with the trapdoor. Lighting another candle with the first, he turned to go, but I stepped in front of him.

"Want me to stay?" He grinned at me and winked.

"No, Choley, I want to thank you. You're giving up a profitable business to help me."

"Who says I'm giving up anything? Figured I'd have to leave someday if my smuggling was discovered, so I made plans long ago, just in case. Money, escape routes, new city, everything waiting until needed." He grinned again. "Guess now's as good a time as any to move on."

"But—but you don't have to help. Why?"

The grin crumbled to a somber stare, and a quiet sigh escaped his thick chest. "I've guarded caravans through deserts so hot my sweat sizzled as it fell to the sand. I've climbed through mountains so cold I thought I'd lose fingers and toes, avoiding border patrols out to stop smugglers. I've fought wars for causes I didn't believe in, just for the money. Nothing I've done ever made a difference in the world, made it better. Now I have a chance to save one life." He stood tall, almost regal as he gazed at me.

"And ..." he paused, eyes narrowed, "I watched my brother and his wife and their two children die of Quick Fever, life sucked out of them like a weasel sucks eggs. In a week's time I lost all the family I had." His eyes glinted with the anger his voice revealed. "And Dask deliberately exposed you to Quick Fever, to make certain you died! That's why I'm helping you!"

He disappeared behind the curtain. Moments later, I heard the side door open and latch again.

A warmth swirled in my chest. The good in humans always surprised me. A person here or there still gave me hope that humans would someday value compassion as much as the Jin had.

I stripped off my boots and cloak, unbuckled my sword, then lay down on the wide, firm bed. Staring at the candle-wraiths playing on the ceiling, I wondered if our plan would work, if I'd ever see Fi again.

A quiet baritone voice cut through my dreams. "Elan, we have to go."

I opened my eyes to see Choley standing in the doorway, curtain draped against his arm. "Time already?" I asked.

"Yes. What we have to do requires dark." He let the curtain drop between us.

I dressed and hurried to the main room.

Choley was opening the trapdoor as I arrived. "I've got a wagon and three extra horses tied up outside. We'll put Dask in a barrel and sneak him out of Thallingar with the rest of the supplies I've packed."

I handed him a lit candle as he started down the ladder. "What about the message?"

"Won't be delivered till a couple of hours before sunset. The Innocents won't have enough time for a sneak attack." He gave me a wink. "Don't worry. Nothing can go wrong." As he reached the bottom, I heard him mumble, "I hope."

When I joined him in the secret room, he was pouring a cup of wine. "Take off his gag," Choley said.

Dask was bleary-eyed but still angry. As soon as I removed the cloth, he cursed me with plague after plague.

Choley held the cup in front of Dask's face. "Thirsty?"

Dask turned his curses on the tavern keep, but Choley just smiled and tossed back a few of his own. "Look, priest, you can drink this wine and fall asleep, or I can pound you unconscious. That'll take longer and feel lots worse—for you, that is. I'd enjoy it. So what'll it be?"

Dask snickered. I guess he didn't think Choley would really hit him. Dask was wrong. His jaw sounded like pottery breaking as Choley's hand smashed against it. Green eyes rolled back into a head which wobbled like a poppy with a broken stem. I thought Dask would've been out for hours from a blow like that. Instead, his eyes focused on Choley, fear glittering emerald bright.

"Thirsty now?" Choley asked.

Dask opened his mouth and swallowed as Choley held the cup.

"Good." Choley turned to me. "When he's out, we'll leave."

Dask became slack-jawed and dull-eyed in moments and was soon limp as a rag doll. His breathing slowed, and his lids closed, but he smiled in his sleep.

Choley hefted Dask over his shoulders and climbed the ladder. I followed, shut the trapdoor, and went to the side entrance. I snuffed the candle and cracked the door enough to check the alley, hidden in the gray light before dawn. No movement, no sound, no gleam of eye or steel. I opened the door. Choley carried Dask to the wagon parked beside the door, shoved him into a barrel, and secured the lid. We piled bundles around it, then climbed onto the driver's bench.

Dawn blushed the sky as we reached the western gate. A caravan waited for the first shaft of sunlight announcing a new day and the opening of the gates. I was edgy as we passed the sentries, but they didn't stop us. We followed the caravan, just another wagon on the western trade route.

We reached the mouth of the western pass through the Yorbid Mountains—the site chosen for the trade—in two hours. Choley showed me his secret path into the mountains. We took Dask's barrel off the wagon and hid it in a crevice, then Choley drove farther up the path. I stayed behind to watch Dask and set traps to block pursuit. Beyond that, all I could do was wait and hope.

The westering sun was hot on my back when Choley took Dask from the barrel. He was as unwieldy as wet clay and about as cooperative. It took both Choley and me to lever him out.

When Dask was sitting on reddish sand at the mountains' base, I noticed something was wrong with him. He looked like a sack of grain, even acted like one, not moving from the position in which he'd been placed. I thought he might still be asleep and shook him. There was no reaction. He was a shapeless heap, moving only when moved. I grabbed his chin and forced his eyes to meet mine.

That's when I saw it—that subtle lack of awareness I was so familiar with. I'd seen it in my sister's eyes. I felt sick and wanted to scream at Choley. He'd put Dream Dust in the wine, too much, causing brain damage. I could do nothing for Dask. My healing power had its limits.

"Why?" I cried as I turned on Choley. "You didn't have to destroy his mind! I just wanted my sister back alive!"

Choley glared at me. "You really think the Innocents would give up Fi for him without a good reason? They're sacrificing someone tonight. It has to be one of the childminded. Better him than her."

I started to argue, but he cut me off.

"Suppose we'd traded him for her, and he'd told them about Fi's visions. You think they'd let any of us live? Now, at least, we'll survive, and he'll see his god face-to-face. I'd say he's getting what he deserves."

My vision rippled like heat waves above desert sands. My soul cried, but I knew he was right.

Dust clouds from the east distracted me. The Innocents had come to make the trade, about ten riders. Hopefully, one of them was Fi. I took my dagger from its sheath, knelt behind Dask, and held the blade to his throat.

Choley took his bow from his shoulder, knocked an arrow, and aimed it at the lead rider. "Stop there," Choley called when they were fifty feet away. "Where's the woman?"

The lead rider signaled. A man rode forward, leading a horse. Fi's wrists were tied to the pommel. She looked pale but unharmed. I had to grit my teeth to keep from crying out.

The leader shrugged back his hood. It was the chief priest Royan. *He* was the leader of the Innocents. "We've honored our part," he growled, "but we require proof of the truth of your claim before we complete the exchange."

I looked askance at Choley. What did Royan mean?

Choley didn't relax his aim even a fraction. "Examine him. He has visions and is touched by the gods."

Cautiously, Royan dismounted and walked toward me and Dask. I watched the chief priest like a desert viper. Royan stooped before us, gave me a cold and deadly glare, then searched Dask's face.

Dask startled both of us by speaking, his voice high-pitched and awed. "Blue flame. Blue flame touched me. Touched the hurt and made it go away."

I trembled and nearly dropped the dagger. Even now, Dask remembered my healing power. His words meant our deaths.

To my surprise, Royan's eyes grew wide. He sucked air through his beard-hidden mouth. "He is indeed touched by the gods! We will have our sacrifice!"

I almost gave a prayer of gratitude to the Jin gods, except I didn't believe in them anymore.

Quickly, the Innocents cut Fi's ropes, and two men built like stone towers set Dask in her place. Royan stared at me. His voice was ants crawling on my skin. "We'll remember you."

He wheeled his horse and galloped toward Thallingar, followed by the others.

Fi ran to my open arms, and I hugged her so hard she whimpered. "Fi, are you all right? Did they hurt you?"

"Time for that later." Choley's eyes flitted across the landscape. "I don't want to stay here, just in case."

We mounted our horses and followed the secret path, now half-shadowed. As we rode, I thought about Dask and felt an ache in my chest, a hollow feeling like despair. Dask had tried to kill me and Fi for his god's sake. Choley had ruined Dask's mind from a sense of poetic justice. Royan hadn't cared who suffered as long as he had his proper sacrifice. I'd just wanted to save my sister's life.

I'd been among the humans for years. I'd served them, fought them, killed them, but I'd never understand them.

PROMISE TO ANGEL
by Stephanie Shaver

Stephanie says of herself that she is, "short, brown-haired, freckled, and inclined to stay that way." To which I add that she is not too short (we're all rather short around here), but I believe that Stephanie's no shorter than anyone else; I am probably shorter than she is. Stephanie speaks of brown hair, which sounds nondescript, but hers is rich and darkly brownish-black in a flood over her shoulders. She has a very sweet, untrained voice and sings all over the house while she works. Since she has moved into my house, we have discovered that she's a night person, going to bed when I am getting up, and vice versa. Personally, I can't imagine why anyone would want to stay up all night, but Stephanie is unabashed about it.

She's been working on getting her first novel, *Shadowstrike,* ready for submission, and has acquired a boyfriend named Ron who came to visit and help us when we were doing a large mailing for the magazine. Stephanie and Raul (our token male in the household) spend a good deal of time teasing each other. My own kids are grown and gone—my youngest is 28—and the behavior between the two of them makes life very interesting and baffling to our other housemate Jane, who is an only child and unused to ordinary sibling rivalry. I am mostly amused by it.

Anyhow, no matter where she lives, Stephanie's short stories are all good. This isn't as short as some, but I think it holds its length well.

Silver hair split around T'ia's hands like molten silk as she bent her head downward, her elbows resting on the table, her fingers digging into the loose flow of hair. She had silvered early in life, and in a strange fashion. Only the tips and the crown of her head had turned that strange, shimmering, night-metallic color; the rest was raven's wing black. A sign, her teacher had once told her, of one of the royal houses in her blood.

Mother would kill me if she saw me right now, T'ia mused as she tried to still the pounding in her temples. *Of course, Mother died when I was still a babe, so there's really no way to prove that statement, but still, all the tales I heard of the great Commander of the combined Aestern army and navy, Sabra Kinier, seem to point toward that general conclusion. . .*

T'ia sighed and shook her head, swinging her hair over her shoulder with a minimum of movement, so as not to start the little gremlin in her brain from acting up again.

Mother fought no matter what. Her greatest

pride was that she never retreated from a single battle. No matter the odds, she never lost. A superb tactician, a brilliant strategist. . . .

And I, her "heir" to the military genius, am a healer.

Sabra Kinier had been a fighter, a philosopher of war, and a legend in her time. That her daughter turned out to be a healer was not only ironic, it was nearly sacrilegious.

That I also left the homeland she so valiantly saved is almost worse, the Aestern woman thought as she stared out a window that looked upon the Ravern streets of Par, capital of Ravenbek. *But it seemed like a good idea at the time. . . .*

It was more than that—and she knew it. Running away from her home in the Aest had saved her from a life of nothingness. Had she stayed, she would have been delivered to the Imperator of the land as His personal healer, cloistered within the City of Footfalls, forgotten and lost until her death, or the Imperator's, which was one and the same since the dead lord's servants were buried, still alive, with Him in His tomb, so as to serve Him in death as they did in life.

Some life! she thought. She lifted her head briefly to reach across the table and pour herself some lavender-flower tea, the kind that eased headaches. From the smell of it, it had steeped long enough to impart its properties into the hot water, and, though the lavender wasn't what would shoo away the little hammer-wielding gremlin in her head, it at least made the concoction taste better.

If that is possible, she added wryly to herself.

Steam curled from the cup as she grimaced and sipped the bitter stuff. She momentarily played with the idea of sweetening it, like Raverners did, and then decided with a wrinkle of her nose that that would only make it worse. She had never understood the Ravern desire to overpower their drink with cloying honey-sugar or oily milk-and-cream. Ah, well. . . .

The sound of a door opening made her muscles freeze momentarily, and then she saw a familiar face coming through her front door and felt relief sweep her.

Really, she told herself, *you are far too jumpy. As if the Imperator could find you here? Or maybe it is the headaches. You have been having them so often, lately—and for what reason?*

With a wince, T'ia realized that her jaw was clenched, and set about loosening it. *Well, there's one reason,* she thought, returning her attention to the man who had just walked into her home/shop.

"Hello, Anjilo," she said calmly, taking care to pronounce his name correctly without any Aestern inflections.

The black-haired, green-eyed Guardsman smiled cockily and swept into a bow. "Mistress T'ia!" he exclaimed, his voice setting her head pounding again. She winced.

"Anjilo, please, I have a terrible headache. Would you be so kind as to keep your voice to as slight a volume as you can manage?"

A look of surprise washed the tall, young man's face and he bowed low. Then he straightened and sat down across from her at her crude table.

She took a moment to look at Anjilo, and ponder on how much he reminded her of a man she had known so many years ago. The man who had given her a gift of a silver ring that even now rested on her middle right-hand finger. The man who had shown her that there was a world outside the tiny hut she had lived in all her life. The man whom she had sought after she came here to Ravenbek, but never found.

And who I still search for ... but, somehow, I have become stuck in this town. She blinked. *I wonder how that happened—and I wonder if I could even bring myself to leave, now that I have a good business and gold flowing into my pockets daily?*

She shrugged mentally, decided it didn't matter, and returned her attention to the young man.

"And what brings you here, Anjilo?" she asked politely, sipping the tea.

Anjilo seemed to consider the question, then said softly, "Mistress, what do you know of children?"

I know that I can have none, she thought bitterly, but only answered, "Quite a bit. They need healing more often than adults."

"I ... found one on patrol today."

She cocked a brow. "Found?" she asked.

He nodded vigorously. "A young boy," he said. "A young boy who is very hurt—outside and ... inside, I think."

T'ia's eyes narrowed, her brows cramping together. She was suddenly aware that her headache had stopped.

But tea did not work so quick as that. . . .

"Where did you find this boy?"

"The District."

"What district?"

"*The* District," he replied intently.

"Oh." *That* District. The part of town where no one willingly went—not even to die. "What were you doing *there?*"

"Well, there was a fight—and someone got killed—and the two who did it, they got away— and I followed—"

"And wound up there. I'm shocked you stayed long enough to find a boy."

"I didn't," he replied. "The boy appeared in front of me."

"What?" She frowned, not understanding.

"I mean he—appeared. Like—like—*wizardry*—in front of me."

Her frown deepened. She stood, then, set her tea to the side, and reached behind her for her cloak. "Come," she said softly, firmly. "Take me to this boy-who-appears-like-wizardry."

The child had lank blond hair, sorrowfully heartbreaking blue eyes, sallow skin, and bruises all over his body. And he trembled—like an aspen leaf in a hard wind.

Anjilo had taken her to his personal home, one of the apartments granted to the senior guardsmen. It was small, but clean, with a single bed pushed against the farthest wall and a heavy curtain over the lone window screening out most of the light.

"Hello," she said softly and saw no reaction. She had yet to touch the boy.

To Anjilo she said, "How did you bring him back?"

"In my arms," the guardsman replied.

"Ah," she said gently, keeping her voice even and neutral. Then she reached forward and touched him.

The boy looked up, his blue eyes almost a match for her near-crystal colored set. Blind man's eyes, Anjilo had called them when he first met her and she had healed him of injuries no common practitioner could have helped.

Something in the boy's face shifted, moved, as if he were recognizing someone he had thought lost.

"Mother?" he asked.

She shook her head and touched one hand to his face, brushing his temples lightly. Reaching out with something other than her hands to touch more than skin—

Cuts, bruises, fractured ribs, sores. The diagnosis of what was wrong with his body swept her in a fever-chilly wave that made her shudder momentarily. Wrapped in her silk robes of green and blue, it was hard to see that she trembled at all, which was half the purpose of such garments in the first place.

"Mother?" the boy repeated as she turned his wrist over and placed one finger against the life-node point, starting to stream the healing energy into him.

"No, child, not your mother," she murmured, and her heart wrenched, as the words reminded her of what she could never be.

His head dipped slightly as the first wave of healing began to scour his wounds, mending skin and bone and drawing his ill body back toward health. She heard Anjilo's sharply intaken breath through the shallow trance she used when healing.

Enchantress, they call me, she thought. *Mage and more—but do they not know that my powers are nothing like a wizard's? My source is nothing at all like the magister's Source? Aye—of course not. To them, all magic—whether of the self or the Source—is the same magic. . . .*

She cut off the flow of energy, and opened her arms as the boy slid against her, falling into the slumber that normally followed an Aestern mystic's healing. She held him close, for once ignoring the dirtiness that so prevailed in Ravern society, and that especially clung to the hair and skin and clothing of the boy.

"I will need to take him with me," she said, "to do any more."

"Yes, Mistress T'ia."

"Very good. And, Anjilo," she added, a note of irritation creeping into her voice.

"Yes, mistress?"

"Stop calling me mistress! I'm younger than *you*."

She had Anjilo escort her back home due to the falling wings of Lady Night's cloak around the city, and she had *him* carry the boy as punishment for having called her by an elder's title throughout the day. She didn't look *that* old . . . did she?

Carefully, Anjilo set the boy in bed, and she went into the kitchen to boil water as he did so. She still feared the large, open hearths favored by the Raverners, but she had to admit that they boiled water quicker than anything back in the Aest.

"Mis— I mean, T'ia?"

"Yes, Anjilo?" she asked, turning toward him.

"I know I should have brought this up earlier, but I—well, I don't have much money, and. . . ."

She looked him square in the eyes, reading the truth there, and shrugged. "My business is good. I can allow you to owe me a favor instead of money."

He nodded. "Thank you."

"Now, go home. You must be up early tomorrow, I assume, and I must be going to work." Her headache, she realized, was coming back. "Go!" she shooed, and the too-tall guardsman ducked his head like a shy adolescent and walked out the door.

Alone again, T'ia sank gratefully into a chair and put her head into her hands. The pain was double the normal agony; the gremlin must have invited some friends over. She reached across to the cold tea she had left sitting on the table, and then stopped as a scream filled her home.

She jumped like a startled rabbit, then reprimanded herself for behaving so. Businesslike, she hoisted her long robes into her hand, and swished her way into the bedroom. It did not escape her notice that, as she drew closer to the boy, her headache increased.

The boy was thrashing in her bed, his face contorted, tears streaming down his cheeks. Sorrow plunged itself, death-water cold, into her heart, and she caught her breath even as she caught up energy around herself and drew a shimmering veil of protection down around the boy.

The sorrow—and the headache—died with an almost audible snap, and T'ia knelt down next to the boy, her eyes huge.

One magic—but both very different. This one is the first I have seen since I came to this place with traces of something other than Ravern magic, traces of my own type of spells, yet his hair is fair and his face nothing like an Aesterner—what in Halcyon's name is going on?

She touched the boy's face, and he trembled, pulling into a curled ball. With a negative shake of her head, T'ia straightened him.

His eyes snapped open, his face naked with fear.

"Mother," he rasped, tears still streaming down his face. T'ia knew the words were not addressed at her, it was more of a statement. The boy had been dreaming about his mother.

"What is your name?" she asked, stroking his damp hair away from his face.

The boy looked down, looked up. "Angel," he whispered. "What is yours?" His voice had the quality of someone who did not speak often.

'T'ia," she replied.

He nodded slowly. "Tee-aye-ah," he said, pronouncing each syllable.

She smiled. "Stay awake," she ordered, and left the room.

The water was boiling by then, and she threw some herbs into the kettle to steep, then took another pan filled with water and a washcloth and went back into the room.

He was sitting up in the bed, trying to stand. She pushed him back down.

"Sit. You are in no condition to move."

He shook his head. "No—I must leave. They will kill you—"

Her hand, plunged into the lukewarm water, froze where it was, and she stared at him.

"Who will?" she asked sternly.

He paled. "I—I have to go—"

"Sit!" she ordered, her voice backed up with Aestern sorcery, and he had no other choice but to sit back down on the bed.

"Now," she said crisply, wringing out the cloth. "Who is trying to kill you—or me—or whatever?"

He bowed his head, but she caught his chin and raised it, then began wiping his face. He wrinkled his nose with blatant disdain, but otherwise endured the severe washing.

"Alva," he said shakily as she scrubbed his ears. The boy was filthy!

"Strip," she ordered absently. Then she asked, "Why is Alva trying to kill you?"

"Not *me*," he said, dutifully removing his rags. "*You.*"

"Why?"

"Be—because—you have me—and I belong to him—"

Her look pinned him, and his words broke

away and melted. "You *belong* to him? I see no marks of slavery on you. And by the laws of even this land you are too young to belong to another, little one."

He sighed, said nothing, removed his shirt.

A frown rippled over her features as she stared at the numerous scars that ripped his young body, then began washing his chest.

"It is illegal for you to 'belong' to these ones-who-would-murder-me-for-healing-you." There was a word for such people in her language. In this one, it was just a handful of words strung together.

He nodded, eyes downcast.

"So why do you not seek out the King's guards?"

"Because that is who owns me."

Her hand froze again from where it scrubbed his chest.

"The *King's* guards?" she said dubiously.

"Well . . . not really. . . ."

"Then who?"

He did not answer.

"Who?"

Silence.

She sighed, hating to do it, but being forced to. . . .

"Who?" she demanded, and drew the answer out of him with her mysticism.

"The King's assassins," he whispered, new tears streaming down his cheeks.

Oh, dear gods. "The King's assassins," she repeated slowly. "Why?"

His jaw clenched. "Because of my magic," he said, speaking the answer though she knew he did not want to.

"The magic to appear?"

He nodded.

"The magic to disappear?"

"And make others do so," he murmured, his voice a thread that was nearly lost in the twilight.

On impulse, T'ia reached out and drew a flower of light into being in the palm of her hand. It was a mystic's simple trick, and it illuminated the entire room.

He caught his breath, and she saw in his eyes that he knew this magic to be like to his own.

"Can you do this, as well?" she asked softly.

He nodded.

"Could your mother do this?"

He paused, then shakily nodded. "But not much," he admitted.

"Did she teach you to do this?"

"A little," he whispered. "She taught me that, and a little of the Aestern language, but I don't remember all of it."

"Where is she?"

"Dead." A sea of sorrow in his voice.

"How old were you when she died?"

"Too young to know my age."

"Your father?"

He shook his head. "She was a whore."

"And how did these assassins find you?" she asked, her soul seething with anger. Some pieces of the puzzle were fitting together now. If his mother had been ... one-of-*those*-women, then there was always the possibility that he simply did not breed the Aestern blood true. His mother could have been half-blood herself and still looked Aestern. Gods knew that T'ia's blood was mingled, yet she was almost indistinguishable from a "full-blooded" Aesterner.

Hist, Wandermind! she chided herself. *The boy speaks.*

"I—I was alone on the streets after she died. And I was hungry. So I used to wrap myself in—in—" he frowned. "She called it a cloak of mist. I used to do it, and when I did, no one could see me. So I would use it to steal food. And—one day—I had gone so long without food, that, when I finally sat down and dropped the cloak—I—I didn't know there was someone in the alley, and they—it was Alva. He asked me how I'd done it, and when I wouldn't tell him, he sliced me—here—" he touched a scar on his chest, "—with his knife. And he hurt me—t–til I did. Then he asked me if I could do it to others—and I–I said yes, I could. And he—he confiscated me in the name of the King."

The boy's voice trembled with tears. "He said that I was unique. He said that mages can make people disappear, but that when I did it, mages couldn't sense it. I don't understand that but—but they fed me—kinda—and—"

She silenced him with a hand. "It is true. Ravern mages are not the same as Aestern mages. The magic is not the same. An Aestern mage's spells are different from a Raverner's. Raverners are more powerful because their power comes from outside them, from a place called the Source, but an Aesterner's magic is more flexible because it comes from the *self*. Do you understand? No? Well, take a Ravern mage's heavenbolt. It will fry you to a crisp, yes? But a Ravern mage cannot control the frying. He cannot make a roast with it. He has to create other spells to do that. An Aestern mage must put skeins and skeins of power into a spell to kill someone—like turning a man's skin into fire. It takes much energy, for an Aestern mage must draw upon her *self* to do something like that. But she can also, with a minimal amount of effort, cook a roast with the same spell."

The child's face transformed with enlightenment as she explained the differences of mysticism and wizardry to him. After a while, he said, "*That's* why I felt so weak today! I'd never put the cloak around myself and *two* people at a time. No wonder I couldn't keep up with them. Is that why I fell in front of your friend—because I was doing it to so many people?"

She furrowed her brow, nodding in answer to his question, while her mind spun into a sudden circle of understanding. So *that* was why they wanted the boy—to kill Ravern mages? It made sense. If they used another Ravern mage to throw invisibility—or the "cloak" as the boy called it—around an assassin, he would be seen by the mage he intended to kill, or at least the victim-mage would sense the Source magic nearby and become wary, especially if he suspected that the King had put a contract out on his head. But with an Aestern spell woven of self-magic—the magic that a Source-tuned wizard simply could not sense—around the assassins. . . .

They would never see it coming. Literally.

"T'ia," he whispered, "they're coming."

She snapped her head around to look at him. Did the boy have the Sight? Could he see the future as well?

"How do you mean that?" she asked sharply, and he seemed to understand what she meant.

"I mean that they will be coming. I don't know when. Just that they will."

She nodded grimly.

"You must let me go."

She laughed. "No, no, I must not."

"They'll kill you!"

She smiled and stroked his hair. Tears rattled in his eyes.

"No, they will not," she said.

"But—!"

"Angel," and her voice was soft again, but backed by granite, "this I promise you. They will *never* take you back from me. Do you understand that?"

Tears melted down his cheeks. He nodded.

"Good." She stood and brushed his tears away with the edge of her robe. "Finish bathing," she nodded toward the pan, "and when I return we will prepare for those-who-must-use-children-to-kill."

The food was hot, and he ate it all. T'ia herself was too wrapped in plans to truly taste what she had prepared. She was weakened by the day of healing and talking and folding the wings of her shields around this boy. Had she the time she would teach him how to do it to himself, but she didn't, so she couldn't.

I should sleep, she thought, but knew she wouldn't. The boy would—she flowed healing into him again, so he really had no choice—and when she was done, she went into her kitchen, picked up the cold cup of tea, and stared into the dark.

I am dead. What can I do against a guild of assassins, much less the King's assassins? I have no allies other than Anjilo, and he is a King's guard.

Of course, there *was* one thing she could do. She could go back to the Aest, give herself to the Imperator and hope that maybe, *maybe,* the Imperator would not only spare her life and forgive her rebellious actions, but also apprentice the boy to someone who could teach him the way of the *ai-sa,* a healer-bodyguard. Like her, only she was no longer officially *ai-sa.* Yet another title she had abandoned—only this one had been voluntary.

But she dropped that idea as soon as she conceived it. Give Angel into a slavery that she could almost guarantee would be worse than what he had already endured? Never! She was surprised how fierce her loyalties were toward the boy, but she had to admit that she felt kinship to this Angel who was a slave in spirit, if not in name.

Like I was.

She let *that* thought drop away into stillness. Turned to a new one.

But if not the Aest, and not Ravenbek . . . where?

She stared down at her hands, at a ring that glittered silver on her finger, and considered it.

A mouthful of tea slid into her belly like a leaden clump of ice. Some drinks were excellent chilled. This was not one of them.

She pondered in the darkness, the moons rising until they came to the hour that was midnight and then, silently, T'ia stood, changed into lighter clothes, and slipped out of the house.

There was no sign of anyone following her as she made her winding way through the now treacherous-seeming streets of Par and to the senior guardsmen's flat. With tools that were illegal in most kingdoms, she coaxed the door lock open adeptly (a random skill she had "picked" up in her travels), and slipped inside. No guards. Who set a guard in a house filled with them?

Anjilo was sleeping as she entered and crouched down by his bed.

"Anjilo. Waken."

He sat up with a start, and stared at her. She looked back at him, scanning his face, and decided.

"I am leaving."

"Hunh—what?" Sleep thickened his young, velvety voice.

"I said, Anjilo, that I am leaving."

"What—what for?"

In calm, simple words she told him, and watched his face as she spoke. It suddenly occurred to her that the boy may have been lying—making up some sort of elaborate story—

No. No one bore such marks of beating without a reason. And no one carried themself like a broken cur without cause.

After a long silence, Anjilo asked, "Where will you go?"

"I cannot tell you, Anjilo."

He stared into her eyes and knew that it was not because of trust that she would not reveal the place where she would be taking Angel. If Anjilo knew, and they found Anjilo, and interrogated him . . . no man was immune to torture. Sooner or later, if only to stop the pain, he would tell them.

With a sigh, Anjilo laid back against his pillows. "All right, T'ia. If you decide to leave in the night, go by the north gate. The guard there is a friend of mind, and a few coins will get you out."

She blinked, then smiled, now realizing why she had come here.

"Thank you, Anjilo."

A hand reached out of the darkness and touched hers, clenched it in a form of farewell. "Gods go with you."

"At this time, Anjilo," T'ia replied with mild amusement, though the currents that ran beneath her voice were anything but amused, "I don't need Their presence, I just need one of Their miracles."

She returned home to find the child still sleeping. Still safe.

We must leave.

The words were a near-frantic litany in her mind, but none of that panic penetrated the composure that floated around her like an aura. The healer's aura.

She had much already prepared. She had long feared that the Imperator would find her and try to drag her back to the Aest, and had anticipated it in advance by keeping "emergency supplies" on hand and nearby should a hasty departure be necessary.

She sighed. How angry her mother would be if she knew that T'ia planned on running—again. But T'ia had to admit that, sometimes, retreat was the only plan of action that worked.

The one tactical lesson my proud mother never learned. Which is why her body is ash now. Had she not tried to take those bandits single-handed when they ambushed her. . . .

Well, no use dwelling on another's mistakes. T'ia became busy packing bags with food and herbs and other necessities. She shivered, aware of how cold her little two room home was. Teeth chattering, she crossed over to the hearth and knelt down before it. She stoked the embers into life, feeding wood into the dancing, licking flames.

Now, back to packing—

And it was at that precise moment, when she was pushing herself up from where she crouched by the hearth, that the door to her home exploded off its hinges.

T'ia had a brief appreciation of how intense pain could be as splinters of wood slivered into her body. She saw a dark silhouette outlined against the now ragged doorway, saw the robes that signified a mage, and saw hands raised and bristling with Ravern Source-magic.

Unthinking, T'ia's hand dipped into a place inside her robes, came out with a small knife no bigger than her longest finger. The little weapon looked like a blade that someone had forgotten to put a handle to. It flew gracefully through the air, and she heard a solid *thunk!* as it landed in the man's throat.

There was a sputtering gurgle, and whatever spell the man had been in the middle of casting died. So did he.

Shaking, the healer ignored the bile rising in her throat from having actually *killed* a man, rolled to her feet, and hurried into the bedroom. The boy was sitting up in bed, his eyes huge, the covers clenched to his chest.

"Get dressed," she ordered in a low voice, extending herself outward—to Sense—to See—

No. The mage was the only one they had sent. This time.

Quickly, Angel dressed and obeyed T'ia when she handed him a pack. The door, thank the gods, had exploded soundlessly enough, or else there would have been a racket coming from the neighbors by now.

"T'ia," she heard Angel say, "you're bleeding."

"Hush, child, and help me with this body."

It was true, she was bleeding, but she could be worse. Had she not moved over to the hearth when she did, there was a good chance that some of those larger pieces of wood could have impaled her or knocked her out. As it was, the most she had was a scattering of splinters in her body that could be extracted. Painful, but it would not kill her.

Together, they dragged the man into the sleeping room. T'ia had dealt with dead weight before—healer she was, but even for some, she was not the best. Death's healing had won over hers a few times. Not many, but enough so that she knew what a dying body felt like, what it looked like under her hands.

"Come, now," she said softly. "We must go."

He nodded as she shouldered a pack and, then, shyly, he took her hand.

She smiled down at him and, together, the two left the healer's home.

Streets.

T'ia moved down them rapidly, Angel's hand in hers, the stars that were embroidered into the fabric of Lady Night's cloak glittering above them.

Something sinister was whispering in T'ia's ear, something that said that the King's so called assassins would not let her leave so easily. Something made her neck prickle, her skin crawl. Something. . . .

Perhaps it was her highly-trained mind, already tuned into paranoia, or perhaps it was a damned fool's luck, but she managed to trip and fall, carrying Angel with her, just as the quarrel hissed through the air where her head had been and buried itself into a stone wall directly across from her.

She pushed Angel behind her, dipped into her robes, and pulled out another hiltless knife as shadows detached themselves from an alley across from her. Five shadows—six knives. *Make them last,* she thought, and flung the first one.

It sang as it landed in the man's chest, and he grunted and fell. The one with the crossbow cursed and began to reload. The remaining three charged.

She got one last knife off—it skimmed through the air and plucked the man in the arm but failed to find anything vital—before they were on her, and then she found herself slipping into the old patterns of the hand-fighting that was a trademark of the *ai-sa*.

There was a snap as she circular-parried the first man's knife with the flat of her palm and broke his wrist in the process. He howled and dropped, writhing in pain. The second—his sword raised to slash—fell with a set of stiffened fingers in the sternum and then a downward kick toward his thrashing body that caught his windpipe and snapped it.

But the last one . . . he was smiling, waiting his turn with an insane patience. He carried a twin set of knives in either hand, and both danced wickedly in the light. T'ia wondered briefly when the damned crossbow was going to pluck her and end it all—and then she wasn't wondering anything. She was fighting for her life.

"Alva," she heard Angel whisper, and nodded grimly as she tried to hook the man's legs out from underneath him.

He danced away from her and she felt the edge of a knife slice through her silk robe and draw blood. She parried the other one with her forearm, then knife-handed toward his belly.

He danced back again, smiling still, teeth white and bright and hard in his face. He knew he was winning. And that was the damnable part of it.

T'ia swallowed painfully, aware of sweat and blood pouring down her body, aware of how weak she was. She had not fought in so long—she had always been more of a healer than a warrior. It was all a matter of time before this young fool stopped smiling and playing and slit her throat. And then she would fall—and her promise to Angel would be broken.

No. No! By the gods, you cannot do this to me.

You took my childhood, and you nearly stole my life. You cannot *steal this boy's life, too!*

Of course, there was one other thing she could do. It would mean her life—but it would also mean Alva's. It was a final spell, a desperate spell, an explosion of all her self-energy that would consume her body as well as Alva's. It was a last-ditch effort, but it was effective. . . .

Another knife slid against her forearm; shallow cuts that stung, not killed. She snap-kicked at his knee, but again, eellike, he slid away and dodged.

Bastard!

A knife jabbed at her ribs, slicing shallowly, and she tried to take advantage of his position and move in closer to him. No luck; he just slid away, his laughter mocking her. T'ia felt her breath flagging, her sides aching terribly, and it was at that moment that she knew the gods had left her with one choice. Her time was up. There was a brief flash of insight, a weary sigh from her soul. It was now, she realized, or never.

Alva moved forward, the intent to cause more suffering spread across his face with glee. She ground her teeth, feeling a trickle of triumph in knowing that this was the last time he would ever make another person suffer on a whim.

Knives flashed, went to strike—

"Angel! RUN!" T'ia screamed as she gathered the power to blast that damned smile off Alva's face—

And the fluid knife-dancer stiffened.

She blinked, watching as the smile slid away from the man's face, only now seeing the dark shadow that loomed over Alva, only now seeing the tip of a Guardsman's sword sticking out of the assassin's sternum.

From behind, the swordsman twisted his blade. There was a popping sound, and blood dribbled down the assassin-turned-assassinated's shirt. He slid off the sword slowly, going first to his knees, then to Death.

T'ia licked her lips, seeing only now that the crossbowman, also, lay still, his blood pooling in the shadows of an alley. The one with the broken wrist, too, had died, as soundlessly as Alva and the other did.

"Mistress," Anjilo said, and bowed.

She smiled, relief washing her features, her self-energy resettling as the spell aborted.

Anjilo toed the stiffening remains of Alva with disdain. "If this is the sort of scum my King hires," he said softly, "he is no King I wish to work for."

"That is a safe assumption," T'ia said dryly, her whole body shaking. "How did you find us?"

"It wasn't so hard," Anjilo replied with a shrug. "I got to your home not long after you left; the blood on that body was still wet. And I knew you'd taken my advice when the north side of town started growing quiet and the Guard patrols thinned out, then died altogether."

T'ia cocked her head to one side, abruptly realizing that, despite the sound of men dying, despite the combat and her scream, not a single door or window had opened, no dogs had barked, and there were no Guards to be seen.

Par, it seemed, was a more dangerous city than she had thought.

"Should I assume you are going with us?" she asked.

"You said I owed you a favor."

She glanced at Alva's body. "*That* I considered an absolving of your debt."

He grinned, flashing broad teeth. "That? That wasn't a favor, ma'am. That was a *pleasure*."

Nodding thoughtfully, she turned to Angel. He

was trembling, staring at Alva, staring at the blood that lapped around T'ia's soft boots.

T'ia caught his eyes, held them. Took them away from the ungraceful death that sprawled at her feet, took them away from the life-fluid, cooling on the cobblestones. Told her promise to him again, with her eyes, with her face, with the sweat and blood that mingled on her body.

"Come, child, we must be gone," she said, and opened her arms to him.

Angel nodded, a tiny movement, smiled minutely, and wrapped his arms around her waist, and she heard a distinct little "mother" float up from where he had buried his face against her stomach.

"Ready?" Anjilo asked.

"Yes," she said, wrapping the wings of her cloak around the child. "I think we are."

They left by the north, slipping through the gates to the the road and the cool night. Though they set a brisk pace, they would have to rest soon, for neither Angel or T'ia was up to so much walking. However, barring periodic rests, T'ia was certain they could make it to the Baryanka Sylvan, and seek shelter beneath the trees before dawn broke.

Running again, she thought briefly, and smiled at the wind. *Dearest gods—mother would not be proud.*

She played with the silver ring on her left hand. Not the one the stranger had given her—that was on her right hand, on the finger of friendship. No. This was a different ring, resting on the finger of wisdom, given to her by another man. Not a stranger. She smiled at it as they walked.

No, mother would not be proud.

She laughed to herself.

But father would.

SHADOW HARPER
by Cynthia McQuillin

When I first published this writer—about thirteen years ago now—she was very young, probably not thirty yet. Now she's beginning to have very attractive patches of gray appear in her dark hair.

I ask myself sometimes, "Is there anything this gifted young woman can't do?" She's living in our house, with her friend Jane; Jane is a massage therapist who is almost as good at rearranging our discombobulated bodies as she is at unscrambling our embarrassingly frisky souls with her music. Cynthia—with or without Jane—has made for us some fascinating tapes. Cynthia does not herself play a harp, but she shares with me the delusion that she *ought* to be able to play one without having to learn how. As I said, she and I are very *old* friends.

All of her stories have an unexpected flavor—they are never quite as simple as they seem at first.

Fiona paced anxiously from window to window, looking down on the starkly lit landscape. The light pouring through the unglazed openings made silver swirls of the dust her skirts swept up as she crossed the cold stone floor. Pushing a lock of auburn hair from her eyes, she paused to stare out of the largest of the three windows. The world looked very different from this perspective than it had that afternoon from the hillside below,

Returning from the cheese market with supplies for her mother's inn, Fiona had let the pleasant weather and the beauty of the rolling dales lure her from the safety of the road.

"Foolish daydreamer," her mother often scolded her. "That fanciful temperament of yours will be your bane, or mine." But Fiona could no more still the wild heart within her than she could have been unkind. Besides, dinner time was far away and what harm would it do to while away an hour on such a pretty day. But then she had heard the distant chime of a wire-strung harp. Ensorcelled by the sound, she discarded cap, shawl, and shopping basket in unaccustomed abandon, to dance after the harper's wondrous music. It had led her to the haunted ruin of this ancient fort.

Though Fiona had lived her entire life in the shadow of these hills, she had never seen nor heard of such a ruin. Yet here it sat, a weathered sandstone edifice crouching like a great ginger cat atop the highest mound. Its single dark tower thrust skyward with an air of foreboding, but even this could not deter her from entering the ancient keep.

Curiosity led her to explore its silent halls, but something more compelling had drawn her to the tower stairs, urging her upward until she stood in this very room. Then, that remarkable compulsion had released her, leaving Fiona feeling light-headed and weak. Suddenly weary from the long climb, she sat down on the floor with her back against the wall, to rest for awhile. But scarcely had Fiona settled herself, when she fell into a deep, dreamless sleep, to wake when the moon had risen.

Now, as she stood trembling in the chilly night air and wondering what to do, it seemed that she could hear the entrancing harp-song once again. But as she listened more closely, she realized that the sad, sweet sound of a human voice had been added to the threads of the harper's melodic tapestry.

"See me, hear me, you can't touch me.
Time stands like a wall.
I'm the shadow of a memory,
And you can't touch me at all."

Enchanted by his deep, vibrant tenor, Fiona was drawn to the doorway. She paused for only a moment before carefully picking her way down the ancient stone stairway. The atmosphere of the place seemed to thicken as she moved through it, though the hallway gradually lightened as she went. The singer's voice was stronger now, and she began to catch tantalizing glimpses of a ghostly figure moving in the shadows just ahead of her. Strange in his outmoded style of dress, the harper was handsome—slender and supple as a willow.

"Stop running away!" Fiona cried at last, unable to overtake him no matter how quickly she followed. Frustration warred with weariness as she plunked herself down on the steps of what had been the dais of the dining hall. The chill from the hard stones made her tremble as she surveyed the long-abandoned room. It seemed cavernous and bleak. Tapestries hung in dusty tatters on the unfinished stone walls, and the trestle table had been overturned, its planks scattered about the room. Only a few of the chairs remained more or less intact.

Diverted from her examination by the sound of footfalls nearby, Fiona leaped to her feet, demanding, "Why do you taunt me?"

"There is more of a haunt about me than a taunt," came the reply from the dais beside her. The harper's speaking voice was as pleasing as his song. Startled, Fiona turned to see a very solid looking young man eyeing her with a wistful expression. He held a small harp cradled protectively in one arm. His eyes were the blue of certain April skies, and his straight, black hair swept back from his forehead to hang well below his shoulders. In the moonlight which bathed the room, his features glowed with an unearthly brightness.

In fact, Fiona realized, everything in the chamber was glowing. Shadows played cheerfully across exquisite velvets and brocades as ghostly candles lit the room. Puzzled, she bent to examine the fine needlework of a brightly-colored rug which became solid even as she touched it. It hadn't been there a moment before, of that she was certain.

"Who ... what are you?" Fiona said, turning back to face the harper. Her voice was hoarse with alarm, barely a whisper.

"Colin Songbird at your service, sweet maiden." He made a gallant bow, flashing her a smile that might have melted the heart of a less experienced lass. Taking her hand, he led her to a brocaded sea-green couch. There he seated her with an elegant gesture, and took his place on the harper's stool at her feet. "What is your pleasure, my lady?"

"I'm hardly a lady, Master Colin." Her tone was wry as she gestured to her blouse of unbleached linen, leather girdle, and skirt of brown wool. Only the fine needlework on the bodice and sleeves set her above the commonest peasant. In contrast, he wore crimson and blue, his tabard stiff with gilt threads among the blue, and his boots dyed crimson to match his tunic.

"To me there is no finer lady than the flame-haired beauty I see before me." He spoke with the charming insincerity of his profession, striking a chord as he gazed soulfully into her clear gray eyes. But many a harper had sung for a meal or a round at her mother's table; so Fiona's attention was for Colin's harp rather than his flattery. The wood was highly figured maple which glowed with golden ripples of light the color of amber. No gilding or inlay was needed to enhance the beauty of the harp's materials and craftsmanship.

"What a lovely instrument." Her hand reached out of its own volition, to stroke the lustrous frame. Fiona was surprised to find that the wood was warm to the touch, seeming to vibrate slightly, almost like a living thing.

"She is beautiful." Colin smiled sadly, stroking the harp just as Fiona had. "Her name is Clarion. She was the gift of a jealous queen."

"The Faerie Queen!" Fiona's eyes were wide as she drew back her hand in alarm. Had she doomed herself by touching the Faerie gift?

"Have no fear, sweet maiden. Her curse binds none but me."

"You may call me by my name, which is Fiona, if you please," she said, annoyed by his casual endearments. "But, tell me how you came to be cursed, Master Harper?"

"Now that is a sad story, Fiona, and an old one. It began with my ascension to the post of King's Own Harper in the court of Finn Oleran."

"That would have been close to a century ago!"

"Truly. And I was a fine harper even then, though as vain a young man as ever you will meet, I'm afraid." Though his tone was contrite his expression was hardly repentant. "Thinking myself more valued by the King than I was, I set my heart on the hand of Lady Megan, Oleran's niece, and his ward."

"You were ambitious, then, as well as vain." Noting the disapproval in her tone, Colin changed his tack.

"You wound me, girl!" he said, casting his eyes to the floor with a sigh. "It wasn't for station or wealth that I loved Megan, but for her own self. She had a quality of spirit that I have seldom seen in another, and a rare sweetness. Had she consented, I would have fled the court with her, to follow the vagabond road."

"Forgive me, Colin. I only meant to tease you." Fiona spoke softly, taken in by his pretense.

"I can see that now. You've a kind heart for all your sharp tongue," he smiled at her. "Unfortunately, Seamus the Raven discovered my liking for Megan, and plotted to use it against me. Seamus had long sought to bring me into disfavor with the king and claim my post for his own.

"One evening, as we sat to drink at Oleran's table, Seamus made his play. 'The King's niece would never stoop to wed a songbird, no matter how pretty his plumage,' he taunted me. His voice, though soft, was harper-trained and carried clearly. A hush fell over the company. 'You're a fool, Colin, you may as well admit it. The Lady Megan may have a passing fancy for the King's

Harper, but she will wed whatever man of title Oleran chooses.'

"Stung by his remarks, and well into my cups, I grew reckless and boastful. ' 'Tis your envy that speaks, Seamus, for a songbird may charm any woman he pleases with the sweetness of his song. But a raven, that croaking harbinger of ill-omen, would be hard pressed to please any but a hedge-witch,' I replied.

" 'Do you then claim to hold Megan's heart, bold rascal?' Oleran inquired, having overheard our exchange along with the rest of the table, as Seamus intended.

" 'I spoke in generalities, Majesty. But it is true that I love Megan above all others, and crave her hand in honorable marriage.' Nettled by Seamus' glee at my discomfiture and made overly candid by the drink, I had spoken my true thoughts, seeing the trap too late. It was plain that Oleran was ill-pleased with such presumption, and thinking to put me in my place, he made this wager.

" 'If you woo and win the lady I shall name, I will grant you Megan's hand. If, however, you fail to return to me within a fortnight with some token of your success, you will forfeit your place in this court and in my favor.'

" 'Name the woman!' said I, without hesitation. 'To wed fair Megan, I shall win her, be she maid or crone.'

" 'Done!' Oleran grinned wickedly. 'Return to me with a love token from the Faerie Queen, and Megan's hand is yours.'

"Now I ask you, Fiona, what could I do?"

"Men are fools, when it comes to women and their own pride," she said, shaking her head.

"True enough," Colin agreed with a rueful grin. "But, being true to my nature, as every man must, I took up the challenge. Rising up the next day, as early as my whiskey-sodden head would allow, I donned my finest clothes, took my harp in hand and set off down the Southern Path.

"After riding for quite some time, I came to the edge of Elam's Wood, and there I left the road to enter the Faerie Hills. Knowing, from the legends I sang, that Faeries danced in rings beneath the full moon and loved mortal music above all else, I felt myself well prepared. My success seemed assured, if only I could keep my wits about me."

"Only a fool or a harper would believe his own ballads!" Fiona chided. "Were not True Thomas and Tamlynn both beloved of the Faerie Queen?"

"No need to remind *me*, Fiona," he winced. "But if you are done belaboring me for my gullibility, perhaps you'll allow me to finish my tale?" Suppressing a smile, she folded her hands in her lap and adopted a more attentive demeanor.

"I had only walked a short way when I spied this fort. There was no sign of anyone about, but though the tower and the galleries below appeared deserted and ancient, all stood in good repair and there was an air of expectancy about the place. 'This must be the work of the Sidhe,' said I, and sat myself down to wait. And what do you think happened then? Why, I fell asleep, and when I woke the moon was already high.

"It was then that I heard the most beautiful, unearthly music. The manic sound of pipe and fiddle led me to this hall, where I beheld slender, quicksilver men and women cavorting to the songs of earth and air. They danced with wild abandon, their faces and forms seeming to melt from one beautiful shape to another. But the most beautiful was the Queen of Air and Darkness, sitting regal upon her argent throne. The hall, so cold and empty before, was awash with the full moon's light, and there were tables laden with every food and drink a man could crave. What a sight it was!

"As I stepped into that fine company, the music died away and a quiet murmur ran through the crowd, the dancers clearing a path to the dais where Titania sat with her court all about her.

" 'Most Beautiful Queen of the Night, allow this lowly bard to intrude upon your entertainment,' said I, making my deepest reverence.

" 'And what, pray tell, may be the name of this lowly bard?' Her eyes glittered like starlight and her smile was chilling in its perfection.

" 'Colin Songbird, harper to his Glorious Majesty Oleran.' I rose to meet her gaze.

" 'What business have you with this court, King's Harper?'

" 'Being an honest harper, I seek to prove the truth of what I sing. So many balladeers have immortalized Blessed Titania, whose beauty is beyond compare, and whose hospitality is renowned, that I have come to see the Queen of Air and Darkness for myself.'

" 'And now that you have seen?' She leaned slightly forward, eager to hear my reply.

" 'I am overwhelmed, sweet Majesty! Not one ballad comes near to doing justice to your grace and beauty. May a poor mortal crave a boon of the Faerie Queen?'

" 'Pray, Master Harper, speak on.'

" 'Grant me leave to share your company for but a short while, that I may publish a truer account of your gracious self.' This seemed to amuse her.

" 'As you wish, Master Harper. And since you choose to join our company, will you grace us with a song?'

"I could hardly have asked for more. Choosing carefully from among my store, I settled on a ballad I had written earlier that spring, a love song for Megan. Pretty and passionate as it was, the tune pleased the Faerie Queen, and she bade me join the pipes and fiddles to play out the revel. I harped as I had never done before, for how could I do otherwise in such company?

"After the last chord had sounded and the dancers drifted from the hall, Titania invited me to her chambers. I woke the next morning clasped in her slender arms, and she declared herself well pleased with *all* my talents, heaping treasures of every variety upon me, as tokens of her affection. What a lover she was—subtle as a woman, yet bold as a man—taking the shape of every beautiful woman who ever lived, save one." Colin's eyes clouded with longing for a moment. "Still, my heart was Megan's and I could not forsake my dear one, even for such a lover as the Faerie Queen.

"But when I rose, thinking to be on my way, Titania turned such sad, loving eyes upon me, saying, 'My days are so empty, and I shall miss the sweetness of your songs if you go.' So I stayed.

" 'Only a few days more,' she would whisper each time I grew restless.

"When I realized my fortnight was nearly gone I begged the Queen for leave to journey to the mortal lands. Knowing now she would never willingly let me go, I thought to trick her, swearing I would return within one cycle of the moon if she granted my request. Loath as she was to trust me, she finally tired of my pleas and agreed.

"At our hour of parting, she presented me with Clarion, saying that the harp's voice, finer than that of any instrument crafted by mortal hands, would remind me of my pledge and speed me safely back to her side. What a trophy Clarion would make to parade before Seamus and the others! I thought, setting off at once for Oleran's court with a light heart and a heavy sack.

"But when I returned I found that everything had changed. Though I had been gone less than two weeks time and had eaten not one morsel of faerie food, Oleran was fifteen years in his grave, and I was all but forgotten. Worst of all, Megan was an old woman, twenty years wed to my rival, Seamus; while I was still a young man, even as you see me now.

"Furious, I hurried back to keep my moonlight tryst, but the Queen of Faeries found no docile, grateful lover when she returned for me. Instead I railed at her for deceiving me into forsaking all I held dear. Swearing that I had never loved any woman but Megan, and cursing Titania for a whore, I vowed by the Holy Mother of All that I would never return to play for Faerie revels, nor share a Faerie's bed.

" 'Mortal Fool!' she shrieked, seeming to grow as tall and terrible as a storm cloud. Her face was as grim and hideous as death. 'Why do you say these things to me, when you know they are untrue? I would have given you both sun and moon or whatever other bauble you fancied, had you been true, but you betrayed me!

" 'Was it not you yourself, Master Colin, who came all uninvited to my court, begging leave to join our revels and our company?

" 'You gladly partook of the pleasures I offered you, accepting every gift I gave with no thought of refusal, and now you have the ill-grace to cry "I have been deceived," and deny all that I have given you.

" 'So be it, Colin Songbird! Out of your own mouth has come your doom.' She raised her left hand to curse me then. 'As you are no longer a part of your world, so you shall no longer be a part of ours, but will walk like a shadow through the years, bound between the worlds. Untouched you will be, and untouching, always alone.' Then the Faerie Queen turned as if to go.

" 'No, Sweet Titania!' I pleaded, realizing too late what I had done. 'This is too cruel. I spoke in the heat of anger; forgive me!'

" 'That I cannot do,' she replied coldly, "but for the sake of your songs and the Faerie harp you bear, I will be merciful. Though you are lost to both worlds, your music shall remain a part of both; and if ever one comes seeking you under the full moon's light, then you may once more walk in the land of men, but only then. Beyond that time you shall be no more than an echo in the wind.' Then, wrapping herself in shadows, she was gone.

"To my horror, I found myself unable to walk beyond these fortress walls. For a hundred years have I waited here alone, playing songs that no one hears."

"But *I* heard you, Colin. It was your song that brought me here to break the Faerie's curse!"

"Then, as you have heard my song in spirit, sweet savior, come let me play for you in the flesh!" He smiled adoringly into her eyes.

"Yes, please," she said, longing to share the enchantment of his song once again.

He lifted the harp with a grateful look and began to play. His fingers capered across the silver strings like dancing spiders, and the resulting ripple of sound pierced Fiona with its sweetness. Then he began to sing, and her heart flew up like a bird. When his song was done, Colin laid the harp aside and rose to sit beside her. Gazing fondly at her freckled face, he drew her to him and whispered fiercely, "Lie with me, Fiona. I am chilled to death by time, and your flesh is firm and warm."

Charmed by the ardor with which he spoke and the memory of his song, Fiona surrendered herself to his embrace, and was soon lost in his caresses. Colin proved as tender and passionate as his songs, and when desire was quenched at last, the pair collapsed in happy exhaustion upon the floor of the dining hall to sleep. Fiona woke just before dawn, to find herself alone in the midst of a scattering of tumbled stones, all that truly remained of the fort. Colin's voice, and Clarion's, echoed sadly through the ragged walls, his words fading as the sun's light touched the hillside.

"See me, hear me, you can't touch me . . ."

As the final note died away Fiona felt cold fingers tighten for a moment around her heart. She understood, at last, the full extent of the curse the Faerie Queen had laid upon her faithless harper, and how limited had been her mercy.

"I'll be back, Colin," she murmured as she rose, touched by his plight. "When the moon is full, I'll return." Vain and thoughtless as he was, the foolish harper had never deserved such a cruel fate. She paused for just a moment to look back with a wistful smile as she remembered Colin's face soft with spent desire. Then, Fiona turned her back on the ruin and started down the hill for home.

THE STONE FACE, THE GIANT, AND THE PARADOX
by Vera Nazarian

Vera Nazarian was the first of the extremely young writers who have become my trademark (Stephanie Shaver being the youngest so far, I think). Vera did not tell me her age; I discovered how old she was only when her first contract came back countersigned by her parents.

In her updated biography she mentioned that she had the pleasure of meeting me personally at a convention I hosted last April. I don't remember much about it (my mother had just died the day before); the whole con was a blur in my mind.

But I retained a mental snapshot, of Vera and the dark crimson dress she wore, and her lovely dark hair, done up in something (braids?), around her vivid face.

She adds that this story is the first she has ever composed directly on the computer. She is still working doing Tech support, but adds that she has found, "the perfect way to catch up on writing—my lunch hour! Yes, indeed, my own sacred time, at last! That's when no customers may nag about life, computers, and the pursuit of laser quality, and I get to eat my sandwich with one hand, type with the other, and keep my phone off the hook. Often that's the only time during the day I get a writing opportunity."

She says she has one new dog to report, a Lhasa Apso, and one new cat, making a grand total of eight.

She would like to dedicate this story to Stella Thompson.

B rushing a constant sprinkling of ants off her bare knees, Janéh crouched on the grassy bank of the wild pool, mesmerized by her own reflection on the still water. On the surface of the waters, her face floated pixielike out of the upside-down sky. It watched her back from a unique angle only her perfect twin self could achieve. It had beautiful odd almond-eyes of the Faerie, with a distant look imprinted on them. And it was perfectly immobile.

Janéh hated her face. It was the blank countenance of a strange young woman without shame or fear or humanity—the heritage of her fey father who had appeared to her beautiful half-wit mother, like the Green Man of the Forest, on a lazy sun-drenched afternoon in May. On that same day, with the buzzing of bees, and a warm fragrant breeze blowing over two sinuous, sweetly wrestling bodies, Janéh was conceived, while the sun played through the trees. Her simple mother, Mireah, was later known to mumble, in her more lucid moments, that he had been "glorious like spring itself", and "bright," and he "promised to return."

Mireah died, waiting for him to return, while Janéh grew to early womanhood. Janéh had a face that never cried, never smiled, not even when she felt such emotions inside. She wore a mask of locked features that frightened little children of the village where she lived. They would see her, and start their running game, terrified and yet enjoying the sense of terror deep in their naive wicked minds. "The Stone Face!" they cried, and ran about squealing, in little ruffian gangs.

Janéh ignored them always as she passed, straight-backed and fey, and looking straight ahead of her. The little beastlings never knew that, out of pity, she avoided turning her swamp-hued almond eyes directly on them. They also did not know or even suspect that she could run faster than any of them, and could catch them, if she wanted, easier than a breeze.

The adults of the village knew a bit more about Janéh than their offspring. The blacksmith's son had watched her once, hidden in a thicket, as she raced through the forest glade, like the wind itself, and her feet—he claimed—had left no imprint on the moss-covered earth. "She must have been chasing the stag, and she ran beside it!" he later swore to his fellow drinkers in the tavern. Not many believed the blacksmith's son, for he was known to tell a tale brighter than the rainbow. Besides, it was well-known that the blacksmith's son, Gihen, preferred tales and songs and his reed-pipes, to pursuing his father's trade. This did not go over too well with the villagers, who were not too frivolous themselves, but hard-working and simple like the earth.

But the villagers were more ready to believe when Ailan, the son of the richest merchant in these parts, came back from his deer hunt empty-handed, his beautiful dark eyes flashing in anger.

"It was Mad Mireah's daughter," he told them. "She helped the stag escape me by spooking it, and then ran after it! The witch, the fey changeling—she runs like a wild beast of the forest! It was her, I tell you, I wouldn't mistake her ugly Stone Face anywhere."

Ailan never mentioned to anyone, however, that he had been aware of her for seasons now, watching with occult hunger the stone-frozen unearthly mask, and her Faerie eyes. He had been watching ever since he had once looked fully into her eyes many a winter ago, when they were still children, and saw a *mystery*. At that time also, he still knew no names for desires that were just beginning to move inside him.

And it was for that reason that he often went hunting in these parts, knowing that she roamed the forest like a wild creature. Often he caught glimpses of her through the trees, and once even saw her pale body as she swam in the little thicket-hidden pool. The sight of her body imprinted on his retina like fire, and sent demons of want leaping in the very core of him. And because even then Ailan did not know—or would not let himself know—his own deepest self, in that instant he hated Janéh, hated with a passion the sight of her lithe whiteness that seemed untouched by the sun despite exposure to the elements.

Janéh lived alone on the fringes of the village, in the house where Mireah died. The young girl remained there because she had nowhere else to go, and because, despite her isolation, she considered it her home. When Janéh passed through the village, she hardly ever spoke to the folk on the streets. When she did speak, it was in a rarely soft voice. Also, she had learned well, instinctively, to avert her eyes, so as to avert unnecessary attention and cruel mockery from the likes of Ailan.

Lamira and Nellis, daughters of the baker, who used to play with her sometimes when they were children, would speak kindly with Janéh when she came in to the bake shop to make a purchase. Often, she would receive the bread from the shop in exchange for berries or wild herbs that she was famous for gathering. The baker's daughters used the fresh herbs and succulent berries of the forest as ingredients in their baked goods. However, they usually talked to her only when the baker was not looking.

In the village tavern, Radiene the tavernkeeper, smiled at Janéh only when the tavern was half-empty, and no one could see his expression. Janéh dutifully came to sweep the floors and counters there daily, and in exchange, Radiene would give her a generous sum of four silver coins every month. He was also one of the few who dared to strike up a conversation with the girl everyone thought Faerie-born.

Janéh had, at first glance, a simple manner about her, almost like her mother. She spoke so little, some customers thought she was a mute. And yet, Radiene knew, there was wisdom lurking in her slanted fey eyes—for, once he actually glanced inside he found humor, sharp wit, and of all things, compassion.

"Why don't you ever smile, Janéh?" he once jokingly said, when no one was looking. "I know folks have not been fair to you around here, but you are a good, hard-working girl, reasonable and with all your wits about you—unlike your poor departed mother, bless her soul. You should stand up for yourself more when people laugh, you know. If you don't, folks get the wrong ideas. It's a sad world, it is, but you must be friendly. Or they'll grow to mistrust you even more. And then, it'll be no turning back. . . ."

Janéh stopped scrubbing the counter top and raised her Stone Face and slanted almond eyes to stare directly at him. The moment froze and distorted. And it seemed to Radiene in that odd instant of shimmering time that the Forest itself, crawling with *things* had touched him then, encroached into his own soul, with a chill of the pine-needle floor and mossy trunks of great trees, with a hiss of wind through branches of monolithic oaks, and with the silent alienation of falling leaves as they swooned gently toward the earth.

The moment had passed. And Janéh answered his question very simply. "Master Radiene," she said, "thank you for the advice. I want to tell you a truth which may sound odd to you. I never smile because I—*cannot.* Not even when my eyes are laughing wildly. In the same way, I cannot weep, or express surprise. *I cannot move my facial features beyond blinking or barely parting my lips.* In truth, everyone is right to call me 'Stone Face.' Because I am that."

And again she proceeded to polish the counter with earnest zeal, averting her gaze and allowing her dark swamp-brown hair to obscure the Stone Face.

But Radiene felt a novel fear. And although still kindly disposed, he never again dared to speak thus to Janéh.

The small quiet pool was at the edge of the forest closest to her, and Janéh liked to come often near its still waters. When no more work was left to be done, she would come and sit and look into the murky depths, trying to fathom the very bot-

tom of it, past the mirror surface that reflected
back at her the hated Stone Face.

As she sat thus, she would also glance now and
then at the diligent rows of scurrying ants all
around her on the grassy bank. When they
crawled on her, she took deep breaths and simply
blew them away, or gently brushed them off her,
for it never occurred to her to harm the tiny creatures of the forest. She was a Giant, and they, the
little ones, helpless before her. Therefore, it was
she who had to tread lightest, to control her physical presence, so as not to overwhelm.

Sometimes, hares came hopping past her in the
grass—so still she was—and drank warily from
the pond. At other times, a stag showed its ant-
lered head, and lapped the clean water at the farthest edges of the bank.

Once Janéh saw a man walk past, with a light
step and voice uplifted in song. She knew Gihen
immediately, having seen him before in the forest,
and her eyes danced in acknowledgment, while
her face-mask remained still and rigid. The blacksmith's son grinned at her and winked, all alone
singing like a lark, and proceeded on his way.

And another time, she saw a different man,
haughty and loud, the sound of his boots crashing
through the stillness. He wore hunter's green, and
carried a crossbow, with heavy feral arrows meant
for a stag slung behind him. She recognized Ailan
of the village and pretended not to see him, while
he halted in his tracks and stared at her, breath in-
drawn. He thought she did not realize he stood
there, and revealed such a look in his eyes, which
she had never seen him show when others were
present. She had always thought he simply hated
her, mocked her for her silent ways, but what she
saw then was naked lust.

Soon afterward, she noticed the hunter often in

these parts, and always he would halt by the pool
to see if she was there, before proceeding on his
way. Often he carried a bleeding carcass of the
slain prey with him, seeing which Janéh's throat
constricted into an anguished knot. Only—while
it rent her insides, her frozen Stone Face remained
like the surface of the still water.

Most recently, there was talk in the village that
Ailan was in pursuit of a great living stag. Janéh
believed she herself had seen the elusive creature
once or twice, and thought it was more noble than
any other sight of the forest.

On the day of his planned hunt, Janéh became
the stag's shadow, following the animal through
the forest so that the stag itself did not sense her.
Never did Janéh think it unusual that she could
move more silently than silence itself, or that she
could match the beast's pace at will. There was
only the occasional realization (when, throughout
the day, the stag grew tired and stopped to feed
upon the forest green) that the world also swung
to a momentary halt, and then appeared to fall out
from underneath her feet, while the sky spun
gently and settled like a slowing carousel around
the orb of the sun.

When the hunter arrived, the stag had paused to
drink, and Janéh crouched right beside the creature, paces away. Ailan cocked his arrow. But
with a scream that was torn out of her by pain itself, Janéh jumped forward to frighten the stag
who took off like the wind. The woman in turn
went running after the beast—alongside it—while
branches and tree trunks flew past, and the forest
blurred all around.

The hunter, Ailan, was left far behind, burning,
furious, and his hissing arrow flew amiss.

For the rest of the day, Janéh never left the wild

creature's side. She only returned to the village at dusk.

Odd looks greeted her from passersby. In the tavern, everyone stared, and the talk grew quiet until she again left, having come only for her pay. It did not take long for Janéh to sense some wrongness, an emotion of brewing chill, even though she did not see Ailan anywhere, only perceived a *flavor* of him in the talk of the villagers. A psychic scent of displeasure started to waft on the wind, together with a trace of ghostly anger, of one man's raging voice that rang in her head. All this Janéh knew, being—she thought—fey and inhuman. She never heard Ailan's physical voice, never had to hear the actual words repeated by anyone on the streets. She simply knew that he had told certain *things* about her to everyone in the village.

She was to receive the odd looks for the next several days, as she went about her tasks, and still there was nothing overtly amiss. At least, nothing that seemed to apply to her directly.

Until a half moon's turn later, it came crashing down on them all, the doom.

The elders of the village spoke in hushed tones. The children stopped playing on the streets, and hid their sweet wicked faces to stare from behind shuttered windows at the wind-blown streets.

It was the time they said, after the Cycle of a hundred autumns, that the Great One was stirring, and you could feel it in the wind. It was in the way the stag ran. And in the way the Faerie-born revealed their normally hidden fey powers to the rest of the mortals.

The Giant was coming.

"It is bad luck that Mad Mireah's daughter lives among us," said Farista, the most beautiful maiden in the village, as she took the bread from Lamira, the baker's daughter.

Since the baker himself stood there, sorting the fresh wheat loaves, Lamira said nothing, as always she said nothing to defy her father. But, as always, the nonact of silence allowed a slithering feeling of guilt to start up in her, to chew at her gut. For, inaction also is betrayal. And Janéh, sad Janéh of the grotesque ugly-beautiful mask face had been Lamira's friend.

But then came a fresh strong voice, like Lamira's unexpressed conscience itself. Gihen, the blacksmith-never-to-be came into the bake shop, slamming the door and making the tiny entry bells dance like angry bees.

"What's this talk of bad luck I hear everywhere I go, good friends?" he exclaimed. "Not you also, Farista my Fair? Spreading rumors of that poor girl. Tsk, tsk—here, Nellis, Lamira, get me a sourdough or two, if you please—"

Farista snorted daintily. "Rumors, is that what you think?" she said in a chilly tone. "They say she drove away Ailan's great stag, for she runs like the devil's own mare. They say she turned her Face to look at him, and now Ailan is cursed. He lies in bed all day, and there is a pallor sickness upon him. They say his bright eyes have lost their black fire. . . ."

"They say the Fool sits on the Dung-hill, and the Cow dances on the Pot of Gold! Pah! Believe only what you know," sang Gihen, his wild baritone breaking out while Farista, Lamira, Nellis, and the baker all jumped back from the living onslaught of it.

"Out, out, ruffian, clown, you!" The potbellied baker shooed him out. "Go sing outside with your crazy Cows, you greatest Fool! I pity your father."

"And I pity your lovely daughters," retorted Gihen as he grabbed his baked goods and ran for the door, laughing.

Outside, his laughter stilled, for there was sorrow on the wind.

In the tavern, that incorporeal sorrow was drowned with ale, while somebody said rudely: "What foul witch-luck! I've heard the Great One comes at such times as these. It's a sign of such, for Mad Mireah's daughter lives among us."

"It is true," someone else noted. "Supposedly, He comes forth from the distant mountains where He sleeps for centuries until an unusually strong presence of Faerie kind awakens Him, pulls Him from the Sleep. It's happening now, they say. The breath of Faerie is too definite on the wind. Soon He will come to stomp on us, on the village, on all our lives, for to him, we are but ants. . . . And all because Mad Mireah's daughter lives and witches among us!"

Radiene straightened his apron over his bulky frame and poured from the tap, silent.

And then someone else said: "Well, so she does. And what are we going to do about it?"

"Yes. What is everyone going to do about this living curse among us, this Janéh, whose mother lay with the devil himself?!"

All heads turned as Bremand, father of Ailan, and the man who owned half the village, entered the tavern. Bremand stood tall in his rich fur-trimmed clothing, his graying hair topped by a hat of ermine. Bremand threw a regal glance around the room, until his heavy eyes met those of Radiene.

"Tavernkeeper," he said, "is that unfortunate still in your employ?"

"If you mean Janéh, yes, she is," answered Radiene quietly.

"Then I demand you let her go immediately, wash your hands of her, and forbid her to come into this establishment!"

Radiene frowned, and shifted his bulk, straightening himself involuntarily. "Isn't that for me to decide, Master Bremand?" he said in a low voice.

"Such a decision will not be necessary. Sirs!"

All heads turned again, for Janéh, Mireah's daughter herself, stood on the threshold of the tavern, just behind Bremand.

She looked different somehow. Everyone blinked, trying to fathom that difference, but then it occurred to them that she no longer wore women's long skirts, or dirty smock and apron. She no longer had her hair tied in a plain sorry knot at the back of her head. Instead, loose and fine, it came down her back, like long spiderwebs. And she was clad like a man, in coarse pants and doublet. No weapons she bore, and yet she stood, ready to do battle, a soldier.

Janéh stared with her horrific blank Face at them all. And then she began to speak, in a tone of voice that none had ever heard from her—loud, forceful, brazen.

"Master Radiene! I thank you from the depths of my devil heart for allowing me to work here all this time. But now, friend, find another tavern scullion."

She turned to Bremand who, standing so near her, almost shrank away. "So, Master Bremand. How is your handsome son?"

"How dare you, hell-spawn! Even now you extend your witch thoughts to my Ailan. He is already bedridden in his chamber, from the unspeakable evil you had called upon him, the death-will, the beastly apathy—"

"The beastly lust," said Janéh. "That, and hurt pride."

"What?" The merchant stared.

"Your son lusts after me and pursues me, for more moons now than I can count. But he is proud, very much like you. Even admitting the lust to himself is unthinkable. And to others? What would all of you think? That Stone Face, ugly wicked Stone Face, has such an effect on fair Ailan who can have his pick of the best? Even I think him sick and perverted in desiring this—this—" Janéh struck herself on the chest, the only sign of fury being her trembling fist. "This pathetic creature with no heart, frozen in a stillness worse than death."

"Then maybe death it is that you should have, witch!" Bremand cried in rage, "Death, clean and holy to purge us of your presence, to drive off the fey curses of your Faerie kind, to free my son!"

"Yes! Kill the witch!"

". . . Let us stone her! . . ."

". . . Kill! . . ."

Radiene heard the swelling of voices all around, felt the almost physical hate, but felt immobilized somehow, both in voice and movement. And incidentally, he began to perceive a rhythmic sound. Was it only blood rushing in his temples?

Janéh stood meanwhile, silent, and she looked at them with her Stone Face. Finally she opened her tight beautiful immobile lips, only once, to say with surprising calm: "I have done nothing. . . ."

But they did not hear her, for they were arguing whether to burn her in the center of the village, or to hang her before the church.

It was then that the first truly audible great rumble came from a distance, a persistent rhythmic sound that in its initial birthing they did not sense. But as it grew in intensity, it culminated at last in thunder. It made the glasses ring and dance on the tables, while the ground shook under each hammerlike blow.

Then, Gihen came into the tavern, dramatic, wild-faced—or, more so than was his usual manner—and he stood before them all, saying nothing, simply pointing outside with his hand.

And above the sudden general silence, arose Janéh's clear voice, calm, sardonic, and binding. "At last, then. Those are His Footsteps. You were all correct, and it is all my fault. He is here. The Giant has indeed awoken, and is hurrying all the way here to greet me. Or is it, to eat me? Or, to eat all of us and stomp us into pulp? Why, could it really be that I, poor Stone Face, whether Faerie-born or not, am so pivotal to the scheme of things, that a Giant has nothing better to do with his time?"

And in the continuing silence, the woman with the Stone Face, without twitching a muscle, or cracking her face-mask, laughed.

"Well then, idiots who would kill me for your own fear," she said finally, "I suppose I must go and meet Him."

And with that, she turned, slipping past Bremand, past Gihen, past the tavern doorway like a mist, and was gone.

While outside, growing louder by an increment of miles, the Giant Footsteps thundered, and the whole village and the earth on which it stood, quaked.

Outside, the wind was strong. There was a light haze over the village and the horizon, where the sun was beginning its slow evening landing, while the sky shimmered like a mother-of-pearl mirage.

Janéh stood outside and blinked, for in the delicate haze nothing was as it seemed. In her unfaithful vision, faraway mountains momentarily rose and sank like yeast dough, while the clouds shifted and tore themselves into filaments of cotton.

For that reason she almost doubted the sight of the swiftly approaching shadow—yet another shifting mountain—which loomed from the far West, and which brought with its approach, rhythmic thunder.

She blinked, the wind drying out her eyes, and her thoughts raced ahead of her, out and above. And somewhere in the far distance they met with a great *presence*. Her thoughts—the winged things—sprang to *it* like offspring, and blended, giving her multidimensional sight. She could sense the *old one's* pattern of awareness. Through *it*, she towered over the land, her eyelids brushing the cloud mass, her brows like snow-capped peaks, and her lips the fissure-caves of a mountain.

So immobile, so rigid the Giant *face,* that Janéh felt a sudden unexpected affinity. For she also felt thus; she, too, knew the frozen immobility of features that was beyond humanity.

Villagers gathered around her like frightened beastly children, yet Janéh did not know them, was only halfway there with them, and halfway thundering high above the earth.

The Giant shadow loomed, and in passing, momentarily eclipsed the sunset. Like encroaching night, the *being* swung *its* arms as *it* took each step, and eddying winds curled and wound into sudden vortex-funnels with each great swing, while the land trembled. . . .

. . . *Dreaming* . . .

Janéh heard the Giant thoughts swoon like clouds, from high above. And she thought she saw panoramic memory-glimpses of ancient deserts bathed with a white younger sun, of seas that used to exist where mountains now reposed, of mountains being born, and of endless ancient sand. . . .

And now and then, there were instants of sight encompassing great Cities of old, of legend, of great human Fleets upon long-dead oceans, as they fought each other like tiny ants, among the glittering aquamarine waves. And when the waters washed over it all and receded, again there was only sand. . . .

And there was another intimate *awareness*. . . . Only—just before Janéh could fathom its secret, she was slammed back into the full physical presence of her own being, as wild human cries arose all around her.

The people of this village watched from their temporary safety of distance as the Giant's feet crushed the barley fields of the neighboring settlements, only leagues away. The Giant moved slowly, like a dream-walker, and yet drew near with the swiftness of a heartbeat. And as the monolithic human form neared, *it* appeared less and less human, and more and more like a walking mountain—like a craggy brown mountain rockside hewn in the vague humanoid outline. The Giant never bothered to look down upon the destruction that *it* wrought, never flinched as *it* stepped upon toy houses and dispersing human insects. *Its* eyes—or the blotches of concave darkness that appeared to be in place of *its* eyes—*its* eyes were shut closed.

"Look!" the villagers cried, pointing. "They are trying to burn the monster!"

And at that point distant fiery projectiles were seen flying like tiny bees to harmlessly sting the Giant form, as the residents of one neighbor village attempted to fight back.

"We must get away!" cried others. "In minutes,

that thing will be upon our own village. Load the wagons!"

Janéh stood like a rock, mesmerized, while all about her panic erupted.

"My goods, my precious warehouses!" cried Bremand. "Fifty gold pieces to anyone who would load my goods! A hundred for a wagon!"

But for once, no one listened to the richest man in the village. Instead, as he stood dazed with greed, someone ran into him on their way down the street. Bremand's fine ermine hat got knocked down from his head, and was instantly stomped in the dirt.

"We don't need your gold, Master Bremand," a man said then, "and you don't need it either. Let it be! Go instead, and save your son who lies ill."

Janéh felt a firm grip on her arm, and focused at last. Radiene was pulling her, with a worried face. "Best be on your way, too, girl!" he said, "Like everyone. . . . Get away while you still can. Look, gods have apparently intervened, striking us all down, but giving you this chance. . . . Hurry now, and bless you!" He tarried for an instant more, gave her hand another squeeze, and was on his way.

"Bless you also, Radiene," she whispered at his wide back. She blinked again, stared at the sunset. She felt light, almost reluctant to be fully present *here* in her body, for her winged thoughts still made her buoyant, still cried out to lift her like a feather to soar with the Giant *one*.

"So, what kind of a Fairy are you anyway, girl?" The mocking baritone voice came from behind, breathing over her shoulder, and she turned sharply, startled, almost knocking noses with Gihen, the blacksmith's son.

He stood, outrageous, calm like a mule, hands on hips, and regarded her with very steady clear eyes. She wondered for a moment why he was not running like everyone else. But then she remembered that this one was as crazy as she—or more so.

"I said, what kind of a Fairy—"

"I heard you the first time, don't shout. And don't call me 'girl,' either. You know very well I am Stone Face." She answered him in a similar manner, falling into the easy sarcasm automatically, as though she'd been saying such things all her life, not just since this afternoon. But then, Janéh realized suddenly, she'd *thought* sarcastic thoughts all her life, simply never voiced them before today. Her speech, too, had been frozen into a blank pattern—just like her face.

"I don't like 'Stone Face,' " said Gihen, while the earth around them pounded. "I don't like names that distort the truth, or don't fit things. Since I don't believe that you are Stone Face, even 'girl' sounds better. But forgive me, Janéh. What I was trying to say is, being so called Faerie-born, how come you do nothing now?"

"Do nothing?" said Janéh, "First of all, you Singing Fool of a blacksmith, I'm not even sure *what* I am—stark mad, or Faerie-born! No matter what you and everyone else may believe. Second, what would you like me to do, challenge the Giant to a duel? I might actually hurt the poor thing as He treads on my Stone Face and finds instead an unbreakable hard spot. . . ."

But Gihen watched her seriously, and he said, "Your eyes are like wild swamp water. Fathomless. Unreal."

"Oh, and is that supposed to be poetic and make me swoon?"

"No. It is supposed to make you think. Because it's true. And it simply means that you are—

despite what you say—one of the Facric folk.
And you can't even admit it to yourself."

"Fine, supposing I am. . . . Shall we spend another hour standing here arguing about it?"

"I wouldn't advise it, Fairy Janéh," he answered. "Unless you would like to be stepped on.
In approximately five more minutes."

"What then would you suggest, blacksmith-
poet?"

"I suggest you make up your own mind. And
by the way, since now I'm not leaving you until
you do, you'd better make it up fast. And make
sure it's a safe and satisfying solution for both of
us."

Another time, and Janéh would've been furious
with this one. But not now. Because he stood so
steady and still, with folded hands. And what he
said actually made sense and rang true. And
because none of them had anything more to
lose, except time.

Janéh brought her hands up to touch her face,
to feel the cool skin of it—while all around,
screaming people and horses and wagons rushed
about, children cried in real fear, and the sunset
burned. Her Stone Face felt the same as always.
Immobile fine muscle around her eyes. And no
curve came to her lips when she tried to force
them into the grimace of a smile

. . . *Dreaming* . . .

The Giant was so near. In six more steps *it*
would tower over the church spire on the outskirts
of their village.

Janéh rubbed her cheek. And then she felt a
tiny sharp sting. By reflex she smote herself in
that place, but luckily missed the tiny ant that got
simply transferred from one section of her body
to another, and continued to run down her hand.

As always, she did not kill the little one, simply blew on her arm, and the ant was airborne.

And then it came to her, the answer that was there all along.

The Giant was Dreaming.

All she had to do was bite it into awareness in a way that she knew she could. In her own unique way, of the Faerie.

Janéh closed her eyes, and her thoughts sprang heavenward like small warm winds. With her thoughts, she raced higher and higher, until she was near the *great one*. And she found herself again floating among the ancient dream memory images.

Listen! her thought cried. *Awake and listen, ancient one!*

But the feebleness of her spirit-call surprised Janéh herself. The Giant's dream images, floating cumulus-cloud visions of ancient land and sea, were so much stronger, so prevalent, that in the dream-vapor her single thought sank and drowned.

What makes one feel an ant's bite? A poison? Its tiny focused intensity? Intent?

Janéh gathered herself, shaped her winged thoughts into a single precise arrow, and then, in spirit, flew. Her bright Faerie-human essence rose, crossing the distance of miles, circling the great plateau trunks of mountain that were its legs, past the torso that was one solid abysmal cliff wall, and around the Giant's wizened head of white-capped granite. She neared the cavernous Rock Face with caved-in spots of darkness where eyes should be. She rose past the forehead of limestone, veined with silver ore around the brows.

And then the woman-arrow sank, dived and pierced the cheek of the Giant Stone Face, and she called it with all her will, called it in the ancient way.

A heartbeat of eternal silence.

And then the moving mountain stopped. On the very outskirts of their village, the Giant stood motionless, silhouetted against the sunset. And the aura of Dreams around it became a great funnel tornado. The Dreams whirled with an ever-intensifying centripetal force, and finally sank into the recesses of the great *being*.

In their place, a flower of *presence* bloomed forth. Dark eye-caves shook and eyelid-portals swung open to reveal Faerie *light*. A monolithic arm lifted, and a cupola-palm rested against the stone cheek to touch the place where the thought-arrow found its true bite. The Giant was Awake at last.

And as she found her essence cupped in the heart of this ancient indescribable thought-flower, Janéh knew at last the things that had always simmered just out of reach of her own awareness—things that were her fey heritage, and things that were simply deeper aspects of her humanity. Like a thin but unbreakable rime of frost, they had surrounded her since birth, waiting to break free upon her self-realization, and always hovering at the outer surface, containing her emotions and making her face into a living mask. Like miniature replicas of the Giant dreams, they accompanied her always—fluttering subliminal butterflies of Faerie power and human emotion, imprisoned by her self-denial, and in turn imprisoning her true self.

But now they were free. . . .

Janéh's thought essence flared like a lantern in the dark, expanded into a cloud of *sensation* while, at the same time, Janéh's mortal body, miles away, began trembling with a fever.

Gihen watched with a mixture of pity and awe as the fey woman before him shook, then suddenly doubled over and covered her Stone Face with her shivering hands. When he attempted to assist her, she struggled, brushing him off with inhuman strength. And she continued holding her face, as she began to collapse onto the ground. In the end, Janéh lay in the fetal position, palms covering the Stone Face, harsh feral sobs rending her, gasping for air. And he could only stand there and do nothing.

In contrast to her body's agony, Janéh's mind-presence flowered in an ecstasy of freedom. The Giant *being* surrounded her with a warmth of *presence,* and she knew it was both *male* and *female,* sky and earth, day and night. She also knew, at last and without a doubt, that the Giant's being was indeed connected somehow to her own self.

I have returned, my daughter. As I had promised once I would. To complete what I had started in you. You, who were conceived by the force of one of my Dreams taking human form, the one that visited your mother in a spring long gone. . . .

You see, without me, you would not be. And without you, I would have nothing to draw me to life, nothing to perpetuate this new Cycle. For, I come when my own blood calls. Only mine own, Faerie, can call me into the world. Only mine own, Faerie, can stop me. I come to be Wakened and then to be Thwarted and put down, back to the Slumber of time. I am the Timekeeper of the world, awakening at each End and Beginning, to mark the Passage of things, as must be done, now and always.

"You are the earth, and the forest, and you are my father," spoke Janéh's soul in understanding.

And then, unfurling its spirit-wings, her essence once again soared, and flew. She left the haven of the Giant's *presence*, to return to her flesh and complete her own self, at last.

Janéh took in a shuddering gasp of air, and raised her tear-streaked face to look up at the world of angry sunset and a man's still shadow falling over her.

Where the Giant had stood, there were but dark clouds quickly dissolving, as though an invisible gale-wind had come to drive them away, only to replace everything by empty skies and an odd silence.

"It has been accomplished," said Gihen quietly, looking down at her. "Like the songs and stories had told. Like the legend."

"You hardly know what you're talking about, blacksmith-poet," responded Janéh tiredly, wiping dirt-smudged tears and blowing her nose in her sleeve.

But Gihen ignored her words. Instead, he stared at the smudged face before him upon which a host of very definite grimaces succeeded one another as she cleared her throat, and then was replaced by an even more definite smile.

A *smile!*

The Stone Face was grinning at him, stone no longer, and as human as anything he had ever seen.

"I am different. . . ." she reverently whispered then, running her fingers in awe over the curved apple of her cheek, and stood up from the ground, "Look! I am—"

He looked indeed, and saw her true at last— saw what he had always known she was. The only thing left of the old were her slanted weird almond eyes. . . .

At that moment there was much shouting all

around them, as more and more people picked up a cry.

"It is her! Janéh has saved us!"

". . . The Giant is gone . . . Faerie-born magic has saved us!"

Gihen laughed, shaking his head. "Pathetic, isn't it? Yes, now they admit it. And as always knowing so little, they have made an instant heroine. Where only an hour ago they were ready to kill."

"But you—blacksmith-poet. You do *know*. Had always known, haven't you? Your fool's songs had been fragments of wisdom—"

Janéh could say nothing more, although she wanted to say so many things to him, because at that moment, she saw Bremand the merchant approaching them all, and at his side, the stiff haughty figure of his son.

Ailan did not look ill. In fact, having come out of hiding, he appeared rather healthy and well-rested, even elegant. And his always proud beautiful eyes now shone with an even greater eternal ice.

One thing was different, however.

It is said that eventually there comes a balance in all things. Eventually, justice has odd ways of manifesting itself in this world, human mortal and Faerie. When truth is denied, it still struggles to be, and in the process, transforms the very object of denial.

Ailan had struggled so hard to deny, even to himself, what he had felt toward Janéh—an emotion that in its uncorrupted form might even have evolved into love—that the inevitable change had taken hold of him.

Thus, he now stood looking at them all, fair and tall as always. But his raven locks framed a blank absolute Stone Face.

WORMWOOD
by Laura J. Underwood

Laura Underwood is "one of *ours*" in a special way; we've printed several harp-centered short stories about the magical harp Glynnanis and her elvish owner. Laura lives in Tennessee; a good place for a writer (just ask Andre Norton, who is trying to set up a writer's retreat up there).

What I really want to know is . . . when will she write the story of how the harp Glynannis came to her owner? I think all my readership wants that, but, while we're waiting for her to get her creative juices in gear, here's "Wormwood." I scarcely need remind this audience that a worm—or "wyrm"—is another name for a dragon. Dragons often seem the bane of my existence when I'm reading the slush (five dragons in a day are not at all unusual), but if they were all as good as this, I wouldn't object so dramatically.

The gray gelding refused to take another step into the dark forest, in spite of Brona's persistent heels. Not that she blamed the stupid beast. The air was alive with a mixture of odors, the stench of carnage and sulfuric bite that told her she must have been close to the lair.

Grumbling over the witless state of horses in general, she dismounted. She tethered the gelding to a tree with a slip knot that would keep him from wandering while giving her the advantage of freeing him quickly, should she be forced to flee. Killing wyrms was not the easiest way to make a living, but a mercenary had to take what fate offered if she wanted coin in her pouch and food in her belly. There hadn't been a real war in years, and Brona had no desire to tie herself to one master for very long. The road and battle were the only life she had known since she left her family farm at fifteen. That was more summers ago than she cared to count now.

She checked her gear with practiced ease, pulling the round helm over her short, dark tresses that were picking up threads of silver here and there. Her armor was a mix of chainmail and boiled leather, and she made sure each buckle was firmly latched. Not that armor would matter if the wyrm was large enough to spit acid. The Baron of Dramlair had ordered his own smith to sharpen Brona's sword at no cost. In fact, everyone in town seemed quite eager to please her. *Why not,* she mused. The wyrm was laying waste to any who ventured through the depths of the forest to reach the open fields beyond where wormwood grew in abundance. That precious hoard was part of the local economy. Dramlair was reknowned through the kingdoms for its fine wines and liqueurs, but without the only supply of absinthe for miles, they were doomed. It was natural for them to heap respect on the warrior woman who took their offer to trade the wyrm's head for a pouch full of gold. The Baron could afford to be generous. It would save him the cost of his men-at-arms to let a freelance mercenary battle the monster.

Well, the gear was in good order, and Brona was rested, feeling quite alert. Sword in hand, she picked her way cautiously through the tangle of trees. Mentally, she noted this would not be the best place to battle the wyrm, though it would be helpful were she forced to flee.

She paused when she reached a clearing. There, she crouched on a rim of rock that overhung a small canyon. A stream wound through its center, forming a pool near the mouth of the cave. A number of carcasses lay about that opening, mostly cattle. They were clean to the bone, though one ox showed signs of recent savaging. Brona frowned in thought. So the wyrm was well fed. And its lair was a good distance farther off the road then she would have thought. The legless beasts were not fond of traveling too far from their lairs, and slithering through the woods she had just passed would not have been an easy task.

Then why is it going all that way to feed on the villagers, too?

Movement near the mouth of the canyon broke Brona's thoughts. She shifted her focus from the cave to the slim figure in a long, tattered robe picking a path along the stream bed. *A girl!* Hardly more than fourteen by Brona's figuring. What in the name of the Black Realms was she doing making straight for the wyrm's lair?

Brona rose, quickly searching and finding a small trail leading down into the ravine. She made her way to it, clambering as quietly as she could until she was in the canyon.

Her rapid approach got the girl's attention, for she stopped and narrowed pale blue eyes up at the swordswoman. Arms crossed, the lass waited, looking rather put out by the intrusion.

"Fool girl!" Brona hissed with a quick glance toward the cave. "Get out of here while you can! This is a wyrm's lair, and you'll make a tasty snack for the beast if you don't leave!"

Those pale eyes glimmered with amusement over a sneer. The girl pushed back coils of long red-gold hair.

"Just who are you?" she asked as nonchalantly as if she were inquiring to a servant about the lateness of her tea.

"I'm Brona MacMorgan," Brona said, seizing the girl's arm in a tight grasp and starting for the end of the canyon, "and I've no time for fancy talk. I've no desire to feed the wyrm's maw, so come on, child."

"You're hurting me!" the girl said.

"Better my hand than the wyrm. . . ."

Brona did not finish her words. She heard the girl speaking what sounded like panicky gibberish before a force lashed at the mercenary like a tongue of lightning. Pain lanced every nerve of her skin. By the gods, had she been spat on by the wyrm?

When the pain cleared, Brona was sitting on the ground, looking up at the lass who straightened out her tattered robes with a pout. "Sorry," she said, "but you shouldn't have done that. And anyway, you're not really hurt. The spell just makes you think so. My name is Trea."

She folded her hands and cocked her head.

"Trea," Brona said and cast a quick glance toward the cave. "We really should leave here now, child. I've work to do, and all this noise will bring the wyrm on us."

"Oh, you don't have to worry about the wyrm. As long as I am out here, you'll never see it."

Brona frowned and picked herself up from the ground. *This girl is about as witless as my horse,* she thought. "And just why is that?" she asked.

Trea smiled and held up her hand. She whispered a word, and a ball of golden flames filled the outstretched palm. By the Pigs of Loren, the girl was a sorceress!

"You're one of the magefolk!" Brona said.

"Exactly," Trea said, shaking out the flames. "The wyrm is mine. I conjured it."

"Why?" Brona said.

Pain flickered briefly across Trea's face. "Come," she said. "I was about to have lunch. If you'll join me, I'll tell you my tale."

She stepped onto a flat rock near the mouth of the cave. With gestures and whispered words, she brought forth a table set with a small feast, and two stools. Trea offered Brona first choice. She immediately selected the seat that would allow her to watch the mouth of the cave, drawing her sword and placing it within quick reach. Trea shook her head and sat on the other stool, helping herself to a few bits of bread and nibbling as though she wasn't really hungry.

"Why did you conjure the wyrm?" Brona asked once more.

Trea sighed. "Revenge," she said.

"Revenge?" Brona repeated. "On who? For what?"

The pale eyes grew hard as topaz as the young sorceress' face drew into a frown. "On my father, the Baron of Dramlair, for the murder of my nurse Amalea."

Brona nearly dropped the wedge of cheese she started to bite into. "The Baron is your father?"

"Aye . . . as much of a father as he can claim,"

Trea said bitterly. "I was *got* by him, true enough, but whether my mother was his former wife or one of her maids, no one will say. He is not a man to withhold his favors in the pious name of fidelity. It is rumored my mother died birthing me. In either case, because father didn't care about anything but his sons, I was handed over to Amalea from the day I was born. Even though she had already raised half a dozen of his offspring, I was her favorite.

"Amalea was lovely. It was hard to tell just how old she was. From early on, I knew why. She was one well versed in the arts of magic, and from the day of my birth, she sensed that same power in me. She taught me to use what the gods had gifted me with while I was quite young."

"Why did he kill her?" Brona asked.

Trea looked away. "As I said, Amalea was beautiful, and that beauty sent men's hearts to thundering with lust—including my father's. But Amalea was not interested in his favors. She was careful never to let herself be alone with him, knowing his reputation. She always told me a truly devout sorceress cannot give in to the worldly pleasures of the flesh."

Trea's delicate hands were ravaging a sweet roll into small crumbs.

"Still, my father pursued her," she said. "He could not believe she would refuse him. But she did in front of others, and that turned his heart and mind bitter against her."

Like wormwood, Brona thought and glanced at the cave. Still no sign of the wyrm. The beast must have sated itself on the ox and been sleeping off its gorge. Or maybe the little sorceress wiping crumbs out of her lap could keep it at bay.

"About a month ago, my father fell to drinking heavily of the absinthe-flavored liqueur for which

Dramlair is famed," Trea went on softly. "Those of his friends who were with him say his words were like venom each time he mentioned Amalea. He worked himself into a rage that could not be stilled."

Trea paused, pain tightening her face. "Forgive me," she said. "I . . ."

"Take your time," Brona encouraged, though she had a feeling she knew how the tale would end.

"In a drunken rage, he stormed our quarters in the old tower," Trea said, and tears began spilling down her cheeks. "Amalea tried to lock him out, but he broke down her door. He came at her, calling her every foul name he knew, and when she tried to escape, he seized her, forcing her down on the bed and strangling her with his bare hands.

"My room was just down the hall. I came as fast as I could, but I was too late. He was rising from her bed even as I entered the room. . . ."

She pressed hands to her face. Slowly, Brona reached across to touch the red-gold hair. It spilled through the mercenary's sword-callused hand, fine as silk.

"He told everyone she threatened him with magic, and he only killed her in his own defence," Trea sobbed. "Only I knew he had lied. I would have known had Amalea used her powers to save herself."

"Why *didn't* she use magic to save herself?" Brona said.

Pale eyes blinked at the mercenary as Trea's hands fell away from her face. "Amalea always told me that magic used to harm others demands a heavy toll."

"But you have used magic to conjure the wyrm."

Trea swallowed, nodding. "And I will gladly pay the price, so long as my father pays as well."

Brona frowned. "But you are hurting innocent folk. If you conjured the wyrm to kill your father, why come out here and harry the peasants? He's not going to come here himself as long as he can hire swords to kill the beast for him."

"I know," Trea said. "I had hoped he would worry about his manhood enough to come battle it himself. Instead, he hides in the walls of his keep, and sends others to do his dirty work. I had to flee the keep that night, you see. I was afraid he would have second thoughts about my life. After all, I'm the only one who knows he murdered her."

"Then why not send the wyrm against him there and unconjure it once it had fulfilled its task?" Brona said.

"It's not quite as simple as that," Trea said. She wiped her own tears on her ragged sleeve. "The wyrm will go where I tell it, but I must be there as well. And it cannot be unconjured—only killed. Besides, my father knows I've fled because of him. I crept back into town the other day, and learned that my father has spread rumors that I also tried to end his life and have fled to avoid his justice."

Brona frowned. She had heard the Baron was placing a bounty on some head or another, but she was never asked to be a party to the taking.

"I will be murdered if I am found," Trea said. "And I must not be found before the wyrm ends my father's life. Please. I know you were offered gold to kill the beast, but you must not do so until I see vengeance justly rewards him."

Brona sighed. "But if the Baron dies, I doubt I will see my pay," she said.

Trea looked worried. "If gold is all you care

about, I'll gladly give you that. I know where my
father keeps his personal treasures. I can show
you where if you'll just help me."

"I'm not a thief," Brona said. "I work for my
gold."

"Then help me get into the keep," Trea said
with a thoughtful look. "In fact, I know exactly
how you can get me in and be paid for your trouble."

"How?"

"You could take my body to my father and say
you found me here. He will give you gold for
that."

"And how do I convince him you're a corpse?"
Brona said.

"Leave that to me. There's enough ox blood
here to play the ruse. If I control my breathing,
he'll never see through the deceit until it's too
late."

"What about the wyrm?" Brona said, glancing
toward the cave. "How do we get it there?"

"It will come when I call," Trea said.

Brona shrugged. The plan still seemed far
fetched and dangerous. "And how do I know I
won't be blamed for his death—or for yours?"

Trea's eyes turned cold. "Because once the
wyrm kills father, you can kill the wyrm. They
will count you a hero in Dramlair and probably
pay you as well."

"And what price will you pay?"

"You need not concern yourself with that,"
Trea said. "I have already resigned myself to my
fate."

At so young an age, too, Brona thought. That
hardly seemed right, but there was no swaying the
lass. And Brona could see no other recourse than
to go straight into the lair and kill the wyrm now.
She rather doubted the little sorceress would al-

low that. Having already been stung by Trea's magic, Brona did not want to consider just how much damage she could really do.

"All right," she said. "We'll try your plan and see. But it it fails . . ."

"It will be on my head," Trea said.

And mine, if I'm not careful, Brona thought. Still, she could do no more than help the lass make ready. The gray gelding was not happy to carry two, nor did it care for the stench of the ox blood Trea brought in a large phial. Not far from the town gates, while still in the woods, they paused long enough for Trea to generously coat herself and her rope with the blood. Brona padded a space behind her saddle with blankets and carefully wrapped the girl in one before binding her in place with loose lengths of rope, just in case she needed to slip free and escape.

The afternoon sun was sinking toward the walls of Dramlair as Brona rode into town. The curious stares of the guards followed her arrival. She ignored them, riding directly into the keep itself.

"I am here to see the Baron," Brona said to the guard at the keep's gatehouse.

"Is the wyrm dead already?" he asked.

"I have yet to find the wyrm," Brona said, dismounting and loosening her bundle. She lifted Trea from across the saddle. The little sorceress was surprisingly light on Brona's shoulders. "But I have found his daughter Trea."

That got her a wagonload of attention. She was practically carried into the Baron's private study. He stood before his desk, waving the servants and men out of the room. His red-brown beard bristled around his tight mouth, but his eyes—pale as Trea's—flickered restlessly over the mercenary and her bundle as he crossed the room to lock the doors at her back.

"They say you found my daughter," he said, slowly pacing back to his desk. His hand gestured almost contemptuously toward the bundle. "Is that her?"

Brona nodded and came forward, gently laying her bundle on the desk. She drew back one corner of the blanket to reveal Trea's blood-streaked face. A flash of relief seemed to fill the Baron's eyes before he turned a harder gaze on the mercenary.

"What happened to her?" he asked with a dark scowl.

Brona shrugged, calmly meeting the stare. "She is as I found her, my lord—at the lair of the wyrm."

"And the wyrm? Is it dead?"

"No, my lord," Brona said. "I will soon enough see to that. I thought it more important to bring your daughter to you at once. After all, I heard a pound of gold coins had been offered for her return. Naught was said of whether she should be dead or alive."

A faint smile gleamed. "Yes, I suppose you would have heard that," he said and sneered. "But I am more interested in the wyrm that killed her and is still a threat to my people and their livelihood. Just where is the monster?"

"Here, Father," Trea said.

The Baron gasped and threw himself back. "What treachery is this?" he hissed as his dead daughter rose. Brona drew back, too, slipping her sword free in preparation as Trea raised her arms and called words of power into the air. As soon as the wyrm came to finish the Baron . . .

Then Brona froze, for Trea began to glow with golden light, and her body was stretching into a long and sinuous form twice the length of the desk. Her rope and the blankets fell away from the red-gold scales that covered her skin. Brona cursed and watched as the petite features of the sorceress shifted into the malicious visage of the wyrm.

The Baron ran for his sword. Too late, for the wyrm writhed off the desk and struck at him like a snake. He tried to defend himself, pummeling the beast in vain. The golden-red coils wrapped around him as the wyrm sank fangs into his throat. His screams were cut off as he and the wyrm tumbled to the floor.

Hissing, the creature uncoiled itself from around the corpse, releasing its death grip on the Baron's throat. Rising, it turned topaz eyes on Brona.

By the gods, this was not what she had expected. The wyrm writhed and slithered across the floor, rearing before the mercenary. Dimly, she heard the thunder of men at the bolted door as she met the beast's hypnotic stare.

"Now, warrior woman," it hissed. *"Slay me now!"*

"But, you . . ." Brona began.

"I cannot be allowed to live on," it said. *"This is the price for my misuse of power. For the sake of those innocents who died in my quest for revenge, and for the sake of those who will die if this incarnation continues to live, you must keep your word and kill the wyrm! Or the wyrm must kill you as well. . . ."*

The beast rose over Brona's head, preparing to strike, exposing its soft underbelly to the mercenary's startled gaze. Brona struck first, her steel easily penetrating to find the creature's heart. There was a terrible scream that cut her soul, and the spew of warm ichor before the wyrm collapsed on the floor. Then the door broke open behind her, and guards poured in through the gap.

"The wyrm!" one cried, and in no time, that word filled the halls of Dramlair's keep. Servants and guards alike came running to see the beast that had slain their master.

Brona told them the wyrm came for the girl's carcass and devoured her before it could be stopped. That she and the Baron fought the monster, and the Baron died in valiant battle. They listened eagerly to her tale, never doubting words. They even paid her the gold she'd been promised and allowed her to leave Dramlair.

No more wyrms, Brona decided as she passed through the forest again. Perhaps, she should seek a quiet keep and offer her fealty to its lord. She was weary of life on the road, and she'd sooner starve than take gold to butcher another wyrm. The killing of Trea would sit as bitter as wormwood in Brona's belly for a long time to come.

SILVERBLADE
by Deborah Wheeler

Deborah, like the two writers mentioned next—Mercedes Lackey and Diana Paxson—goes back with me a *very* long way. At present she's retired as a chiropractor and turned to full-time writing, and has two daughters who are my honorary grandchildren. Sarah was a toddler back when Don Wollheim gave me the job of editing this anthology; now she is almost fifteen and Rose will be in third grade. How times flies; it seems only a few weeks ago that I sat with Deborah, watching Rose trying very hard to stand—falling down and trying again. I could almost feel the intelligence working behind that little face.

Deborah has a book out from DAW; it's called *Jaydium* and is "very much better than likely," in the immortal words of the Reverend Patrick Bronte. She also has another one, called *Northlight,* which, by the time this anthology comes out, should already be on the bookshelves; it's scheduled for February of 1995.

Silhouetted against the twin-mooned amber sky, a woman in trail-stained leathers reached the last dusty ridge, moving quickly despite the sword strapped across her back. As she stood panting at the edge of the cliff, she shook lank, ginger-colored hair back from her face and shaded her eyes with one hand, scanning the valley from the strip of harbor to the abandoned farms to the inland hills behind her. Below, tantalizingly close, sat the Western Keep which she had been summoned to fortify. The ancient stone walls looked sound enough, invulnerable to assault. Any human assault, that is. The Dark Ones inching their way up the valley were another matter.

People called them *dragons* or *devil-spawn* or simply *monsters*, but no one knew what the Dark Ones truly were. Taller than a haystack, blacker than pitch, relentless, untiring, armored with impenetrable carapaces and capable of spitting fiery acid, they seemed more insect than reptile. Some said that Barzon, Duke of the Eastern Marches, had bargained with a necromancer for their aid, then they had swallowed him up and seized his lands for their own. Whatever the truth, the western kingdom of Creston-var now also lay in waste and Wynne's Queen was in exile.

Wynne cursed under her breath as she hurried back down the trail. These days it seemed she'd spent her whole life fighting the Dark Ones, although she'd never faced more than a single one before.

She found her team resting in a dry riverbed beside a clump of thorn trees, a dozen men and women armed with rough-forged bronze or iron swords. Their single remaining pack animal bent its scrawny neck to nibble the yellowed grass.

Aldair, Wynne's second, heaved himself to his feet.

"How close?" he asked.

"An hour away, maybe less. There's no way we can reach the Keep before they do. Not with enough time for the gates to be barred after us. They'd be fools to let us in."

"They'll take the Keep at the last," he said. "You know that, Silverblade."

Silverblade, he called her, calling her not by her own name, but by her sword.

Wynne felt his aged eyes on her, measuring her as they had not done since she was a skinny, arrogant teenager, demanding sword lessons from her mother's old teacher. What did he see when he looked at her now—Wynne herself, or only his memories of her mother, who'd carried Silverblade before her? Did he see anything at all beyond the sword?

She ran her fingers through her hair and rubbed her neck. "There's precious little to live for these days, old friend. The Queen safe on the Islands. Sarai and the other youngsters at the Keep. A good death with as many demons as we can take with us. . . ." But it was the sword speaking, not the woman.

Wynne frowned. She didn't like to break up her team, not even so close to their goal. The day before, they'd finished off a cluster of demons which had strayed from their convoy. But they'd lost two good fighters and one, the boy who'd joined them just a few months ago, was down with a splintered lower leg. Nathi was swabbing his broken skin with a poultice of the last of their healing herbs. The pungent smell tinged the air.

"Jon, Nathi, Tia, you come with me," Wynne said. "Aldair, you and the others make for the

Keep. Put the boy on the pony. We'll try to buy you enough time."

They settled into formation behind her, these three who'd been with her the longest. As they broke into a run across the valley floor, Wynne reached over her shoulder to draw Silverblade. It felt light, almost alive in her hands. Her mother had said it held magic, although Wynne doubted it. The blade was no ordinary metal, certainly not iron, or even costly southern steel, but silver-white, razor-edged, never rusting.

Tia-the-dancer ran silently in her usual place at Wynne's side. What she would have been if the Dark Ones hadn't come boiling out of the east ten years ago—a real dancer or just an ordinary farmwoman with a fat husband and four children—Wynne couldn't guess.

The convoy crept along the unpaved road that led to the Keep gates, the three giants moving in single file, rattling and hissing. Their bodies slithered over the naked red-dust path on huge segmented claws. The smaller demons spread out, killing every living thing they found; others nestled amid the Dark Ones' weirdly sculpted projections like deformed wings. Some looked like goblins, others horned scorpions. As Wynne's team approached, they scuttled to the ground and took up defensive positions.

Jon and Nathi veered toward a man-high demon, while Tia slashed at another with her short bronze sword. She danced away from its clumsy swipe, drawing it off to give Wynne a clear field.

Wynne scrambled up the nearest Dark One, leaping from one ornate chitinous shape to the next. The giant monster swerved and one eyeless, wedge-shaped head whipped around on its articulated neck, its jaws snapping and reeking of brimstone. She kept climbing. Where the weight-bearing claw joined the main body, she found a flexible collar as long as her forearm. The chitin resisted her thrust for a moment, then the blade slid in, as if slicing a fruit with a stiff rind but succulent interior.

Suddenly Nathi tripped, and the nearest demon lunged for her. As Jon yelled a warning, Tia darted in, stepping lightly off the angular claw. She somersaulted through the air and landed, taking off at a run just as the demon swiveled toward her, spitting acid.

Wynne heard Nathi's cry and knew she'd been wounded. She jerked the sword free in a spurt of yellow blood, jumped down, and sprinted away. The Dark One came to a hissing, staggering halt, both heads thrashing, limping heavily on its crippled claw. Abruptly, the demons broke off their attack and came swarming back.

"Come on!" Wynne called.

Jon hauled Nathi to her feet and, supporting his injured companion, raced after her, Tia guarding the rear.

The convoy had still not moved by the time the four humans reached the Keep. Nathi, although still on her feet, was stumbling, and they were all breathing hard. The parapets looked empty, as if deserted. For a moment, Wynne wondered if the Keepfolk were too frightened to let them in. Then the gates parted and Aldair beckoned to them.

Behind him stood the rest of Wynne's troops, a few oldsters, a scattering of grim-eyed fighters, many of them crippled, and a handful of frightened children, strays or orphans probably. They were maybe thirty in all, counting the older children. The Keep was designed for a much large force; beside the enormous well, a handful of striped goats looked up, tails flicking.

"Momma!" Eight-year-old Sarai, her hair an unruly crop of sunshine, catapulted across the courtyard, scattering chickens.

It has been a year since Wynne sent her daughter to the fragile safety of the Keep and Sarai had lost all traces of her baby softness. For a moment she looked utterly unfamiliar, a changeling. Wynne saw not a slender child with serious eyes, but the shadow of a man now dead. She had been only seventeen during that brief loving, snatched between battles across the midland plains. Her mother had been alive then, and Wynne not yet Silverblade.

Wynne gave Sarai an awkward pat on the shoulder before she turned back to Aldair.

"Is this—there have to be more than this. What about the other northern companies—Lauren's, Sell's? They started out before us."

"They never came, Warlady. We held on as best we could." One of the Keepfolk stepped forward. She peered at Wynne through her one remaining good eye, the other hidden beneath a knotted scar. A short dagger was slung around her neck. "The Queen set off for the Islands at midsummer. She took the best of what we had left." There was no hint of censure in the old woman's voice. "Everyone thought we'd be reinforced before now."

Wynne glanced at the walls, measuring how few could defend them, marking the position and steepness of the stairs. The granite stones had been fitted so closely that not even a sprig of wall-ivy could take root.

"Supplies we've got," the old woman said, "but empty walls can't keep those devils out."

"We can hold them, if no one gets careless." Wynne let the sword speak again. "Aldair, I want sentries posted and hot food for our people. A healer for Nathi, if there is one. How's the boy with the leg?"

"He can't fight."

"Then put him where he can do some good. Get everyone else on the walls, the older children as supply runners. You know what to do."

He nodded and headed off toward the main hall. The Keepfolk dispersed, leaving Wynne standing there with Sarai.

Wynne looked down at her daughter. "I—ah—don't have time to play now."

"Oh, Momma, I'm too *old* to play. Can I see the sword?"

Wynne pulled Silverblade over her shoulder and held it flat as sunlight danced over its silver-white surfaces. "Some day it will be yours."

"Is it really magic?" Sarai reached for the hilt.

"Don't—" Wynne started to say. *Don't be in such a hurry to grow up.* But the words seemed as futile now as when her own mother had said them.

Wynne sat in the central hall, eating stew with cracker-bread and hot spiced fruit. Above them, the minstrels' gallery sat forlorn, perhaps dreaming of the days when Queens listened to music as they dined. A few weavings remained on the walls, too worn to be worth hauling away; some bore the coats-of-arms of noble families which no longer existed. Nathi, her thigh bandaged, sat across the table. Wynne remembered that she'd lost children to the Dark Ones.

"—says it's all over now, but I know she's wrong because we never had *Silverblade* fighting with us before," Sarai chirped. "I'm going to kill giant monsters when I'm big. Just like Momma!"

"Leave the Dark Ones to grown-ups," Wynne snapped.

Sarai favored her with an indignant grimace. "You're going to kill them all and not leave any for me. That's not fair!"

Aldair nudged Wynne's other elbow and said in a low voice, "You were just like that at her age." He added, to Sarai, "There'll be plenty to go around, little love."

A voice ghosted from outside: "They're here!"

Wynne scrambled to her feet. Sarai pulled at her sleeve, as if wanting to begin killing immediately.

"No," Wynne said in as gentle a tone as she could manage. "I need you to be a good girl and go with the others. I can't fight and keep an eye on you at the same time."

The girl's gray eyes smoldered. "Don't *need* an eye kept on me!"

"A good soldier follows orders, no?" said Nathi, drawing Sarai toward the inner chambers. "Your mum's our captain, did you know that? We all do what she says."

Wynne glanced over her shoulder, startled by how easily Nathi managed Sarai's mood. But she had no time for wondering now. She hurried out into the courtyard and up the narrow stairs to the parapet. The Dark Ones had already reached the trampled ground below the gates. Demons swarmed up the walls, soundless except for the unnerving slither of chitin over stone. The rigid tips of their claws found holds in crevices too shallow for human fingers and toes.

"Here they come!" Aldair shouted.

Wynne's heart pounded and her muscles quivered in anticipation. She sliced through the probing claw of the topmost demon and sent it toppling to the ground. The fallen demons picked themselves up and began climbing again, making hissing, creaking noises. Down below, one of the two unwounded giants spewed acid on the metal bands, while the other began battering at the gates.

Wynne chanted her battle cry as she slashed and thrust at the demons. The sword sang in her hands, warm, supple, a thing of living light. Deep within her, something answered. Quicksilver scintillated along her veins. She could feel its fire streaming all through her, down her arms and legs.

The Dark One kept pounding at the gate, sending ominous echoes through the courtyard. Demons kept coming and Wynne kept fighting. She lost her sense of time. Then suddenly, for a moment, the parapets were empty. Wynne glanced around for her team and could not see Tia-the-dancer anywhere near her post. Jon and Nathi, stationed too far apart for decent teamwork, shouted encouragement to one another.

Breath rasping in her throat, Wynne lowered her sword. There were no demons within attack range, and the booming at the gates had stopped. From the courtyard came a high-pitched wail, a child's imitation of her own war cry. A small, golden-headed figure darted toward the gates, staggering under an unwieldy bronze sword.

Wynne raced down the stairs, taking them two and three at a time, slipping and stumbling but somehow keeping her balance. She sprinted across the yard, reaching the child just as Aldair appeared on the other side of the courtyard.

Sarai turned a suddenly whitened face to her mother. "I was going out," she faltered, "to fight. Like you, Momma." Her lower lip quivered. She dropped the sword.

Outrage drove Wynne beyond speech. She could not think of what to say. She stood there, shaking Sarai with one hand while brandishing a naked blade in her face, and trembling with anger as much as her daughter was with fear.

"Silverblade!" Aldair halted at her side and pointed to the gates.

Wynne stifled a cry of alarm. The massive wooden gates sagged on their hinges, no longer capable of resisting a determined thrust. The metal, pitted and eroded, smoked. Outside, the giant thrust itself against them with renewed vigor.

The other defenders had come down from their posts into the empty yard, the livestock having disappeared at the first assault on the gates. The wounded and children stood in a knot just outside the hall. The old woman who spoke for the Keep stepped forward. Her face was ashen. "This is the end, isn't it, Warlady? Do you think it's any kinder to them," jutting her chin in the direction of the children, "to be hunted one by one? Wouldn't it be easier to go all at once?"

Wynne glanced down at Sarai, now standing in the curve of Aldair's arm, looking up at her with mixed tears and rebellion. A little dagger hung from her neck, a dagger such as everyone in the Keep wore. Silently they waited for her signal.

She lifted the sword above her head, tilting it so the metal gleamed in the sun. This time, its beauty seemed a pale shadow, its promise of magic a hollow lie.

What's the use of fighting on? The very best I've been able to do is wound them. Not kill, only slow them down. Here is not one but three, and such darkness in my soul. . . .

But something made her hesitate for a few crucial moments. The bronze hinges shrieked like an animal in agony. The gates splintered and gave way.

"Get behind me—all of you!" Wynne shouted. She heard rather than saw them obey.

Demons swarmed through, spreading out to half-encircle the stunned humans. Majestically, the Dark Ones swept in to take possession of the Keep. Their segmented necks swiveled from side to side, blind heads bobbing.

There was a quick movement near the top of the foremost giant as a demon which had nestled there broke free and clambered to the ground. It stood on two legs, had two arms and a discernible head. An eerie parody of speech, distorted by the chitinous coverings of its head, issued from it.

"Par-r-rley."

Wynne almost dropped her sword in astonishment. In all the years she'd fought the Dark Ones and their demons, she'd never heard them make anything like human speech, only that infernal hissing and booming.

"Stay where you are!" she cried.

Slowly the words came, strained but decipherable. "We wish—a trade. We offer—safe passage."

"Given half a chance, we can outrun them and reach the Islands," Aldair said.

"What do you want?" Wynne called out, not taking her eyes off the manlike demon.

The demon raised one claw arm and pointed at her.

Behind Wynne, Nathi cried out and someone else shouted, "Never!"

Wynne hesitated. Could she trust them? No, but she could bargain with them long enough to let the others escape. Then ... Her blood turned cold. What could they possibly want with her? A war trophy, a slave?

I will do it, no matter what the cost. I will buy life for Sarai. Then I will find a way to die.

She thought she would tremble as she nodded, but she didn't. She turned her head and saw Jon standing beside Aldair, and Nathi beyond him with tears in her eyes. Tia would have chosen death rather than this moment.

Wynne kept herself and her sword between the Dark Ones and the refugees. They left behind everything but their weapons. The demons scuttled back and forth at a careful distance, but made no effort to interfere. Step by step, the ragged band crept across the courtyard and through the ravaged gates.

Once they were in the open, Wynne paused, looking over the narrow valley leading to the harbor. She didn't want the others to leave her alone, and yet they must. And quickly, too, before the full impact of what she'd done overtook her.

Sarai, her face covered with dust and tears, wriggled to the front. "Momma, why are they letting us go?"

"They're letting *you* go, little love. You must be brave and strong."

What am I doing to her, so young? Will she spend her life trying to live up to her martyred mother?

Even as I did?

She bent to kiss the child's forehead and then handed Silverblade to Aldair. "The Dark Ones may have me, but not the sword. You must keep it for Sarai."

Aldair met her gaze. All the color had bleached from his eyes and he looked like a man at the end of his strength. Perhaps he was. He'd trained two generations for Silverblade, only to see them die.

Sarai slipped her hand through his elbow. "Will you teach me to use it, the way you taught Momma?"

Aldair squared his shoulders and placed his hand over hers. His eyes looked grim and sad; he would find some way to go on. And then, Jon and Nathi hurried the rest of them toward the harbor.

Once back at the Keep, the Dark Ones gathered around her. Their bulk blotted out the sun. She shivered from an inner chill. Without the sword which had never left her since the day she took it from her mother's body, she felt naked. She'd borne Silverblade so long, she wasn't sure who she was without it.

The manlike demon raised both upper appendages to the knobs along its vestigial neck. With a crack and a twist, the entire head section popped off.

A human face emerged, milky and withered, crowned with wisps of hair. A scar ran across one temple and down the cheek. His eyes shone dully, and his mouth was compressed into a lipless line.

"Who are you? Are you," Wynne wet her lips, "a prisoner, too?"

"A prisoner? No . . ." Without the echoing effect of the helmet, his voice creaked. His expression seemed hollow, as if all emotion had been stripped from him.

"Where are we?" he asked, looking up at the empty parapets.

"The Western Keep. Creston-var." She blinked, realizing. "You mean you *don't know?*"

He shook his head, his pale eyes wandering. "I was like you. Once." His breathing took on a new, hoarser quality. "I had a name. Barzon. I had . . . sons."

Barzon! The Duke who made a pact with the black wizard? "What are you doing with the Dark Ones? What do they want? How do we fight them? How do we win?" Wynne wanted to grab the old man and shake the answers out of him.

Her fingers curled into fists, but she kept them at her side.

"That was all a long time ago. They put things in my mind. Dreams. I woke up and I was old. I don't know where my boys are. I have to find them." His skin was gray, his lips almost blue. A light sheen of sweat covered his face. "Come on, it's time."

Wynne drew back. "Not until you answer me— what do they want with us? With you, with me? How can I fight them?"

Barzon's words wheezed through his throat, one rusty syllable at a time. "If you see them. Tell them. I did it all for them."

It was no use. Whatever was left of the old man's mind was now lost in the past.

Before her stood an unwounded giant. It held a helmet, breastplate, gauntlets, other things that looked like armor. Wynne froze. It was one thing to see Barzon peel away his armor, and quite another that in a few moments she herself would be encased—no, *entombed*—in chitin.

The demons inched closer, forming a funnel toward the giant with the armor. Wynne recoiled, but found herself held fast. Barzon, behind her, grabbed her arms and pinioned them in a grip like a death rigor.

"They have—no purpose—of their own." Barzon's breath hissed in her ears.

The Dark One extended the helmet toward her, closer and closer until it was only inches from her face. Gasping, Wynne threw her head back. The chitin brushed her forehead.

Wynne suddenly found herself floating above her body. Strange sensations flooded her, so vivid they seemed like her own memories . . . darkness, a fire-lit cavern. Slow waking, each moment an avalanche of pain. Compulsion: resistance. Sleep rising again in her—then a kernel of will—alien, irresistible, coruscating through her like lightning. Daylight, gold. The slow march from marsh to plain, scything through field and underbrush alike, stripping trees until only stubble remained. Pausing to sweep away the soft-bodied pests, to mend wounds from their prickles. Moving on and on, driven by the burning, tenacious ember.

Still Wynne struggled to hold on to her own human thoughts. It would be so easy to let go, to drift on the dreams. . . .

The helmet dropped lower. Somewhere within her, a last spark of resistance flared. She looked on the bodies in the Dark One's vision, tossed aside like so much garbage. A patch of straw-colored hair caught the light. Like Sarai's hair. Like her mother's.

The first Silverblade had taken most of a convoy with her when she fell. When Wynne pulled her from the pile of tangled bodies, all she could think was, *Where's the sword that will make me Silverblade?*

I am still Silverblade!

Wynne twisted away from the helmet with all her strength. The light was so thick and bright she staggered under its weight. She ducked, then lashed out with a snapping side kick that sent the helmet flying from the Dark One's claws.

She grabbed Barzon's shoulders and shoved. He cried out, a harsh, gurgling rattle, and crumpled to the ground. His weight jerked her to her knees. His face had gone from blue-tinged to waxy, and only a crescent of white showed between his half-closed eyelids. His mouth fell open, his lips pulled back slightly from his yellowed teeth. He lay utterly still, not a flutter of his eyeballs, not a quiver of breath.

The demons scuttled back while Wynne knelt

and touched one finger to the side of his neck. His flesh felt like warm clay.

She was still close enough to the giant to smell its dry, slithery scent. Dimly she felt its obsession falter.

Drawing her legs under her, Wynne lunged for the shattered gates. Sarai crouched behind a massive fallen beam, staring at her with such awe-struck worship that Wynne's heart leaped in her chest. Had she ever looked like that, watching her own mother fight?

Once she'd moved, the demons swept into action. Two of them circled her, cutting her off, closing in, one to each side. Wynne retreated one step, then another.

Suddenly, a demon spotted Sarai and swerved toward her.

Wynne jumped in its direction, then skittered to a halt. What did she think she was doing, attacking it with her bare hands? Behind her, the Dark Ones boomed and hissed.

"Run!" she cried.

Silverblade! Without thinking, she reached for the sword that was not there.

Sarai pulled the dagger from around her neck and scrambled to her feet, plain in the demon's path. The demon stretched out its serrated claws and scuttled closer. Sarai held her little blade in front of her. Her face had gone white, mouth set, her stance steady as she waited for the demon to close the distance.

Even as she screamed and hurled herself after it, Wynne watched the next few moments unfold in her mind, as she'd seen so many others in the past. The ebony claws ripping flesh, the spurting blood, the heart-sickening *thump!* as the body— Sarai's body—hit the ground. The pale gold hair tangled in the dust.

The Dark Ones loomed above her like a wall of tidal blackness. She could feel their desperation like caustic over her skin. They would bury her under their hissing, thrashing mass, and buy her death with their own.

Silverblade! The world turned molten. Fire raced along her veins. Air sizzled past her ears as her feet pummeled the earth. She brought her hands together as if grasping a sword hilt—

Flames burst from her fingers, forming a blade of pure white light. Wildness, hot and sweet like fire and music together, surged through her, sweeping away every other feeling, searing her to the core. She gave herself over to it.

Chunks of chitin armor went flying and yellow blood sprayed the ground as Wynne sliced through the demon's head section. She whirled, facing the black wall of Dark Ones. The other demons, in retreat, huddled at their feet. They cast eerie shadows in the light of the blade.

Wynne's body shook with the power coursing through her. Madness or funeral pyre, she didn't care, just so long as the Dark Ones kept shuffling backward.

"Momma?" A small voice cut through the roaring inferno.

The fire raged all through her now, consuming her from within as it leaped ever higher and brighter from her hands.

"Momma, come now!"

The flames faltered and the image of the sword dimmed. Wynne's vision cleared. She felt as if she were waking from a fever. She wavered on her feet. Her nostrils filled with the stench of burnt chitin.

Wynne ran to Sarai and pulled her toward the gates. Demons rumbled after them, claws churning the dust. Sarai scrambled to keep up, then slipped suddenly and fell. Her hand jerked from Wynne's grasp.

Grabbing Sarai's wrist and ankle, Wynne heaved the child's body across her own shoulders and raced for the harbor. The road sloped downward, uneven. She stumbled, regained her footing, somehow held on to her daughter. Pain shot through her thigh muscles, but she kept moving, one step after another. Each breath seared her lungs. She heard only the sound of her laboring heart.

They were near the bottom of the long sloping trail leading to the harbor. A few oar-boats bobbed alongside the low wooden pier. In the other direction, the Dark Ones were just starting down the last incline.

As they reached the pier, Wynne made out the outlines of the nearest islands jutting above the glass-calm sea. The oar-boats all looked reasonably seaworthy. Sarai jumped nimbly into the nearest one.

Wynne guided the boat away from the pier and aimed it toward the nearest island. The oars slipped through the water with a weight and rhythm of their own. The air smelled fresh and salty-wild. Sarai sat in the back of the boat, hands laced around her knees, sea-breeze ruffling her yellow hair.

Wynne rowed, calling up the last of her strength as the Dark Ones clattered on to the pier and stopped there, hissing, eyeless heads thrashing. She felt in her bones how much they hated the water. She felt, too, the fervor seeping from them. Without Barzon's consuming ambition, without her own hatred to drive them, they were rapidly sinking once more into somnolence.

Wynne's spirits soared as she realized what she'd done. Now she could lead her people from the Islands to beat the Dark Ones back to the wastes that spawned them. Sarai's children would farm their own lands without fear.

"Momma." Sarai's eyes were as bright as stars. "I saved your life back there, didn't I?"

Wynne's mouth smiled of its own accord. *My warrior daughter.*

"So I'm the next Silverblade, aren't I?"

Wynne rocked back with the motion of the boat, for a moment unable to speak.

"So when do I get the sword?" Sarai asked.

Not while I'm still Silverblade!

She couldn't tell any more whose voice echoed through her mind—her own, her mother's, Sarai's. If she'd had the sword at that moment, she would have thrown it into the ocean.

Her arms kept rowing of their own accord. The waves rippled against the sides of the oar-boat. Sarai sat there, eyes glowering, arms folded tightly across her chest.

"It's—it's not—we don't need the sword any more." Wynne stopped. It was no use. Her words sounded hollow even to her own ears.

Sarai's lips were drawn tight and her eyebrows pulled together until they looked almost straight.

I should have died like my mother. It's too late.

Numbly, Wynne pulled the oars in and let the little boat drift along the current. Her arms felt so heavy, her vision blurred. Wetness slipped down her cheeks. Sea spray, nothing more.

What if she had let the fire have her, would it have been any worse? Would she have felt so empty, so barren of heart, so like a burned-out shell?

Sarai slid forward in the boat, slipped her arms around Wynne's waist and laid her head on her breast. At first Wynne sat stiffly, as if she didn't know how to hug back. She felt her daughter's breath, coming in jagged little gulps. Then something broke open inside her and she, too, began to cry.

A DRAGON IN DISTRESS

*by Mercedes Lackey
and Elisabeth Waters*

Misty and Lisa have been friends for a long time, and this year they were both very busy, so they decided to collaborate on this story, which is both one of Misty's Tarma/Kethry stories and a sequel to Lisa's "The Birthday Gift" in *Sword and Sorceress IX*. Misty, along with her husband, artist Larry Dixon, was Guest of Honor at the Fantasy Worlds Festival last April, so she and Lisa were in the same place at the same time. Lisa was doing most of the running of the convention, especially after my mother died the morning before it started, but she spent an extra night at the hotel after the convention ended so that she and Misty could write this story.

At the moment I believe that Misty is in the middle of her seventh and eighth trilogies (yes, simultaneously), and she has so many short stories in print that I lost track long ago.

Lisa has about thirty short stories and one novel in print. The novel, *Changing Fate,* is about a shapechanger. As I mentioned in my introduction to "Skins" earlier in this volume, the story of a shapechanger can be an indication of an obsessive desire to change one's life. Now, if Heather, who works for me part-time, writes a short story on the subject, and Lisa, who works for me full-time and lives in my household, writes an entire novel, does this say something about life in my vicinity? Or does it mean something else? I'm strictly diurnal—I never see either of them when the moon is full. . . .

66 "A h, my heart, and a-a-a-ah my heart
        My heart it is so sore,
        Since I must needs from my love depart,
And know no cause wherefore . . ."

The light tenor voice wafted into the cave with the spring breeze from the ledge outside where the prince had been spending his days for the past two weeks. Unfortunately, since both of the cave's occupants were tone deaf, the melody was wasted on them. The words, however, were another matter.

Princess Rowena, who was sitting cross-legged on the floor going out of her mind with boredom, looked up at her companion. "Do you suppose that means he's going away now?" she asked hopefully. "He's been out there for quite a while."

The dragon smiled, an expression that did not look as forbidding as one might suppose. Her life had become much more amusing since Rowena had moved in with her, following the receipt of a birthday gift from her Aunt Frideswide which had been chosen with more poetic license than common sense. Boredom was the bane of a near-immortal's existence, which was probably why the dragon had agreed to foster Rowena when the princess had decided she did not wish to return home. So far the arrangement was working out quite well for both of them, although there were occasional drawbacks—such as the prince outside.

"I'm afraid not," the dragon replied calmly, using two foreclaws to pick up a particularly fine emerald from the pile of gems in the girl's lap and twist it so that it sparkled in the light from the fire in the back of the cave. "He's been here only two weeks, but he strikes me as the persistent type. He could be here all summer—perhaps even until the snow falls." Her voice was wise with centuries of experience. "Princes as a whole talk a lot, sing romantic ballad after romantic ballad—"

"—after romantic ballad. Maybe he'd like to perish gallantly for love," Rowena suggested brightly, then sobered under the dragon's glare. "All right, it's not all that funny, but I'm getting very tired of being cooped up in here."

She sighed, which added an opal to the pile of gold coins and jewels in her lap. "Unrequited love is hell. And if he finds out about this—" she gestured at the gems which fell from her lips with each word she spoke, "he'll never leave."

"Just don't ask me to kill him," the dragon said tartly. "Those stupid princes taste dreadful, and they're difficult to digest."

Rowena giggled. "Especially if you eat their armor." Then she sobered. "You don't think he knows about the spell, do you?"

The spell in question was the birthday gift which had resulted in Rowena's sudden desire to leave home. Originally it had been the standard fairy-tale version, where every word spoken produced a flower or a jewel. After Rowena left home and moved in with the dragon (that afternoon), the dragon, who had given Frideswide the original spell, had modified it somewhat, substituting gold coins for the flowers. Unlike roses, gold coins had no thorns, so Rowena was relieved by the change and more than happy to give the dragon the coins for her bed.

The young prince outside sang on. He could scarcely have found a less appreciative audience.

"It's not that I *want* him dead," Rowena sighed. "And I know that knights don't cook evenly and they're hard to digest. But still, it's a pain to be stuck here inside for weeks on end, especially when the weather is so beautiful outside. And if he doesn't go away soon, all the berries will be gone, and I wanted to pick a lot of them before the season ends. It's not fair!"

"True," the dragon agreed. "It's not as if he is a real guest. We're not obliged to entertain him or arrange our schedules to suit him."

"And it's all so pointless. Why did he come here to 'rescue' me?" Rowena frowned fiercely. "I don't need to be rescued! I'm much happier here than I ever was at home."

"You might wish to marry someday," the dragon offered, sounding amused, "and you don't get many opportunities to meet young men living alone here with me."

"If I were ever to marry, which I don't plan on," Rowena said firmly, "I'm sure I would want a husband who had some sense of self-preservation. Camping out on a ledge just outside a dragon's lair does not betoken any great degree of intelligence."

That actually provoked a snicker from the dragon. "You might try explaining that to him."

"Sure I could," Rowena said sarcastically. "I tried that four—or was it five—princes ago. That particular idiot insisted that I was bewitched and begged me to come away with him so that I could be freed from the nonexistent spell you have me under."

She grinned up at the dragon, in a lightning change of mood. "Besides," she pointed out, "it's very difficult to talk to anyone face-to-face without having him find out about Aunt Frideswide's birthday present."

It had been quite a shock for Rowena to wake up in this condition on her fourteen birthday. The gems were all right, but the rose thorns *hurt*. And she had known immediately what her fate would be if anyone discovered that she was producing something more rewarding than flowers; she'd have been locked in the palace treasury and forced to talk herself into exhaustion. Ordinarily, Rowena was something of a chatterbox, but there were limits!

Fortunately the dragon had carried her off that afternoon, before anyone at the castle realized why Rowena had locked herself in her room and was refusing to talk.

"There's a full moon tonight," Rowena said, still trying to find a way out of her current trap. "And I think he goes somewhere else at night to sleep, because I never hear him on the ledge after dark." She looked up at the dragon again with a touch of defiance. "I'm going to sneak out tonight and pick some berries; there's enough light for that at full moon. And if I don't get out of here for a little while, I *am* going to lose what's left of my mind!"

"Very well," the dragon agreed. "Just be sure that you're back before dawn."

"I shall," Rowena said grimly, "I've no desire to be carried off by anyone or anything, let alone some stupid prince."

Rowena left that night, and the dragon, listening carefully, heard no sounds of pursuit. But the girl was not back the next morning. This was enough to worry any foster-mother, of whatever species. The dragon left the cave two hours after dawn and flew a search pattern until midday. She couldn't see Rowena anywhere, and she knew that her search had covered more area than a human on foot could have gone in the time since Rowena left. There was also no sign of the prince or his horse. This could only mean one thing.

It was time to panic.

Rowena sat in the corner of a small, damp, uncomfortable cave and glared at her captor. Her wrists and ankles were firmly tied, although he had at least had the consideration to tie her wrists in front of her. And even with her ankles tied together she could still kick well enough to make him keep his distance from her. In face, his shins were bruising nicely, and Rowena felt a certain amount of satisfaction in that.

"I am sorry for the lack of comfort in our accommodations, your highness," he said, "but if we leave this cave, the dragon is certain to find us."

Rowena bit her lips. She would have loved to tell this idiot what she thought of him, his ancestry, his morals, and his singing, but she didn't dare open her mouth. He didn't know about the spell, and she needed to keep it that way. It had been dark when he grabbed her, so he hadn't seen the pearl that appeared when she screamed, and she'd kept quite ever since. Of course, she had struggled and tried to run, which was why he had tied her up. So now she was wedged into this cave with him and his horse, until either the dragon found them or he felt safe enough to try to leave it.

"But you are safe with me," he continued, "and as soon as possible I shall take you home and ask your father for your hand in honorable marriage. I am Prince Florian of Astrefiore, at thy service, Princess." The prince stepped forward to make his bow, keeping a wary eye on Rowena's bound feet. "My eldest brother was among the guests at your birthday party when you were carried off, and he came home and told us of your abduction—and of how your own father forbade all of the princes gathered there to attempt your rescue!" He looked thoroughly indignant. "As it is the clear duty of a prince to rescue such an innocent victim, and as King Mark's unnatural command was not binding on me, I set out for the mountain where the dragon laired." He smiled sheepishly. "I'm a better minstrel than a fighter, so I'm just as glad that you were able to creep away without my having to fight the dragon. Of course," he added hastily, "I would fight the beast if it were necessary to insure your safety."

Chivalry is dead, Rowena thought morosely. *It's been replaced by total idiocy.*

Two women, one dark and one amber-haired, guided their horses on a barely-perceptible deer track that threaded its way through decidedly unnatural trees. Fortunately, *this* set of trees whimpered and shrank away from the riders. They could, all too easily, have been reaching toward the women and their mares with avid hunger.

The last lot had, after all.

"I thought you knew your way around the Pelagirs," the dark-haired one said, rather crossly. Her companion didn't answer, but then, the remark had not been aimed at her.

:I did,: came a purely mental reply, in a tone of affronted dignity. *:It is not my fault that the forest has changed. That is the nature of Pelagir territory that has no Hawkbrother Vale nearby. You never asked me if I thought I could still find my way around this area.:*

The head of the speaker emerged from the underbrush, and the bushes there squeaked with alarm and pulled away. He was tall, dark, would have told you himself that he was a handsome fellow, and he was not human.

Nor was he a male in the strictest accounting. Warrl was a *kyree* neuter, a magically-made species with the coat and heads of wolves, the bodies of the great hunting cats of the plains, the size of a young calf, and all of the intelligence of a human.

Of course, Warrl would have insisted that he was far more intelligent than any human.

Right now, his spirit-bonded friend, the Shin'a'in warrior Tarma shena Tale'sedrin, would have argued for the superior intelligence of the calf.

"Let it be, *she'enedra,*" her companion, the sorceress Kethry, advised. "We're not in any danger."

"Now," Tarma replied darkly, though she did not elaborate. She didn't have to; Kethry already knew what the Pelagirs were like. This was not the first time that they had penetrated the wild lands where magic wars of long ago had warped and twisted the plants, the animals, and even the land itself into something strange, unrecognizable, and often deadly.

It wouldn't have been so bad if they had actually been in the forest on purpose—but they weren't. They were *supposed* to be on the way to Kata'shin'a'in, but the familiar road had inexplicably dwindled to a track, then a path, and now had become nothing more than a game trail. Trying to turn around hadn't worked either; the trail vanished altogether when they tried that. Clearly, something wanted them to go in this direction, something magical. Tarma was hardly pleased. It was bad enough that much of their time was spent satisfying the demands of Kethry's mage-sword, Need—but to have some unknown magician trying to herd them to a completely unknown destination was intolerable! She was beginning to feel like some poor character in a play, bullied toward a confrontation known to the audience, but not to her.

She did not particularly like the feeling.

Suddenly the track opened up into a clearing. She urged her battlemare into it, disliking the whimpering trees and eager to put some distance between herself and them—and then reined the mare in abruptly when she saw what stood in the center of the clearing.

It was a doorway without a building, a beautifully formed arch of white stone taller than three tall men, and wide enough for a cart to pass through with space on either side. There was only one problem.

It shouldn't be here. There wasn't a single sign of the hand of man for leagues and leagues around.

Warrl stood directly in front of the portal, staring at it as if caught in a spell of fascination. All around the clearing, the whimpering trees with their thick, palm-sized leaves pulled their branches toward their trunks and shivered.

Kethry brought her mare up beside her partner's, surveyed the clearing, and wrinkled her brow in consternation. "The path ends here, doesn't it," she stated.

Tarma nodded gloomily. "And I'll bet you that if we try to retrace our steps, there won't *be* a path. We've been herded here like a couple of sheep—"

She would have said more, except that the space inside the doorway suddenly changed. Instead of the other side of the clearing, there was nothing there but darkness, a black void that Tarma shrank from without knowing why she did so. Whatever *that* thing was, she wanted no further part of it!

She started to turn her horse's head, determined to ride through and even over whatever animate plants wanted to get in her way—

But suddenly Kethry gave an all-too-familiar cry of pain, and spurred her mare straight at the archway. Warrl was right on her horse's heels, and in a heartbeat, the two of them were swallowed up in the blackness between the white stone pillars.

With a heartfelt curse, Tarma spurred her horse after, and followed.

"Warrl, I don't think we're in the Pelagirs anymore—" Tarma said weakly, looking around at the rocky and mountainous slope ahead of her. Sunlight blazed down from a sun near the zenith on the graveled path where their horses stood—it had been near sunset in the clearing.

Warrl did not dignify the observation with even a snort of derision.

It was possible to deduce some of what had just happened; Tarma had heard about magical doors into other places, often called Gates or Portals; obviously that doorway back in the clearing had been one such device. Something had made it active—and once active, whatever was on the other side had called to Kethry through the medium of the sword she wore, a blade called Need.

The sword responded to women in crisis, as the runes on her blade explained: *Woman's Need calls me/As woman's Need made me./Her Need must I answer/As my maker bade me.* Kethry had accepted a kind of soul-bonding with the sword as the price of the aid the blade gave her—Kethry, though completely untrained as a swordswoman, became an expert when the blade took over, and if she was wounded, the blade could and would heal just about anything. As a result, the greater the urgency of the woman in trouble, the worse the sympathetic pain Kethry would experience, unless and until she rode to that woman's aid.

Very nice for the women they helped, but not too damned convenient for Tarma and her partner.

No point in trying to throw the sword away, either; the farther Kethry got from it, the more it would call to her, and much too strongly to be denied. Relief would only come when Kethry found a successor to pass the blade on to—and even then, the sword would have to accept the new candidate.

"Where?" Tarma asked her partner curtly. Kethry shook her head as if to clear it, closed her eyes for a moment, and pointed up the slope.

"There," she said, her soft voice giving no hint of the firm will behind her pretty face and emerald eyes. "Whoever's in trouble, she's up there, and she is—must be—practically out of her mind with it. She's also a mage, but not of a kind that I recognize; that must be how she brought us here."

"Lovely," Tarma muttered. She stood up in her stirrups, and surveyed the countryside again. It was singularly unprepossessing. The rocky slopes boasted nothing much in the way of vegetation except for thick patches of blackberry bushes. At least, Tarma assumed they were blackberry bushes. There were berries in various stages of ripeness, from yellow-green to darkest plum, showing clearly against the foliage. If they were like the blackberry bushes of home, they'd be as thick with thorns as with berries. Tarma's long-dead love had called them "wait-a-moment bushes," because that was what anyone who tried to force his way through them was reduced to calling out, over and over again.

There appeared to be a path of sorts ahead of them, leading up to a cave with a generous ledge outside it. That was the direction Kethry was pointing.

There were no armies camped outside that cave, no signs of horses or other beasts of burden, no fires; whoever was in that cave was probably alone or, if captive, guarded by one or two people at the most. There was nothing to be lost in riding straight up to the cave mouth and taking a look. Very few people outside the Shin'a'in Clans knew just what it was that Tarma and her partner rode—battlesteeds were easily the equivalent of two ordinary human fighters apiece, and when you added in Warrl, you had a force the equal of any seven fighters. So if there *was* anyone nasty up there, he was going to get a major shock if he tried a direct confrontation. And just at the moment, Tarma rather hoped he would. She was truly in a mood to kill something.

"Let's go," she said, "I want to get this over with." And as her partner blinked in surprise at her apparent impulsiveness, she sent her mare trotting up the path to the cave.

She had been supposing all this time that her adversaries would, of course, be human, so when the monster snaked its head and neck out of the cave mouth, all she could do for a moment was to freeze in place.

The monster seemed just as surprised as she was; it stared at her with its mouth—a mouth well-appointed with daggerlike teeth—dropping wide open in shock. Unfortunately, that only gave Tarma a much better look at all those teeth.

Whatever it was, it *wasn't* a creature like anything *she* had ever heard of before—except, perhaps, a cold-drake. This thing was the wrong color, but the size was right, and the long neck, and, of course, all the teeth.

There was, presumably, a female being held captive somewhere in that cave. Maybe the monster was saving her for dinner, later; maybe it was just there to guard her. Whatever, the woman's distress held Kethry here until she was freed—and that held Tarma and Warrl. Tarma did the only thing a Swordsworn warrior could, under the circumstances.

She drew her sword, and with a Shin'a'in battle cry, spurred her horse into a charge while the monster was still caught off guard. That is, she *started* to charge. Kethry's shriek made her rein her mare in so quickly that the poor beast's hooves skidded and she slid to a most undignified stop.

"Tarma! Stop!" Kethry cried in real pain. *"Don't! Need wants us to help the dragon!"*

"Dragons," Tarma muttered, staring at their hostess in disbelief over a nice hot cup of tea. "Tea-drinking dragons. I must be out of my mind."

The dragon ignored her, as she had ignored Tarma every other time she had muttered something similar. It—she—was a very polite dragon, although a deeply distressed dragon.

She had every right to be distressed, though how that distress and the spell she had cast to bring her some help had interacted to open a portal between *her* world—which was obviously not the one that held Shin'a'in, since there were no such things as dragons in Tarma's world—and their world was a mystery White Winds Adepts would probably be debating for the next century or more. That didn't matter. What did was what she and Kethry were going to do about the situation that brought them here, since obviously the magic that had done so would not release them until they had.

"I'm dreadfully sorry now that I built the spell that way," the dragon was saying apologetically. "But I thought I would probably be dragging in some reluctant knight or other, and—well— historically my kind and theirs do not exactly get along. I built in coercions, and now I can't get rid of them."

Kethry nodded wisely, as Tarma sighed. "At least the track isn't even cold by Warrl's standards," Tarma put in. "I have to admit that you couldn't have deliberately selected anyone more fit to get Rowena back to you in a reasonable amount of time if you'd tried."

Warrl nodded. :*I really should get on the scent now,*: he said, his tone as sympathetic as Tarma had ever heard. :*Rowena is probably terribly frightened—*:

"Rowena is probably furious," the dragon corrected. "And if she starts telling him what she thinks of him—"

The dragon's voice broke on a sob, and her talons tightened on her own oversized mug until it broke, period. Tarma did not finish the sentence, for the dragon had revealed Rowena's "little talent" to explain why they were going to have to find the girl quickly. *Princes are always hard up for cash, especially younger princes. Once he finds out he has the equivalent of a mint and a mine in his hands, he'll lock her up so tight they'll have to send daylight to her by messenger.*

:*I'm on my way,*: Warrl said hastily, not wanting to be subjected to another bout of draconic tears and hysteria. The last bout had been quite enough for him.

I would never have guessed that dragons could cry.

Warrl vanished with alacrity, and Tarma decided to change the subject before the dragon broke down again. "Look, this idiot can't have gotten far with her. She *isn't* going to cooperate, and he is going to be far too gallant and polite to knock her over the head and bundle her off unconscious."

"That—that's true," the dragon sniffled. "Rowena didn't think much of him before, and by now, her estimate of his character has probably placed him somewhere below spotted newts. If he's lucky, she hasn't done anything to him that's permanent."

"Well, given that, how do you want us to get her loose?" Tarma asked. "I don't think *you* ought to appear; he might try something desperate."

The dragon winced, but nodded.

"We need to be smart about this," Kethry mused. "I—"

Then she flushed, and grinned. "You *did* say that her father forbade anyone to go after her?"

The dragon nodded again.

"Well," Kethry said slyly. "I have an idea that would provide the perfect explanation for *why* he did that, and possibly even prevent anything like this from happening in the future. Provided, of course, that your fosterling doesn't mind her reputation being totally destroyed."

Tarma looked closely at her partner, and as often happened, realized precisely what the sorceress meant; after all, it was an assumption—incorrect as it happened—that was often applied to her and Kethry. *Oh my ears! If she's thinking what I think she's thinking—*

The dragon lifted her head high, and cocked it to one side. "I don't think she would mind if it kept princes off the ledge, but what—"

:I've found her,: Warrl trumpeted in their minds. *:They aren't far away at all. Hurry up, though, I think His Highness is getting impatient.:*

"Let's go" Tarma said, jumping to her feet. "I want to get this over with. We'll explain on the way."

This prince, if not a complete idiot, was certainly the most incompetent person Tarma had ever seen. He hadn't left any kind of a guard on the trail outside the cave he'd hidden in, he'd picked a hiding place barely an hour away from the dragon's own cave, and he wasn't paying any attention to anything going on outside. *I guess this just proves that the gods watch out for fools and the mad,* she thought in disgust, as Warrl drove his horse off. *I can't think of any other reason why he's still alive.*

The sound of his horse galloping off—the fool hadn't even *hobbled* it!—finally brought him out of the entrance of the cave. He stared in shock at the sight of two grim-faced, armed women—with swords drawn—waiting for him.

Tarma was going to be the one challenging him, because Need had a tendency to overreact and they *didn't* want to kill or even hurt him. And right now, caught between the distress of the female dragon hidden out of sight behind them and Rowena's emotional state in the cave in front of them, Kethry would not be able to restrain the sword if she had to fight the boy.

Of course, there was the chance that he was a much, much better fighter than they thought. He could even be better than Tarma. In that case, they were not going to play fair. Kethry would move in and deal with him. Hopefully, she would be able to keep Need from inflicting anything too permanent.

"Stand forth, kidnapper!" Tarma growled menacingly. "I, Tarma shena Tale'sedrin, do challenge you as a cad and a miscreant. I challenge you for the welfare of the lady you have stolen. I challenge you to single combat for the hand of my lady and my love, the Princess Rowena!"

The look on the boy's face when she got to those final few words was almost enough to make her break out laughing. His eyes bulged, and his mouth dropped open, giving him an uncanny resemblance to a startled frog. The green surcoat he wore only heightened the resemblance.

"I—ah—" His mouth moved, but nothing more came out of it.

Tarma took advantage of his mental state to advance on him. He barely got his blade up in time to deflect her first move; he never saw the second. Her blow to the side of his head laid him out flat.

"Now what?" Kethry asked.

Tarma shrugged. "Go free the girl and explain the situation to her. *She's* the injured party. Let her decide what she wants to do with him. Personally, all I want is out of here."

:*He is a very good musician,*: Warrl put in wistfully. :*Truly a marvelous minstrel. I don't suppose—*:

"NO!" snapped Tarma, Kethry, and the dragon, all together.

From her position in the cave, Rowena had been able to hear clearly everything that was going on, but it didn't make much sense to her. First that incredibly odd looking animal had crept in and scared off the horse. She had seen it quite clearly, although she hadn't recognized it. It was like nothing she had ever seen before.

Warning the prince about what was happening to his horse was not something *she* was going to do; she didn't owe *him* any favors. She was prepared to watch the horse gnawed to bare bones before she opened her mouth, but she was just as happy when it was merely chased away—after all, none of this was the horse's fault.

But her mouth dropped open in astonishment when she heard the challenge. *Who is Tarma shena Tale'sedrin?* she wondered. *And what does she mean "my lady and my love"—I've never even* met *her!*

Then a very pretty young woman with amber hair came into the cave, cut her loose, helped her to her feet and held her up until the numbness wore off and Rowena could walk again. "It's all right, Rowena," she said soothingly. "My name is Kethry, my partner is Tarma, and I think you may have seen Warrl earlier. Your foster-mother hired us to rescue you."

Rowena had several questions about this "rescue party," but she didn't know if it was safe to talk yet. So she remained silent as she followed Kethry out of the cave into the sunlight. The prince lay on the ground, but Rowena didn't spare enough attention to determine whether he was dead or merely unconscious. Kethry had obviously been telling the truth about who hired them;

the dragon was perched on the trail, just beyond the cave. Rowena ran to her and flung both arms around as much dragon as she could reach, which was most of one foreleg.

A scaly chin dropped down to pat the top of her head and then pulled back. "My poor child," the dragon said. "Have you managed to keep your mouth shut all this time?" Rowena nodded, her head still pressed firmly against the dragon's leg. "I'm impressed," the dragon chuckled. "I know it wasn't easy for you. But you can talk now. He's unconscious—"

"Not dead?" Rowena asked in mock disappointment, carefully palming two jewels.

"Rowena!" the dragon reproved her. "And Tarma and Kethry and Warrl know about your peculiar talent."

Rowena turned to look at them. Kethry smiled sympathetically. "It must be awkward sometimes," she said.

Rowena nodded. "But it's not so bad since the Lady Dragon modified the spell to get rid of the flowers," she said, carefully catching the jewels and coins in her cupped hands. "The rose thorns in the original spell really hurt!" She looked at Tarma. "Why did you call me your lady and your love? I don't understand that part—we've never met before, have we?"

Tarma chuckled. "That was to discourage further royal attempts at 'rescuing' you," she explained. "If you are thought to be a lover of women, most princes won't want you."

"What's a lover of women?" Rowena asked, still puzzled.

Tarma sighed, and Kethry giggled. "Oh," Rowena said, realizing the class of information involved. "That's one of those 'you'll understand when you're older' things, isn't it?"

"Something like that," Kethry replied. "The idea is that when the prince tells this story, people won't bother you anymore."

"There's just one problem with that," Rowena said. "He's a minstrel—he's not going to tell *anything* accurately—or even close to it!"

"Damn," Tarma said. "She's right. We know how strange a story can become when a minstrel gets hold of it."

The prince stirred and groaned. "What happened?" He looked around, saw the dragon, and promptly fainted.

Rowena sighed. "He's a frog," she said firmly.

Pop! Everyone blinked at the sound, then looked at the figure on the ground. The prince was gone, replaced by a frog.

"How did you do that?" the dragon asked in surprise.

Rowena shrugged. "I don't know," she said. "He just seemed like a frog to me."

The dragon sighed. "I guess I'll have to start giving you lessons in magic. Wild talents are dangerous."

"So are some tame ones," Rowena retorted. "Look at my Aunt Frideswide."

"Can you change him back?" Kethry asked.

Rowena shrugged again. "I don't know," she said. "I don't particularly want to change him back, either—not after the way he treated me!"

"Well, you have to do something with him," Tarma said, "or he'll be outside your cave every time you look."

Rowena looked up at the dragon. "Can you do something with him?"

The dragon thought for a minute. "I'll set up a transport circle, and send him to wherever he's wanted or needed."

Rowena nodded. "Let's hope there's somebody

who wants him, then." She turned to Kethry. "You said that you were hired to rescue me. Did you," she looked from them to the dragon, "agree on a price?"

"We're actually getting paid?" Tarma said incredulously.

Rowena handed Tarma the jewels that had fallen into her hands with every word she had spoken since they had rescued her. "Would you prefer coins for the rest?" Tarma nodded, apparently unable to speak. Rowena cupped her hands in front of her face and chanted softly. When she lowered her hands, they were full of gold coins. She handed them to Kethry, who put them into her belt pouch. Tarma, still staring at the jewels, followed her example.

"Are you sure this is going to work?" Kethry asked the dragon anxiously, as she, Tarma, Warrl, and their horses took their places in the carefully scribed magic circle.

The dragon could only shrug. "I can only hope. I am not entirely certain how I brought you here in the first place."

"Just get on with it," Tarma said, addressing a private and fervent prayer to the Star-eyed. The dragon closed her eyes, and inscribed a complicated figure in the air with one talon.

Then the world went black.

But instead of reappearing in the clearing in the Pelagirs, Tarma found herself standing alone, in a place of softly glowing mist, on a path of light. *The Moonpaths!* she thought, startled, *But why*—

"So," said a familiar voice, a hollow tenor, pleasant enough, but echoing as if the speaker stood in the bottom of a well. "Finally, we find you. Your spirits have been wandering, Younger Sister—wandering quite out of our world."

"What?" she asked, startled.

"You have traveled in spirit to a very distant place," her *leshy'a Kalendral* teacher told her. "Oh, do not mistake me, your venture was quite real, and as you know, you affected the world in which you walked quite decisively—but your true body was lying in your camp, where you were overcome by the dust of *gade'shata*. You, and your *she'enedra* both, your horses and your *kyree*." He tilted his head to one side. "We bent a rule for you, we, your teachers, and guarded you while you walked."

Tarma blanched. *Gade'shata* mushrooms produced a cloud of spores which were incredibly potent. Shamans sometimes used them to walk through other worlds and times, though at their peril. If she and Kethry had survived an encounter with those potent fungi, they were fortunate indeed!

"I shall not ask where you walked," the spirit-Kal'enedral continued. "You could only have been drawn to one who needed you profoundly. I will only say that you have been fortunate to have escaped this with a whole soul, and if I were you, I should be very careful to watch where I stepped in the future."

And before she could reply, the world vanished again. Only this time, she found herself lying cramped and cold on wet grass, soaked from head to toe by a sudden rainfall. She dragged herself to her feet with the help of a nearby sapling, scraping her wet hair out of her eyes as she looked around.

The mares were tethered nearby, shaking their heads as if dazed, the imprint of their bodies still marking the grass beside them. Kethry was blinking and sitting up; Warrl scrubbing at his eyes with his paws. It looked as if they had just made camp, for the remains of a fire smoldered in the light rain—and just beyond the fire, Tarma spotted the flattened shapes of decomposing fungi, their spores depleted. *The mushrooms,* she thought dazedly. *We camped next to the mushrooms, and the heat of the fire set their spores loose. Oh, the gods watch over fools and the mad!*

"What—was it a dream?" Kethry asked, dazedly.

"Yes—and no," Tarma croaked. "Let's get out of here while we can. I'll explain it to you on the road."

Kethry sighed. "It figures. Any job involving Need where we get paid would *have* to be a dream."

STONE SPIRIT
by Diana L. Paxson

Diana has had a story in every anthology I've ever edited, in addition to being a very successful novelist in her own right. Most of the members of our family, including Diana and me, have both Native American and Germanic ancestry—and in "Stone Spirit" she has drawn on both traditions. Diana is also one of my best friends and more successful writers. She has a novel in print, *The White Raven,* about Tristan, one of King Arthur's knights—really more about Iseult and Branwen—as well as such unlikely subjects as King Lear, *The Serpent's Tooth,* which is much less grim than Shakespeare's play. Like this story, her most recent novel, *The Wolf and the Raven,* a retelling of the story of Seigfreid and Brunhild, uses a Germanic background. I love her books and she likes mine; it's very nice to belong to at least one Mutual Admiration Society.

Diana is younger than I, but her older son, Ian, just married and he and his wife are expecting a child, so Diana will beat me to being a grandmother.

"**Y**our lady is a powerful seidhkona," said the young man. "But did she mean to prophesy that I would gain glory fighting for King Eric or against him?" He smoothed his mustache and moved closer to Bera, who frowned and edged away again.

After a seidh session folk often asked her help in understanding the sometimes cryptic replies Groa made to their questions. Two years of following the wisewoman from farm to steading throughout Norway had taught Bera enough of myth and meaning to interpret some of the symbolism, and she did her best to help when she sensed real need. But men, especially young ones who would never have dared to accost the seidhkona, sometimes seemed to find Groa's young apprentice a challenge to their virility.

At least this attempt at flirtation had been covered by a real concern. Eric Blood-Ax, driven from Norway by his young half-brother Hakon eight years before, had taken to raiding his former subjects between stints as under-king of Northumbria. This young man—his name was Arnor, the eldest son from a neighboring farmhold—was not alone in his confusion.

"The gods do not offer men their gifts like a valkyrie presenting a drinking horn," she said blandly. "Your answer is a ladle—it is up to you to find the cauldron."

"I have a fine, large ladle," he said, reaching for her. "If you will uncover your cauldron—"

Bera, realizing too late that her kenning had been badly chosen, blushed furiously. "Not for you!" she exclaimed. As she turned, she met the amused gaze of another man, his head black as the kettle and shoulder-high to the rest of the warriors.

Scowling, she drew herself up, wishing she herself were taller, and stalked past him, seeking Groa's side. Bera had fought too hard for the independence the seidhkona's life promised her to give it up for any man. She heard laughter behind her, but she did not turn. She had been told that she looked like a small brown bear when she was angry. Any man who had spoken to her just then would have felt her claws.

The dark man was still watching her. She glared back at him, then turned to Ranveig, the holder's daughter, who sat on her other side.

"Who is the svart-alf? Does he not know that staring is unmannerly?"

The other girl stiffled a laugh. "No doubt he thinks himself beyond such courtesies. He is Kon Grípirsson, one of King Hakon's court-men. But be wary how you speak to him—he is supposed to be a runemaster."

Bera snorted. "If he tries any sorcery on me, he will find that we women have our own magic!"

She thought she had spoken softly, but later, when they had taken up the boards and folk were sitting around the fire, he rose up to block her way as she was bringing Groa a horn of ale.

"So—you don't think much of me or my magic?" Standing, he was not much taller than she. Outland blood there, thought Bera, like her own. He had the same air of being willing to take on all comers whatever the odds that she had noticed often in small dogs, or short men. She supposed it was a compliment that he should think her a worthy adversary.

"Did I say that?" she asked sweetly. "It is only

that in my experience, the masters of galdor are scornful of any sorcery but their own."

"I am not scornful—" he shrugged. "But seidh is woman's magic, and I never met the woman yet who could say from one day to the next just how she spices her stews. You have power, I admit it, but its application depends on your mood, your energy." He shrugged once more. "You have no control."

"Why didn't you add, 'the phase of the moon'?" she asked dangerously. "You know nothing! Cannot you understand that to deal with such powers as we face daily requires a discipline as great as any warrior's? I have been with Groa for two years, and I am only beginning to master the skills of a seidhkona. And you, I suppose, do nothing but study rules and formulas. How do you raise the might to empower your spells?"

Kon's hair might be as black as soot, but his skin was milky fair. It showed his flush beautifully. Clearly, he was searching for some rejoinder that would crush her utterly, but before he could find it, the master of the hall called for their attention so that the toasts could begin. Scowling, he returned to his place, and Bera continued around the hearth to hand her mistress the horn.

Some hours later, when Bera was beginning to lean sleepily against Groa's shoulder, the boasting had given way to the telling of tales. Suddenly she found herself sitting up again, blinking.

What had he said? *The duergar....* Memory flickered, an image of rough gray limbs fading into stone. There had been trolls across the fjord from her father's holding, but she had learned not to speak about seeing them. What did these folk have to do with the People of the Hills?

"The dwarf-kin carried off the maiden—my grandfather's youngest sister Alfhild," said

Reidar, their host and the owner of the farm. "And with her the great gold-banded drinking horn that my great-grandfather had from Halvdan the Black. When he tried to follow, her young brother was crushed by falling stones, and since that day no man who has tried the hill but has lost life or limb."

Arnor's gaze focused on Bera. "I could get in—" he mumbled, lifting the horn to make his vow.

Kon's gaze followed his. "Don't be a fool!" He gripped Arnor's wrist with a strength that obviously surprised the warrior. "Did you not hear? No ordinary human strength will prevail against the Invisible!"

"You think you could do better, little man?" growled Arnor, pulling his arm away.

"Perhaps . . ." Kon's pale eyes narrowed. "Mind can prevail where muscle fails, and there are few powers that can stand against the runes, rightly applied."

Arnor snorted scornfully. "I will wager my roan stallion against your gold arm ring that I can find a way into the hill and bring back the horn!"

"If it's still there," said someone. There was a babble of commentary as men began to make their own bets on the side.

"I forbid it!" cried Reidar. "What the earth folk have, let them hold!"

"A wager, then," answered Kon grimly, ignoring him. "At tomorrow's dawning I will meet you on the hill."

The seidhkona glanced at Bera. "What have you been up to, child, to set these young fools to snorting and pawing the air like two stallions?" She had been a big woman, beginning to stoop a little now, her face worn by the years to beauty like a river stone.

"I did nothing!" Bera exclaimed indignantly. Reidar was protesting that he had meant no challenge, and would pay no mannbot in compensation if they should get their deaths on the hill.

"Perhaps not," said Groa with a sigh. "Neither does the mare. It is enough that you are young and touched already by power."

Bera stared at her. She had never thought herself fair, and therefore never worried about men's response to her. But Groa, despite her age, had a presence more compelling than beauty. If she herself was beginning to acquire the same glamour, then she would indeed be responsible if these young men died. They had made their brags where all could hear. No word from her now could stop them. But perhaps, she smiled as she thought of the herbs in her pack, there was another way.

As always after a night's feasting, the women were the first to stir. From the cupboard bed against the wall that she shared with Groa, Bera listened to the sounds as the maids drew back the bar on the great door and began to make up the fire and smiled, wondering how long her two swains would sleep. They had been flattered to accept the mead she brought them the night before, its heavy sweetness disguising the taste of the herbs she had mixed in. With the sleep charm she had sung into the drink to keep them from noticing, the young men should slumber until the sun was high.

Carefully, so as not to wake the seidhkona, Bera parted the woven bedcurtains and eased through, clutching her outer clothes. She shivered as cool air touched her bare arms, for summer was drawing to a close and the nights were already cold, and pulled her woolen hanging skirt over the linen undergown in which she had slept, fastening the straps with the bronze turtle brooches Groa had given her at Yule. She would wait until Groa woke to find the comb and deal with the sleep-tangled masses of her brown hair. One of the girls brought her a beaker of mulled ale, and she drank gratefully, smiling a little as the warriors who slept on the benches beside the hearth began to mumble and stir.

Arnor lay sprawled on the straw with his cloak tangled around him, snoring. She glanced at the other recumbent forms, seeking the black head of the king's man.

"Are ye looking for Kon Grípirsson?" asked one of the girls. "He's off to the hill. Yon sleeping pig will be wild when he wakes and learns he's lost his wager after all!"

Bera felt the blood leave her face and then flame back again. The sleeping draught had worked—there was Arnor to prove it! How had the other man resisted her spell? She shut her eyes, remembering how he had looked when she offered him the mead. His eyes grew luminous when he smiled. They had distracted her. But she remembered now that before he drank he had made a sign and muttered something over the horn; she had thought it a blessing.

A runespell against magic! Bera thought furiously. But he had not seemed to suspect her. Perhaps the precaution had become habitual for a king's man.

"When?" she said fiercely. "When did he go?"

The girl's eyes widened. "When we unbarred the door."

Not so long, then. If she ran, she might catch him. Swearing, Bera yanked her heavy shawl from its hook and hurried toward the door, leaving the maid to stare after her.

* * *

Reidar's farmstead lay inland, on the lower slopes of the spine of mountains that lift like a keel between Norway and the land of the Swedes. Beyond the home pasture the forest clung to the roots of the mountains, and Ymir's bones thrust in a great outcrop of gray stone through trees whose leaves were already beginning to flame with the golds and reds of fall. Plain in the dew-wet grass Bera could see Kon's footsteps. But even without them she would have recognized in that huge, domed boulder the earth-folks' hall.

As she drew closer, she saw that its face was pitted and worn. The morning light cast the base of the rock into deep shadow, and as she drew nearer, Bera realized that the stone itself had split. The overhang deepened into a chasm that led within. Kon's prints were still wet on the stone. Scrambling upward, she called his name.

Something moved in the shadows. She stilled, and as her eyes adjusted, she saw a man's shape against the lightless opening of a cave. Why was he standing there? Bera took a careful step forward, and froze again as he whirled, steel flashing as his knife came up to guard.

"Oh—" he said a moment later when they both had got their breath again. "It is you. You should have called."

She sniffed and pulled her shawl up against the chill air that flowed from the blackness beyond. "Who were you expecting? Arnor?"

"Isn't he with you?"

"Didn't you see him?" she replied indignantly. "He won't stir before noon. I meant you to sleep as well!" Her heart gave an unaccustomed skip as something in his face altered.

"Living with kings teaches one to be careful. When your herbs began to make me sleepy, I stuck a finger down my throat to bring the drink up again. I was angry. I thought you wanted Arnor to win."

Bera sighed. "I suppose it's enough if it worked on one of you. You can come away now with your honor intact."

"No." He gestured toward the rock face. "I came for honor, but that doesn't matter now. Do you understand what is here?"

Now that her eyes had adjusted, Bera could see symbols etched into the stone: stick figures with swords and sun-shields in their hands, animals and ships and a great hand. Traces of red coloring still showed in the grooves.

"Are those runes?" she pointed at some of the smaller shapes.

"Some of them—the runes that were before the runes, perhaps. That is why I want to go inside. This place is old, Bera. Who knows what wisdom is hidden here?"

"Or what dangers!" she said tartly. "The dead do not lightly give up their secrets."

"I have fought draugs and bound them within their howes! A few earth-bound souls will not disturb me!"

"Then you are a fool!" she exclaimed.

"And you are afraid!" he replied.

"I have walked the road to Hel and returned. I have spoken to spirits and faced beings you cannot imagine, runemaster! Do not speak to me of fear!"

Kon grinned. "Then I challenge you! If you are so courageous, and if your magic is so powerful, come with me into the cave!"

All the reasons she should not go were quite apparent. But as she met Kon's bright stare, Bera knew only that this arrogant master of galdor must not be allowed to scorn the skills that Groa had taught her. She picked up one of the torches that Kon had brought with him, and grinning, he reached into his pouch for flint and steel.

It was cold in the caves, colder than the grave, the even, bone-numbing chill of a place that that never sees the sun. But at least it was dry, and the torch flared out in streamers of flame as a fresh draught stirred the air. Kon had given Bera his cloak when she started shivering; if he was cold as well, he was refusing to show it. Presently, Bera thought, she would make him wear it for a while, but for the moment he might as well suffer the consequences of his own stubborn pride.

There were gnawed bones and animal droppings near the entrance, and the passage beyond it was scattered with fallen stones, but a path was worn into the rock beneath them, and here and there someone had hacked away an impeding outcrop of stone. Men, or other things manlike in form, had passed this way. And from time to time, where the passage divided, they would find another of those not-quite-runes.

"They say that Odin gave runes to all the kindreds when he came down from the Tree," said Kon once when they paused to rest. "But not whether they were the same runes. I look at these, and I can almost understand them, then my mind flinches away. Perhaps these are the ones he gave the ducrgar."

Bera nodded. It might be so. The dwarf-kin were the children of earth, born of the maggots that fed on Ymir's flesh when the holy gods made Midgard from the giant's body and bones. Duergar, huldre-folk, trolls, and the shells of men—earth held them all. She told herself that the sounds that sometimes stirred the silence of the caves were only wind, but more and more it seemed to her there were words in that whisper-

ing, though not in any language she could understand.

Here there were no daymarks by which to measure time's passing. It seemed forever that Kon
and Bera crept through that murmuring silence,
crawling sometimes where the passage shrank
around them, working their way ever deeper into
the hill. They encountered no opposition from
foes dead or living, but senses that had nothing to
do with the physical communicated to Bera an in-
creasing unease.

Kon's intent features showed no sign of trouble. Were her seidh-trained senses sharper, or was
she deceived by her own fear? The first torch
burned down and they lighted another. There were
two more. When the second torch was finished,
thought Bera, she would make him turn back.

Her stomach was reminding her how long it
had been since she put food into it when they
eased around a spur of stone and found that fallen
rock had blocked the path.

"That's the end of it, then," said Bera.

"Don't sound so pleased, and don't be so sure."
Kon leaned closer to the stones. "I can feel air
coming through."

"Let the powers that dwell here keep their secrets," she answered, her nerves twitching with
tension. "We've proven our courage."

Kon straightened and turned to her. "I told
you—I'm not here to prove anything. I want to
know!"

"I know enough," whispered Bera. "Something
is wakening. We should go."

"Just a few stones—" He grabbed one and
tossed it aside. The clatter seemed loud in the silence. Bera held the torch high, feeling her heart
pound in her breast. "Look—" He stood aside and
she peered through the opening. In the darkness

beyond it something gleamed. Grunting, Kon burrowed into the rockpile, flinging the stones behind him until there was a space big enough for a human to pass.

"Well?" Kon's smile flickered like sunlight and her heart leaped in answer despite her fear. In another moment he was scrambling through the opening. *We'll be safer if we stick together,* she told herself, and followed him.

Because of the torch, it took her longer to get through. When she succeeded, she saw that Kon was standing still, staring. Bera lifted the torch and blinked as light sparked and glinted from the cavern floor. *A king's treasure,* she thought, making out the shapes of a helm and spearheads, two-handled bronze jugs, a tarnished silver bowl. Where dessicated leather had split, a scattering of gold coin spilled across the floor. Here, deep in the earth, it was too dry for rust and too cold for mold to grow. Only a thin film of dust dimmed the splendor of the hoard.

"How old?" she whispered. She had heard tales of helms like this one, a framework of gilded bronze over hard leather with the figure of a wild boar fixed to the arch above the crown, but no one wore them now. "Are we the first to see these things since they were hidden here?"

"Not quite." Something in his voice warned her. Bera turned, and the torchlight gleamed on something that lay apart from the rest of the hoard. It was a drinking horn, tipped and banded with worked gold. Bera caught her breath, and then realized that the hand holding it was only skin stretched over bone.

Carefully she stepped nearer. The body was that of a young woman, her face mercifully hidden by waves of still-golden hair. Her clothing was in tatters, but as Bera looked more closely she could see that it had not decayed, but been torn away. Reidmar's ancestress had been attacked by someone, or something, before she died.

Kon took the torch and turned in a slow circle. "There——" he said hoarsely. The half-blocked passage through which they had entered was not the only entrance to the cavern. The torch showed a sloping floor and curved walls broken by several dark fissures. Near one of them lay the body of a man.

What remained of the girl's clothing was good cloth, but the man had been dressed in coarse woolens and badly cured skins. Light flickered on features still set in a snarl, and Bera looked quickly away.

"She was abducted, but not by the trolls," said Kon. "He must have been a beggar or a wolf's head, a desperate man who saw his chance to steal the horn."

"Did she surprise him so that he had to take her hostage, or did he want her from the beginning?" The damage to the girl's clothing made it clear enough how he had used her before she died. "If they were trapped here by the rockfall, why didn't he clear it away?"

"I don't know," said Kon. He turned back to the hoard. Bera shuddered as the air grew suddenly colder, and senses that had been distracted by their discovery suddenly screamed alarm.

"Don't touch it!" she exclaimed. In the torchlight she saw his eyes widening in question, and the golden arm ring in his hand. Then wind blasted suddenly through the cavern and the torch went out.

"Stay where you are——" Kon's voice shook only a little. She heard the scrape of leather as he moved toward her. Bera blinked, willing her eyes to adjust to the darkness. But this was not the human world where there was always some illumination, even in the darkest storm. These depths had never seen the sun. The blackness around her consumed even the memory of light. She jumped, then sighed as he touched her foot and sat back again.

"Just a moment, and I'll get the torch rekindled." She heard him fumbling with his pouchstrings. Then he swore. "I put the flints and striker back," he muttered, "I know it!" She heard the click and rustle as he searched again.

"If you hadn't insisted—" she began.

"I didn't force you to come with me!" he cut her off. His fingers closed on her ankle; at the touch, terror surged through her.

"Let me go!" She jerked away and lurched into the darkness, her flesh shrinking from hot breath and hard fingers and pain. "Please, don't hurt me—"

"Bitch!" he exclaimed, then stopped on a sob. "Bera—stop. I didn't mean—" And then, "It's them, Alfhild and her abductor. You're feeing their memories!"

Bera shook her head, trying to deny the oaths that echoed through the darkness, the screaming that went on and on. *"Groa!"* her spirit cried. *"Help me!"*

She never knew if somehow the seidhkona heard, or if her name alone had been enough to waken memory, but it seemed to Bera that she heard her teacher's patient voice once more. *"The breath is Ond, the spirit of life that Odin gave ... breathe in ... and out ... in ... and out.... Your breath is your power. ..."*

With each breath she drew in stillness, each exhalation thrust the terror farther away. At last there came a time when she could hear Kon gently calling her name.

"I hear you . . ." she whispered. "It is all right now. . . ."

"I'm going to crawl back to the rockfall," his voice trembled with his own struggle for control. "My flints might have fallen out when I crawled through. . . . Stay where you are."

Bera could not have moved if she would. Legs that suddenly had not the strength to bear her gave way and she sank down upon the cold cave floor. The small sounds Kon made among the rocks only seemed to intensify the surrounding silence. She became acutely aware of her own fragility, surrounded by this dreadful weight of stone. Surely this was a doorway to Niflheim, that dark cold place to the north below Midgard where nothing lived, or moved, or grew.

Kon and I both boasted of our magic, she thought grimly, *but neither one of us can summon so much as a spark of flame!*

After a long time she heard Kon's sigh of defeat. Tracking her by her breathing, he felt his way back across the cavern floor to her side. This time it was Bera who reached out, drawing him into her arms, drawing strength from the solid warmth of his body. She could feel his heart beating against her own.

"We can get out of this cavern," he said softly. "But I had memorized the dwarf-runes and counted on reading them to find my way back through the passages. We can try to leave, and risk losing ourselves further in the darkness, or my knife will give us a clean death here. Think about it while I rest. I will abide by your will."

A pity you did not say that when I first caught up with you! Bera thought bitterly, but she bit back the words.

Her ears rang with the silence. At first she resisted it, afraid of being overwhelmed by Alfhild's terror once more. But presently she found pity replacing her fear. *"Be at peace, sweet ghost,"* she thought then, *"though I do not know the way out of this darkness, I have walked between the worlds. If my wyrd is now to fare to Hella's kingdom, I will show you the way."*

Gradually her inner stillness deepened. Now she could hear once more the whisper of air against stone that had sounded like voices. She supposed that her senses, deprived of stimulation, were trying to impose meaning on whatever they could find. Or was it all imagination? She remembered suddenly what Groa had told her. Everything had spirit. The nisse dwelt in the waterfall; the armadhr watched over the harvest; the tomte guarded the hearthfire.

There was spirit even in stone. The svart-alfs, the duergar, lived in the deep places of the world. Freyja herself had sought these depths to lie with the dwarves who forged the golden necklace, Brisingamen.

"Lady of Life and Luck and Love—" her spirit cried. *"Get me back to Midgard and you may claim your own offering!"* She held her breath then, listening, and thought she heard an echo of golden laughter.

Then the air was filled by a rush of sound. Or was it thoughts she was receiving? Bera struggled to comprehend feelings for which humans had no senses, and concepts for which they had no words. She looked through visible darkness, tasted the sweet strength of stone.

When she could think again, Kon was shaking her, calling her name. Bera reached up to touch his face.

"Kon, do you remember the dwarf-runes?

Show me one—draw it on my hand!" She could feel his amazement, but after a moment she felt the angular shape upon her skin, and in the same moment heard with her inner senses the sound that was its name. She sucked in breath and sang out the word. And very faintly, from somewhere in the distance, came an echo of sound.

"It is the rune!" Kon said hoarsely. "That is its name—I can feel the rightness of it, and the stone is answering! What have you done?"

"I am no rune mistress, but I sing to the spirits. The thoughts of those who live in stone are strange beyond imagining, but if you can give me the shapes, the duergar will give me the sounds, and they will sing us home."

Before they left the cavern Bera felt her way to what remained of Alfhild and gave the poor body a blessing. And then, for she had felt the regret that bound the ghost to the cave, she lifted the gold-banded drinking horn from the dessicated hands. She felt them fall into dust as she touched them, and a sigh of release as the spirit sought its home. But from the hoard they took nothing, for they had learned to their cost the power of its warding spells.

And then step by careful step, they felt their way along the passages that led toward the world of men. At each fork and turning, Kon traced the shape of a dwarf-rune on Bera's hand and she sang out a word that had never before been shaped by human tongue. The sounds passed through her like a wind, but she wondered if Kon, who had made the shapes his own, was committing the names to memory. When after a time the passage widened and they paused to rest, she asked him if it was so.

"I was trained to remember such things," Kon

replied. "But the word is nothing without meaning, and Bera, as you sing each rune, as much as
a human can, I glimpse its essence! Odin has
walked even here! The runes that he gave the
duergar tell of stress and structure, of density and
duration, of the inner nature of the elements from
which the gods shaped our world. Does that
sound like madness?"

"Not to me," she answered. "For somehow I
have ceased to fear the dark. I can feel the shape
of the space around me, and each kind of rock we
come to sings like a different harpstring. I think
that if I could sing the right note my own shape
would alter and I could move through the stone as
a fish swims in the sea!"

"Do not try it!" he exclaimed, putting his arms
around her. "The shape you have now is far too
fair!"

Bera laughed then, though her pulse was racing, and they resumed their journey toward the
day.

A time came when Bera found her feet dragging and began to wonder if her strength would
last. The way down had not seemed so long—it
came to her that perhaps the duergar were leading
them astray, and for the moment it took to thrust
that thought away she could no longer hear the
song. It was the strain of all she had been
through, she told herself. Surely Freyja would not
abandon her!

Kon felt her falter and slipped his arm around
her, and supported by his strength she went on.
He was arrogant, she thought, leaning against
him, but no more so than any other man, and he
had done his best to atone.

Bera did not know how long they climbed after
that, for time was a concept she had willed herself
to forget. But suddenly Kon halted. She started to

ask him why when she realized she was hearing a new sound, hearing it with her fleshly ears.

"The farm folk—" Kon's voice cracked. "They are calling at the entrance to the caves." He cleared his throat and for the first time sang out himself, first one dwarf-rune and then another. Bera listened to the echoes and sensed completion and balance, as of something in right relation to its surroundings, and then to her inner hearing came a sound like laughter.

Kon pulled her forward. Not caring if they bumped against the rough walls or tripped on stones, they scrambled up the passageway.

They had entered the caves in the morning. But when Kon and Bera squeezed through the opening and out into the open air at last the torches of the sunset had been lit and all the western heavens were ablaze. Bera cried out and hid her face against Kon's shoulder, feeling as if the light were burning into her brain.

"Let her be—" came Groa's voice from somewhere close by. "Her eyes cannot bear the light after so long, but they will recover soon."

Bera whimpered, and felt herself pillowed on the older woman's soft breast, breathing in the familiar scent of the herbs with which Groa washed her hair.

"By all the gods," she heard the holder say, "this is a wonder. It was just past noon when the seidhkona started up, crying out that you two were in danger, and made us come up here. We saw the marks in the dust where you went in and then we understood her, right enough, but we would have given you up for lost, lad. It was the wisewoman who would not let us cease calling."

"There, my darling," murmured Groa, patting Bera's back as if she were a child, "it will be better soon."

Bera burst into tears, and it was not until much later that she could explain that she wept because she could no longer hear the singing of the stones.

The seidhkona and her pupil stayed at Reidar's farmstead for eight days. The holder would have welcomed them for longer, for the whole winter even, grateful as he was for the return of the family's legendary horn. Arnor had taken himself and his shame homeward the next day, but Kon Grípirsson remained.

For the first few days Bera felt as if she had been beaten all over her body, and it was some time before she could bear the full light of the sun. She asked Groa how to fulfill the pledge she had made to the goddess, and wondered why the older woman answered that the Lady would no doubt find a way to let her know what she wanted, and then smiled.

It was not until the evening before they were supposed to leave that Bera began to understand. She had gone out to look at the sunset, but instead she found herself gazing eastward, toward the gray dome of stone.

"Do you miss the duergar's music?" asked a quiet voice beside her. "In my dreams I still hear the sound of your voice singing out the runes. And I feel the sweetness of you in my arms, and then I wake and weep because I am alone. Bera, can't you forgive me? You have scarcely said two words to me since we came down from the hill."

"There is nothing to forgive," she said slowly, still looking toward the mountain.

"You almost died because of me!" Kon exclaimed.

"It it had not been for me, you would never have gone to the hill," Bera replied.

"We were both foolish, then," he said, a little

more steadily, "and we were both wise. It took your magic and mine together to get us out of there"

And a little help from the goddess, thought Bera, smiling. And in that moment she understood the need of the man who stood beside her, and knew what Freyja wanted as an offering. She turned to face him.

A pulse was beating in Kon's throat and suddenly the hammer-beat of her own heart was the same. His fingers brushed the curling hair back from her brows, tender as if he reached out to stroke some wild thing, then slid down across the soft skin of her neck to her breast. Bera sighed, lifting her face to receive his kiss, and as Kon's arms closed around her she heard music once more.

"Stay with me!"

It was morning. Kon stood with Bera in the farmyard, watching as Reidar's man settled the chest that held the seidhkona's clothing into the wagon and came back to pick up Bera's, which sat waiting by the door.

"Bera, you accused me once of not honoring your magic. You proved its worth, but I think the value of mine was proved to you as well. What power in the world can stand against us if are together?"

"Together?" Bera looked at him, and felt her flesh tingle with memory. "As your wife? You think we would be equals, but in the king's household what work would there be for me?" She fought to keep her voice from trembling. She had lain awake for long the night before, working through what she would do if he should ask this of her, what she must say.

"I love you," Kon said simply. His black hair

glinted with inky lights in the sun. "We can do what you wish, go where you say—"

She shook her head. "I would not take you from your work, my love, and you must not seek to draw me from mine. I still have much to learn. The people need their seeress. There is no one who would need me as much if I went with you."

"Except for me," he said bitterly. "Does that mean nothing?"

"It means to me what it means to you," she whispered. "My body will ache for yours in the nights to come, and my spirit will mourn, but this is where my weird drives me. Cannot you understand?"

"Up there, in the mountain, I thought the stone was unyielding," Kon said grimly, "but you are harder. And yet there was a song in it. I will remember that, and so must you."

He smiled suddenly, so sweetly that Bera almost forgot her resolve. "We will meet again. I have seen it in the runes."

Which runes? Bera wondered. But as she opened her senses to the beauty of the day it seemed as if the very earth beneath her feet were singing and she knew it was true.

GARDEN OF GLORIES
by Jennifer Roberson

Jennifer's first story in print appeared in *Sword and Sorceress I,* and she had a story in every volume through VI, by which time her novel writing career was in high gear. She has two bestselling fantasy series: the eight-volume "Chronicles of the Cheysuli" and the four-volume "Sword Dancer" saga. She made her mainstream hardcover debut with *Lady of the Forest,* a historical reinterpretation of the Robin Hood legend, emphasizing Marian's role. But when I started *Marion Zimmer Bradley's Fantasy Magazine*, she still made time in her busy schedule to write a story for my first issue, as well as the cover story for issue #16.

Her forthcoming novels include *The Golden Key* (a fantasy collaboration with Melanie Rawn and Kate Elliot), *Glen of Sorrows* (a historical novel set in seventeenth century Scotland,) and a new fantasy trilogy: *Prince of Night, Queen of Sleep,* and *King of Dreams.* I'm looking forward to reading them.

Feidra surveyed the courtyard garden with a practiced eye. But it was a soft eye, not seeking now to find fault; she had found fault already, had corrected it, and thus was given leave to take pleasure in what she had wrought.

"Magic," she said, and grinned. "Merris would laugh."

Merris would. Merris was like that. She said what she would say, laughed when she would laugh, ridiculed against her taste that which was another's.

It did not disturb Feidra. Merris was Merris. Feidra was—Feidra. Her pleasures were her own, if predictable; her powers insignificant among those others counted as real, as worthy, as meaningful within the context of their lives. Small lives, she thought, if painted with bloodier colors; hers was far more fruitful, the subtlety more peaceful.

Fruit. Feidra's smile broadened. The courtyard would offer its bounty in good time: oranges, sweet and juicy; lemons for their tartness; grapefruits for her breakfast. For now the trees bloomed, buzzing with bees; Feidra loved the sound. Let others have their shouts, their war cries, their songs of steel and death.

Rank upon rank of terraced, brick-bordered gardens formed stair-steps up the hand-smoothed walls. As militaristic, Feidra thought, in their arrangement as Merris was in war. Foliage matched hue for hue, for texture, for height; the colors and size of petals delicate as often as blatant. But the militancy of her gardens ruled with perhaps more kindness than the sere desert scape of Merris' life; a spirit found peace, not warfare, in the ripe beauty of Feidra's garden. A different kind of glory than that Merris courted.

She closed her eyes. The sun was warm on her

face, wholly seductive, suggesting refuge in indolence, in irresponsibility after too much time spent in work; and it was due her, she felt, after ministrations. All the importunate weeds pulled, the untamed roses checked into order out of rank chaos, the upstart vines coaxed to the challenge of new trellises, the hummingbirds welcomed with a little sugar and water set out in a clay bowl rimmed in crimson glaze. The bees would water there, too, drawn by the sweetness, but Feidra did not mind. Let them share as they would. Or not. It was the way of the world.

Spring yet, but warming toward summer. For now the days were temperate, seductive in full measure after the cold of winter. She knew of few people who could ignore the days, the warmth, and the erotica of the season, to keep within their homes.

She was barefoot. Clay tiles beneath her feet warmed in the sunlight. Damp earth dried on flesh, turning to crusted mud that would flake off as she walked. She did not doubt her face bore testament also to her offices, and did not care.

Merris, of course, would laugh. Merris would toss her a damp cloth and say, with excess irony, that she should clean her face; that the daughter of their father was required to be clean, so she might catch a man.

But Feidra had caught a man. Like a fish she had hooked him, and brought him home to dinner. Like a fish, he had rotted, offending her home, her garden, and she had eventually put him out of both, disposing of him, his things, like a fish left out of water too long now reeking in the sun. Unwanted under her roof.

Feidra smiled. Her face was dirty and she did not care. She had caught a man, as her father had wanted. And she had let him go.

Merris would not believe it.

* * *

The corbies crowded, stealing the breath from her. But better breath than blood; there was too much blood in the grass for them to deal with hers, still mostly in her body, and she had bound her wounds. None so bad as to die from; she would be well enough. But the spirit, knowing loss, bled yet, and would, until she fashioned in her mind a victory out of defeat.

It would require time, and healing. Time Merris had aplenty now, for the victor had picked the spoils, stealing from dead and dying what wealth could be judged to spend; a silver pin, a ring, boots, a fine-hilted knife. They were soldiers, not merchants; there was little to fill a purse save what commerce would result from the aftermath of war.

They had believed her dead, and she had not disabused them of it. She had made no sound, offered no resistance, as they tore the pin from her tunic, worked the boots from her feet, pulled the ring from her finger. A poor ring, worth little, save in its giver; but Kendig was dead, and what she had of him was muttered over by enemies for its lack of value, but put into purses regardless.

What she had of him, too, was the heart that yet beat in her breast, and that she could not forget. Forgive, perhaps, someday; she had hoped they would die together when the day came for it, pledged like man and wife at the pulpit of battle, but he had died without her. And left her to live after all, so she could feel his blood drying into the weave of her tunic, crusting on her face.

Feidra, she thought, would bring her a bowl of cool citrus-scented water and a cloth to be sopped in it, to wash the blood away while she let Merris brood. It was what she did so well, did Feidra:

ministering to others when lured out of her garden; and brooding was, always, what Merris was better at.

Brooding. And battle.

The corbies crowded. She lacked a pin, boots, a ring; had lost sword and knife as well. But she lived, and would; it was for her to survive, to recover, to fight again at need.

Feidra would grieve for Kendig. Feidra did not know him, but would grieve nonetheless. Her gift was to make things live. Her curse was to watch them die.

Feidra would grieve, as well, for the sister who spurned men who looked on women as weaklings, but who had found a man nonetheless who treated her as his equal in battle as well as in bed. He was hard come by, was Kendig, and harder to keep; Feidra had had her choice among the men who came to call, but Merris never knew it. Nor had wanted it.

She shifted, biting her lip. He was heavy, was dead Kendig; they had learned to fit themselves to one another in all the ways a man and woman could, but they had not planned for death. They had not teased death, mocking its aspect, its ascendancy, and now Kendig's body, all the stilled parts of his body, was manifestly heavier, more awkward than imagined.

Merris cursed the corbies as she dragged herself from beneath the butchered body. It was the price of war, was death; she and Kendig had challenged death aplenty, yet never courted it. They had not loved it that much, offering only respect as soldiers did.

But death was blind to the difference, to the semantics of their lives. Death loved Kendig, too. Merris, death ignored.

* * *

The bench was warm beneath Feidra's buttocks clad only in loose-woven linen. Unlike stone, wood caught and imprisoned the sun until it turned away its face, and so Feidra, shut-eyed, catlike, reveled in it: bare muddy toes against spring-warmed stone clad in its raiment of petals; the buttocks, so nearly naked, content upon the wood, her spine equally pleased to rest against a wall. Near her ear a bee buzzed its office: to lift from the blossom the nectar that would give life to another plant; that would, in its bounty, give flavor to the honey.

The world was livid crimson beyond the fragile lids. A sorry shield, she thought, made of flesh and lashes, not at all like the studded shield Merris carried in war to turn back the blades, the arrows, the stones of the enemy. If Feidra raised *her* shield, no enemy would come to call; only the brilliance of the day, and the promise of the season.

She knew her garden, her courtyard. She knew its sounds, its smells. She knew the moment someone arrived at her gate. The day altered its song, the shadow muted sunlight.

"Come in," Feidra invited, not raising the fleshly shield. "Share the day with me. It is too glorious to waste."

"Glory," Merris said, "is dependent on one's taste."

Feidra stood up all at once. The sun, let into her eyes, dazzled her a moment, so that all she saw was a figure at the gate with a hand upon the iron as if it could not let go.

She took inventory of her sister as she did of her garden. Weeds to pull, she thought, and thorns to cut back, and dry soil to water so Merris might bloom again, restored from the hostility of a long season left untended, the sterility of drought.

Merris was, had always been, the less beautiful of them, in the ways a man counted. But Feidra, who knew better, counted beauty in the spirit, in the strength of a stubborn will. Merris was thin, severe, honed keen and clean by battle; as sharp in tongue and wit as the steel of her blades. But as true, also, if less kind than some might prefer.

Feidra blinked. Blades. Gone.

Merris, come home again. With no weapons at all.

"You lost," she said abruptly.

Merris did not flinch. "This time, yes. Next time, we will win."

"We?"

A shrug, quickly accomplished: a casual hitch of a shoulder. "Whoever I take service with. Whoever will have me."

Feidra no longer felt the warmth of the clay tiles as she crossed the courtyard. The callused hand still gripped the iron. Feidra put hers upon it. Callus upon callus. One hand wielded a sword, the other a trowel.

"Come in," Feidra said. "Do you expect ceremony?"

The edged smile was faint. "If I did, I would not have come. I know the woman who lives here."

Feidra smiled. She wanted to laugh, but could find no heart for it. Merris cherished honesty, as cruel as it was kind. She stepped back and unlatched the gate, iron grinding on iron. "She lives here yet," Feidra said, "if alone."

Merris stilled into stone. "Is he dead, then? Edvik?"

"Oh, no . . . not so far as I know." She knew it was not the sort of answer Merris expected. "When last I saw him, he was quite alive."

"Ah. Drinking again, is he?" Merris stepped

through the gate into the courtyard. "A pretty place for a man, no? He need do nothing but enjoy your bounty as well as your body. And no earning of it, no right to either."

Feidra shut the gate again. "He had right. Once. The priestess bound us."

"Father wanted you *un*bound," Merris said dryly, "and immediately. Of all the men who came, you chose him."

"He was pretty," Feidra said, repeating to her sister what she had said to herself so often. "He was all the things I believed I wanted. And, for a time, did want." She set the latch again, smiling to herself as Merris stilled into silence. The courtyard and its glories did that to a soul. "There are men, and there are men. Some are worth the trouble."

"Not Edvik," Merris muttered.

"No, not Edvik. But what is life for, save to make mistakes so we may learn from them?"

Merris cast a wary eye upon her. The scar beside it lent a wicked glint. "Philosophy, from you? Father would despair."

Feidra laughed. "Father despaired of me the day I wed Edvik."

Merris' mouth hooked wryly. "His despair of you was of markedly shorter duration than his despair of me."

"Your choice," Feidra reminded. "Will you come into the house?" She thought so. Merris found little beauty in the glory of her garden. Beauty, to Merris, was steel freshly honed, and the vulgar harshness of the army. There she thrived, even as Feidra would not.

"No," Merris said. "No, let it be here. I detest roofs."

"Ah, but there is a roof even here," Feidra pointed out, glancing at the array of overhead lattices bent beneath ivy and the trailing limbs of roses. They required shoring up; it was her next project.

"A singularly more attractive roof than tile and timber," Merris demurred. "And closer to hand than the table inside."

Feidra saw why such was important as Merris moved to the bench. She had lost the lithe elegance of her step, the understated power that was her personal gift. "You are hurt."

"*Was* hurt," Merris corrected succinctly, seating herself with care upon the sun-warmed bench. "Mostly healed; I took time for it before setting out."

But there was tension in the line of her shoulders, and Feidra was not fooled. "Well, then. Shall I bring refreshment? Would your pride countenance care?"

As a child, Merris had been serious. But now she smiled. It puckered the scar by her eye. "My pride, just now, countenances much. Bring out what you will, and sit. It will do me well just being still a while."

Feidra agreed wholeheartedly, but said nothing of it.

Merris was still and took relief of it, but the courtyard was not. It was a living thing, if judged by context other than that of warfare; she had not looked upon a garden as anything but time wasted, effort expended, and fair prey to an army bent on seeking good ground. Too many times gardens had been broken apart by a siege, or beaten beneath hooves and boots. Feidra's folly, she thought, to believe a life could be governed by the shapeshifting of the seasons. What governed life was death, and a soul's avoidance of it.

Better to die of a purpose than to justify one's life by the color of a flower.

But it was warm in the garden, and redolent of citrus. The hard green knobs depended already in clusters from bee-beleagered blossoms; they would swell, alter color, and ripen—and one day she need only pluck an orange from a tree to have juice in her cup, or the sweet fragile pulp bursting to flavor within her mouth.

It was a long way from war, here in Feidra's garden. A long way from the world Merris had made her own. What could she tell her sister? What *should* she tell her sister, that Feidra might understand? That any woman could, who was raised to different needs.

Merris smiled. Her skull found purchase against the wall of Feidra's little house. Ivy importuned itself within the strands of her hair, finding little lattice; she cropped her hair man-short so as not to interfere in the practice of her trade.

She had described to Kendig once the house they had grown up in, alone but for their father. How Feidra, in her youth, acquired her mother's habits without knowing how; their mother had died when they were very young. Their father had believed his wife returned to them in the small ways of the household, and sought physical pleasures elsewhere if not another wife. He had Feidra for all but bed. For a son, he had Merris.

Except she was born a woman.

The smile died away from her mouth. How he had misunderstood. How he had shouted, and threatened, and beaten, though with a lighter hand than most. Had cajoled, had pleaded, and thundered. But she had stood firm amidst the wreckage of what had been their love. Her duty, she said, was different; he had Feidra for his household, and Merris for a war.

But a man would change that, her father assured her. She need only look to a man, and once she had one she would set aside foolish thoughts and comfort herself as a woman should: pleasing a man, tending a house, bearing his children.

Until one day it killed her, in spirit if not in body. But he had not said that. It was not necessary. She had known it from the beginning.

In war, all unexpectedly, she had found a man. And in war she had lost him. Unexpectedly.

A clink of pottery, and Feidra came through the door with cups in one hand and a pitcher in the other. It was too early for citrus, but watered wine would do. Grapes were another of the things Feidra tended.

Feidra poured in silence, handing the cup to Merris. Merris accepted with grave thanks, invoked the Goddess' blessing briefly in soldier's argot, and drank. It slid down her throat as it always did when made of Feidra's grapes: sweet and smooth and soothing.

"Edvik did not drink you dry, I see."

Feidra smiled and sipped from her own cup. "No," she answered. "But he had little time for it, once I told him to go."

A slow stirring of anger on her sister's behalf. "And how long this time?"

Feidra arched elegant, eloquent brows.

"How long before you open the gate to him as you opened it to me?"

"Oh," Feidra said, "that is done between us."

It was casual, lacking defense, stripped of explanation. It was Feidra's way.

But Merris snorted disbelief. "Done, is it? You and Edvik? He must be dead, save you deny it."

"He may be dead. But I think not; someone would come to tell me." Feidra settled beside her, sharing the warmth of the day.

Merris frowned. "How can it be done? Unless ..." She paused a long moment, considering offense unintended but nonetheless real. But they were sisters, and honest; sometimes to a fault. "Is there another, then? Have you come to your senses at last?"

Feidra shrugged. "No other."

"For you, I mean." And dryly, "I would expect it of Edvik."

"No, there is no other for me. For Edvik, perhaps, but that does not matter. . . ." Her sideways glance was amused. "Is it so difficult to believe I might at last be a woman without a man?"

"*You?*"

Feidra laughed. She sipped. She enjoyed the moment.

"Not you," Merris declared. Then, "Oh, but it will not last."

"Perhaps. Perhaps not. I am not counting the days." Feidra sighed and persuaded ivy to disassociate itself from her ear, where it courted her curls. "How many times have you told me a woman requires no man to be whole? To be accepted for herself?"

"Many times," Merris answered, "but not so many of late. It has been three years since I was last here."

Feidra frowned. "And two since I put Edvik out."

It astounded Merris. "Two years? Alone? You?" She paused. "Are you ill?" she asked severely.

Her sister smiled the smile of a cat. "You mimic Father, now. He should live again, to hear you."

"But ..." Merris shut her mouth, it displeased her to know she claimed any part of him. "Feidra—surely others have come to call."

"Of course they have," Feidra said matter-of-factly. "But I am content."

"Alone."

"Alone." She glanced at her sister. "You, of all people, should know the pleasure of that."

"Pleasure? I would say: necessity." And thought then of Kendig, knowing herself a liar even to herself.

"You've always been so strong," Feidra said reflectively. "You stood up to Father, refused to be what he expected you to be. And went off to make your own way. I envied you that strength, that freedom . . . I had so little of either."

"But—you *wanted* to get married!"

"Of course I did. I regret none of it."

Merris twisted her mouth. "Not even Edvik?"

"Oh, I might have wished later I had been wiser in my choosing, but I *did* the choosing. In fact, I found my strength and my freedom. Father gave in at last."

The irony was habitual. "Probably because he feared his only remaining daughter would follow her elder sister."

"Oh, no, he knew better." Feidra grinned. "Can you see me on a battlefield taking to task a soldier for crushing the grass beneath his boots?"

"And trying summarily to restore it?" Merris grinned back. "You should hire on to those who have lost their gardens to war; you would be rich in short order!"

"Perhaps I should," Feidra said, but Merris knew she would not. Her work was here. Her strength, her magic, was rooted in her courtyard.

"So, for two years you have lived without a man." Merris scratched at the healing scar beside her left eye. "I would not believe it had anyone else said so."

"Nor did Edvik, at first. He came back twenty-one times."

"And on the twenty-second?"

Feidra's expression was serious. "There was no twenty-second. He believed me, then."

"Or was too drunk to care any more."

"He says not. The townfolk say not. But it no longer matters." Feidra said contentedly, "I tend my house for me."

Merris grunted. "For now."

"For now. I swore no oath. I am not opposed to men, you see, only to curtailment of the spirit." She paused. "But you know about that."

"I know," Merris said, and felt hollow inside.

"And so now I understand what it is you tried to tell me, so many years ago. That a woman should be what she is, and not what men—fathers, brothers, or husbands—would have her be."

Quietly Merris said, "But there is compromise."

"*You* say so? You?" Feidra laughed. "You are the most uncompromising soul I know!"

Merris made no answer.

"Merris—you let no man dictate what you should be."

"No."

"You follow your own desires."

"Yes."

"And are happy for it!"

Merris sighed. "Sometimes. Sometimes—not so happy."

"When are you not?" Feidra challenged, then amended her tone. "Oh, I am sorry . . . surely you do not find happiness in war. In—killing."

"No, not happiness. Competency. Control." Merris cradled the pottery cup in both palms, scraping baked clay against the horn of her hands.

"A feeling of worth, that I can do what I am best at, and be honored for it."

"Killing."

"Fighting," Merris corrected. "Earning my pay in service to another."

"And do you believe in them all? These lords you serve, these causes?"

"I am not a whore," Merris answered, knowing it would hurt her. "If there is peace won before a battle, it pleases me. But all too often there is not, and I am left to fight."

"Do you shock the enemy? Do you win because of that?"

Merris smiled briefly. "I win because I am good."

"At killing."

Merris set down the cup. "I am not made for gardens," she said, "any more than you are made for war. Kendig understood."

Eventually Feidra asked, "Who is Kendig?"

"Was," she said tautly. "My sword-mate. My bed-mate. The only man I have ever been able—and free—to love." She waited for no blurt of shock, no comment of disbelief, but looked straightly at her sister. "I came because I knew you could offer a child more than I. That you *would*."

Color fled from Feidra. The blossoms behind her were made lewdly lurid by the pallor of her face.

"I know it grieved you," Merris said gently, "that there would be no children. I could not perceive it; war is no place for a child, nor a mother who kills men. A warrior's mind does not shape itself to think of bearing children. And so I did not. And then there was Kendig. And now—there is a child."

Feidra's breathing was ragged.

"What else is there to do?" Merris asked. "Our magic is alien to one another. I am dark, and you are light. I am death, and you are life."

"Merris."

"The child will be what it is meant to be. But I am less forgiving, less tolerant than you. The first time my daughter restored a boot-crushed flower, I would ridicule her for it. And I refuse to be my father."

Sharply: "And on the day your son picks up a trowel and wields it as a sword?"

Merris smiled. "It need not be a son."

The cup fell from Feidra's hands and shattered against the tile. "Oh . . . oh, Merris . . ."

"This is your gift," her sister declared, "this magic you have wrought here in your courtyard. A child should have a choice."

"But—you need not go! You need not leave it to me!" Spots of livid color blazed in Feidra's cheeks. "You need not desert your child!"

"I am a soldier," Merris said. "It is all I know."

"But you could live here, with me! Or—" Feidra made shift to repair the potential schism, "—or not, if you prefer; there are *other* houses—"

"But no gardens such as this." Merris bent down and picked up, one by one, the shards of shattered cup. She set the pieces into her sister's lap, into cool, sun-bleached linen. "She—or he—will thrive in Feidra's garden."

Feidra stared blindly at the little pile of clay. One by one she picked up the shards and pieced them, like a puzzle, together again. In her palms the cup was whole—and did not break apart when she set it onto the bench between them.

"You see?" Merris said. "Kendig knew what I was. He loved me for it. I know what you are, and love you equally." She set one hand into her sister's curly hair, cupping her skull, and leaned her scarred forehead against Feidra's milky brow. "This is your glory," she whispered. "It has no weakness, but strength; it is different, that is all." She swallowed painfully. "Permit my child to have a chance to know it. To know and respect the difference."

In silence, when she could, Feidra nodded. And the tears that dampened her cheeks also dampened her sister's, falling at last to stain the spring-warmed, petal-clad tile beneath their dusty feet.

STEALING THE POWER
by Linda J. Dunn

Linda says that she always planned to be a writer until she "married someone who didn't approve of such nonsense." It won't surprise any writer to learn that this was not a marriage 'until death do us part,' although it did last long enough to produce two children. While surviving divorce, single motherhood, full-time work, and part-time college, Linda discovered word processors, which renewed her determination to make enough spare time to write.

"Seven years and one supportive husband later" Linda sold her first story. This one is her fifth sale in a year-and-a-half of professional writing. She lives with her husband and children in a rural community with "the usual assortment of cats" and is writing children's fantasy books.

Solveig cringed as she heard her father's cries.

Why doesn't he ever listen to me? Really listen?

"I demand to know the meaning of this!" Her father held up a rather sickly looking lizard and dangled it before her eyes.

"I tried to tell you last night, Father, but you were too busy—"

"Busy? Of course I was busy. That demon wizard who's been sucking the magic out of all the other wizards will be here shortly and you want to waste my time with idle gossip?"

"It was no idle gossip, Father. What I have to say is very important."

"It can't be any more important than this." He shook the little lizard by its tail. "The spell's gone bad. This was supposed to be a mighty dragon to protect us. Instead, all I've got a tiny lizard. Did you gather the herbs just before the dawn, as I instructed?"

"Yes, Father."

"And those three strands of hair were your own, right? You plucked them out by the roots as I instructed and didn't just comb them out?"

"Yes, Father, but—"

"Silence! I need to think. If you followed my orders, then it must be something I did wrong myself. We should have a dragon here. Not this thing."

"Father, I—"

"Quite, I say. Fool woman. That spell of confusion I put over the woods won't deter Bela for long. He could be here any moment."

"He reached the woods last night."

"What? Why didn't you tell me this?"

"I *tried* to warn you. You kept telling me to be quiet and leave you alone. So I did."

"All right. Never mind that now. I must hurry. There's no time for another dragon, but perhaps I can find something else in the book to save us."

Solveig caught the little lizard as her father tossed it over his shoulder and rushed back to his room. She shook her head and slipped it into her pocket.

Her father was a nice man, but hopelessly incompetent when it came to magic. Were their home any less isolated, he'd have been laughed out of the craft years ago.

And now everyone looked to him to save them from the evil wizard Bela. There seemed no chance of success.

Each time Bela conquered another wizard, he folded their energy in with his own. Now he was so powerful that none of the greatest wizards could possibly have hoped to defeat him.

And they were already vanquished. The only remaining wizard in all the seven kingdoms was Taliesin, Solveig's father.

Solveig stepped outside the hut and took a deep breath. The morning air smelled of poison from the swamps, but she could still detect the movement of Bela through the woods. No doubt he never even tried to dismiss her father's weak spell. He had time. This was the last wizard. He would want to enjoy his hunt and stretch out the suspense for as long as possible.

She began removing her clothes as she called out to her father. Bela would be there in minutes. There was no time for another spell. Either the magic made last night would be successful or they were all doomed.

"Taliesin," a voice called. "I'm here. Are you ready to be absorbed by me?"

Her father stepped forward, trying to present a dignified finish to his otherwise undignified life.

Bela laughed as her father chanted a spell. A weak protection charm that wouldn't save a mouse from a hungry cat.

Poor Father.

Solveig watched Bela closely as she removed the last of her garments and slipped the little lizard onto her shoulder. Surely he knew she was there. But was he prepared to face her again? Did Bela suspect? She was doomed if he did.

"Of course I know you're there, Solveig. What a strange name your father picked for you. It means, 'Dark Power.' Did you know that?"

"I knew." Solveig stepped forward and tried not to blush as her father's voice faltered and then failed.

Bela stared at her naked form for a moment and then laughed. "You're a fool if you think you can sway me to protect your father. I seduced you last night only so your father wouldn't have a virgin cow anymore. Hasn't it been a little harsh these last few years? Virgin's hair. Virgin's blood. Virgin's spittle. Is there any part of your body that hasn't been picked or prodded to produce a little something extra for your father's spells?

"You're free now, Solveig. Run before I decide to turn you into a chicken and cook you for dinner."

He laughed again and Solveig felt her cheeks growing hot. She closed her eyes and started singing softly, allowing her voice to build to a shrill screech that caused Bela to stuff his fingers in his ears.

"Now, Father." She turned to him as the little lizard slid down her shoulder and wrapped itself around her upper arm. "Now say the enchantment for the dragon. Quickly."

"But, Solveig—"

"Now!"

He fumbled through his book, speaking quickly and mumbling some of the words. Solveig prayed he got enough of it right.

Bela laughed. "You expect to scare me with shrill screaming and mutterings about dragons. Dragons are gone, my dear. I defeated them all."

A strange look came over his face as Solveig felt the change. She spread her arms and felt the little lizard digging into her flesh. Her knees buckled and then there were no knees at all. She felt herself flying and looked down at the wicked wizard below.

Who seduced who? She laughed. In dragon-speak it came out as a roll of fire.

"I've beaten dragons before," Bela shouted, shaking a fist at her. "Even magical ones. Don't expect to take me so easily."

He raised both arms and pointed. Solveig gasped as the energy filled her dragon body. Her scales glowed a soft pink and then orange. She felt power flowing through every part of her body and laughed as she flew higher and higher.

It had worked. Bela had defeated himself with his own wizardry. Now Solveig had the power of all the greatest wizards and Bela, too.

She was free now. Free to be whatever she wished in this world. Dragon, sorceress, even an ordinary girl if she so desired. She could marry and have daughters who could learn her skills—if she wanted to follow her mother's path.

She returned to land at the same spot where she had transformed only minutes before. Her wings folded and the scales faded. Once again, she stood before them naked and human.

"It was my mother who named me Solveig," she said to Bela. "And 'dark power' suits me well."

She folded up her clothes and placed them in a

basket. The lizard was still tightly coiled around her arm. No longer a living creature but a picture burned into her arm forever.

She kissed her father. "Thank you for everything. I told you once that someday you would be the greatest wizard in the land. Now I'm right."

Tears trickled down her father's cheeks. "The price you paid was too high. You cannot go back."

She smiled. "I have no wish to go back. I knew exactly what I was giving up and what I was gaining when I allowed Bela to think he was seducing me."

She turned her head to look at Bela.

This time it was her turn to laugh as the strong man of a few minutes ago grew older and deformed. He looked at his gnarled, trembling hands and screamed, fleeing into the woods.

With the loss of his magic came the loss of his immortality spells. Soon he would be little more than a feeble-minded old man begging for a living. One could almost feel sorry for him.

Almost. But not quite.

She turned to her father. "There wasn't time to tell you. I wasn't even certain it would work. But you were no match for him, not when he had the strength of our best wizards."

He nodded grimly. "But now what of you?"

She shrugged. "I'm a shapechanger now. Like my mother before me. You said she was a werehawk. You've granted me the form of a dragon."

She reached up to kiss him. "Good-bye for now. I'll return someday when I've found my mother and my destiny."

Solveig wiped a tear from the corner of his eyes.

"I had hoped you would never leave me. Your

mother promised to come back someday and the years since have been very lonely."

"No one can own another person," she told him, "and a child has to leave home sometime. I will come back. Someday we will both return. You'll see." She stepped back, holding the basket firmly between her teeth, and spreading her arms for the change.

She felt guilty about leaving her father alone to fend for himself but not guilty enough to stay. It was going to be good to see the world at last.

THE LOST PATH
by Patricia Duffy Novak

Patricia is still an Associate Professor of Agricultural Economics at Auburn University, where her husband Jim also teaches. Their daughter Sylvia is four now.

One of the side benefits of editing this anthology series is watching my writers' children grow up. Patricia made her first sale to me about the time Sylvia was born; she's had stories in *Sword and Sorceress IX* and *Sword and Sorceress X* as well as *Marion Zimmer Bradley's Fantasy Magazine* and several of the Darkover anthologies.

She is now beginning to write a novel about Alvyn and Kaitlyn.

Kaitlyn the Gray peered through the gloom, in the direction indicated by her companion, Alvyn the White. A hundred yards or so from the path, a small light did indeed twinkle. Too regular for a cook fire, it had to be a lamp.

"See?" Alvyn said happily. "I told you we'd find a place to stay."

"I think we'd be better off going back to that last town," Kaitlyn said. "We don't know what kind of folk live out here. It might not be safe."

"Go back to that town! Five miles or more, you're talking. What harm could there be in staying here? We can outsmart any country farmers."

She clucked her tongue. "If we're so smart, how did we end up in this mess? You got us lost, remember? And I'm probably a bigger fool for letting you talk me into taking this trip without a guide."

"I did not get us lost," he said firmly, a statement he had been making for hours, ever since they realized the road to Tinkertown was nowhere to be found. "No guide could have done better. The path to Tinkertown should have branched from this road, just before the stream. Either the map is wrong or someone's moved the path."

Kaitlyn used the least-soiled corner of her robe to wipe the travel dust from her face, declining to argue the issue any further in spite of the ludicrous nature of Alvyn's self-defense. Moved the path, indeed!

Back at Wizard's Keep, Alvyn had made this adventuring business sound exciting and fun. Now, all her old reservations returned in spades. He'd promised her they would arrive in Tinkertown today, to take their first real jobs as apprentice brew-spellers. Instead, they were wandering about the countryside, hungry, tired, and dirty.

She looked again at the steady glow of golden light, brighter now against the darkening twilight. It should have looked welcoming, but something made her want to say no, to insist they continue backtracking until they came to that town. But logic was on Alvyn's side, for once. There really was no harm in asking for lodging at the farm. "All right," she said reluctantly, "we'll stop here if they'll have us."

She followed Alvyn as he left the path and headed toward the light. But her feet had never been as nimble as his. "Bloody Heck," said Kaitlyn, as she stumbled over a tree root and nearly went sprawling.

Alvyn put a steadying hand under her elbow. "If you're going to curse, do it right. I could teach you some real oaths."

"No, thanks," she said, with the beginning of a smile. She could never stay mad at Alvyn for long. "And you a White wizard. What would anyone think if they heard you?"

He grinned, a flash of teeth in the darkness. "You know the truth about the robes."

Indeed she did know—that the power a wizard most desired was often the power most unsafe to summon. She, not the irreverent Alvyn, had wanted the White robes, the way of Good, but her very desire had kept her from that path. Kaitlyn was still unhappy with the choice she had made, but at least she was not a Blue wizard, summoning the powers of night and darkness. *Power is power,* the Masters always said, *yours to use for good or evil, no matter the source.* They said that, but Kaitlyn never truly believed them.

"Well, here we are," Alvyn said, as they came to a neat-looking farmhouse. A few seconds after his knock, a slim, blonde woman in long skirts opened the farmhouse door. In the shadowy light, her features were somewhat obscured, but Kaitlyn saw that she was both young and beautiful.

The woman looked them over and smiled. "Wizards," she said, pleasantly, glancing at their distinctive, if somewhat travel-stained, robes.

"What a nice surprise. We get so few visitors here."

Alvyn elbowed Kaitlyn covertly, as if to say, "See, I told you so," as the pair followed their hostess into the house, a compact but tidy structure. Comfortably furnished, too, Kaitlyn noted, as they passed into the parlor, where a larger lamp glowed brightly.

"My name is Angelin," the woman said. In the stronger light, Kaitlyn could see her clearly. Her complexion was flawless, her lips full and red. But her eyes seemed oddly out of place in that young face. Hard and blue, seeming to have a life of their own.

"Alvyn the White," said Alvyn, extending a grimy hand, which the woman took and held a moment longer than necessary. "And this is my companion, Kaitlyn the Gray. We're traveling to Tinkertown, but have lost our way in the woods."

Angelin nodded curtly at Kaitlyn, then turned her gaze back to Alvyn. "Tomorrow, I will set you on the proper path, good sir. But tonight you must stay here and rest. Unfortunately, my father isn't here to welcome you properly, but I will do what I can to ease your weariness."

A smile played along the edges of Angelin's mouth, as she slanted a glance at Alvyn. Flirtatious, Kaitlyn thought. Odd to find such behavior in a country girl. It more befitted a tavern wench. She glanced at Alvyn, who was grinning foolishly at the woman. Evidently, he didn't find their hostess' behavior unusual. Rather, he seemed to revel in the attention.

"We appreciate your kindness," Kaitlyn said. "We will gladly pay you with coin or with a service."

Angelin raised a white hand to her breast, as if to indicate revulsion at the notion of payment.

"The pleasure of your company is payment enough." She took Alvyn's arm. "Come," she said to him, "you may use my room to refresh yourself. Upstairs, in the loft. Then I will bring you dinner." She started to lead Alvyn away, and Kaitlyn stood in place, nonplussed, wondering what she should do with herself.

But then, Angelin turned and looked over her shoulder at Kaitlyn, as if on second thought. "Oh," she said, "My father's room is vacant for the night. You can find it, I'm sure." With her free hand she pointed back toward the hallway.

"I'm sure," Kaitlyn echoed, working hard to keep her temper in check. She had never before encountered such rudeness! Of course, she'd only left the safe haven of Wizard's Keep a handful of days before, and there were—she knew quite well—quite a few experiences she lacked. She gave a mental shrug and turned to find her own quarters, noting before she did that Angelin's long fingers were gently massaging Alvyn's arm.

The room Kaitlyn had been assigned was large and comfortable, with its own water barrel and wash tub, and even a privy closet. Towels and soap had been laid out, ready for a bather. Luxury indeed after the cheap inns in which she'd passed the last few nights. No doubt Angelin's father liked a good soak after a hot day in the fields. Odd, though, that there was no trace of a man's previous occupancy—no clothes, no boots, no personal belongings of any kind.

Kaitlyn filled the tub with water from the barrel, then shrugged out of her dirty robe and breeches and unbraided her hair. A good wash would make her feel better, she told herself as she submerged herself in the cool water and scrubbed vigorously. She hadn't felt really clean since they'd left the Keep.

Still, something continued to trouble her. Alvyn's easy desertion, maybe. But it was ridiculous to be upset about that. He was free to do what he wanted. There were no ties between them other than friendship and a sympathy of magic that allowed them to work together well.

When she finished bathing, she toweled herself dry and put on a more-or-less clean set of clothing. She caught her damp hair back in a wooden clip, then feeling far more presentable than she had upon arrival, wandered back to the parlor.

Alvyn wasn't there, nor was Angelin. Kaitlyn paced the room for a minute. Darn it, the woman had promised them dinner. Or was that offer for Alvyn alone?

And what was he up to, all this time? He was, after all, supposed to be her traveling companion. No matter how they squabbled, she'd never desert him like this.

From upstairs, in the loft, came the sound of muffled laughter. The first laugh was light and high; the second, deeper and male. Kaitlyn had known Alvyn for almost a dozen years—they'd arrived at Wizard's Keep on the same day, two frightened children—but she'd never heard him laugh that way before. And she didn't like it.

"Alvyn," she called up the stairs. "Are you all right?"

A few moments later, Angelin appeared at the head of the stairway, looking distinctly annoyed, but her voice, when she spoke, was pleasant. "We'll be right there, Mistress Kaitlyn. Make yourself at home."

True to her word, Angelin appeared a few minutes later, followed by a much-improved-looking Alvyn. His dark hair was washed and slicked neatly against his head. And like her, he'd donned his least soiled robe. All and all, she supposed he wasn't a bad looking young man. Kind of handsome, really. And he was a wizard, to boot. No doubt there was a certain attractiveness in him. Bar maids and tavern girls had flirted with him often enough. But he'd never seemed to notice. Now, though, his face bore an idiotic and bemused expression as he followed Angelin into the parlor, not even glancing at Kaitlyn.

"Be seated, young Master," Angelin simpered, patting a chair. "And you, too, Mistress." She gave Kaitlyn a quick glance, then returned her attention to Alvyn. "Now, then, let me see about supper. Our kitchen is a humble room. I'll bring our repast to you, here.'

"Well, what do you think?" Kaitlyn asked, as soon as Angelin left them.

"Huh?"

"Odd situation, don't you think? A woman all alone out here. Her father nowhere to be seen."

Alvyn frowned. "What did you say? I'm sorry. I wasn't listening." All the while, his eyes were fixed on the doorway through which Angelin had passed, as if he could think of nothing other than her return.

About him, Kaitlyn detected the not-so-subtle odor of wine and wondered if he was drunk. "Alvyn, what's the matter with you?"

He shook his head, but said nothing. Kaitlyn, disgusted, lapsed into silence.

Angelin returned with a platter piled high with bread, cheese, dried meat, and sliced fruit. She set the platter on the room's one table, then disappeared again, only to return a few seconds later with three glasses and a jug of wine.

"Lovely," Alvyn murmured, staring at Angelin instead of the food.

While Angelin poured the wine, Kaitlyn built herself a thick sandwich. Alvyn remained seated, staring at Angelin. "Aren't you hungry?" Kaitlyn said.

"What?" Alvyn didn't shift his gaze.

"Oh, never mind."

"Let me wait on you, Master Alvyn," Angelin said, as she handed a glass of wine to Kaitlyn. It was a heavy, red color, with an acid odor—much like the odor that had emanated from Alvyn. The wine reminded Kaitlyn, incongruously, of blood. She touched her tongue once, then twice, to the liquid, and set the glass down. Alvyn, she noted, drank his cup dry.

The bread was yeasty and pungent, and the cheese full flavored and delicious. But the sight of Angelin fawning over Alvyn—even going so far as to hand feed him bits of fruit and cheese—was almost more than Kaitlyn could stomach. She had been ravenous; now she could barely manage to finish her sandwich. By all the Gods, she thought she would vomit if she had to witness much more of this bizarre flirtation.

"I'm tired," she said. Getting no response, she rose.

Her action caught Angelin's attention. "But, Mistress, you haven't finished your wine. Drink it, I pray you. It will speed you to your rest."

Kaitlyn stooped to pick up the glass. "I'll drink it in my room. Thank you?"

"You promise?" Angelin's blue eyes held an odd intensity.

"Yes," said Kaitlyn, with absolutely no intention of complying Nothing in her wizard's oath precluded convenient lies on social occasions.

As soon as she got to her room, she tossed the contents of the glass into the privy.

Unable to sleep, Kaitlyn lay in bed, listening to the sounds of laughter coming from the parlor. Then, the thump of feet on the stairs leading to the loft. They were up there together now, she supposed. Try as she might, she could not quite stop her mind from manufacturing pictures of what they might be doing.

It was not so much that Alvyn had found Angelin attractive that annoyed her; at least, that's what she told herself. It was the way he had ignored her, as if she no longer mattered. All those years of friendship coming to nothing when a pretty girl beckoned. She thought of Alvyn's face, blank and stupid, as he waited for Angelin to return from the kitchen. He was absolutely besotted, bewitched by that simpering blonde she-goat.

Bewitched. Kaitlyn bolted upright in the bed. All those tavern wenches, some of them as pretty as Angelin, had won not so much as a second glance from Alvyn. Why was he so intrigued by this particular woman? Was there magic here?

Quietly, she slid out of bed and into her robe. She calmed her mind and reached for the source of her own power—the neutral forces.

And tapped nothing. Not a trace of power.

Her heart lurched. A power void was impossible. If the Gray forces were untouchable, then another force blocked her efforts.

She reached into her pack and pulled out the four little power stones—red, gray, white, and blue. Normally, they would all be glowing, some more brightly than others, but now three were dark; only the blue glowed, and that one burned with a surprising intensity.

Oh, Gods. She almost cried aloud. The force that blocked her own magic was the Blue, the one power of the four she could not summon. By her oath, she was forbidden to summon any power other than the one chosen for her in the Great Test. She had learned that she had the power to summon three powers, White, Gray and Red. Of these, only the Gray was safe for her; either Red or White would lead to disaster. The Blue, though, she had not been able to summon at all. She remembered Master Fen's gentle admonition on the day of her Test: "You have never shown much respect for the Dark powers."

Not, "You have never shown any talent with the Dark powers." Rather, "You lack respect." Did she, in fact, have the talent to summon the Dark powers, a talent she had blocked because of her profound distaste?

But none of that mattered now. She put her head in her hands, sunk in misery. What would become of Alvyn? A White wizard, caught in a Blue trap. Angelin would suck his power, leaving him permanently disabled, never again able to summon the forces—if he survived at all.

She should have known. By all the Gods, she should have known. If she had not been so stubborn about the lost path and so angry by what she thought was Alvyn's betrayal, she would have realized that he was bespelled. Master Fen, her favorite of the teachers at Wizard's Keep, had warned her to beware of her pride. And now her pride had led to Alvyn's ruin.

No. She would not give in without battle. Whether she could draw her power or not, she would have to try and save him.

Barefoot, she crept from her room and mounted the stairs to the loft, not yet knowing what she would do. At the top of the stairs, she found not a door, but an invisible wall, a summoning of the dark powers into a tangible barrier. Kaitlyn pushed and struggled, but she could not pass.

She felt a wash of despair, and the darkness

seemed to reach into her very soul, opening a path inside her that had previously been shut. Despair and darkness. The power of hate.

With hardly a thought about the oath she was breaking, Kaitlyn reached. And something flooded her. A power unlike any other she had experienced. Not evil, exactly, but a dark and terrible presence. She extended a hand, and the barrier that had seemed so real only moments before crumbled at her touch.

She strode forward, into the loft, where the soft glow of the rising moon shone through the single window, onto the bed. Angelin was crouched there, naked, like some dangerous animal, while Alvyn lay still and quiet in the sheets.

For a heartbreaking moment, Kaitlyn thought she was too late. Then Alvyn's hand moved and his eyelid twitched. Not dead. But whether he was harmed or not, Kaitlyn could not tell.

"I know what you are, Angelin," Kaitlyn said. "Succubus. Witch. Breaker of Oaths."

Angelin gave a low growl as she rose from the bed. Her face was no longer the face of a beautiful girl, but rather the face of a hag. Only her eyes—the hard blue eyes—remained unchanged.

The thing on the bed raised its hand. "You lied to me, girl. You didn't drink your wine. Even so, you will not stop me." Gone was the light, girlish voice, replaced by a guttural snarl.

The creature drew a web of power into her upraised hand, then hurled it at Kaitlyn. Instead of resisting the blow, Kaitlyn pulled in the power, letting it flow through her. "You cannot harm me, witch. I am Kaitlyn the Gray of Wizard's Keep."

With another growl, the creature launched itself at Kaitlyn, almost catching her off guard. But she saw the flicker of motion just in time and moved with the force of the blow, physical this time, and the witch, not Kaitlyn, went sprawling.

The Blue power was dissipating. Kaitlyn could feel it wane in strength. And she called for her own true power, the Gray force, and heard it answer. Her fingers began to move in weaving motions, but before she could set her trap, the witch rose from the floor.

"I curse you, Kaitlyn the Gray," the witch said. "You are apostate now. Oath breaker. No better than I."

With that, the creature pulled the last shreds of the Dark power about itself and vanished.

"Well, there's the path, right where you said it should be. I owe you an apology, Alvyn." Where brambles and bushes had seemed to grow the day before, now there was an open road, complete with a sign saying, "Four Miles to Tinkertown."

Alvyn nodded glumly. His face was pale and drawn; all the color had drained from his lips and his eyes were deeply shadowed. It would be a day or two, Kaitlyn suspected, before he fully recovered from the spell. She was almost certain the witch had put her own blood into the wine; Alvyn would not be entirely free of her influence until his body had time to neutralize the poison.

"Illusion," he said, with a sigh. "Dark illusion. That witch set it to trap us, and I didn't detect it. I feel like a fool. If I had only checked my stones."

"No, it was my fault. I should have trusted you about the path, instead of arguing and getting mad. Then maybe we'd have thought about traps."

"You weren't the one who almost fell into that creature's hands forever. That was my stupidity alone."

"No." Kaitlyn shook her head emphatically. "All the witch's power was focused on you. You were probably more than half-bespelled as soon as you laid eyes on her. I should've been watching out for you, but I was too stubborn and angry."

"But you saved my life, Kaitlyn. That's all that matters to me."

She shook her head, unable to let go of her guilt. "Well, here's the road. How are you fixed for coins?"

He put a hand into his pocket and pulled out a small scattering of coppers. "Four pence, and— what's this?" He looked hopeful for a moment, then puzzled. "A laundry marker. I must have left something at Wizard's Keep. Odd, I thought I packed all my clothes before we left."

She suppressed a groan. Leave it to Alvyn to worry about laundry at a time like this. "You'd better take some more money." She handed him two silver pieces.

He stared at her, then tried to give back the coins. "Why are you giving me these? You hold onto them. You've always been better with money. I'll just spend it in a tavern or on some craziness. At least that's what you always tell me."

"You'll have to manage your own money from now on. I'm not going with you, Alvyn. I'm going back to the Keep."

"What?" He looked up, his dark eyes enormous in his too pale face. "I thought you said you didn't blame me for what happened? I'm sorry Kaitlyn. I wouldn't hurt you for the world. Not if I could help it."

She swallowed, feeling the hot sting of tears behind her eyes. "That's not it," she said. "I broke my oath."

"What?" He frowned in puzzlement. She had told him already the gist of what had happened in her battle with the witch, but he had been groggy and debilitated and may not have remembered much.

"I summoned the Blue forces. Against my oath."

"But you did it to save me."

"Nevertheless, I am an oath-breaker."

"I'll come with you."

She shook her head. "The beer-makers are waiting for us. We took a job. At least one of us should honor that commitment."

"Kaitlyn, please—"

"Alvyn, this is hard enough. Please don't make it any harder. I'll be all right, I promise, whatever the Masters decide." They could strip her of her robe and her powers; she expected nothing less for what she'd done. But she prayed they would allow her to do penance, instead. She desperately wanted a second chance. "Please go now," she said.

He took a step toward her, reaching, as if he would touch her. Then he stopped—perhaps reading the pain in her eyes, pain which she wished to keep private. "Good luck, Kaitlyn. May the Gods watch over you."

"Good-bye," she whispered, and stood for a moment, watching him walk down the path.

She moved from the gloom of the tower into the sunlight, dark green penitent's robe swishing behind her in the warm late-summer breeze. For one month, she had been shut in the tower, wrestling with her own soul, trying to sift through the competing desires that threatened to tear her apart. Today was the first day she had been allowed outside, the most difficult part of her penance behind her.

She blinked in the sunlight, her eyes smarting in the unaccustomed glare. Master Fen had sent word she had a visitor, but she could see no one in the tower's small yard.

"Up here."

Her eyes followed the sound. There was Alvyn perched in a tree, his White robes tangled in the branches. She suppressed a smile, not thinking humor appropriate to her present situation. "Very dignified."

He shrugged. "I got bored waiting." With a pull on his robe, he freed himself and dropped to the ground beside her.

"How long have you been here?"

"In the tree? About ten minutes. At the Keep, nearly a month. I got here not long after you did, but no one would let me see you. Until now."

"And your job?"

"I resigned. Said there was an emergency at the Tower I had to take care of."

"An emergency?"

"Well, more of a mystery. You remember that laundry marker?"

She frowned, the reference eluding her.

"The marker. I showed it to you on the path. I couldn't rest until I found out what I had forgotten here."

Now she remembered. She stared at him, incredulous, but his face betrayed no sign of teasing. "And?"

"A cape belonging to my old roommate, Finn. He'd asked me to drop it off, and I did, but forgot to give him the marker. He'd already reclaimed the item. Mystery solved."

His face remained impassive. By all the Gods, Kaitlyn thought, is he telling the truth? She shook her head; short tufts of hair tickled her neck. Her long braid had been one of the sacrifices of her penitence. "You came all this way back to the Keep for the sake of a laundry marker?"

Now the smile broke through, lighting his dark features. "Gods, you should see your face. Did you really believe that stupid story?"

"You've done sillier things."

"I?" He raised a hand to his chest in a gesture of outraged innocence. "I'm not the one who got my head shaved." He squinted at her. "But you know, your hair doesn't look half bad short."

She waved aside the compliment. "So why did you come? It wasn't for my sake, I hope."

He colored slightly, and the smile left his eyes. Kaitlyn wanted to bite her tongue. "That came out wrong," she said. "I'm delighted—truly—to see you. But you never wanted to stay at Wizard's Keep. You must have other things to do than wait here while I finish my penance."

He shook his head. "We're supposed to be partners."

"I don't know when I'll be able to leave. There are still so many things I have to sort out." Like the color of the robe she would wear when she finished her penance. She'd felt the Blue power surge through her, making her stronger than she'd ever dreamed. The Gray forces would never serve her as well. In her tests during penance she had seen that the Blue way was safe for her to follow, but still there was her revulsion, her antipathy for the Dark path.

"I'll wait," he said. "I've always been more patient than you. Besides, I've been taking classes. I might go for the next rank." He shrugged. "And that witch is still out there somewhere. I'm not that eager to face her again, at least not until I master the check-spell ward."

"I'm sorry I failed you, Alvyn," she said, after a moment's silence. "I know how much you wanted that job. You're giving up a lot for my sake."

He grinned. "Yup. Like all that free beer. Real beer, too, not that gingery nonsense they serve in the dining hall here. Seems to me, after all this, the least you can do is come with me to the village and treat me to a mug of ale."

She nodded. Yes, she could do that. Her month of confinement was officially over. But then another thought struck her. "Alvyn, I don't have any money. Not a farthing." Every cent she'd had, she'd paid in fines, part of her penance.

He groaned. "Well, then, it will have to be my treat."

"Your treat? You have money?"

He laughed. "You always underestimate me, Kaitlyn. On my way back from Tinkertown I performed a few odd jobs here and there. And I've been working some around the countryside. There's a good living to be made with this wizard stuff."

He offered his arm, in an exaggeratedly courtly fashion. "Coming?"

She took the arm he offered—and smiled for the first time in what had seemed like years.

WINTER ROSES
by Patricia Sayre McCoy

Patricia Sayre McCoy has one husband, no children, and "the ubiquitous writer's cat, a very bossy Siamese Burmese cross." She also has an identical twin sister.

She has a Masters degree in Library Science and a day job as Head of Cataloging at the D'Angelo Law Library of the University of Chicago. She once explained her job to her grandmother as telling people what numbers to write on the spines of library books, and her grandmother said: "They pay you for that?" They certainly *should* pay her for that; it's incredibly difficult to classify books so that anyone looking for them can find them. My secretary gave up years ago and settled for cataloging my books so that *she* could find them. When I want a book, I have to get her to find it for me.

This is Patricia's first sale, and I hope it will be only the first of many.

Halayn knelt before the old hermit. Putting her palms together, she bowed low, touching her forehead to the cave's icy floor.

"Grandfather," she said softly, "I've brought you dinner and hot tea. Please honor this one with your presence."

The old man opened his eyes, a broad grin lighting his face.

"And did you bring lump sugar to sweeten it, too?" he asked.

"No, Old One," Halayn sighed. "I forgot."

"Forgot my sugar, Granddaughter? That is very unlike you."

Halayn bowed again. "Forgive me, Grandfather. I was distracted. There are strange voices on the winds tonight. The snow beast roams far."

The old man swirled the tea leaves in the translucent cup and studied the patterns forming. Beckoning Halayn closer, he leaned over the cup and breathed gently. A film formed on the surface of the tea. Gradually it stilled and faint pictures formed. The hermit nodded to the girl and she leaned over the cup, gazing intently, eyes unfocusing as she entered a trance.

"What do you see?" he asked.

"White, swirling white in a blizzard force wind. Silver, flashing silver claws in the storm. Oh, and red, warm and thick, staining the white snow."

Frightened, Halayn drew back. She had never seen so clearly before. But what did it mean? Whose blood was that on the snow? Did the vision reveal what was happening or only what might happen? With mounting horror, she remembered the snow beast's cries. It was happening now, she knew.

Shuddering, she looked away. "The snow beast is abroad tonight."

"Yes," the old man agreed. "It is hunting. We must be swift."

Gathering his woolly coat close, he led the way out of the cave and into the storm. Halayn adjusted her veil and followed, shivering.

Swiftly the storm blew down the mountain and a clear cold moon shone on the fresh snow fields. The snow thinned as they sought the high lairs of the snow beast well above the tree line. Finally, Halayn spotted blood on the rocks.

Carefully, for they were close to the awful creature's territory, the old man and girl drew closer. Leaning against a black boulder lay the body of a slim young man. One hand clutched his side, where the bright heart's blood seeped through tightly clenched fingers. The other hand held a long, intricately carved box of dark wood.

"Oh, Grandfather, he's so young," Halayn breathed, kneeling beside the youth. "Can you heal him?"

The old man knelt, too, laying one hand on the youth's forehead. He moaned and opened his eyes.

"Surely I am dead and am now in Paradise," he murmured. gazing at Halayn. Flustered, she drew back, replacing her veil with one hand while the other pried the box loose and took his hot hand in her cool one. Her fingers sought the pulse point. It was very faint. Halayn raised her eyes to her grandfather's and he slowly closed his eyes. The youth was dying, the poison from the snow beast's claws spreading too rapidly. Another moan brought her attention back to the young man. He smiled grimly, pale with pain.

"I am dying, aren't I?" he asked. At her nod, he continued. "I forgot to burn incense to the mountain god. I was so close. I have found Yulan's blue roses."

Suddenly he lunged forward and caught Halayn's hands.

"Deliver them for me!" he cried. "I swore terrible oaths on my parents' graves that I would be the one to find the blue roses. They beggared themselves for me, so that I could win the princess of my dreams."

"Surely any roses you have are dead by now," Halayn began, but he shook his head.

"The magic of the box keeps them as fresh as the moment they were picked. Please, give them to her. I love her so."

He sagged against the rock, blood trickling from his mouth. Halayn cast her veil over her head as she gently closed his eyes.

Later, as the final rocks were placed on the cairn, the old man handed her the strange box. She stared at it in surprise.

"Why give this to me?" she asked.

"You cannot refuse a man's dying request," he said in surprise.

"But to give it to Princess Yulan!" she protested. "Even if there were such a thing as a blue rose, she doesn't deserve it."

"That is not for us to judge," he replied. "But the ghosts of this boy's parents will be cursed to roam forever if his vow is not fulfilled."

"Who is she, to have blue roses that bring men's deaths?"

"Who are we to say she should not have them?"

Halayn sighed. She could argue with her grandfather forever and not have the last word. She nodded.

"Very well, Grandfather. I will take Yulan her roses."

The next morning Halayn left the mountain hermitage. The heavy wool coat, high boots, and thick trousers felt strange after the freedom of loose robes and veils. But there were more storms in the future and her grandfather had said she was not yet ready to face them so unprotected. Other things felt unfamiliar, too. Her very body felt like someone else's.

In appearance it was. Where once a slim, almond-eyed mountain girl had been was a tall, doe-eyed youth. His legs were longer, his shoulders broader, even his skin was redder and darker than her smooth gold. They had argued about it last night, her grandfather and she, but for once she had had the last word.

Yulan would have her roses from the hand of her young suitor. Drawing on her powers of illusion, Halayn had shaped herself into an image of the young man. It had been hard, especially after the change had begun and she began to feel the alterations. Startled, she had broken her concentration and lost the new shape.

"All this world is an illusion," she had breathed, returning to her trance. "The mind shapes the illusion it wishes. I wish to be Halayn no longer, but the youth we buried. I will be like him. I will."

This time, when she felt the change begin, she was prepared and did not lose the trance. Gradually her body and features shifted, rearranged themselves, until the youth stood where the girl had been. It was done.

Borrowing clothes from her grandfather's earlier acolyte, she began the long trek from the mountains, called the Pillars of the Sky, to the glittering courts of the princess in the plains below. It was a journey that would take her many weeks. As soon as she reached the first valley, she bought a fine horse, and richer robes and boots. Nothing was too fine to honor the sacrifice of the two old people for their only son. Yulan would receive her roses from the prince indeed.

After four weeks, she reached a town in the settled lands of the great plains that bordered the desert surrounding Yulan's home. Trade routes led across the sandy waste, and she hastened to find a caravan crossing the desert that she could join. Halayn paused outside the finest caravansary in town. She had never been so far from home before, she thought nervously. What if her disguise were discovered? What would happen to her then, among all these strangers?

"O great prince, your exalted self blocks the door for the more humble among us."

Startled, Halayn turned. A caravan driver, tall and sturdy, stood beside her, half bowing, his free hand making extravagant gestures toward the open door.

"My apologies," she said. "I was wondering what to do."

"Why, enter, of course," the man replied, eyes twinkling merrily. "What else does one do in a doorway, if one has not just exited, that is?"

She laughed. This would be all right, she thought. People were the same everywhere. They would see what she wanted them to see. Still, she wished the dead youth had not been quite so comely. It could cause difficulties.

"It is the doorway to a humble inn, great prince, and not the door to the nether hells. Enter, leave, or step aside, but you are still blocking the door," the man said, his gestures now more impatient. "I would like to drink before the sun goes down. Crossing the desert is thirsty work."

Embarrassed, Halayn quickly stepped aside. He bowed mockingly again, and vanished into the dim, smoky interior. Halayn peered inside, and stepped back again. Should she enter or not? Was another inn perhaps better for her purposes? How could she tell? She looked inside again but saw nothing to help her.

Turning away, she walked down the dusty street, glancing inside the other caravansaries. But they showed her little more than the first one had. All were dim and smoky, and all were full of men drinking. Only now, in the time it had taken her to walk the one street of the trading post, they had had ample time to get drunk. Sighing in frustration and indecision, Halayn found herself back at the door of the first inn, nervously peering inside and back at the darkening street. Behind her, she heard voices.

"Looks rich enough to me," one of them said. "Look at that coat and boots. Let's take him."

"But who was the big driver with him earlier, hm?" a second voice asked. "His kind don't travel alone. He's just slipped his guards for a bit."

"So take him now," the first voice urged, sounding much closer.

Halayn eased her dagger free from her sash. Would they guess she didn't really know how to use it? Drawing a deep breath, she turned and shouted, one booted foot flying up to trip the first attacker. As he fell, she clipped him behind the ear with a stiffened hand and looked around for the other one. He was sprawled unconscious in the dust.

"I think that's worth a drink, don't you, master?" the caravan driver asked, grinning toothily. "A properly grateful master would agree I deserve something."

"I think you've already had your drink," Halayn replied, replacing her dagger. "And I haven't hired you for anything."

"I think you should, though."

"Indeed?"

"Well, you can obviously use the protection. And I am an experienced guide and driver. Ask anyone here, they'll tell you."

Halayn looked at the bodies of the two attackers. They were much bigger than she was, with well muscled arms and many knife scars. She looked at her rescuer. He didn't look much better, she thought. He did have fewer scars though.

"All right, I'll hire you," she said firmly. "Who are you?"

"Durman, King of the Caravans, at your service, fair prince," he replied, bowing to the dust, truly a humble servant. But he spoiled the gesture of subservience with a big grin. Halayn held out her hand and pulled him up.

"I thought I had hired a guide, not a clown, Durman, King of Caravans," she remarked as she entered the caravansary. "What do you recommend for dinner here?"

"Anything that can be carried with you, fair prince," he answered. "I think trouble is brewing."

Halayn looked toward the corner he indicated. A group of men, servants from their garb, were drinking and shouting, the same as any others. She turned a puzzled glance toward Durman.

"What?" she began, but he hushed her.

"Listen," he whispered. "They talk of Kotien and the Princess Yulan. Such talk is not safe here."

"Why?"

"Come with me to my camels and I will tell you what it is safe to know."

After collecting travel food, mostly dried meats and bread, she followed Durman to his camp outside the town. He had a fire banked and only needed a few minutes to get it blazing again. Setting a kettle over the coals, he gestured for her to sit on one of the camel saddles placed around the fire.

"So," she began, spreading her coarse napkin over her lap and taking up her food, "tell me what those men were saying that is so dangerous."

"It is always dangerous to speak of Princess Yulan," he replied. "There have been many executions and the people are turning against her."

"Executions?" Halayn asked.

"Suitors, fair prince," he explained. "She demands blue roses from anyone foolish enough to court her. Those who enter her service and swear to bring the blue roses are executed if they do not. And many have been executed."

"Why would any man want such a frightful wife?" Halayn asked, remembering too late that she was posing as such a suitor.

"That I do not know," Durman said softly. "It is said that she is very rich and very beautiful. I cannot say, as I have never seen her. Nor wish to."

"Beauty is an illusion of this world," Halayn murmured. "It does not last beyond death. Only the soul does. And hers must be truly horrible."

Durman glanced at her sharply. "I think you speak the truth," he agreed. "So tell me, then, why you seek her."

"I have not said that I do," she replied, startled.

"Why else are you here, at a camp on the edge of the world? And I recognize the box you carry. Gossip says that a powerful sorcerer made it for a young prince who sought the blue roses."

"I am not a prince," Halayn said.

Durman eyed her levelly for a long moment. "So you do not deny the rest," he said finally.

"My parents were old," she began, when he stopped her with a raised hand.

"If I am to guide you, you will tell me the

truth," he said. "You are not a prince and they are not your parents. You are not a suitor. So what are you?"

"A seeker for justice," she replied and let the illusion drop. In place of the young prince sat a younger woman.

Durman gasped and stared at her, then nodded.

"Good," he declared. "A woman will be able to withstand her enchantments. And you are a powerful illusionist. But do you have the roses in the box?"

Halayn shrugged. "I have not opened it. But the dead youth, whose image I wore, said he had found them. He was taking them back to her when the snow beast attacked him."

"Well, we will find out when you present them to her," Durman said. "So we must sleep early if we are to be away in good time tomorrow."

Halayn and Durman arrived at the great gates of Kotien, on the western edge of the great desert. Having only skirted the edges, Halayn was in awe of the desert travelers she saw leaving the city, endless lines of camels heavily loaded, bound for the cities of the western empires far out of mind. Others too, left the great gates, but these skulked fearfully in the shadows, looking constantly behind them. As they drew near, Halayn saw one of them suddenly break free of the crowd and run toward the caravan. A handful of city guards followed closely behind, though, and he was dragged screaming and weeping, back into the city, to disappear behind the high stone walls. Halayn had stopped to stare, but Durman seized her arm and hurried her toward the gates.

"What," she began, but Durman hushed her with a sharp gesture.

"Say nothing here," he whispered. "The walls have ears."

Halayn nodded and followed him as he led the way to an inn where he was well known. Inside, he bargained for two rooms and then motioned Halayn to follow the serving girl to her room. He went outside again to arrange stabling for the horses and lodging for the camels.

In her room, Halayn dismissed the girl and began to examine the room. One large window looked out on a square, a market square from its size. Only now there were no booths or tents set up, as night had almost fallen. The square was deserted in the coolness of the early evening, the only movement a few ravens gliding past tall spikes. Halayn idly followed their flight, gasping suddenly as the round lumps on the spikes became heads. She swung away from the window, hand over her mouth, as the largest raven landed and began to feast.

Durman walked in as she finished vomiting into the pot in the corner. His eyes narrowed as he strode toward the window. Cursing under his breath, he swept the shutters closed and firmly latched them.

"Those are new," he remarked.

Halayn lifted a pale face and grimaced. "Why do they keep coming?" she gasped.

"The townsfolk speak of witchcraft and magic," he said, "but not too loudly. Not all the heads are suitors."

"The man we saw as we entered?"

Durman nodded. "Most likely. He must have spoken against Princess Yulan. The city guards are most vigilant."

Halayn sat on the narrow bed, absently shifting until she found a comfortable position on the lumpy mattress.

"This must be stopped," she declared. "Such a monstrous evil should not be allowed to continue."

"Many agree with you," Durman said, "But what can be done? She has too many loyal guards around her. Several attempts on her life have been made. All were foiled and the attackers savagely punished. Nothing less than an army could hope to defeat her. And do not forget the sorcery. I have heard that she is protected with powerful spells, too."

"Truth is the most powerful spell," Halayn replied. "I have a plan. But you must help me. How do I get into the palace?"

"Simply tell the guards that you have brought blue roses for the Princess and they will let you in," Durman said. "She fears no one and is ever greedy for the roses."

"Very well then, that is what we shall do. Tomorrow morning when the palace gates open, go and announce me. Then you may leave. I only hired you to guide me. You do not have to accompany me further."

Durman bowed deeply. "That is true, but I have a great desire to see the end of this. I will come with you to the palace if you will have me. Such a great prince as yourself must have at least one manservant, after all!"

The next morning dawned fair and clear. Here on the edge of the desert, the sun rose early, and work began before the heat of the day grew too great. Halayn nervously adjusted her coats of fine brocade in rare colors, heavily embroidered in exotic patterns. Red leather boots, finely tooled and inlaid with gold and precious turquoise completed her costume. Durman handed her an ebony riding crop tipped with more turquoise and picked up the carved box. He, too, was finely dressed, as befitted a prince's servant, but in more subdued colors and fabrics.

They joined the morning crowd mounted on fine horses, with a hired man walking ahead clearing a path and announcing, "Make way for Prince Kirat, Prince of far Rimpal. Make way for the prince!" Behind them marched an impressive array of retainers, servants and pack beasts, none of whom actually existed, except in the imagination of the viewers. Halayn had worked hard on her illusions the night before.

At the gates of the palace, a tall eunuch met them. Word had been carried swiftly to the palace (helped on its way by Durman's generosity in the taverns the night before) and he was aware that another suitor had brought roses for Princess Yulan. He halted the procession with one hand raised, bowing and mumbling official nonsense. Inside the gates, undersecretaries frantically combed the ancient palace records, feverishly searching for any mention of Rimpal. Halayn smiled secretly. Her plan was working.

Durman let the wait stretch into nearly half an hour before announcing to the eunuch, now fretful and nervous, that his prince had been kept waiting too long and would see the princess now or leave. The eunuch stared, aghast. No one had ever made such demands before.

"The Princess Yulan is not a common woman summoned for show," he began, but Durman cut him off.

"And neither is the Great Prince Kirat a common man, to be kept waiting at the door like a beggar. He has been insulted enough."

"But I have never heard of Rimpal," the eunuch whispered in anguish. "How can I let just anyone into Her Royal Highness's presence? Princes of Parsia and far Hind have courted her, not to mention many of our own princes of Han. Who is this Prince of Rimpal?"

"One who really has blue roses, fool," Halayn spoke sharply, "I will leave now and your ungrateful princess can send for them herself if she truly wishes them."

As she turned her horse away, the crowd groaned and hissed. Forcing his way to her side, Durman threw her a secret grin. The first part of the plan was working perfectly. They had an audience now. As Halayn and Durman turned down the street and prepared to leave, a frantic servant rushed up to the eunuch and waved a message in front of him. The eunuch read it, paled noticeably and hurried after Halayn. Although they had deliberately slowed their horses, the eunuch was fat from years of rich food and little activity, and was almost unable to deliver the message.

"Oh, Great Prince," he gasped, "forgive this ignorant one. Her Royal Highness, Princess Yulan requests that you join her in the Court of Peaceful Serenity and show her the wonder you have brought from the far off, glorious kingdom of Rimpal."

So saying, he collapsed in the dust. Halayn barely glanced at him as she turned her horse and returned to the palace gates, which opened for her this time. Inside, more silk-clad retainers rushed forward to take the horses' reins and lead them to the Court of Peaceful Serenity.

Halayn was only half aware of the rich tapestries, paintings and furniture that lined the halls as they went deeper and deeper into the palace, past the reception rooms and into the private areas. Soon the eunuchs were replaced by fair serving girls and ladies in waiting, all dressed in pale robes with shimmering headdresses of pearl and feathers.

At the end of a long hallway, the doors opened onto an interior garden shaded by apricot trees just coming into bloom in the sheltered courtyard. Beside the central pool, a slender woman waited, surrounded by younger girls playing musical instruments or singing. As Halayn entered, the woman looked up. Halayn drew a deep breath. She was indeed beautiful, with almond eyes of deep brown, fine golden skin without a flaw, and rosy cheeks. It took a close look to see the hardness in those lovely eyes.

Halayn bowed as Durman knelt behind her. The maidens left off their music and clustered around Princess Yulan as she rose and extended one slim hand.

"I have been told that you bring blue roses for me," she said, her soft voice almost a whisper. "I would see them now. You know that I have sworn to marry the prince who brings me blue roses, but those that fail die."

Halayn bowed again and placed the box in her hand. "It is so, Princess."

Yulan paused, hand on the lid. "And you accept the conditions?"

"I do."

"Very well, then," she said, slowly opening the box. "Let us see what you have brought."

A hush fell over the courtyard as she reached inside and brought out two perfect, white blossoms. Durman smothered a curse, glancing frantically at Halayn. One of the maidens gasped, but quickly muffled it behind her hand, as Yulan glared at her. Yulan herself, for one moment, looked disappointed. Only Halayn's expression remained the same.

"They are not blue roses, Highness," one of the guards finally said, stepping up beside Halayn. "Shall I take him to the execution grounds now?"

Yulan looked at Halayn, eyes thoughtful. Something about this prince was different from the others. She would be sorry to see him die. Taking a deep breath, she raised one imperial hand.

"You are wrong, Guard Commander," she said clearly. "The roses are blue."

And in her hand, the roses were, indeed, a clear sky blue. Smiling, she held out her other hand to Halayn. "Come, my Prince. I will show you to your people. Tomorrow we will be wed."

"I think not, Highness," Halayn replied.

Yulan stared. He had refused her!

The Guard Commander spoke. "Every prince in the land wished to marry Princess Yulan!"

"But I do not," Halayn replied. "I do not wish such a cruel wife."

Turning to Yulan, she continued, "I know your secret, Princess and it is ugly. Any rose would have been a blue rose in your hands. How many men have you killed through your capriciousness?"

"My father would have married me to an old man," Yulan snarled at Halayn. "I was too young for him. So I thought of the roses."

"Not all the heads on your gates were old, Princess," Halayn replied. "There is blood on your hands, and I will have no more of you."

Gesturing to Durman, Halayn turned in a swirl of coat tails and stalked out of the courtyard. Behind her, Yulan held up two slender hands that slowly dripped blood. Screams followed them as they left.

AMBER
by Syne Mitchell

I always try to end these anthologies with
something short and amusing. This story was
originally submitted to *Marion Zimmer
Bradley's Fantasy Magazine,* and I started to
reject it for its lack of fantasy content. But
then I realized that while it wouldn't do at all
for my magazine, it was perfect for *Sword and
Sorceress.* We then had to call Syne and get
permission for the change of market, which
also involved holding the story for over six
months, since I wasn't reading for *Sword and
Sorceress* then. (I read for my magazine year
round, but I work on the anthology only for a
couple of months in the spring.) It's always
easier if something is submitted to the correct
market in the first place.

Syne is currently residing in Madison, Wis-
consin, which is where she ran out of money
while touring the country. She says that she is
"still very much female" and owns "the requi-
site cat, Shades."

"**Y**ou will kill Master Chin," Saibel said, lounging in her perfumed bath water. She dipped one hand into the pink-tinged liquid and brought up a handful of bubbles. "And in the agonizingly slow final moments of dying I want him to know that it was I, Saibel of the Fifth House of Astur, that ordered his death." She blew lightly and the bubbles flew from her fingertips.

Amber did not change her posture, kneeling before Lady Saibel's sunken alabaster tub. Behind her dark mask, her mind raced.

Yet she had sworn a year's contract to the soft, rich woman in the tub. She must kill Master Chin or face her own death in dishonor if she did not follow her mistress' word to the letter.

Master Chin was the same as she remembered. His round face was at once aged and ageless. He smiled and nodded when he opened the door. Amber remembered that it was he who had given her the name she now bore, after the unusual color of her eyes.

"You do this feeble old man honor, little one," Chin said, "It has been too long since my little wharf rat has graced my threshold." He looked her over. "You look fitting for the Ansazi. Your skill brings honor to my teachings."

"I am only glad that the child you rescued could prove worthy of your teachings." Amber bowed and offered the clay jug she held "I have brought you a gift as well as my regards."

"You know my vices only too well," he chuckled, taking the jar. He carried it across the spartan room and set it to warm in front of the tiny fireplace.

Amber's eyes followed his smooth movements. She held her back very straight.

"So, little one, why do you pay this old man the honor of your company?" Master Chin asked, setting a second pallet near the fire.

Amber knelt on the cushion. "It has been too long since I visited you," she answered. "I have missed our conversations. Tell me what you have been doing these past few years."

The old man spoke of his importing business and how it had flourished to his competitor's detriment. He spoke of grandchildren born and sons buried.

"But I forget the wine," he said. He leaned forward and pulled the cork.

Despite her companion's new wealth, nothing had changed. Amber found the wine cups in the chest where they were always kept. She ran her hands along the smooth porcelain, glazed blue with tiny five-lobed flowers ringing the lip.

With efficient movements he filled the two cups.

The young assassin lifted the cup to her lips and watched as the old man drank deeply.

"A most fine wine," he commented, "from the south fields, I'd wager."

Amber nodded, not meeting his eyes.

"Do you remember the first time that you stole from my larder?" the old man asked between sips.

"Yes, foster father. You asked me how I had stolen your wine out of a locked cabinet," she replied, "and I said that I had clever hands."

"And then you asked me how I had known who had stolen it, and I told you that it was better to have a clever mind than clever hands."

Amber nodded, "I was afraid that you would turn me over to the magistrates. But instead you took me into your household, and raised me as your own daughter."

"But, my young friend, enough talk of old

times. What has become of you since we last met?"

"I've fallen upon evil times," Amber said, "After completing my training I was unable to find work. Only one would hire me, such a young and untried Ansazi. I work for a mean-spirited and dishonorable mistress and she has given me a task that I do not like." Amber met Master Chin's gaze.

"Tell me, child, if your oath does not prevent it, what is this task?"

"I must kill an old friend."

Master Chin rose to his feet slowly. He set the saki cup on the mantle. His hands fell to his sides. His posture was relaxed.

"I am ready for you," he said.

"I only wish that my orders were so honorable," Amber said from where she sat. "She who sent me asked that you have an agonizingly long death. The wine was poisoned."

Chin sat down heavily on the stone floor. His black eyes looked into Amber's yellow ones.

"How long, little friend, does this old man have?"

Amber's voice was soft, "The poison I used is very slow-acting, as my mistress indicated. The dose I measured out will kill you in about twenty—" she paused for breath, "—years."

The old man shook his head in disbelief. Then, a hearty laugh rumbled out of his chest.

Amber explained Saibel's instructions and how she had interpreted them, bringing another bout of laughter from Master Chin.

"Ah, my child. You have surpassed my teaching."

The old man was still chuckling to himself as she left.

* * *

The air was steamy and heavy with the sandalwood perfume that Saibel favored. Amber's dark-haired mistress was wearing a red silk dressing gown. Her body was still damp from the bath and it clung to her skin.

"Is he dead?" Saibel asked, stroking her long hair with a tortoiseshell comb.

"He has been poisoned, Mistress," Amber answered.

The rich woman turned, "How did he die?" she asked, licking her lips.

"The poison I used was very slow-acting. I told him that it was you who had ordered his death. When I left him, he was on the floor, convulsing."

"Excellent," Saibel purred, "the shipping business is now mine."

Amber was not surprised to find herself unemployed a week later. Saibel had mysteriously drowned in her bath. But then, Master Chin had always been a resourceful man.

MARION ZIMMER BRADLEY

THE DARKOVER NOVELS

☐ DARKOVER LANDFALL	UE2234—$3.99
☐ HAWKMISTRESS!	UE2239—$4.99
☐ STORMQUEEN!	UE2310—$4.99
☐ TWO TO CONQUER	UE2174—$4.99
☐ THE HEIRS OF HAMMERFELL	UE2451—$4.99
☐ THE SHATTERED CHAIN	UE2308—$4.50
☐ THENDARA HOUSE	UE2240—$4.99
☐ CITY OF SORCERY	UE2332—$4.99
☐ REDISCOVERY*	UE2529—$4.99
☐ REDISCOVERY (hardcover)*	UE2561—$18.00
☐ THE SPELL SWORD	UE2237—$3.99
☐ THE FORBIDDEN TOWER	UE2373—$4.99
☐ STAR OF DANGER	UE2607—$4.99
☐ THE WINDS OF DARKOVER	
& THE PLANET SAVERS	UE2630—$4.99
☐ THE BLOODY SUN	UE2603—$4.99
☐ THE HERITAGE OF HASTUR	UE2413—$4.99
☐ SHARRA'S EXILE	UE2309—$4.99
☐ THE WORLD WRECKERS	UE2629—$4.99

*with Mercedes Lackey

Buy them at your local bookstore or use this convenient coupon for ordering.

PENGUIN USA P.O. Box 999—Dep. #17109, Bergenfield, New Jersey 07621

Please send me the DAW BOOKS I have checked above, for which I am enclosing
$_____ (please add $2.00 to cover postage and handling). Send check or money
order (no cash or C.O.D.'s) or charge by Mastercard or VISA (with a $15.00 minimum). Prices and
numbers are subject to change without notice.

Card #_____ Exp. Date _____

Signature_____

Name_____

Address_____

City _____ State _____ Zip Code _____

For faster service when ordering by credit card call 1-800-253-6476

Allow a minimum of 4-6 weeks for delivery. This offer is subject to change without notice.

FANTASY ANTHOLOGIES

Buy them at your local bookstore or use this convenient coupon for ordering.

PENGUIN USA P.O. Box 999—Dep. #17109, Bergenfield, New Jersey 07621

Please send me the DAW BOOKS I have checked above, for which I am enclosing
$_____ (please add $2.00 to cover postage and handling). Send check or money order (no cash or C.O.D.'s) or charge by Mastercard or VISA (with a $15.00 minimum). Prices and numbers are subject to change without notice.

Card #_____ Exp. Date _____
Signature_____
Name_____
Address_____
City _____ State _____ Zip Code _____

For faster service when ordering by credit card call **1-800-253-6476**

Allow a minimum of 4-6 weeks for delivery. This offer is subject to change without notice.

Mercedes Lackey

The Novels of Valdemar

☐ THE BLACK GRYPHON* (hardcover)   UE2577—$22.00
☐ THE BLACK GRYPHON*   UE2643—$5.99
☐ THE WHITE GRYPHON* (hardcover)   UE2631—$21.95

☐ MAGIC'S PAWN   UE2352—$4.99
☐ MAGIC'S PROMISE   UE2401—$4.99
☐ MAGIC'S PRICE   UE2426—$4.99

☐ THE OATHBOUND   UE2285—$4.99
☐ OATHBREAKERS   UE2319—$4.99

☐ BY THE SWORD   UE2463—$5.99

☐ ARROWS OF THE QUEEN   UE2378—$4.99
☐ ARROW'S FLIGHT   UE2377—$4.99
☐ ARROW'S FALL   UE2400—$4.99

☐ WINDS OF FATE   UE2516—$5.99
☐ WINDS OF CHANGE (hardcover)   UE2534—$20.00
☐ WINDS OF CHANGE   UE2563—$5.99
☐ WINDS OF FURY (hardcover)   UE2562—$20.00
☐ WINDS OF FURY   UE2612—$5.99

☐ STORM WARNING (hardcover)   UE2611—$21.95
☐ STORM WARNING   UE2661—$5.99
☐ STORM RISING (hardcover)   UE2660—$21.95

*with Larry Dixon

Buy them at your local bookstore or use this convenient coupon for ordering.

PENGUIN USA P.O. Box 999—Dep. #17109, Bergenfield, New Jersey 07621

Please send me the DAW BOOKS I have checked above, for which I am enclosing
$_____ (please add $2.00 to cover postage and handling). Send check or money
order (no cash or C.O.D.'s) or charge by Mastercard or VISA (with a $15.00 minimum). Prices and
numbers are subject to change without notice.

Card #_____ Exp. Date _____
Signature_____
Name_____
Address_____
City _____ State _____ Zip Code _____

For faster service when ordering by credit card call **1-800-253-6476**

Allow a minimum of 4-6 weeks for delivery. This offer is subject to change without notice.

Jennifer Roberson

THE NOVELS OF TIGER AND DEL

Tiger and Del, he a Sword-Dancer of the South, she of the North, each a master of secret sword-magic. Together, they would challenge wizards' spells and other deadly traps on a perilous quest of honor.

CHRONICLES OF THE CHEYSULI

This superb fantasy series about a race of warriors gifted with the ability to assume animal shapes at will presents the Cheysuli, fated to answer the call of magic in their blood, fulfilling an ancient prophecy which could spell salvation or ruin.

Buy them at your local bookstore or use this convenient coupon for ordering.

PENGUIN USA P.O. Box 999—Dep. #17109, Bergenfield, New Jersey 07621

Please send me the DAW BOOKS I have checked above, for which I am enclosing $_____ (please add $2.00 to cover postage and handling). Send check or money order (no cash or C.O.D.'s) or charge by Mastercard or VISA (with a $15.00 minimum). Prices and numbers are subject to change without notice.

Card #_____ Exp. Date _____
Signature_____
Name_____
Address_____
City _____ State _____ Zip Code _____

For faster service when ordering by credit card call 1-800-253-6476

Allow a minimum of 4-6 weeks for delivery. This offer is subject to change without notice.

Melanie Rawn

EXILES
☐ **THE RUINS OF AMBRAI: Book 1**   UE2668—$5.99
☐ **THE RUINS OF AMBRAI: Book 1** (hardcover)   UE2619—$20.95

Three Mageborn sisters bound together by ties of their ancient Blood Line are forced to take their stands on opposing sides of a conflict between two powerful schools of magic. Together, the sisters will fight their own private war, and the victors will determine whether or not the Wild Magic and the Wraithen-beasts are once again loosed to wreak havoc upon their world.

THE DRAGON PRINCE NOVELS
☐ **DRAGON PRINCE : Book 1**   UE2450—$5.99
☐ **THE STAR SCROLL: Book 2**   UE2349—$5.99
☐ **SUNRUNNER'S FIRE: Book 3**   UE2403—$5.99

THE DRAGON STAR NOVELS
☐ **STRONGHOLD: Book 1**   UE2482—$5.99
☐ **STRONGHOLD: Book 1** (hardcover)   UE2440—$21.95
☐ **THE DRAGON TOKEN: Book 2**   UE2542—$5.99
☐ **SKYBOWL: Book 3**   UE2595—$5.99
☐ **SKYBOWL: Book 3** (hardcover)   UE2541—$22.00

Buy them at your local bookstore or use this convenient coupon for ordering.

PENGUIN USA   P.O. Box 999—Dep. #17109, Bergenfield, New Jersey 07621

Please send me the DAW BOOKS I have checked above, for which I am enclosing
$_____ (please add $2.00 to cover postage and handling). Send check or money order (no cash or C.O.D.'s) or charge by Mastercard or VISA (with a $15.00 minimum). Prices and numbers are subject to change without notice.

Card #_____ Exp. Date _____
Signature_____
Name_____
Address_____
City _____ State _____ Zip Code _____

For faster service when ordering by credit card call **1-800-253-6476**

Allow a minimum of 4-6 weeks for delivery. This offer is subject to change without notice.